Paul A. Kazakov was born at 19:40 hours on March 6, 1946, at the United Nations Relief and Rehabilitation Administration Stateless Working Camp at Furstenwald, Germany (American Zone), which previously housed his parents as slave labor workers before the end of the Second World War. The family emigrated to Canada on April 21, 1950, aboard the U.S.N.S. General J.H. McRae and eventually settled in Southern Alberta.

The author obtained a B.Ed., B.A. & S. and LL.B. He was initially employed as a sessional lecturer in law for the Faculty of Commerce at the University of Calgary. He was admitted to the bar in 1981 and practiced in the civil litigation field until he retired on June 15, 2020.

Upon his retirement, he took up creative writing and *Hard Kisses, Bitter Tears* is his first completed work, inspired by some of the events which transpired in his parents' lives.

The author visited the Soviet Union/Russian Federation in 1983, 1985 and 2003, both before and after the dissolution of the USSR. He has recently completed a legal trilogy and is currently working on another story set in the Soviet Union/Russian Federation during the period from 1985 to 2000 – from Gorbachev's 'perestroika' to Yeltsin's 'Vouchers' and 'Shares for Loans' to Putin's ascendency. Its working title is *'The Oligarch'*.

To my muse, Nancy Brager, and my dear son, Mark.

For Cindy
(Thanks for all your
help)
Hope you enjoy my first
published work.

Paul   Oct. 12/21

Paul A. Kazakov

HARD KISSES, BITTER TEARS

AUSTIN MACAULEY PUBLISHERS™

LONDON * CAMBRIDGE * NEW YORK * SHARJAH

Ordering Information
Quantity sales: Special discounts are available on quantity purchases by corporations, associations, and others. For details, contact the publisher at the address below.

Publisher's Cataloging-in-Publication data
Kazakov, Paul A.
Hard Kisses, Bitter Tears

ISBN 9781649796455 (Paperback)
ISBN 9781649796462 (ePub e-book)

Library of Congress Control Number: 2021916650

www.austinmacauley.com/us

First Published (2021)
Austin Macauley Publishers LLC
40 Wall Street, 33rd Floor, Suite 3302
New York, NY 10005
USA

mail-usa@austinmacauley.com
+1 (646) 5125767

In memory of my father,
Afanas Larionovich Kazakov.
D.O.B. – 17 January 1907
D.O.D. – 30 August 1976

Principal Characters

Larion Daneelivich Sulupin
- First Lieutenant in the Soviet Army (also referred to by his familiar name 'Louyna' by his family and close friends

Tamara Dimitriova Sulupin
- Wife of Larion Daneelivich Sulupin

Dimitri Aleksyevich Shanin
- *Kolkhoz'* manager and Tamara's father

'Old Valodya'
- The Shanin's *'adopted'* grandfather and Larion's mentor

Olga and Ivan Kertinsky
- Local *NKVD/SS* informers in Xhotimsk, Belarus, SSR

Boris Mikhailovich Tunov
- Local chief of police and Tamara's godfather

Julius Ivanovich Martov
- Instructor at the *Frunze Military Academy* in Moscow

Gregory Andreivich Galkovskiy
- Colonel of Larion's battalion in Finland and in the Ukraine

General Vasily Vinogradov
- Larion's divisional commander in Finland and the Ukraine

Major Dimitri Tynlenev
- General Vinogradov's adjutant

Nikolai Pavlovskiy
- Partisan commander in the Ukraine

Irina Karzhova
- Partisan sniper and Galkovskiy's companion

Tanya Akulich	- Partisan sniper and Tynlenev's companion
Dr. Gerasimov	- Tamara's family doctor
Sturmbannfuhrer Gersdorff	- *SS* major and commander of the Xhotimsk *SS* company
Natalia Vishlova	- Partisan commander in Belarus
Oberst Elias Schalburg	- *SS* colonel and Gersdorff's superior officer
Sturmbannfuhrer Kampfe	- *SS* major and Schalburg's adjutant
Lieutenant Thornton	- US lieutenant who liberated the Furstenwald Work Camp
Helmut Seiz	- Wehrmacht soldier and Schalburg's associate
Albert Nesterenko	- Canadian farm owner and Displaced Person Sponsor.

Prologue

This is an account respecting a part of the life of Larion Daneelivich Sulupin, but the reader is asked to be patient and endure some brief historical background to this story. Any expressed opinions are solely those of the author.

The twentieth century was distinguished by many things, but primarily by two world wars and, in particular, the Second World War, where it is conservatively estimated that about sixty-five million souls perished. Of that number, at least twenty-five million were Russian.

The Versailles Treaty was executed on 28 June 1919 and it ended the First World War. The War also dismantled four empires: the German Empire, governed by the Hohenzollern dynasty that had its origins in Prussia in the eleventh century; the Austro-Hungarian Empire, governed for centuries by the Hapsburg dynasty that also had its origins in the eleventh century; the Ottoman Empire, originated in the thirteenth century and after it had conquered the Byzantine Empire in 1453, governed Turkey and the Middle East for centuries as well; the Russian Empire, which had been governed by the Romanov dynasty since 1613.

Interestingly, the principals who controlled the events that led up to the Second World War and who dictated the evolution and resolution of that deadly conflict were all born in the preceding century, primarily in the 1870s and 1880s. Three of them died under different circumstances in the month of April of 1945.

Assassinations by anarchists in the later part of the nineteenth and early part of the twentieth century became rather commonplace and included the following: Tsar Alexander II – 13 March 1881 (even though he had emancipated the Russian serfs); King Umberto of Italy – 29 July 1900; American President William McKinley – 6 September 1901. However, it was the assassination of Archduke Franz Ferdinand, heir to the Hapsburg throne, by a Bosnian anarchist named Gavrilo Princip at Sarajevo on 28 June 1914, which precipitated a sequence of events that led inevitably to the outbreak of the First World War.

Adolph Hitler was born in the Austro-Hungarian Empire on 20 April 1889. His initial popular appeal was to redress the inequity of the Versailles treaty which reduced Germany's land mass in Europe and stripped it of its colonial empire, which was ceded to the victors or their allies. The victorious Allies imposed unconscionable reparations on Germany, referred to as the 'Weimar Republic' once the Kaiser was forced to abdicate. The war was followed by the Influenza Epidemic in 1918 and 1919, then the Great Depression infected the world economy after 1929. The nascent Weimar Republic became doomed and that permitted the ascension of Hitler to seize dictatorial power from 30 January 1933, until he committed suicide in the Fuhrerbunker on 30 April 1945.

Interestingly, the winning allies, primarily England and France, also dismantled the Austria-Hungarian empire into a multiplicity of European ethnic states. They also dismantled the Ottoman Empire which had allied itself with the Hapsburgs and the Hohenzollerns. They divided the Middle East into a number of individual states which they then proceeded to 'administer' as 'protectorates'.

Arthur Balfour, the English Foreign Secretary, even declared on 2 November 1917, some twelve months before the war actually ended, that Palestine was to be dedicated as the eventual home for European Jewry, subject to two important conditions: firstly, nothing was to prejudice the civil and religious rights of the existing non-Jewish communities in Palestine and secondly, nothing was to prejudice the rights and political status enjoyed by Jews in any other country. Balfour did not bother to consult the Muslim and the Jewish populations who had cohabited in Palestine for the preceding two millennia in relative peace, if they were inclined to accede to this proposal.

The Balfour Declaration of 1917 could be cynically interpreted by some as an anti-Semitic decision primarily intended to rid Europe of Jews. Conversely, others could interpret the decision as a belated moral attempt to repatriate the Jews of Europe to their ancestral homeland which they were compelled to abandon during the Roman-enforced 'scattering' between 66-70 CE.

After the Roman Diaspora and the adoption of Christianity as the state religion in 313 CE, the various nation states in Europe conveniently overlooked the fact that Jesus was a Jew and initiated various practices of anti-Semitic discrimination, however, the Jews persevered.

In 1290, England expelled all Jews who did not convert to Christianity and it was not until Cromwell executed Charles I in 1649 and established the Commonwealth, 1649 to 1660, that Jews were encouraged to emigrate to England and even afforded some religious tolerance. In 1492, Spain expelled its Jewish and Muslim populations who were not prepared to convert after the Moors were defeated in Granada. France also practiced its own form of anti-Semitism by forcing Jews to reside collectively in urban ghettos. The French Revolution of 1789 permitted the Christians and the Jews to make some reciprocal accommodations. The Christian 'revolutionaries' set aside numerous discriminatory practices and the Jews modified a number of traditional religious practices which they hoped would make them more acceptable and conforming as 'Reformed Jews'.

But England also gave the world Winston Spencer Churchill, who was born on 30 November 1874, and he died peacefully on 24 January 1965. A brilliant, though an imperfect man, whose failings included the belief that England's Empire was its 'God-given Right' to govern in perpetuity.

He became Prime Minister on 10 May 1940, and by 26 May 1940, he was forced to deal with the forced evacuation from Dunkirk of about 338000 soldiers of the British Expeditionary Force, which was sent to France after war was declared on Nazi Germany in September of 1939. Subsequently, under pressure from Stalin to open up a second front in the West, on 19 August 1942, Churchill authorized the misguided invasion at Dieppe.

After Dunkirk and Dieppe, Churchill seemed reluctant to engage Hitler's Wehrmacht directly in Europe. Thereafter, he continued to oppose an invasion in France and lobbied for an invasion in Northern Africa to protect Britain's Suez access to India and its other colonial possessions. Then he pressed for an invasion of Sicily and Italy. In 1943, he continued to recommend an invasion through the Balkans (the 'soft underbelly' of Europe, in his opinion), to intervene with Soviet Russia's advance on Germany from the east and to belatedly prevent Stalin from achieving sole dominance over eastern Europe.

However, Churchill had an unparalleled mastery of the English language which he was able to marshal to inspire the English people to stand up to Hitler when the rest of Europe had either capitulated with sycophantic leaders or which Hitler had destroyed militarily by the 'blitzkrieg' (the 'lightning war'). Hitler did not intend to have the Second World War degenerate into a trench stalemate extending for hundreds of miles and lasting for years, as in the First World War.

Churchill's eloquent counterpart in America was Franklin D. Roosevelt, who was born on 30 January 1882 and he died in office on 12 April 1945, after winning his fourth presidential term. Roosevelt, like Churchill, was a moral counterpoint to individuals such as Hitler and Mussolini. Despite his paralysis from polio, which he contracted in about 1929, he towered above his fascist European contemporaries. His oratory was able to persuade his country to initially assist England in her defense against Hitler's Nazi onslaught.

Subsequently, he led his countrymen into another European War and defended America from the Japanese 'War Lords' in the Pacific as well. One error was not to support the candidacy of his Vice-President, Henry A. Wallace, in the 1944 election. Wallace had incurred the wrath of senior southern party leaders for his opposition to southern segregation. In 1940, Roosevelt threatened to withdraw his own candidacy if Wallace was not confirmed as his running mate. Unfortunately, in 1944, his health was too frail.

Those southern party leaders appointed an undistinguished Missouri Senator, Harry Truman, a man inclined to racial slurs and business failures, to succeed Roosevelt after his election as President for the fourth time. However, in July of 1948, when he became aware of Negro soldiers being thrown off military buses and beaten in Mississippi, Truman signed Executive Orders #9980 and #9981, voiding racial discrimination in the federal civil service and in the armed forces. It was a forerunner of President Johnson's 'Civil Rights Act' of 1964. He also dealt with the Berlin 'Air Lift' and the Korean War.

There were other players such as Benito Mussolini who was born on 29 July 1883, and who was executed by his own countrymen and hung up by his legs on 28 April 1945.

He had created the concept of 'fascism' in 1919 and it inspired other far-right dictators such as Francisco Franco in Spain, Antonio Salazar in Portugal, and Hitler in Germany. He was a vain, delusional man who wore elevated heels to increase his short physical stature and shaved his balding head to try to convey personal strength and conviction of purpose. His principal delusion was that he was going to remake the Mediterranean into a latter-day 'Roman Lake'.

The final principal character was Harry S. Truman, born on 8 May 1884, and he died on 26 December 1972. He made the unenviable decision to utilize atomic weapons for the first time on 9 August 1945. However, Japan was already near defeat and it was more concerned about Soviet Russia, which declared war on 8 August 1945.

Stalin had committed to Roosevelt that he would attack Manchuria after the European War ended and he fulfilled his promise on 26 August 1945. Truman's decision to bomb Hiroshima was primarily intended to intimidate Stalin by demonstrating America's 'Super Weapon' than to force Japan into an unconditional surrender. In fact, the Potsdam Conference was delayed until after the first atomic test was conducted on 16 July 1945.

Truman also repudiated Roosevelt's wartime financial commitments to Stalin and declared his 'Truman Doctrine' policy of containment of the Soviet Russia. Truman was the first American President to use the 'Atomic Threat' to try to establish American hegemony. But Stalin's expansionism in Eastern Europe, coupled with Truman's bellicose 'Atomic Threat' and the 'Truman Doctrine' ushered in the 'Cold War' and the arms race for the following forty-five years.

But this is a story in the life of Larion Daneelivich Sulupin, so the principal Russian players should be reviewed briefly, since the First World War also destroyed the Russian Empire. The nineteenth century was rife with new philosophical movements such as anarchism and communism. The former basically preached the destruction of all order by whatever means were available. The latter preached a 'workers' utopia', which was to be achieved by revolution and the overthrow of the ruling class and its accomplice, the church. There was to be an initial dictatorship, but it did promise a democracy, eventually.

On 1 March 1887, Aleksandr Ulyanov was arrested for conspiring to assassinate Tsar Alexander III. The Tsar gave the conspirators the choice of rendering an abject public apology or face execution, notwithstanding the fact that his own father, Alexander II, was assassinated some six years earlier. Ulyanov elected to be executed on 20 May 1887, at the age of 21.

Ulyanov was the older brother of Vladimir Ilyich Ulyanov, born on 22 April 1870, and he was seventeen when the Tsar executed his older brother, but as fate would have it, he not only established a 'Dictatorship of the Proletariat' in November of 1917, he also had the entire Romanov royal family executed on 17 July 1918. Lenin did not intend to have the Romanovs rule Russia again, irrespective of the ultimate outcome of his revolution. The Russian communists also had a penchant for adopting 'noms de guerre'. Just as Vladimir Ulyanov became 'Lenin', Lev Davidovich Bronstein became 'Leon Trotsky' and Joseb Djugashvili became 'Stalin', the 'man of steel'. A short man who, like Mussolini, elected to elevate his physical stature by wearing elevated heels. His left arm was partially disabled because of a childhood accident or possibly a beating from his alcoholic father, who succeeded in destroying all vestiges of human empathy in him.

After all, what can one say about a man who is purported to have said that: "...though the death of a single person can be a tragedy, the death of a million is a mere statistic." He even refused to exchange his son for Field Marshall Paulus after the Soviet victory at Stalingrad in 1943 and his son ended up committing suicide in a Nazi prisoner-of-war camp.

But events do not occur independently. Just as America's entry into the First World War gave the Anglo/French alliance some much-needed military assistance and fresh manpower, the German Empire decided that it had to eliminate the war on its eastern front. They adopted the expedient measure of smuggling Lenin into the turbulent Russian Empire in the hope that he would be able to foment a revolution to overthrow the Romanov's and end its eastern war with Russia.

Lenin succeeded in that goal and the Treaty of Brest-Litovsk with Germany was signed on 3 March 1918, but there was no respite for the Russian populace. Though the First World War ended in the west in November of 1918, Russia had to endure a continued civil war between the 'Red's' (communists) and the 'White's' (monarchist's). The Red's had to also fight the foreign interventionists, including England and America, until 1922. The Baltic states declared their independence and Finland even had the temerity to occupy territory in the Baltic peninsula which the Romanov Tsars had confiscated in the previous century. Japan also occupied Russian territory in the far east until 1925.

Winning a revolution and a civil war was different from actually governing a country. What confronted Lenin was widespread famine and disease, and it was not the most opportune time to implement 'state socialism'. Consequently, Lenin introduced the 'New Economic Policy' whereby individual capitalism was going to be tolerated for a time, but overall economic control would be retained by the 'state'. After enduring almost four years of the First World War and then another five years of civil war and foreign intervention, Lenin fervently believed that this interim proposal would facilitate the economic recovery of the country. There would be ample time, subsequently, to implement total socialism.

Trotsky was not interested in economic theory or plans as much as he was interested in fomenting a world revolution. He had helped create the 'Red Army' and he seemed to be the preeminent person to replace Lenin after his death on 21 January 1924.

Stalin disagreed with Lenin in respect of the implementation of the 'New Economic Policy' since he felt it was a betrayal of the revolution, however, until Lenin died and Trotsky was eliminated, he had to bide his time and effect alliances to eliminate his opponents. Inevitably, he would then turn on those former allies. His initial success was to strip Trotsky of his official positions in 1927 and then drive him into exile in 1929. Trotsky finally ended up in Mexico where Stalin succeeded in having him assassinated on 21 August 1940. Ironically, Trotsky had the last posthumous word since his biographical diatribe against Stalin was published after his death.

In the interim, Stalin proceeded to dismantle Lenin's 'New Economic Policy' and that meant the mass destruction of Lenin's quasi-capitalistic experiment. The 'Kulaks' (Lenin's capitalists) were eliminated as part of Stalin's implementation of complete governmental socialism over agriculture and industry through an accelerated protocol in the form of 'Five Year Plans'. Just as he had finally eliminated Trotsky in Mexico in 1940, his primary goal in the interim was to eliminate all domestic political and military opposition, both real and imagined, in order to consolidate his absolute power until his death on 5 March 1953. He initiated his terror in 1930 and millions of people were enslaved, imprisoned, resettled, or executed in that process, but then those millions were mere 'statistics'. Not surprisingly, Stalin also ended up executing most of his executioners as well.

*****

Russian names seem to be confusing. Take Larion Daneelivich Sulupin, for example. His given name was 'Larion', however, 'Louyna' was his affectionate nickname used by close family members or friends. His last name, 'Sulupin', was his family name. The female equivalent would add a suffix and it would become 'Sulupina'. His middle name, 'Daneelivich', was his patronymic name, adopted from his father's first name, 'Daneel'. Others would address him politely as 'Larion Daneelivich', while others would address him rudely, simply as 'Sulupin'.

Russian history and life seems melancholy to many, but there remains an underlying passion Russians can best know and feel, and which helps them endure and persevere. An emotional farewell is usually expressed as 'Zhestkiye Potselui, Gor'kiye Slezy' (Hard Kisses, Bitter Tears), which is intended to underscore the tender melancholy of an emotional parting between family and close friends.

Part 1
Prelude to War (1935 to 1940)

Chapter 1

Larion Daneelivich Sulupin, 'Louyna' to his mother, was born on 5 May 1917 in Xhotimsk, a small town in the eastern part of 'Belarus' which was to become the 'Byelorussian Soviet Socialist Republic', which in turn formed a small part of the 'Union of Soviet Socialist Republics'. It was bordered by the Ukraine to the south, Poland to the west, Lithuania to the north, and Russia to the east. His father was an engineer and his mother was a teacher. Larion was their only child and they both had high aspirations for their son.

In the spring of 1935, he was completing his compulsory third level of education. He was going to have to decide whether to follow his mother's wish and apply for university entrance to study engineering or follow his father's wish and apply for entrance into a military academy and graduate as a junior second lieutenant. Though his father was an engineer, considering the state of the Soviet Union and Stalin's purges, he ironically believed his son would be more secure in the military.

Whatever decision Larion was to make, he was bound to disappoint one of his parents, but at least he did not have to make that decision for a few months. His present priority was to assist his fellow Soviet comrades with the spring planting and all of his schoolmates, male and female, were given time off from their studies to fulfil that patriotic duty to the Motherland. They were to assist with the planting in the spring and harvesting in the fall. Stalin had directed that it must be so.

Larion's attitude was that if something was unavoidable, then you had to try to make it as enjoyable as possible. Each morning he was up at dawn and after quickly finishing his breakfast and taking the simple lunch of a slice of rye bread with some cheese or meat, when it was available, he would hurry out into the street so that he could be picked up by Valodya.

The old man drove a single old mare pulling a wooden wagon to the *kolkhoz*, the collective farm to the north of the town, each morning and returning after dusk each evening. Valodya happily provided Larion with his required transportation and Larion was sincerely grateful and tried to perform favors for the old man whenever the opportunities presented themselves.

Valodya not only provided Larion with transportation to the collective farm, he also regaled him with ribald stories and gave him an advanced education in Russian curses. Words he had never heard at home. At the collective farm, he followed his daily instructions as well as he could. Most people were inclined to forgive him for his occasional minor errors. Larion would apologize profusely, smile and run his hands through his dark brown curly hair and ask for a second chance to redeem himself.

One contrite look from his smiling face and deep blue eyes assured forgiveness. On this occasion, however, once they left the town, instead of heading to the collective farm, Valodya steered his elderly mare towards the adjoining forest.

"Say, *staryk* (old man)!" Larion asked respectfully. "Where are you taking me today? They are expecting us at the *kolkhoz*."

"Let's just say it is a surprise, my young boy," Valodya answered. "Possibly something new for you to learn as you grow up to become a young man."

They proceeded into the forest thick with birch and other trees. A flock of birds were flushed out by their approach and they swirled among the trees, singing out urgently as they sought new undisturbed refuges. The journey through the forest took about a half hour by Larion's best estimate until they finally came upon a clearing. A couple of men who he was able to recognize appeared to be dismantling some kind of contraption or apparatus which had been set up.

"Valodya, you lazy, old fart." One of the men said in an annoyed fashion. "We thought you would never get here. We have to move the *soma honka* to the new location before the chief of police gets here. The Chief let it be known that they were coming out to the forest today to destroy any illegal stills they may find. Though we all appreciate the chief's consideration in giving us notice, you would think that he would give us a bit more time. Al-though, I guess we should not complain."

"Soma honka?" Larion asked Valodya quizzically. "What the hell is a *'soma honka'*?"

"Watch your language, my young son," the old man replied seriously. "I do not want your parents to think that all I am teaching you is how to curse. As

22

for a *soma honka*, it is what it says it is '*self-made*'. It is our communal 'still' where we make our own vodka. You cannot drink the Soviet vodka. For one thing, it is expensive and for another, we are sure that they add chemicals to it because you get these terrible hangovers. With our homemade brew, all you get is happiness and sweet dreams. You wake up in the morning and you just feel reborn."

"So why are we dismantling it?" Larion asked in a confused reply.

"We and the police have an unspoken understanding. We make the vodka for our own use and there are about twenty of us who contribute to this enterprise, but we do not sell it for a profit. That would make us capitalists and Comrade Stalin would not approve. But we are permitted to sell it to recover our costs and our labor. In return, to maintain public morals and the law, the chief of police has to demonstrate that he is attempting to keep us lawbreakers in check.

"However, he always conveniently lets it be known when he will be staging a raid, which usually gives us sufficient time to dismantle the still and move it to a new location. To show our gratitude to the chief and his police, we arrange to deliver a dozen bottles, anonymously of course, to the police station each month."

It took the two other men, Valodya, and Larion a few hours to complete the dismantling and removal of the still and its sundry appurtenances to its new location. Some other members of their 'vodka commune' would come by the next day and make it operational again. The police would stage their raid and their city and its citizens' morality would be safe-guarded again for a few months.

Valodya then took his mare and wagon to the *kolkhoz*. The collective farm not only raised a variety of grain crops, it also had an apple orchard and raised a variety of chickens and geese, cows and swine. The soil was fertile; however, its productivity was dependent on the worker's collective motivation and that affected the farm's overall efficiency. Though all of the workers were taught Marx's dictum: *From each according to their ability; to each according to their needs.* Not all of the workers were inclined to practice it when they saw that some were not prepared to contribute as much as they could, yet they still expected to receive as much as possible.

As they drove up the main entrance to the collective farm, Larion noticed a young girl exit the manager's office. She had blonde hair and a lithe figure.

A spring gust of wind lifted up her light flowered dress and she casually low-ered her left hand to maintain her modesty, while she lifted her right hand over her eyes to shield them from the setting sun so that she could better observe the two new visitors. As they got closer, Larion recognized her from his school; however, they did not share any classes, so she was a stranger to him.

Valodya may have been old but he was observant and he noticed that Lar-ion was staring at the young girl, who was staring back at him.

"That is Tamara Dimitriova Shanina," he announced, as he stopped his wagon at the front steps. "She is the manager's daughter. She is helping out in the dairy. A pretty young thing, don't you agree, Larion Daneelivich?"

Larion was tongue-tied for a moment. He had never seen her in such close proximity. She kept her full lips pursed as she smiled at them and her light blue eyes glistened in the setting sun. She lifted up her hand to tuck a straying lock of her blonde hair back under the scarf she was wearing.

"Welcome, comrades," she announced in a melodious voice. Though she was staring at Larion, she forced her eyes to respectfully stray to Valodya. "*Dzedushka* (Grandfather), what may I do for you?" she asked the old man respectfully. Larion was not sure if she addressed the old man as grandfather out of personal esteem or out of a familial relationship.

"I have just come back to see if anyone needed a ride back to town, my pretty one," Valodya replied, as his beaming smile revealed several missing front teeth.

Larion was a bit put out. After all, Valodya was old enough to be her grand-father, perhaps even her great-grandfather…and here he was, flirting with her. Something he wished he had the initiative to have done himself when she first spoke to them.

"Well, Valodya…my old friend. Where have you been all day?"

The words were spoken by an older man who had followed Tamara out the front door. Larion assumed that he had to be her father since Tamara affection-ately embraced the man and kissed him on his cheek before she waved a fare-well to everyone and headed off in another direction. But she turned back for a final glance at Larion and he was positive that her departing smile was for him, alone.

"Dimitri Aleksyevich, my most sincere and humble apologies," Valodya replied. "But I was obliged to go to the forest and assist some comrades…if you know what I mean."

"The Chief pursuing lawbreakers again?" the manager asked knowingly.

"That pursuit is never-ending…thank God…I mean *thank Lenin*!"

"Who is your young friend?" Dimitri asked, as he examined Larion closely. He had noticed the young man's gaze following his daughter as she left.

"Comrade Manager, I have the pleasure of introducing you to my young companion, Larion Daneelivich Sulupin. He is going to some university in the fall, but I am trying to teach him some of the nuances of real life before he commences all that book reading," Valodya answered proudly.

"Hopefully, those nuances do not include your unique collection of Russian epithets," Shanin replied. "And you, Larion Daneelivich. Haven't your parents…not to mention old Valodya here…taught you how to greet a new acquaintance properly? How do you think you will be able to shake my hand politely while you remain seated in that wagon?"

Larion immediately attempted to jump off the wagon; however, his left foot got tripped by a piece of rope in the footwell and he ended up rolling onto the ground in front of the surprised manager. He recovered quickly and as he dusted himself off and wiped his right hand on his shirt, he extended his hand in greeting, which the amused manager willingly accepted.

"Sir…Comrade Manager, I mean," Larion sputtered formally. "I have an enormous privilege, which I respectfully request that you would consider bestowing on me."

"Well, Comrade Student," the manager replied is a bemused fashion. "Considering that we have just met, is it not a bit presumptuous of you to impose such a request upon me in this fashion?"

"I apologize, sir, for being presumptuous. I certainly do not mean any disrespect. However, I would be immensely pleased if I am afforded the opportunity of an introduction to your beautiful daughter, Tamara Dimitriova," Larion replied sheepishly.

Though Dimitri remembered enduring a similar shame-filled entreaty when he was Larion's age, it was his only daughter they were discussing and any sympathy he may have been inclined to feel, he decided that it should be suppressed…at least for the moment.

"Well, your request may 'immensely please you', however, I am not sure that it would 'immensely please me'," he replied solemnly. "After all, a father has to exercise extreme caution in such situations. And instead of showing up this morning and fulfilling your duty on the *kolkhoz*, you permitted yourself to aid and abet this geriatric scoundrel and you became his accessory in a serious crime."

"Oh, do not be so unforgiving, Dimitri Aleksyevich," Valodya implored. "Have you forgotten what it was like to be a young boy…I mean, a young man."

"That is the problem, Valodya," the manager replied wryly. "Unfortunately, I have not forgotten." Turning to Larion, he affected a more serious tone. "But why don't you show me how diligently you are able to perform your duties for the balance of this week? Your school respite ends this coming Saturday and perhaps if you work hard and show up for spring seeding celebration on Sunday, you may be fortunate enough to be introduced to my daughter, Tamara."

Chapter 2

True to his word, Larion performed all of his duties in a diligent and expeditious fashion for the remainder of the week. In addition to his regular duties, he even volunteered for additional work in the dairy. He brought in hay for the cows and he was even willing to muck out the stalls and cart the manure away to a stockpile, which would be used to fertilize the fields in the fall.

He did glimpse Tamara on a few of those occasions, but she did not seem to notice him, initially. However, after a few chance encounters she seemed to recall meeting him, since Larion would persistently smile and wave at her and call out her name each time they passed each other. Eventually, she started to return his smile and even waive in reply. Though she was not able to recall meeting him or knowing him, she did not want to be discourteous. He was an attractive young man who seemed to be happy even when he was loading manure onto his cart and then wheeling it away from the dairy.

*****

After dinner on Saturday evening, Larion asked his father for permission to fire up the *banya*, the family sauna his father had built behind their home. The sauna was composed of two small rooms. The outer room was for disrobing, heating the stones, and seeking a brief respite from the steam room. The inner chamber contained the heated stones that were dosed with water until the room filled with steam. There were also fresh cut willow branches one could use to mildly lash oneself, to simulate one's circulation.

Larion wanted to totally purge his body and pores of the grime and the odor he had accumulated by working on the collective farm that past week. He wanted to be pristine for his formal introduction to Tamara and only a sauna would be able to accomplish that. A hot water bath would just not suffice.

Larion's mother noticed that her son seemed to be exceptionally preoccupied with his appearance that weekend. He also asked her to wash his best white shirt and iron his best trousers. He had even borrowed his father's shoe polish to shine his black boots…twice. He tried to comb his unruly curls into submission until they finally relented.

The parents maintained their silence, but they smiled at each other when they exchanged a knowing glance between themselves as Larion kept inspecting the suitability of his shirt, his trousers, and his boots. His mother even offered to share her favorite fragrance she made herself from the flowers of the lilac tree in their front yard, which she combined with other unspecified ingredients into a light lotion. She cautioned him to use it sparingly, pointing out that subtlety in aroma was preferable to excess.

He was obliged to walk to the collective farm on Sunday afternoon, but it was an overcast, cool day, so he did not have to worry about soiling himself with his own perspiration. The walk was approximately three kilometers, but Larion was practically floating with each step. He had only walked one kilometer when Valodya and his old mare came trotting down the road and offered to give him a ride the rest of the way.

"Well, aren't you the young gentleman today. All cleaned up…and you even smell of flowers. Some girl is really going to be impressed with you this evening. Do you have anyone special in mind?" Valodya asked teasingly.

"And I notice that even you seem to have washed and put on some cleaner clothes, old friend," Larion replied in kind. "Are you going to romance some fat old *baba* who will keep you warm at night after the stove fire goes out? Be sure that she is not too round for if she rolls over you, we may be burying you the following morning."

"You should be more respectful to your elders, my young friend," Valodya replied with a smile. "And you need not worry about me getting crushed. After all, I have Cossack blood coursing through these old veins. Even a cow could not crush me. But you should know things like this, because your family has Cossack blood as well."

"So my parents keep reminding me," Larion replied a bit wearily. He was tired of being told of his heritage and its expectations. You had to be able to drink more, fight harder, and assert your superiority at all times, but he believed that they were just being partly serious. His mother did not approve of drinking to excess, but that was the only way his Cossack father knew how to drink. Once a bottle was opened, the drinking did not end until that bottle was empty.

*****

The celebration was to be held in a former church that had been built by some noble on his ancestral estate. The revolution had converted the estate into a collective farm and the former church had been converted into a recreational center. It had been stripped of its icons and the Orthodox crosses that once adorned its onion domed roofs. Now the younger generation put on dances, while their parents used it for non-religious social gatherings, such as celebrating the end of the spring planting.

The regular farm workers had prepared an ample buffet table in the end of the room with traditional warm and cold Russian *zakuski* (appetizers). Cabbage rolls, cheese and potato dumplings, *blini* (crepes) filled with cottage cheese, a variety of salads, sliced sausages, and rye bread. There was ample *sok* (apple juice) and fresh water for the youngsters and the women. Valodya had brought two dozen one-liter bottles of vodka to fortify the liquor supply for the men.

There two musicians to provide the music. A grey-haired old man was playing a *bayon*, a chromatic button accordion, while a middle-aged man was accompanying him on his *balalaika.*

As Larion and Valodya entered the main hall, they noticed that the farm manager and Tamara were standing together, greeting the people who were entering the hall. Chairs had been set around the perimeter of the hall to permit the guests to sit and eat and visit, while the center of the room was reserved for dancing. The atmosphere was quite convivial.

Valodya prodded Larion towards their hosts shamelessly and Shanin decided to affect a severe countenance as Larion came into his view. He knew from personal experience that it was preferable to be firm and stern at the outset, then you could become more relaxed, rather than the other way around. It was always more difficult to impose discipline after laxity.

"Comrade Manager Dimitri Aleksyevich," Valodya announced solemnly. "Allow me to introduce you to my young colleague, Larion Daneelivich Sulupin."

"Ah, yes!" the manager replied sternly. "Yes, I remember. The young man who impertinently sought my leave to 'immensely please him' by affording him the privilege of an introduction to my daughter, Tamara Dimitriova Shanina."

Tamara maintained an enigmatic visage, smiling with closed lips with her hands clasped nervously behind her back, but her light blue eyes were twinkling with amusement at her father's attempt to intimidate her would-be young suitor.

"Well, young man," Dimitri asked ominously. "Do you feel that you have earned the privilege of an introduction to my daughter?"

"I have tried my best and I believe that I have earned that honor, Comrade Manager," Larion replied respectfully, but he could not help injecting some humor into his response. "I believe that I have single-handedly helped to contribute to the serenity of your cows to such an extent that milk production increased substantially this past week."

"Is this true, Tamara?" the manager asked skeptically, turning to his daughter for confirmation.

"Yes, it is true, father," Tamara replied insouciantly. "I can personally attest to the fact that as a result of Larion Daneelivich's dedicated bovine ministrations, the cows seemed to *'moo'* more contentedly as the week went on and milk production increased as well."

"Humm! In that case, Comrade Larion Daneelivich, allow me to introduce you to my daughter, Tamara Dimitriova Shanina. Treat her well, otherwise you may receive an unwanted invitation to visit Siberia."

"I am most pleased to meet your acquaintance, Tamara Dimitriova. Would you care to dine with me and perhaps share a dance later on?" Larion asked politely, affecting a partial bow at the waist and extending his hand to her.

"He does not sound sufficiently *proletarian* to me, Valodya," Dimitri interjected, feigning disappointment. "Perhaps he is a bit too *bourgeois* for my Tamara, don't you think?"

Larion was so preoccupied with Tamara that he was puzzled by the manager's comments and started to get concerned. He was prepared to protest this deemed insult and attempt to confirm his proletarian worthiness.

"That is alright, father," Tamara interceded. "I think I prefer a gentleman with *bourgeois* manners to an unrefined *proletarian*. Lenin, please forgive me," she beseeched facetiously.

"Perhaps you should speak a bit softer, my dear daughter," Dimitri replied seriously as he quickly surveyed the people who were milling about them. "The *NKVD* does not have the capacity to appreciate such comments or such humor."

He gestured with his chin to a morose couple standing nearby by themselves in the company of a dour young man. Tamara immediately became quiet.

"Those people, my dear young friend," Valodya added in a hushed voice by way of explanation and gesturing toward the same glum troika, "are the local representatives of our dear *People's Commissariat for Internal Affairs* (*NKVD*). One word from them and it is off to Siberia, if you are lucky." Turning to Tamara, he added, "You are too young and too pretty to be sent off to Siberia, my dear granddaughter. So please exercise a bit more discretion."

"With your permission, Comrade Manager," Larion asked respectfully, "may I take Tamara to the buffet and get something to eat?"

Dimitri Aleksyevich merely nodded his assent to Larion's request, but he kept watching the dour troika apprehensively.

As they walked away, Larion posed a question to Tamara, "Is Valodya your grandfather?"

"He is my 'adopted' grandfather. My father's parents died when he was quite young in one of the troubles that seems to afflict the Motherland from time to time. Valodya took him in and raised him. He is very dear to both of us."

*****

The evening passed uneventfully. The people ate and drank and engaged in conversation. Soon the center of the hall was cleared to permit interested parties to dance. Tamara took Larion's hand in hers and led him to the dance floor. The males and females formed concentric circles and took turns in dancing for each other. The women placed their hands on their hips and commenced a synchronized footwork in time to the music, spinning in turn as the hems of their dresses blossomed up. The men stood back and watched in admiration and synchronized their own footwork in time to the music as well.

Then the women would stand back and permit the men to show their skills in performing the *hopaka*, an athletic dance attributed to the 'Cossacks', peasants who emancipated themselves from serfdom and escaped to the fringes of the Russian Empire to set up their own culture and civilization. They became expert horsemen and fighters, a necessity in order to maintain their independence. They became so adept militarily that the Tsars eventually retained them as mercenaries to help fight their neighbors, suppress insurrections domestically, and even conduct periodic *pogroms*, which appeared to be an integral facet of Imperial governance.

The *hopaka* entailed the men squatting down and kicking out their legs, one or both at a time, landing on their heels while the dancer supported himself with his hands behind his back. A competition would inevitably develop between the individual male dancers attempting to out-perform each other. Some were so adept that they were able to effect backward and forward flips—all in time to the music while their female counterparts clapped in unison and executed their own synchronized footwork and spins while they watched on in admiration. When both groups became exhausted, they would adjourn and the two musicians would play traditional songs like *Kalinka* or *Ochee Churnayy* (Dark Eyes) to which the assembled crowd would join in as a raucous chorus.

"Tamara Dimitriova," the dour young man announced and extended his right arm and then commanded. "Come, dance with me."

The invitation initially caught Larion unawares and he looked up in surprise. He considered it to be a rude intrusion, but he was reluctant to intervene considering what Tamara's father and adopted grandfather had to say about the dour young man's parents, but he recovered quickly. He was not going to just stand aside and let this usurper take Tamara away from him.

"Allow me to introduce myself," he said, as he rose to his feet. "Larion Daneelivich Sulupin."

The dour young man was not impressed. It was obvious that he was not accustomed to having other people interrupt when he was trying to have a conversation with a young woman who interested him.

"Georgy Ivanovitch Kertinsky," he replied reluctantly and then turned his attention back to Tamara. "So, are you going to dance with me or not?" he asked petulantly.

"Georgy Ivanovich, why don't you dance for me first," Tamara beseeched him. "You do the *hopaka* so beautifully." Effectively deflecting his invitation for the moment.

The flattery worked and as the musicians commenced to play a new song, Georgy assumed control over the center of the dancefloor and commenced an energetic and a very gymnastic version of the Cossack dance. When he finished, he was too exhausted to immediately renew his request that he and Tamara dance together, but he rejoined them with the smug knowledge that his performance was pretty impressive.

Larion immediately jumped up and announced that he thought he could be a bit better. He had thrown down that proverbial gauntlet and the dance duel was about to commence. As he walked to the center of the dancefloor, he did not notice the scowl Georgy Ivanovitch directed at him. Most of the rest of the assembled guests recognized a competition in the making and that the prize was obviously the farm manager's beautiful daughter. They yielded the dancefloor and formed a circle, clapping vigorously to the rhythm of the music, which commenced softly and slowly, but then proceeded to increase in volume and celerity until it came to an abrupt halt. When the music ended, they implored Georgy to dance again and try to surpass Larion's performance. Thereafter for the next fifteen minutes, both Larion and Georgy attempted to outperform each other to the enthusiastic appreciation of the entire assemblage. Georgy had the advantage in being more gymnastic in his performance, while Larion had the advantage of being more artistic.

While Larion was performing one more time, Georgy took the opportunity to try to recuperate. He knew that the competition would have to end soon or he would lose by default in being unable to continue. He had expended considerably more energy than his upstart challenger, however the crowd cheered Larion as much as they cheered him. For his last performance, he did not hold back and for a finale, he completed two backward flips, landing on one knee with his arms extended to the ceiling, which brought the audience gasping in admiration.

Larion was prepared to admit that it was going to be near impossible to outperform until Valodya came to his rescue…with a bottle of vodka. Tamara felt giddy and exhilarated by having the two young men compete for her attention. She merely giggled and clapped her hands to the rhythm of the exuberant music as each one danced for her. Shanin could only grimace in his regret that his daughter was maturing much too quickly.

"Valodya, I can barely stand up right now, the last thing I need is to drink some more. I will just collapse and you will have to carry me home," Larion lamented.

"Oh, my young foolish friend," Valodya answered. "This vodka is not for drinking; it is for dancing." He then proceeded to pour out the liquor in the middle of the marble dancefloor, permitting it to spread out into an ever-enlarging circle. Then to everyone's surprise, he lit the liquor, which burst forth in a light bluish flame as the crowd gasped. Someone shut off the lights, which magnified the intensity of the vodka flames in the center of the room.

"Now you dance in those flames, my young friend, and you shall win!" Valodya commanded.

Without a second thought, Larion jumped into the flames and commenced his final *hopaka*.

It was the fear of getting burned as much as it was his desire to win that drove him on. He decided to make his dance movements quickly to minimize the risk of burns, but he knew he had to devise a novel athletic move to end his performance. The move involved falling backward, arrested by his extended arms behind his back and effecting a high scissors kick with both legs in the air, then as he pulled his legs down in front of him, he pushed off with both hands to lift his torso upright as he landed erect on his feet, his arms proudly extended towards the ceiling in a final triumphant exultation.

The alcohol had pretty much burned out by this point and as he remained standing in the middle of the hall with his hands extended upward, he could feel the warmth and smell his singed shirt and trousers. He had never performed a gymnastic move like that and he was not sure that he would be able to replicate it again, at least not while he was sober, but it worked.

Everyone in the building erupted in a roar of approval and he was besieged by men and women offering their congratulations. As he looked around, he could see Georgy and his parents sulking out of the building. He looked at Valodya and Tamara's father, who stared back at him with incredulity. Tamara was standing beside her father, her hands clasped in front of her chest, beaming proudly.

Finally, after he was able to disengage himself, he went over to Tamara. He looked at her beseechingly, yearning for her approval and she gazed back at him in adoration. Then they both embraced for the first time.

"I did that for you, Tamara Dimitriova," Larion whispered softly into her ear and she embraced him even harder.

"And I graciously thank you...*Louyna*," she whispered back, giving him an innocuous congratulatory kiss on his cheek. "If I may be so bold to address you as such?

Chapter 3

The November 1917 Revolution overthrew the Romanov dynasty and dissolved the Imperial Duma, the lower legislative body in the Imperial government. With the outbreak of civil war, Lenin and his fellow communists attempted to consolidate their political control over Russia. One initial step was to replace the Imperial 'Department for Protecting the Public Security and Order', the verbose title for the Imperial secret police, otherwise known as the 'Okhrana'. The Okhrana had arrested and imprisoned Lenin, Trotsky and Stalin repeatedly in the years preceding 1917. Its more verbose communist replacement was the 'All-Russian Extraordinary Commission for Combatting Counter-Revolution, Profiteering and Sabotage', syncopated in the acronym, the 'CHEKA'.

The principal driving force behind the creation and organization of the communist secret police was Felix Dzerzhinksy, who died on 20 July 1926, at the age of forty-eight. The CHEKA was replaced by the 'People's Commissariat for Internal Affairs', the NKVD, which Stalin granted a plenary monopoly over internal security, imprisonment and execution in 1930, which lasted until the end of the Second World War.

Following Lenin's death in 1924, Dzerhinsky's death in 1926 and Trotsky's exile in 1929, three prominent communist obstacles to Stalin's ascendency to power were eliminated through natural forces. The remaining obstacles would be removed more violently with the assistance and instrumentality of the NKVD and the principals who followed Dzerzhinsky such as Genrikh Yagoda, Nikolai Yezhov, and finally, Laventry Beria, though all ended up being executed themselves. The one surviving principal of the secret police from this turbulent period was Vasili Blokhin, who acted as Stalin's personal chief executioner. He survived Stalin's death in 1953, by a further two years before his own reported suicide in 1955.

Stalin's 'Great Purge' commenced in 1932. It was given additional impetus by the 1934 assassination of Sergei Kirov, one of Lenin's stalwart revolutionary companions and the Communist Party boss of Leningrad. Using that assassination, which he, himself, had orchestrated as a pretext, Stalin proceeded to purge the communist party of potential opponents. Zenoviev and Kamenev, who were instrumental in assisting Stalin in removing Trotsky, were themselves arrested, forced to confess and then executed in 1936. The execution of their families quickly followed.

By 1937, Stalin turned his attention to the military. He had appointed five Field Marshals in 1934, but by the end of the Second World War he had executed three of them, including Mikhail Tukhachevsky, the head of the army, in June of 1937. But true to his form, Stalin then proceeded to have five of the eight military judges who had convicted Tukhachevsky of treason and 'Trotskyism', subsequently convicted and executed, as well.

By 1940, it is estimated that one third of the officer corps were arrested and either executed or imprisoned in the Gulag, which was operated by the NKVD. However, with the disastrous Winter War with Finland in 1939 and the German invasion in 1941, Stalin was forced to be pragmatic and he even redeemed about four thousand officers who were incarcerated in the Gulag and reinstated them back to active duty in the Red Army.

Stalin was also forced to be pragmatic after the outbreak of war with Germany on 22 June 1941, in respect of the partisans. Initially, the Soviet soldiers were expected to fight to the death on the front line. To ensure that loyal servitude, Stalin had the NKVD organize its own military divisions which were composed of 'Rifle Regiments', not armored divisions such as the Waffen SS. The NKVD divisions were strategically placed behind the front line to ensure that no soldier was permitted to retreat. They were to fight to their death or be executed as deserters.

Consequently, the soldiers on the Soviet front line had a difficult choice to make. Either stay in position until the German onslaught overwhelmed and killed them or attempt to retreat and be shot by the NKVD. If they became prisoners of war, that also meant certain death. About 3.3 million Soviet POWs died in Nazi camps.

However, if they could infiltrate past the German front lines and become 'partisans', they could harass the 'Wehrmacht' (Nazi combined naval, land and air force) from behind. Stalin initially considered them to be traitors as well, but once their effectiveness was demonstrated, he deemed them to be an integral part of the defense of the Motherland – at least until the War ended, at which time they were liable to be imprisoned for up to twenty-five years at hard labor or executed.

In respect of the general population, it is estimated that Stalin and his NKVD executed almost 1.2 million people and a further one million were incarcerated in the Gulag. Another one million were 'resettled' for varying terms of servitude in Siberia. Their individual selection was determined not on the basis of their alleged personal sins or failings, but by the economic needs in the various parts of Siberia that Stalin wanted to populate, develop, and industrialize.

Chapter 4

The rest of the school term passed quickly and pleasantly. Larion would meet Tamara as the end of classes each day and Valodya would meet them in front of the school and slowly drive them back to the *kolkhoz*. After a while, Tamara's father even permitted her to invite him in for dinner.

Their relationship was a chaste first-love and simply being in each other's company was sufficient. Holding hands or sharing a kiss seemed to satiate all of their desires. They discussed their respective dreams and made plans on how they would share the remainder of their respective lives together.

The Kertinsky family, however, was neither forgiving, nor forgetful. They felt that Georgy had been humiliated by Larion and they intended to exact their revenge. They had an obligation to the *NKVD* to not only identify potential enemies of the state, but an obligation to recommend candidates for Stalin's monthly quota for *NKVD* disciplinary action in the form of either resettlement in Siberia, imprisonment in the Gulag, or summary execution.

In light of the callous manner, they deemed that Larion had insulted their son, Georgy's parents, with his personal enthusiastic support, decided to submit their denunciation of Larion and his parents as 'undesirables' to the *NKVD* at the provincial (*Oblast*) capital of Mogilev. Though they submitted their denunciation shortly after the event, the provincial NKVD was not able to act on their recommendation for a couple of months. In the interim, Larion, Tamara, her father, and even Valodya had blissfully forgotten the incident and deemed it to be a closed matter.

*****

"Valodya," Larion said as his old friend slowly drove him back to town, "I am starting to feel sorry for your old mare. Perhaps you should retire her and get yourself a new horse. I feel sorry that she has to travel to the *kolkhoz* and back to town each day."

"Don't you worry yourself about my old mare," Valodya replied. "The exercise is good for her, just as a little exercise is good for me. We do not push her to gallop or trot too much, she just walks at her own pace or trots when she feels like it."

As they approached his parent's home, Larion noticed that there were no lights on in the house, which was unusual. He also noticed some of their neighbors were drawing back the curtains and discretely peeking out their window. Valodya noticed one of the neighbors gestured that he should come to his home. Valodya permitted Larion to go to his own residence, while he proceeded to go to see the neighbor, a man he had known for a long period of time.

"Alexi Aleksyevich," he greeted his good friend. "What is with all this furtive peeking and hiding all about?"

His friend quickly hustled him into his home and after checking the street to see if there was any other matter that should concern him, quickly closed the door behind him.

"What is the matter, Alexi?" Valodya inquired. "I swear you seem to be getting more senile with each passing year. They will be sending you to the sanatorium if you are not careful."

But before his friend could answer his question, Larion was anxiously knocking on the door and seeking entrance as well.

"Valodya!" Larion interjected. "There is no one home. My parents are gone. What is going on?" he asked anxiously.

"Please sit down and I will give you some tea and then I will explain what has happened today. This afternoon, a black vehicle bearing Mogilev license plates showed up at your parents' home and took them away. I think you both understand what that means," Alexi replied solemnly.

Valodya and Larion looked at each other with concern. They knew full well what it meant. It had happened several times in the preceding three years. A black car would arrive from Mogilev and people would be taken away, never to be seen again.

"But why?" Larion pleaded. "Why would they take my parents away? My parents have never spoken a harsh word against Lenin or Stalin."

"I do not think the issue is what they may have said about anyone or anything…" Valodya explained. "It probably has more to do with what some people in this town may have said to the *NKVD* in Mogilev, the capital of our *Oblast* (province), about your parents."

"But who?" asked Larion, who was quite confused and bewildered at this development. "Who would do such a vile thing?"

"There is no shortage of vile people when you live in vile times," Alexi suggested ominously. "But the first people who come to my mind are the Kertinskys. They have a vile temperament. They also have the means as NKVD informants and they certainly had the motivation."

"What motivation?" Larion asked. "My parents have never done anything to offend the Kertinskys."

"Perhaps your parents have never done anything to offend them, but what about you!" replied Alexi.

"I have to agree!" added Valodya. "You remember your fiery *hopaka* a couple of months ago? That bastard of theirs...what's his name? Georgy...he has been trying to breed Tamara for the past year and then you not only out-dance him, but you carry her off in your arms...well, figuratively speaking in any case."

"How can I find out where they have taken my parents though? I need to know if I can do something to help them. Possibly bring them back home," Larion pleaded, visibly on the verge of tears.

"When the 'black car' comes to town to take someone away, I have never seen those people return and no one knows where they were taken or even if they are alive or dead," Alexi replied definitively. "Besides that, Larion Daneelivich, those bastards even came to my home and asked me about you, since they were looking for you as well. I did not tell them that it was your habit to ride out to the *kolkhoz* with Valodya and Tamara. I simply pretended to be an old fool who knew nothing."

"You are extremely fortunate that they decided to go back to Mogilev instead of waiting for you to return home. I remember living under the tsars, but that was bearable in comparison to trying to survive in this putrid proletarian paradise. The revolution was supposed to liberate us, but all it did was give the communists their opportunity to really sodomize us. May they all burn in hell for eternity!" Alexi replied and solemnly crossed himself in the Orthodox tradition, right shoulder to left shoulder.

The three remained silent for a moment. Alexi offered to share some tea again, but neither Valodya nor Larion felt thirsty even though both of their mouths were dry and parched. Finally, Larion decided what he had to do.

"My father always taught me to never insult or demean another person. He taught me to be civil, even when I could not sincerely be respectful. But he also taught me that if anyone chose to insult me or slight me in any fashion, I was to seek appropriate retribution. No such insult or slight was to remain un-answered. The Kertinskys have decided to take my parents away from me, my honor demands that I obtain appropriate retribution," Larion pronounced sol-emnly, being fully appreciative of the task he had just assumed for himself, irrespective of the potential risks it posed.

"I believe that you and I should discuss this matter with Dimitri Aleksye-vich and the chief of police. The Kertinskys are not to be trifled with," Valodya finally said.

No!" Larion protested. "I am obliged to exact satisfaction for my family. Otherwise, I would bring dishonor upon my family name." Then he left Alexi's home.

Valodya knew that it was futile to travel back to the *kolkhoz* and relate these developments to Shanin, the *kolkhoz* manager, because it was too late. But he knew he had to inform him because he would know what had to be done. It was obvious that Larion did not appreciate his jeopardy. The chief of police was also Tamara's godfather and notwithstanding the fact that the communists did not formally approve of that archaic relationship, he could provide valuable assistance as well.

*****

Shanin's countenance was anxious and concerned. He had observed his daughter's growing affection for Larion over the preceding months and he had even developed a personal affection for the young man, himself. But having the *NKVD* remove Larion's parents for disciplinary action was something not be trifled with and it could not be easily remedied. Larion should deem himself to be fortunate at having avoided his own arrest…for the time being. But it was imperative that he try to arrange for the boy's personal security before he did something that might prove to be fatal. Family honor became meaningless if one had to die for it. He had to go into town and see his good friend and Tamara's godfather, Chief of Police, Boris Mikhailovitch Tunov.

Shanin knew that Larion was leaning towards studying engineering at university, but he was subject to possible conscription. The communists had introduced it in 1917, to bolster their forces during the Civil War and the Foreign Intervention. If he proceeded to study engineering and then got conscripted, his studies would be interrupted, probably permanently, and his personal status in the Red Army would be that of a lowly infantryman. The minimum age for conscription in 1935 was nineteen, so he would be guaranteed only one year of university studies since there was no exemption or deferment for university students and the minimum term of military service was two years, unless it was extended by the outbreak of hostilities.

If Larion chose to run away, the Soviets had introduced an internal passport system whereby every adult had to carry two critical forms of identification. One document was a photo identification card that contained the bearer's date and place of birth, his full name, and the names of his parents. The other document was a small hand-sized booklet that contained the bearer's work record. It identified where one had worked and in what capacity, and most importantly, his supervisor's assessment of that work performance. In the event any local or national police official stopped him and asked him to produce both documents, failure to comply resulted in immediate arrest, incarceration, and deportation to Siberia as part of Stalin's resettlement program. Shanin knew that since Larion had just turned eighteen, he possessed neither document, but they could be issued by the chief of police in their small town.

After giving it considerable thought, Shanin decided that it was preferable for Larion to enroll in a military academy. It would afford him an opportunity to obtain an advanced education and he would graduate as a junior Second Lieutenant. Although it was the lowest officer rank in the military hierarchy, that status was still infinitely preferable to that of a mere infantryman.

M.V. Frunze had established the first communist military academy in 1918 to train officers for the newly created Red Army which was commanded efficiently by Leon Trotsky. After Frunze's death at the age of forty on 31 October 1925, it was renamed the *Frunze Military Academy* in his honor and it was located in Moscow. Shanin knew that his good friend, the chief of police, had attended that military academy and that he may be able to assist him in getting

Larion admitted to that institution. His only remaining problem was to persuade Larion to follow that advice.

*****

In a small town like Xhotimsk, the chief of police was not only the police chief, but he also had the authority to act as a prosecutor and judge. If the judgment was the imposition of a fine, the fine had to be paid at the local bank, which guaranteed widespread dissemination of that punishment throughout the town within hours. It also provided ample fodder for embellishment by the many gossips in town for several weeks.

"Greetings, Chief Boris Mikhailovich," Shanin addressed his friend formally, since he was in the company of other police officers. "May I speak with you on an urgent matter?"

"Of course, Dimitri Aleksyevich. Let us go to my office," the police chief replied.

While Shanin was explaining Larion's predicament to the police chief, one of his subordinates knocked apologetically at his office door and requested permission to enter. Even though the chief granted that permission, the police constable opened the door but hesitated to cross the threshold until his chief beckoned him to proceed.

"The Kertinskys are outside, sir, and they demand an immediate audience," the constable explained. "It appears that their son did not come home last night and they have been unable to find him today. They fear foul play."

The police chief sighed and looked knowingly at Shanin. His immediate thought was that Shanin's worst fears may have materialized.

"Allow them admission, Constable."

The Kertinskys entered the office imperiously until they noticed Shanin's presence in the room. They immediately halted and looked questioningly at the police chief. They expected privacy. The police chief ignored them and merely inquired as to whether formal introductions were necessary, but both Shanin and the Kertinskys indicated that it was not necessary.

"We would like a private audience, Comrade Chief," the wife stated flatly.

"The constable just advised me that you believe your son is missing and since Comrade Manager Dimitri Aleksyevich operates the *kolkhoz*, I believe he may assist us in having his farm workers check the farm lands and the river that runs through it, for your son."

It was apparent that the Kertinskys were not impressed with the chief's decision, but their concern for their son superseded their deemed slight at being denied their requested privacy. Their simple story was that their son had gone out to meet some friends the previous afternoon and go fishing in the river. But those friends never met him and his whereabouts remained unknown since he left their home. In reply to the chief's query as to whether they were aware of anyone in particular who would want to harm their son, they replied in unison and without hesitation—Larion Sulupin.

Both the chief of police and Shanin exchanged a quick glance between themselves and then the chief decided to make further inquiries of the Kertinskys.

"And Comrade Kertinsky, why would you accuse Larion Daneelivich?" the chief asked.

"There was bad blood between them," the father answered tersely.

"Tell me about this 'bad blood', comrade."

"Well, Sulupin insulted our son at the *kolkhoz*'s celebration of the completion of the spring planting a few months ago," the father replied.

"Tell me about this 'insult', comrade," the chief persisted. "If your son has disappeared and is not out romancing some young girl in town right now, that is a serious charge to make against another person and I require facts…specific facts. I cannot act simply on suspicion."

"Perhaps you cannot act on the basis of suspicion, but we can," the mother spat her words out. She knew her status as an informer for the *NKVD* was well known to the chief of police and she insisted on being afforded the appropriate respect. Her intimation was clear—she may be tempted to submit a recommendation that the chief of police be placed under closer scrutiny himself.

"I was at that celebration, Comrade Chief of Police, and I do not recall any such insult," Shanin volunteered innocently. "The two boys had engaged in a dance competition and both performed admirably. Larion Daneelivich danced last and Georgy Nikolaiovich went home with his parents."

"I believe Sulupin has made our son disappear because the *NKVD* arrested his parents two days ago," the mother continued to spit out her words at the chief of police.

Her comment did not require further discussion since the Kertinskys had basically admitted that they had betrayed Larion's parents to the *NKVD* and they believed that Larion was responsible for their son's disappearance as his act of revenge. Though the chief of police did not fear the Kertinskys because he had his own contacts in the *NKVD* at Mogilev, who had higher status, he also understood that there was no need to be overly confrontational at this time, but he could not resist ridiculing their sense of self-importance.

"And why would Larion Daneelivich want to harm your son because the *NKVD* wanted to question his parents?" the police chief asked innocently.

Both of the Kertinskys merely pursed their lips and scowled in contempt at the impertinent question. The chief of police knew better than to raise such questions in the presence of others.

"I will have to ask you to fill out and sign a formal complaint. In the interim, I shall dispatch a couple of constables to make inquiries in the town." Turning to Shanin, the chief added, "Comrade Manager, I would also ask that you assist us by having some of your employees conduct a search of the *kolkhoz* grounds and perhaps the river bank as well."

Turning back to the Kertinskys, he rose from his seat to indicate that their discussion was over and he was dismissing them.

"I would like to thank you for bringing this matter to my attention and I shall keep you advised of any developments. Thank you."

Chapter 5

Georgy's nude body was found on a riverbank on the grounds of the collective farm a couple of days later. A further search disclosed that his clothes were neatly folded by the river bank upstream near the town, along with his fishing rod and net. The obvious conclusion was that he had tragically drowned when he went swimming. There were no signs of foul play on his body. That official conclusion, however, was not acceptable to the Kertinskys. They were convinced that Larion was involved in their son's death and they intended to exact a proverbial 'eye for an eye'.

*****

Shanin and Tunov concluded that in order to try to save Larion, they had to act quickly and get him out of not only the town and the province, but out of the *Belyorussian Soviet Socialist Republic* itself. The chief of police felt it was prudent that any discussion with Larion should be conducted in the relative seclusion and privacy of the manager's residence at the *kolkhoz,* rather than at the police station, where there were just too many prying eyes and curious ears. They also decided that his removal had to be affected before the Kertinsky funeral was held, which barely gave them two days in which to complete arrangements. All three men wanted to exclude Tamara from their discussion; however, her pleas and tears had the necessary effect and she was permitted to be present, but not participate.

"Larion?" Shanin inquired politely. "If I were to ask you if you had any involvement in the Kertinsky drowning, what would you say?"

Larion looked impassively at Tamara and then her father. "Comrade Manager, you have asked me a hypothetical question, so allow me to reciprocate. If I had some involvement in Kertinsky's tragic drowning, would you really want to know or would you prefer to have me lie to you?"

"Not only a clever answer, Larion, but an appropriate response to end this part of our conversation," the police chief interjected. "However, I have convened this meeting to discuss what you should do at this point in time. You have to understand that notwithstanding the physical evidence that points to an accidental drowning, considering the fact that the Kertinskys reported your parents, they will not cease until their thirst for revenge is satiated and that will only happen when they see you dead."

"I know you were thinking of studying engineering because that was your mother's wish and you would even be following in your father's footsteps," Shanin added. "But I believe that your most secure path would be for you to volunteer to enter the military, instead of waiting to be conscripted. Volunteers are more respected and accorded certain privileges because they are seen to be acting out of their own volition to defend the Motherland, as opposed to conscripts, who are seen as being compelled to serve against their own free will."

"No Father!" Tamara blurted emotionally. "I do not want Larion to die." And then she proceeded to commence to cry.

"Tamara, I want you to sit and listen quietly to what I and Boris Mikhailovich have to say," Shanin stated firmly, hoping that his daughter would be able to contain herself so that Larion would be able to make a logical, rather than an emotional, decision.

"Larion," the chief of police added, "it is imperative that we get you out of Belarus or the Kertinskys will see you dead, one way or the other, and sooner rather than later. I have contacted a colleague who was one of my classmates at the *Frunze Military Academy* in Moscow many years ago. If you volunteer, we can get you admitted as an officer cadet. You will learn military history, strategy, weapons, athletics, and, of course, communist theory, which is mandatory. If you do extremely well and no war erupts in the interim, you may even be selected for admission to the *Moscow Military Academy*, and possibly become…a more senior officer, if fate will have it."

"How long would it take?" Tamara interjected anxiously again, earning anther stern frown from her father.

"The term in the military academy is a continuous two-year period. There are no summer recesses, since the program is quite condensed. The hours of lectures and study are long and tedious, and they will make the days seem even longer. You are awakened at five o'clock in the morning and you only retire at ten o'clock in the evening, usually physically exhausted and mentally spent. This continues seven days a week, fifty-two weeks a year for two years."

"At the end of the two years, you will graduate as a junior Second Lieutenant in the Red Army and if you are fortunate, you will be given the command of a platoon of about fifty soldiers. That means you shall become responsible for not only their welfare, but for their very lives."

"I would like to thank you both," Larion replied solemnly. "I understand that you are doing this for solely for my own protection, but Tamara and I have made our own plans."

"We understand full well," responded the chief of police. "But Dimitri Aleksyevich and I have a collateral motive as well," The chief looked at Tamara, who returned his gaze with tears still welling up in her eyes. "We appreciate the feelings that the two of you seem to have developed for each other, but this is the only way we see whereby it might be possible to safeguard your future happiness. A person's first love can be the sweetest…and the most bitter at the same time. If there is a chance that Dimitri Aleksyevich and I can help the two of you in some way, we feel compelled to try. After all, we were both young and we have also experienced first love as well."

Larion and Tamara rose in unison from the table and embraced each other. Larion could feel her body shudder as she continued to sob while her tears flowed freely down her cheeks.

"Perhaps we should afford the young people some privacy, Boris? Let us go outside and share a Turkish cigar, which has fortuitously found itself in my possession," Shanin suggested quietly, as he placed his right arm around his friend's shoulders and walked him outside.

*****

"Louyna," Tamara implored, "I do not want you to go away. I do not want you to die. I want you here with me. We made plans to marry and have children together, and grow old together in the company of our grandchildren."

Larion gently caressed Tamara's hair and he tried to brush away her tears from her cheek.

"I do not want to go away and I do not want to die. I want to be here with you and marry you and have children together and even grow old together, but we must do what we must do in order for our wishes to have a chance, my love," Larion replied.

Tamara drew back quickly and Larion thought that he had said something to anger her.

"You just called me your 'love', Louyna," Tamara replied with surprise as she attempted to brush away her remaining tears while the joy in her eyes glistened. "You do love me then, don't you?" she asked anxiously.

"Of course, my love," Larion responded. "I knew I loved you from that first moment I saw you standing on those steps, shielding your beautiful blue eyes from the fading glare of the setting sun. I remember how you discretely pulled your billowing skirt against your legs and how you tucked that wayward lock of your golden hair under your scarf. But what I remember most of all was your smile, when you turned back to look at me as you walked away. Those memories shall be forever burned into my heart and my soul. Of course, I love you."

Tamara became overcome with emotion again and she embraced him and drew him tightly to herself.

"But if I go away, will you wait for me?" he asked her tenderly.

"Of course, my love," she responded in kind. "I shall wait for you for as long as it may take, but just promise me that you shall return."

"I promise, my love," Larion replied softly. "I shall return. And if others tell you that I shall not return or that I have died, will you listen to them or will you remember my promise?"

"I will remember your promise, Louyna, but please promise me that you will not forget me. That you will cherish me in your memory until you return so we may be together again. Please promise me."

"I promise you, Tamara," Larion replied and then, as they embraced again, they exchanged their most intense kiss as their respective tears flowed freely down their respective cheeks and slowly intermingled.

*****

Though Shanin and Tunov were standing outside the door sharing the strong pungent smoke of the Turkish cigar, they could not help but overhear the conversation between the two young lovers.

"I believe that Tamara has had the good fortune to not only find herself a true love, but a very promising son-in-law for both of us as well," Tunov observed with some difficulty since he was becoming increasingly unable to control his own emotions. "Life can be so cruel and ironic at times. These two young people meet by chance, fall in love, and now, fate and circumstance compel them to separate and be apart. If there is a God, then they should be able to reunite and meet again, don't you think, my dear friend."

"I am not sure that there is a God, but I know there is 'them'…and there is 'us', and hopefully our personal convictions and strength shall be enough to see this matter through to its appropriate end," Shanin replied quietly, trying to suppress his own emotions.

Chapter 6

The chief of police provided Larion with his required travel documents, his photo identification, and his work record, which was dutifully filled out in glowing terms by the *kolkhoz* manager. The information was sparse, but it was in satisfactory compliance with the existing regulations and insured Larion Daneelivich Sulupin free travel throughout the Soviet Union and most specifically, his train travel from Belarus to Moscow.

The *Frunze Military Academy* was located at 4 Devichego Polya Drive in Moscow. It was an impressive five-story building occupying the entire block, with a generous interior center court, which provided the officer cadets with ample space for weapon training and marching in formation and on rare occasions, an open space to relax in the shade of one of the few trees permitted to grow there.

Their instructors were military officers who were more experienced as soldiers than they were as teachers. The classrooms were large amphitheater rooms arranged in a semi-circular fashion around a solitary lectern located at the base of the room, with rows of seats radiating upward. The lecture rooms accommodated about one hundred students per class. If one wanted to be able to hear what the instructor was saying, it was imperative to arrive early and claim one of the seats on the lower tiers. Otherwise, one had to learn to either become a lip-reader or borrow another classmate's notes, which then had to be laboriously transcribed before the mandatory 'lights-out' at ten o'clock.

The officer cadets would arrive first and punctuality was mandatory. If you were late, you were denied entry because the doors were locked once the instructor entered. That compelled slackers to seek an anonymous refuge in one of the toilet cubicles until the next class. Discovery in the halls meant mandatory punishment and demerits, which was to be avoided at all costs if one desired a good passing grade.

In compliance with strict military protocol, as their officer instructor entered the room, all student cadets rose and stood respectfully at attention until their instructor permitted them to be seated by a curt nod of his head. The instructor would commence to recite his written lecture notes verbatim and the students were obligated to write them down verbatim in their notebooks and memorize them for their bi-weekly written exams. No questions were permitted to be asked except on rare occasions when the instructor would invite a student to offer his own comment on a particular point or be asked a question on some matter that the instructor had lectured on that day.

Those occasions instilled a morbid fear in the student cadets, who were usually so busy writing down the officer's comments that they were not bothering to absorb the logic, if any, of what was being said. Memorizing was a lot easier than actually understanding what was being said. Therefore, on those rare occasions when an instructor would call upon a student to explain the significance of something the instructor had related, it was dreaded by everyone. All of the officer cadets tried to reverentially keep their heads bowed down, their eyes firmly fixed on their notes. Eye contact with the instructor was to be avoided at all costs.

Larion was an exception. The Academy was supposed to be a teaching institution and if he was going to be a good Second Lieutenant graced with the responsibility for the welfare and the lives of the troops under his command, it was imperative that he learn and to learn, one had to understand and occasionally ask questions, even when the officer instructor did not invite such questions.

The standard protocol was that officer cadets were only permitted to ask questions with the permission of the officer instructor, but then there was Larion's 'prerogative'. Larion was inclined to ask questions when he needed clarification, which most officer instructors learned to indulge, but they reciprocated by calling on him to answer their own supplementary questions.

"Officer Cadet Larion Daneelivich, explain the principal error in military judgment which resulted in the stalemate on the western front in the First World War?"

"Officer Cadet Larion Daneelivich, explain the principal error in military judgment which Napoleon committed in his invasion of Russia in 1812."

"Officer Cadet Larion Daneelivich, explain the successful tactics employed by Alexander the Great in his conquest of Persia in the fourth century before the modern era?"

"Officer Cadet Larion Daneelivich, explain what your expectations are on how the next world war is going to be conducted in contrast to the manner in which the first world war was conducted?"

"Officer Cadet Larion Daneelivich, explain your expectations for the effective utilization of aircraft and tanks in any future war?"

Larion attempted to use his acquired knowledge, common sense, and intuition in his attempts to answer the various instructors' questions. Even though his logic was flawed from time to time, most of his instructors were impressed with his attempts, so they continued to call on him more often than other officer cadets and he never shirked his responsibility in attempting to render a response.

The dreariest courses involved a copious study of the teachings of Marx, Lenin, and even Stalin, each week. It was as if the mere recitation and verbatim transcription of those teachings was believed to ensure a sincere conversion. No one, including Larion, dared to ask any questions in those classes. No one dared to raise the apparent contradictions between communist theory and practice. No one questioned the hypocrisy that one of the most repressive, totalitarian regimes on the face of the earth still espoused one of the most libertarian constitutions ever drafted by man.

Though their weekly synchronized marches in the center square was a welcome respite from the daily grind of instruction, the most interesting aspect of their outdoor training involved their introduction to weapons, from pistols to fifty-caliber machine guns, though live ammunition practice was reserved for their bi-weekly visits to the shooting ranges. It was during these outings that they were also obliged to crawl under barbed wire with rifles gripped firmly with both hands while other student cadets were firing machine guns just over their heads.

Larion enjoyed the open air and the physical exertion in climbing up a knotted rope to scale a wooden wall or traversing over a ravine by a single suspended rope bridge or simply running for five kilometers with a fully loaded field pack on his back and holding his rifle in front of him with both hands. There were also daily classes in athletics and gymnastics. The high bar was Larion's favorite apparatus. He loved the sensation of standing below the bar and then jumping up to grasp it tightly with his powdered hands, gradually lifting himself up while keeping his legs perfectly straight and held tightly together. Then gradually swinging them forward and backward until that momentum permitted him to complete an entire 360-degree rotation, faster and faster.

Once his momentum was sufficient, he exhilarated when he released the bar and performed a spin and then re-grasped the bar while continuing his rotation until he would release the bar for the last time and free himself from its axis, spin out, landing on his feet with his arms extended triumphantly. And each time he was successful in completing his dismount, memories of his fiery *hopaka* would come back to his mind, as well as memories of how Tamara had looked at him in wonderment and proud surprise.

He would write her dutifully twice a month with the opening salutation of 'My Love' and end each letter with 'Your Love'. She would respond swiftly, opening and closing her letters in the same fashion. He would explain his daily routine and the things he enjoyed and the things he endured and he always reminded her how much he missed being away from her. She would keep him updated on what was happening in town, on the *kolkhoz* and her own final year of studies.

Most importantly, she tried to keep him informed of the police chief's discrete inquiries as to the status of his parents. The most recent information was that his parents were resettled somewhere in Siberia for a term of ten years. That meant that they were alive and that knowledge gave Larion hope that he may be able to see them again.

In addition to having to endure communist theory, the other most detestable class Larion had to endure was self-defense. The officer teachers only taught in the amphitheater classrooms; the outdoor instruction was conducted mainly by the non-commissioned instructors. Even though officer cadets were not truly 'officers' until they had graduated, they were still deemed to be 'officers of a sort' at the Academy. Therefore, by military protocol, the non-commissioned instructors were duty bound to conclude any statement directed to them with the word "Sir!".

"You are nothing but a useless motherfucker…Sir!"

"Were you born so fucking stupid or has it been a lifetime struggle for you…Sir!"

The first time a non-commissioned instructor swore at him and insulted him and then concluded his insult by addressing him as an 'officer' by stating the word 'Sir!', Larion found it to be disconcerting, but it became routine quite quickly.

There was one non-commissioned instructor who was a senior sergeant, who was particularly brutal. He would instruct an officer cadet to engage him in a fight, usually in the hallway. The cadet, considering the somewhat schizophrenic relationship between instructor and student, would usually be reluctant to defend himself. So the senior sergeant could punch or kick the cadet with impunity, knowing that the student would not defend himself. Nevertheless, his assault would appear to be justified in the name of self-defense instruction.

Larion had decided that if the senior sergeant ever called on him to demonstrate some self-defense techniques, he would not permit him to strike him without being struck back. He had watched him carefully for several weeks and he decided that he should be able to anticipate whether the senior sergeant would try to punch him in the face or to the body or try to kick him.

His favorite move was the flying kick to the chest. He would jump up and forward from one foot and then bend the second leg and then extend it as a kick out into the cadet's chest. The initial kick was sufficient to incapacitate a cadet; however, if it was executed in the hallway, it would also force the cadet's body to ricochet against the wall and cadet would usually collapse in a motionless heap on the floor.

"You have to learn to defend yourself, you useless piece of shit…Sir!" The instructor would announce smugly as he walked away from the comatose cadet, while the other non-commissioned instructors would laugh in unison.

*****

"Officer Cadet Sulupin, you stupid motherfucker…Sir!" The senior sergeant yelled out at Larion without warning. "Defend yourself!"

Larion immediately knew that the senior sergeant was going to try to affect his 'flying kick' to his chest. Without hesitation, he decided on a double feint. He first gestured his body to his right and then immediately feinted that he really intended to shift himself to his left, but then as the senior sergeant was airborne having corrected for the first feint and having committed himself to the second feint, Larion shifted his body back to his right and moved himself out of his assailant's line of attack.

The senior sergeant was powerless from preventing himself from kicking the cement wall. As he crashed his right knee into the wall, Larion struck him with a fierce elbow chop across the back of his neck, which caused his head to strike the wall as well.

"My mother is innocent, Comrade Senior Sergeant…but let the devil fuck your mother," Larion spat out his curse contemptuously at the comatose non-commissioned instructor.

The other non-commissioned instructors ran to minister to the unconscious senior sergeant, but another non-commissioned instructor approached Larion in a menacing fashion. His advance ended quickly when he noticed an officer instructor observing him in the hallway. "I trust you did not intend to try to harm Officer Cadet Larion Daneelivich?" the officer asked rhetorically. "Striking an officer, even an Officer Cadet, could mean summary execution in the field and even years of imprisonment for such an assault in the Academy. Apologize forthwith!"

The junior sergeant instructor apologized obsequiously to Larion, ending his apology with "Officer Cadet, Sir!" and then he proceeded to slink away down the hall.

"And I want to see the senior sergeant in my private chambers at eight hundred hours tomorrow morning and I don't care if you have to bring him to me in a wheelchair."

Turning to Larion, the officer instructor winked at him and smiled.

"I believe that we have a common acquaintance, Officer Cadet Larion Daneelivich," he said. "You remember Comrade Boris Mikhailovich Tunov, I believe that he is the chief of police in your hometown. He asked me to look out for you, but after this demonstration, I believe some of our non-commissioned instructors shall give you a wide berth. I have followed your academic performance and it is most satisfactory. A number of your instructors have passed on their commendations about you as well, but I do not want to inflate your ego too much because you may be obliged to purchase a bigger hat. Carry on with your good work and if you need any assistance or some advice from time to time, do not hesitate to call on me. Allow me to introduce myself: Colonel Julius Ivanovich Martov. I am the senior instructor of this Academy and Boris Mikhailovich's fellow student cadet at this Academy.

Chapter 7

In 1918, the communists declared that May 1st was the 'International Workers Day' and they commenced to celebrate solidarity with international workers, but more importantly, to celebrate Soviet military strength with a massive military parade through the streets of Moscow, ending in front of the assembled communist leaders at the Kremlin in Red Square.

Mikhail Tukhachevsky, born on 4 February 1893 and executed on 12 June 1937, was one of five Marshals who were appointed by Stalin in 1934, of which only two would survive the end of the Second World War. In 1937, he was Chief of Staff of the Red Army. He was a descendant of an impoverished noble family who attended the Aleksandrovskoye Military School and served with the prestigious Semyonovsky Guards Regiment during the First World War. He met Charles de Gaulle as a fellow prisoner in the Bavarian fortress of Ingolstadt. On his fifth escape attempt, he was successful and returned to Russia in time for the October – 1917 revolution, joining the Bolshevik (majority) party and the Red Army. In 1919, he fought successfully against Admiral Kolchak's 'White Army' in the eastern front in Siberia and in 1920, he destroyed the forces of Anton Denikin, another 'White Army' general in the Crimea. Though his participation in the invasion of Poland in 1920 failed, that failure was caused more by a divided leadership than his own personal ineptitude. However, Tukhachevsky did not flinch from violently suppressing uprisings throughout Russia during the civil war. He utilized mass shootings, execution of hostages, destroying villages, creating concentration camps and even utilizing poison gas against some insurgents in forests.

Though his primary goal was to modernize and mechanize the army, and construct a formidable air force, he was not blind to Stalin's machinations in respect of the purges he had expanded after Kirov's assassination in 1934. Tukhachevsky knew that Stalin would eventually turn his attention to the military, which Trotsky had helped create and that meant that Stalin would probably focus in on him, personally.

Stalin was aware of the growing notoriety of his new 'Chief of Army', since the foreign newspapers had even dubbed him the 'Red Napoleon' as he toured western Europe in 1936 and examined their various military installations. He also came to perceive Tukhachevsky as his 'preeminent threat' in 1937.

Genrikh Grigoryevich Yagoda, born 7 November 1891 and executed on 15 March 1938, served as Director of the NKVD from 1934 to 1936. He supervised the initial 'Show Trials' and insured that Stalin's desire for individual signed confessions from the various accused were duly obtained by whatever means which were required. These were usually obtained by torture and the threat of the summary execution of the accused's immediate family, who were usually executed in any case.

Yagoda also used Gulag labor to build the 'White Sea – Baltic Canal', whose construction involved the death of up to twenty-five thousand Gulag prisoners, but Stalin was unimpressed since the canal's shallow depth precluded its use by ocean-going vessels.

Though Yagoda was an ardent supporter of Stalin, by September of 1936, Stalin became disenchanted with what he perceived as lethargy on the part of Yagoda in the implementation of his national 'purge' of real and imagined opponents and replaced him with Nikolai Ivanovich Yezhov. Yagoda had wrongfully assumed that his personal security was assured by certain confidential information he was able to gather from the Tsarist 'Okhrana' secret files, which identified a certain Joseb Djugashvili as a confidential paid informant.

Yagoda's curiosity was piqued by Stalin's repeated successful escapes following his numerous arrests and deportations to Siberia. Those secret files, which Yagoda had retained in his personal possession, confirmed Stalin's duplicity.

Yezhov employed Yagoda's own protocols to obtain his own confession that he was a traitor and a conspirator, but Yagoda was unable to play his trump card – the Okhrana secret files, which he was forced to disgorge on the threat of the execution of his entire immediate family. Stalin's secret remained intact and Yagoda's family were executed or deported to the Gulag in any case.

Yezhov was born on 1 May 1985 and executed on 4 February 1940. He replaced Yagoda on 26 September 1936. He was considerably shorter than even Stalin, but he was a devoted sycophant. Ironically, it was his zeal that eventually resulted in his own downfall. At his show trial, Yezhov had to admit he even had about fourteen thousand former Soviet 'Chekist' officers executed as suspected conspirators. However, Yezhov could be credited for his dubious strength of character in refusing to endorse his own confession. He knew that his family would be executed in any case.

Tukhachevsky, Yagoda, Yezhov, and the other high-profile purge victims had the distinction of being personally executed by Stalin's personal executioner, Vasili Mikhailovich Blokhim, who Stalin personally appointed in 1926. He was in charge of the Kommandatura (Black Works) department of the NKVD, which was located a couple of blocks northeast of the Kremlin. Yezhov was replaced by Stalin's fellow Georgian, Laventiy Pavlovich Beria, a rapist, murderer and pedophile, born on 29 March 1899 and executed on 23 December 1953, about nine months after Stalin's death.

Chapter 8

It was the eve of 1 May 1937, the *International Workers Day Parade*; the officer cadets of the *Frunze Military Academy* were preparing to march in the parade. The student cadets were permitted to end their classes early and focus their attention on ensuring that their uniforms, boots, and unloaded rifles were in formal inspection condition. Therefore, it caught Larion by surprise that Colonel Instructor Julius Ivanovich Martov summoned him to his office.

Larion knocked on his door and being directed to enter, he took one step inside Colonel Martov's office, clicked his heels, and smartly saluted his superior officer instructor.

"At ease, Student Cadet Sulupin," Martov addressed him formally. "Please close the door and be seated. There are certain matters I would like to bring to your attention."

Martov then proceeded to speak hypothetically and in code. A possible military *coup d'état* may be in the works during the May 1st parade. The parade may give certain disgruntled military officials, in collaboration with certain disgruntled *NKVD* officials, the opportunity to seize control of the state. The key elements they would probably want to control would be the Kremlin, the *Zhelezno Stantsiya* (the central railway station), and the national radio station. The *NKVD* officials would be responsible for establishing control over the *NKVD* headquarters.

If this coup were to occur and if it were to be successful, there should be no repercussions that would be of concern to Larion or to the Academy. However, if these machinations were not successful and the coup failed, the bloodbath that would follow would make Comrade Yezhov's recent security excesses pale in comparison.

"I apologize, Comrade Colonel. May I have permission to speak?" Larion asked politely.

"No, Student Cadet Larion Daneelivich Sulupin!" the colonel replied sadly. "It is better that no further words be exchanged between us on this matter. I direct you to keep this information strictly confidential. I will be relying on your intuition and common sense to hopefully see you through whatever may happen tomorrow and in the weeks to follow. You are dismissed."

*****

The events that followed are muddled and confusing. On 1 May 1937, Tukhachevsky was relieved of his command as Chief of Army and demoted to military commander of the Volga Military District. That demotion effectively removed the top military leadership for any proposed coup. Mysteriously, the other top officer corps present in Moscow for the May 1st celebration were arrested by *NKVD* officials before the parade commenced.

Shortly after his demotion and transfer, Tukhachevsky was arrested on 22 May 1937, and returned to Moscow in a prison van. Once there, Yezhov was directed by Stalin to personally attend to his interrogation and obtain a signed confession. Tukhachevsky eventually signed a blood-spattered confession, admitting that he was plotting with others to overthrow Stalin and that he had even been acting as an agent for Hitler's Nazi government.

The forced admission that he was a Nazi agent was just too fatuous to believe, but all Stalin wanted was his signature on a confession making that admission. It is probable that Tukhachevsky, knowing that he would be executed in any event, had agreed to confess as a desperate attempt to save his wife, children, and the remainder of his family; however, they were all summarily executed shortly after his own execution on 12 June 1937.

On the day of the parade, Larion noticed that several of his officer instructors at the Academy were taken away in black cars just hours before the parade was due to start. It appeared that if one received an invitation from Comrade Stalin, it was not an offer that one could refuse.

Otherwise, the May 1st parade proceeded uneventfully, however, upon Larion's return to the Academy, it was obvious that most, if not all, of the officer instructors were absent, including Colonel Julius Ivanovich Martov, and no one dared to ask why or where they went.

That final year of studies was restricted to instruction by the non-commissioned instructors. All regular classroom instruction ceased, with the exception of the classes in Marxist/Leninist Theory. The student cadets' graduation was accelerated and all students graduated as junior second lieutenants and granted a month's leave before having to report for active duty. Larion decided that it was time for him to return home and fulfil his promise to Tamara.

In the months that followed, Stalin and Yezhov proceeded to eviscerate the cream of the officer corps in the Red Army. Yezhov chose to spare no one from First Lieutenants to Field Marshals. As fate would have it, since Larion was simply an officer cadet at the material time, he avoided scrutiny and punishment.

One of the motivating forces behind the 'cleansing' of the Soviet Officer Corps was, no doubt, the fact that it was Trotsky who had created the 'Red Army' during the Civil War and the subsequent foreign intervention. Stalin resented what he perceived as Trotsky's possible lingering influence within the military. This is underscored by the repeated refrain of the condemned admitting that they remained unrepentant *Trotskyites* in their respective confessions. Trotsky remained an obsession for Stalin until his eventual assassination in 1940.

Chapter 9

The train reached Xhotimsk after midnight, but as Larion disembarked, proudly wearing his new officer's uniform, he noticed that Tamara and her father, as well as old Valodya, were waiting at the station to greet him.

Tamara ran and jumped into his arms, almost knocking him down.

"You came back!" she squealed excitedly. "You said you would come back and here you are." She smothered him with kisses, but she could feel that his young body had become more muscled and hardened. His face seemed to have matured as well.

"*Strasvutsia* (greetings), Larion Daneelivich," Shanin announced happily. "It is an immense pleasure to have you back home, safe and sound."

Larion greeted Shanin with an embrace as Tamara's father kissed him on both his cheeks.

"I am sincerely happy to be home…at least for a little while," Larion replied sadly and then turned to greet his old friend, Valodya. "And greetings to you, *staryk* (old man), it is nice to see that you are still alive and well."

"And I assure you, my young friend," Valodya replied. "it is nice to still be alive, if not all that well. After all, I am past seventy years and my life has not been easy, but my health has improved immensely in just seeing you again."

Since the Sulupin home had been assigned by the local communist council to a new family, Shanin decided that Larion should spend his leave at their residence at the *kolkhoz*. The next evening, Tamara would prepare dinner for all of them, including her godfather, Tunov, the chief of police.

*****

"Larion Daneelivich, I have not heard from my old friend, Colonel Martov for a few months," the chief said. "Would you have any news of him?"

Larion described the last discussion he had had with Colonel Martov.

"I can only speculate as to what probably happened to him," Larion replied sadly. "It appears that there was to be an attempted overthrow of the government on the first day of May, which was supposed to coincide with the May 1st parade, but Stalin and the *NKVD* got wind of it and neutralized it. Some officer instructors were taken away even before we left for the parade. When we returned, practically every officer instructor was gone, including Colonel Martov."

"I am sure that you all have heard that Marshall Tukhachevsky, the Chief of Staff, confessed that he was plotting an overthrow of the government and that he was also a Nazi spy. There were rumors that Stalin instructed Yezhov to purge the military of all subversive elements, regardless of rank. I am sure that psychopathic midget is having an orgasm executing all those people. I only hope that Russia does not get involved in any war right now, because we simply do not have the officers to lead the men into battle. It would just end up as a slaughter."

"I doubt if Comrade Stalin would shed any tears," Valodya replied solemnly. "But what will be, will be. If people permit certain individuals to obtain power over them, they cannot say they do not deserve what those leaders decide to mete out to them after."

"That is just sad if that is what happened to Julius Ivanovich," Tunov replied. "He was a good man. I will miss him and his friendship. By the way, he wrote me about your self-defense lesson with that non-commissioned sergeant. Julius said that you taught him well. Congratulations."

"Please let us not speak of politics," Tamara implored the men. "It makes me feel so sad. Larion has come back to me...to us...and for that, we should be happy and rejoice."

"And Comrade Chief—"

The police chief cut Larion off and told him that in light of the fact that he was twenty years of age and had graduated from the *Frunze Military Academy* and was presently an officer in the Soviet Army, he believed that it was appropriate for him to address him in the more familial fashion.

"In that case, Boris Mikhailovich," Larion replied, "do you have any news of my parents?"

"I can confirm that they are alive and well," the chief replied. "Your father is employed, without salary, of course, in an industrial factory helping them redesign their production line. Your mother is teaching, again without salary, at the elementary level. I have not been able to confirm their exact location, but it would be impossible for you to travel and meet them in any case, since they are under disciplinary action.

"They still have eight years to serve on their detention for anti-Soviet behavior. However, I can confirm that the *NKVD* at Mogilev do not intend to pursue any action against you in light of your patriotic act of volunteering to serve in the military and having graduated as a junior second lieutenant. As they told me, they have more repugnant fish to fry than to harass a potential future military hero who has volunteered to protect the Motherland."

"Is there anything that can be done for my parents?" Larion asked.

"Even if the Kertinskys withdrew their allegations, which they would not in any case, it would make no difference," Tunov replied. "The 'Siberian Resettlement Program' is not dependent upon any individual culpability, but economic need. They need engineers and teachers in Siberia and what more economical way to fill those needs but to sentence capable people to ten years penal service without any compensation, other than being provided with the necessities of life. But the important thing is that they are alive and well. I am sure that they are just as hopeful to see you again as you are to see them."

"And what about the Kertinskys?" Larion inquired. "Do they know that I was away at the military academy and that I am a graduated officer?

"Their *NKVD* sources seem to have kept them well informed," Tunov replied. "It was only a week ago that they showed up at my office demanding that I reopen their son's case. I respectfully declined, but I suggest that you keep your distance from those two. The passage of two years has not diminished their hatred for you or their desire to exact revenge. However, if they attempt to threaten you in any way, I want you to notify me immediately. They may come to realize that being informers for the *NKVD* does not give them any blanket immunity."

After dinner, Larion helped Tamara with the dishes while the others retired to the iron bench Shanin had one of his enterprising workers weld and paint. The bench was situated in front of his yard under a chestnut tree. The bench afforded the three older men an opportunity to sit and smoke their strong Turkish cigarettes and watch the summer sun set slowly on the western horizon.

"Look at how red this sunset is," observed Valodya. "My mother always cautioned me that red sunsets are evil omens. We should be careful and beware."

After clearing off the table and cleaning the dishes and cutlery, Larion invited the three smokers back into the house. He wanted to present them with their *podarki* (presents) which he had purchased in Moscow since it was customary for a visitor to give his hosts a gift.

He presented Boris Mikhailovich with a bottle of Moldavian brandy. Then he presented Dimitri Aleksyevich with a new winter jacket. Valodya was presented with a smoking pipe and a pouch of Turkish tobacco so that he could smoke and drive his old mare in a more refined fashion. Finally, he presented Tamara with a small gold Orthodox crucifix suspended on a thin gold chain.

"I did not think that a student cadet was paid while he was at the Academy. How did you happen to accumulate such riches to be able to purchase such expensive gifts?" asked Tunov, as he examined his brandy more closely.

"For that, I have dear old Valodya to thank," Larion replied with a shrewd smile. "Among the many things he tried to teach me, he also taught me how to play cards. When you cannot afford to lose, you learn how to play very carefully and very well, but you still need good fortune. Cards can be very fickle and deceitful at times."

*****

"Let us go for a walk, Tamara. I want to hold your hand and hold you close as the evening becomes cooler." Larion beseeched her politely. "And I want you to tell me what you have done while I have been away these two years."

"My life has been just a routine existence. I get up and eat, and then I help father with his responsibilities…he does not enjoy paperwork, so I have to prepare and file all his reports for the *oblast* general administration. Then I prepare dinner daily and we eat and listen to Radio Moscow. Then we go to bed and the next day, we repeat that same routine. Once a month, we attend a general meeting at Mogilev with all of the other *kolkhoz* managers in our *Oblast* and the comrade leaders alternatively implore or threaten us to increase production; however, they are seldom open to any new suggestions. But before I go to sleep, I reread your last letter and that ensures that I will have sweet dreams."

"That does seem 'routine', my love," Larion replied sympathetically. "But have you considered going to university or continuing your studies at a technical institute?"

"I do not believe that I can leave Father right now. Perhaps in a year or two. After all, I am two years your junior. I still have sufficient time," Tamara reasoned. "And how long do you have to serve before you can be discharged and return to a normal life?"

"Just two years, my dear," Larion answered sadly. "Assuming that the Motherland does not go to war. But enough talk, I just want to look at you…you are so beautiful. I just want to hold you…and I would like to kiss those flower-petal lips of yours. I have dreamed of tasting them for two years."

"In that case, Louyna, please kiss me," Tamara whispered. "After all, I have been waiting two years as well."

*****

A few days later, Valodya took the two of them to town because Larion wanted to see if he could meet some friends. Tamara wanted to go to the supermarket to pick up some items as well. As they entered the market, the store clerks nodded their heads in recognition as Larion walked by and smiled. The store shelves were embarrassingly half empty, just as in Moscow, but at least they were not obliged to line up outside for an hour prior to being given entry.

As they wandered the sparse aisles, they came upon the Kertinskys, who stopped and scowled at Larion, and then quickly turned and walked away.

"Godfather Boris was right," said Tamara, as she watched them stomp out of the store in an agitated manner. "They still hold you responsible and they still despise you."

After the supermarket, they went to the bank and finally to the post office. At the post office, one of the clerks recognized Larion and waved him over.

"Larion Daneelivich, you must see this," he said excitedly. "You have a letter and I think it is from your parents. It came in a couple of weeks ago and I should have returned it, but I held on to it in case you did come back."

As Larion held the letter, it felt as if it was the most precious thing he had ever held in his life. He exchanged a quick look with Tamara and then, after thanking the clerk profusely, they left the post office and went outside to sit on a park bench so that he would have an opportunity to read his parent's letter.

It was dated 15 August 1937 and postmarked from *Krasnoyarsk Krai* (region), which was located in central Siberia, stretching from the Arctic Ocean to the north, to Kazakh SSR and Mongolia to the south. The capital city of the region was Krasnoyarsk, with a population approximating that of Mogilev.

Our Dearest Son,

We send this letter to you not knowing if it will ever reach you, but we can only hope and pray. We are well and though the winters are long and cold, the short summer is warm and pleasant. It reminds us of home.

We want you to know that we are well. Your father is working in an industrial factory and I am happily teaching children in their third form. Whenever I look upon their smiling faces, I believe I see you…wherever you may be.

If fortune permits this letter to reach you, please write back and tell us that you are safe and happy. Restrictions here are not as severe as there, so do write if you can. Though they have forced us to resettle here, we do have more freedom. Until we may be able to meet again, we embrace you intensely and kiss you fiercely.…

Your loving parents.

Tamara could see Larion's tears streak down his cheeks and she held his arm even tighter.

"What a wonderful surprise, Louyna," she whispered. "Perhaps there is a God and He has not forsaken us. You purchased a cross as a gift for me and perhaps God took it as a sign that we have not forsaken Him either. And here, He has given you this small miracle. Words from your parents to console you. I am so happy for you."

*****

Three weeks passed quickly, but both Tamara and Larion knew that their time together was coming to an end. Larion was scheduled to report to his garrison in Leningrad and he had a decision to make before he boarded that train to that northern city on the Baltic Sea. With some trepidation, he decided to proceed. They were seated on that metal bench in front of her father's residence watching the sun set in the west. Larion reached into his pocket, but when he withdrew his hand, it was closed.

"Tamara Dimitriovich Shanina, please close your eyes and open your hand. There is something else I want to give you," he spoke mysteriously.

"Another gift for me?" she replied, a bit surprised. "What is it?"

However, as he dropped it into her hand, she realized that it was a ring. She opened her eyes immediately and as soon as she saw it, her mouth opened and her eyes widened. Then as she closed her hand to ensure that she would not drop the simple gold band, she placed her hands behind his head and kissed him.

"You realize that Father is a bit traditional," she bubbled. "You will have to ask him for permission to marry me, but let's not dawdle. He is home right now. Let's go see him and you may ask him this afternoon."

Tamara grabbed Larion by his hand and pulled him to his feet and pushed him towards the front door.

"Father! Father!" she exclaimed exuberantly. "Louyna has a question for you!" And she displayed the gold ring she held carefully between her thumb and forefinger.

Her father was surprised by her excitement and even more surprised when he saw the ring his daughter so proudly exhibited.

"Well, Larion Daneelivich, what is this all about?" he asked seriously, but he was unable to disguise his personal satisfaction.

"Well, sir!" he replied. "I respectfully ask for your permission to marry your daughter, sir."

"One 'sir' should do, Larion Daneelivich," Dimitri replied. "And you, my young daughter, what do you have to say about all this?"

"Please say yes, Father dear!" Tamara implored him, clasping her hands together in supplication. "Oh, please say yes."

"Hummm," Dimitri responded equivocally. "Marriage is a serious matter…and it should not be rushed into…and have the two of you thought this over…the implications and the responsibilities?"

"Yes, Father! A thousand times yes!" Tamara exclaimed. "Father, will you grant your consent or do you want to break my heart?" she added petulantly.

"And you, young man," Dimitri asked solemnly, "are you prepared to accept my daughter's hand in marriage and all the responsibilities that go with it?"

"I do, sir. I solemnly swear that I do, sir!" Larion replied.

"In that case, I am not going to be held responsible for breaking my daughter's heart. I hereby grant my consent for you, Larion Daneelivich, to marry my daughter, Tamara Dimitriova."

Tamara excitedly embraced her father and then swung around to embrace Larion.

*****

It was decided that they would be married on the next occasion that Larion was able to obtain leave and come back to Xhotimsk. He would provide them with notice so that they could make some modest preparations. A few days later, Tamara, Dimitri, and Valodya went to the train station with him to bid him farewell and a safe journey. Valodya and Dimitri walked a few paces away to give the two youngsters some privacy.

"And you will wait for me?" he entreated her tenderly.

"Yes, I shall, Louyna," she replied. "And you will not forget me?"

"No, my love," Larion replied solemnly. "I promise that I shall return and that I shall not forget you."

Chapter 10

On 23 August 1939, Nazi Germany and Soviet Russia, though totally antithetical to each other in political and economic philosophy, executed the Molotov-Ribbentrop Pact, a non-aggression treaty by which they agreed not to declare war on each other, they also effectively agreed to divide up the Central European countries between themselves. Of the most significance was their decision to divide Poland.

The 'casus belli' for Nazi Germany to invade Poland was Poland's alleged act of sabotage against the 'Gleivitz Radio Tower', which abutted the German-Polish border in southern Germany, on 31 August 1939. The sabotage was actually executed by the *Schutzstaffel* (SS) under the specific direction of Heinrich Himmler, born 7 October 1900 and died by suicide in the Allied's hands on 23 May 1945, and his subordinate, Reinhard Heydrich, born 7 March 1904 and assassinated in Czechoslovakia on 4 June 1942.

Germany proceeded to invade western Poland on 1 September 1939 and Soviet Russia invaded eastern Poland on 17 September 1939. Just as the Nazis fabricated the justification for the invasion of Poland, Stalin had his NKVD stage a bombardment of the small Russian city of Mainila on the Soviet-Finnish border on 26 November 1939, which was followed by the Soviet invasion of Finland on 30 November 1939.

Soviet Russia attacked Finland along the entire border with twenty-one divisions totaling 450000 troops. They were confronted by a frontier that had very few roads and heavy forests, which impeded a speedy advance. Their opponents wore white camouflage uniforms and skis to aid in their camouflage and maneuverability. The Soviet troops wore their regular dark uniforms and basically had to trudge through heavy snow in their military boots. Because of the Soviet superiority in men and equipment, the Finnish troops had to rely upon guerrilla tactics.

The so-called 'Winter War' lasted from 30 November 1939 to 13 March 1940. Though the Red Army was victorious in the end, it was an extremely pyrrhic victory. Soviet casualties were estimated to be about 380000, compared to about 70000 for Finland. Soviet material losses included about 3500 tanks and 500 aircraft, compared to Finland's material losses of about 30 tanks and 60 aircraft. However, Finland agreed to cede about eleven percent of its territory, basically representing the land it annexed during the Russian Revolution and Civil War.

In June of 1940, as Germany proceeded to invade France, Stalin proceeded to invade and annex Lithuania, Estonia, and Latvia, over strenuous American objections.

With the launch of Operation Barbarossa on 22 June 1941, Finland allied itself with Nazi Germany when it invaded northern Soviet Russia and the 'Continuation War' between Finland and Soviet Russia lasted until about 15 September 1944. Finland's casualties totaled about 220000 and Soviet casualties totaled about 825000, while German casualties totaled about 85000, However, once Germany abandoned its Finnish ally because of the Soviet counter-offensive in late 1943, Finland had to sue for peace, which resulted in the payment of substantial reparations and the ceding of additional territory to Stalin's Soviet Russia.

Though Operation Barbarossa initially involved extensive territorial gains for Germany and massive military losses in men and material for Soviet Russia, it ended as a dramatic tactical defeat for Nazi Germany. Its failure to seize Leningrad in the northeast and Moscow in the center and Stalingrad in the southeast, effectively halted Germany's blitzkrieg advance. After those three failures, it was basically in retreat. Furthermore, it resulted in Nazi Germany fighting on three fronts: in the south to try to buttress Mussolini's regime, in the west to try to halt the allied invasion after June of 1944; and in the east, to try to halt the Soviet counter-offensive on Berlin.

Some cynics speculate that the second front in the West was deliberately delayed so that the Nazi fascists and Soviet communists would bleed each other white in the interim. Churchill and Roosevelt had more consideration for human life than Hitler and Stalin; however, after Dunkirk and Dieppe, it did seem that Churchill was less inclined to engage Hitler's Wehrmacht in Europe to relieve the Nazi pressure on Soviet Russia. Churchill's primary concern after the Battle of Britain was the preservation of the British Empire and that meant maintaining control over the Suez Canal. Roosevelt was more sympathetic to Soviet Russia, even referring to Stalin as 'Uncle Joe'; however, he felt compelled to indulge Churchill, even though he believed that both England and France should relinquish their colonial empires in the post-war period. Though England and France had benefited financially from their colonies, the colonies, themselves, did not benefit in a reciprocal measure.

Churchill also seemed to continue to be fixated with his notion of 'the soft underbelly of Europe', which went back to the First World War and his decision, as First Lord of the Admiralty, to initiate the disastrous Gallipoli campaign, which forced him to resign. In the Second World War, rather that supporting the American decision to initiate a western front through an invasion of northern France, he proposed another invasion through the Balkans to intervene, rather than necessarily assist, Stalin's advancing armies from the east after 1943.

Chapter 11

Larion was scheduled to complete his mandatory two-year military term on 1 November 1939. He and Tamara had decided to postpone their marriage until after he completed his service. However, in the event of a commencement of hostilities, that mandatory two-year term would become suspended for the duration of the war. So it was with considerable disappointment that Larion heard the news of Germany's invasion of western Poland, which was quickly followed by Soviet Russia's invasion of eastern Poland. Those events immediately suspended the completion of his military service. He was to remain single and a second lieutenant until further notice.

Dearest One

It is with a heavy heart I write to tell you that it does not appear that I will be able to return soon. War has broken out and I do not know when it will end. We have not yet been mobilized in Leningrad, but the senior officers say that it is inevitable. Apparently, there is territory to be regained which was lost during the revolution…and there are the inevitable old scores to be settled…which undoubtedly shall be remembered and then this settlement of scores shall have to be resettled by others in the future. Though I may be a soldier and an officer, I have grown to hate war. Though they say it is necessary to defend oneself, I keep thinking that there have to be less destructive ways to resolve disputes. But my colleagues remind me that it is not wise to try to negotiate when the other party is shooting bullets at you. It seems that bullets trump words.

I think of you all of the time. I close my eyes and I see your face. I cover my ears, yet I hear your voice. I dream that I hold you in my arms and kiss you. Do not forget me and I shall return to you.

Louyna   *30 September 1939*

The following week, they received their orders to mobilize and move north to the Finnish border. Train transport was arranged for his battalion of three hundred soldiers. It was under the command of Colonel Gregory Andreivich Galkovskiy. He was a dynamic commander. Tall with dark eyebrows and silver white hair which he proudly wore long, just over his ears and down to his collar in the back. He was truly a magnificent man to look at. His voice was a deep baritone, yet it was smoothing to the ear. He was a man who instilled loyalty in his men. There was no risk he would have his men take which he would not willingly assume himself. It was Larion's wish to follow his example and attempt to emulate him as much as possible. Larion wondered at times how his Colonel had been able to escape Vezhov's purge.

The ever-present political attaché to Larion's platoon was Maxim Sergievich Marchenko. He was Ukrainian and a communist zealot. Every thought and every action had to be ideologically pure, at least that is what he taught the troops in Larion's platoon. Larion looked upon him akin to a religious zealot. Instead of ministering to the men's souls, he ministered to the men's minds. Larion and most of his platoon of fifty men knew him to also be a *NKVD* informant, so they treated him with a certain degree of deference and reserve.

*****

Colonel Galkovskiy assembled his company leaders and platoon leaders in a private car so that he would be able to address them. They were to form part of the Eighth Army which was composed of six divisions. Their role in the invasion of Finland was to affect a flanking maneuver around the north shore of Lake Ladoga so as to provide a future enhanced defensive buffer for the City of Leningrad, which was located on the southern shore of the lake.

"Comrade Officers," he stated firmly, "I salute you, since it is appears that we shall soon be at war with Finland. They shall be protecting their homeland, so expect them to fight hard. You must be diligent and try to protect your men as much as you can. Consider them as little children, for in fact, that is what they are. They must obey and carry out your orders, but you should issue orders with prudence and care. You are responsible for your soldiers' lives. Respect that fact and I know you will perform accordingly. Any questions?"

"Comrade Colonel, sir," a company leader asked, "has there been a declaration of war against Finland?"

"Not yet and not formally, Major," Galkovskiy answered wryly. "However, we are moving to the front with hundreds of thousands of troops, so I surmise that this is not just an exercise, especially when one considers the Polish situation right now."

Marchenko could not help himself. He was obliged to contribute a suitable political interjection.

"But Comrade Colonel," he asked sternly, "should you not remind the assembled officers that it is fit and glorious to die for the Motherland?"

It never surprised Galkovskiy how some men were so quick and generous to offer the sacrifice of other men's lives.

"No, I respectfully disagree, Comrade Marchenko," Galkovskiy stated in his booming voice. "If I were to remind my officers of dying, I would remind them that it is their duty to ensure that the other bastard dies for his country."

There was a soft, amused mummer, which Marchenko took as a personal affront and an unforgivable insult.

"However, Comrade Marchenko," Galkovskiy concluded, "if it is your wish to die for the Motherland and I am sure I speak for everyone here—we commend your dedication."

Marchenko's face was flushed with anger. Galkovskiy's comments were inappropriate and disparaging of him, personally. He would pass them on to the appropriate authorities and with some appropriate embellishment. They would stand up as being suitably scandalous to warrant scrutiny and appropriate disposition, but he would remain silent for now. Sooner or later, Galkovskiy would step over that line again and Marchenko intended to have him pay with his head—figuratively or literally, it made no difference to him.

*****

The *Winter War* only lasted three and a half months; however, it was a bloodbath for the Soviet troops who were ambushed relentlessly as they trudged through the Finnish forests, since the roads that did exist were either impassable or death traps. The Soviet troops would be ordered by their inept officers to march in triple file. The Finnish troops would block off and trap those troops on those roads and then proceed to massacre them and scavenge their supplies.

What depressed Larion the most were the Finnish snipers. After denying them the roads and forcing them to trudge through the forests, the Finnish snipers seemed to prefer to secrete themselves up in the heavily foliaged trees and pick off the Soviet soldiers who were laboriously making their way through the heavy snow in dark uniforms, which presented clearly outlined targets against the white snow.

Larion, as an officer, carried a TT-33 Tokarev pistol, which had an eight-shot magazine. He also had an SVT-40 rifle, which had a ten-round magazine and an effective range of five hundred meters. Within the first week, Larion lost five of his troops to snipers and he had to do something, so he convened a meeting with his two non-commissioned officers.

"I believe the sniper who has taken five of our boys this past week is the same man," Larion announced solemnly. "The question is what we can do about it. He seems to be always ahead of us and he always shoots from the trees. He shoots and kills, and that forces us to hunker down. It gets dark early now and he probably comes down from his perch at night and moves ahead a few hundred meters and the following morning he climbs up another tree to shoot again."

One non-commissioned officer spoke up:

"We have been moving to the northwest this past week, but the terrain is going to force us to move in an easterly direction for the next couple of days, according to our maps. The morning sun has been behind us, but for the next couple of days, we will be moving to the east and the sun shall be in front of us."

"So what is the significance of that, Sergeant?"

"A sniper rifle has a longer range than our rifles, but the forest prevents a long-range shot. He needs a clear line of sight, so I believe that he stations himself no more than two or three hundred meters away. Secondly, he shoots from the trees, but the remaining foliage and his camouflage uniform help disguise him. However, the trees are losing their leaves and the early sun has been behind us the last few days and it has made it difficult to discern his hiding place until now.

"If we have a couple of soldiers advance about one hundred and fifty to two hundred meters at night and then bury themselves in the snow, about fifty meters apart, all they would have to do would be wait for the dawn. The sun shall be behind him and they should be able to discover his silhouette in the trees."

"Excellent thinking, Sergeant," Larion replied, duly impressed with the non-commissioned officer's assessment. "But I believe that you and I should test out this theory. Do you object?"

"No Sir!" the Sergeant replied firmly. "The boys are young and scared. It is important to build trust and morale, and show them that their leaders are prepared to assume risks as well."

*****

After darkness fell on the forest, Larion gave instructions to the other non-commissioned officer to maintain their position until at least midmorning. If they were successful, they would come back and rejoin them. If they were not successful, they were to join another platoon and proceed as they may be ordered.

Larion and the Sergeant proceeded into the dark night, moving slowly and silently. Carrying their rifles in both their hands, it was imperative that they travel as quietly as possible. Broken branches or any undue noise was sure to disclose their presence and put the sniper on alert. After advancing about two hundred meters and using hand signals to avoid speaking, Larion and the Sergeant separated and proceeded, as agreed, to advance a further fifty meters, approximately fifty meters apart. Occasionally, Larion would stop and wait to see if he could hear the Sergeant moving in the forest. There was no sound. The night was silent.

After moving to a suitable location partially hidden by thick brush, Larion hid under a bush and covered himself with snow. Once he finished, there was nothing to do but wait for the dawn.

Larion was not aware of how much time had passed. He thought he may have dosed off for a few moments until he was awakened by a bird noisily flying out of a tree about seventy-five meters ahead as if it was disturbed by something or someone. Larion held his breath and looked up at the tree. About ten meters up, he saw a round bundled silhouette clearly outlined by the rising sun. He watched it carefully. There was no point in shooting into that mass if it was not human. If he shot and it was not the sniper, the shot would alert him. He had to be patient.

Ten minutes, then fifteen minutes passed. Finally, Larion saw the dark bundle move. It was human. Larion carefully aimed at the center of the dark mass and shot. Nothing happened. He decided to shoot again. This time, the dark mass fell backwards, crashing down through the branches of the tree and falling to the ground. Larion continued to watch it. It remained unmoving. Larion could hear someone moving to his right towards that tree. He assumed it was his companion. Rising up and maintaining his rifle's aim at the dark mass, Larion cautiously approached it. The sniper remained motionless.

"Good shot, Lieutenant!" the sergeant said. "I could not hear or see anything until I heard your first shot. How did you know it was the sniper when you shot again?"

"Don't tell the boys, Sergeant," Larion replied jokingly, "but I did not know. Since I shot once, the sniper knew that we were here, so a second shot would not prejudice our position any further."

They turned the body over slowly.

"The first shot probably hit him in his abdomen and apparently, he decided to play possum. Your second shot hit him in the face, shattering his left cheekbone. It was the second shot that knocked him out of the tree," the sergeant announced after he had examined the body.

"And look at this, Sergeant," Larion replied as he examined the sniper's rifle. "The stock of the rifle had a total of twenty-three carved notches. Five of the notches appeared to have been carved quite recently."

"We should be safe for a little while, Lieutenant," the sergeant replied. "May I keep his rifle as a souvenir, since it will take our ammunition? If Comrade Marchenko was around, I would not admit that it is superior to my rifle, but its effective range is considerably longer. I would like to carry and use both, as it may be required."

"Since this was your idea, Sergeant, I believe you deserve it," Larion replied.

Chapter 12

Larion would lose half of his original platoon in the subsequent weeks; however, new troops quickly replaced those casualties The Eighth Army was eventually successful in clearing out a wide perimeter around the north side of the lake and finally reaching the Baltic Sea. Now there was nothing further for them to do except wait for further orders. Rumors did reach them that the other armies that were attempting to advance into Finland farther north were sustaining heavy casualties.

Colonel Galkovskiy convened another meeting with his company and platoon commanders.

"Comrades, we have fulfilled our primary objective; however, our High Command has advised me that we are going to advance northward up the peninsula to try to relieve the Seventh Army by a flanking movement from the south. Hopefully, we shall surprise the Finns and relieve the pressure on our fellow comrade soldiers."

"Comrade Colonel, my company is exhausted and I have lost one third of my men and I have not received any replacements," one major replied. "When will the replacements arrive and how much time do we have to recuperate before we advance to the north?"

"I wish I could answer that question, Major," Galkovskiy responded. "But I simply do not have that information right now."

"Your replacements shall be here in two days, Major," Marchenko interjected smugly.

Galkovskiy looked at Marchenko with surprise.

"And Comrade Commissar, how do you know that for a fact?" he asked quietly.

"Because it is my business to know such things," Marchenko replied with satisfaction.

Galkovskiy decided to ignore Marchenko. He saw no need to provide him with further attention and feed his need for self-importance.

"Well, Major," he replied, addressing his company commander. "That should mean that we shall have at least two days to recuperate to prepare for the advance northward."

*****

As Marchenko promised, the replacement soldiers arrived two days later. Marchenko also arrived at Galkovskiy's tent in the company of two uniformed officers who bore the insignia of a *NKVD* regiment. Both Officers held the rank of Captain. Galkovskiy was with Second Lieutenant Sulupin and his company commander when Marchenko arrived.

Galkovskiy rose as the three men entered his tent, while Larion and his company commander remained standing. Marchenko's eyes gleamed with excitement. He was about to exact his revenge.

"Comrade Colonel," he announced tauntingly, "I believe that Comrade Stalin would like to have a chat with you."

Galkovskiy merely looked over inquiringly at the two *NKVD* officers.

"Comrade Colonel, we have orders to escort you back to Leningrad," one of the two officers announced obliquely.

"Really gentlemen, but I have just received orders from my high command that I am to lead my battalion to the north tomorrow morning," Galkovskiy replied, making a brief, but knowing eye contact with his company commander who was standing beside Larion.

"Comrades, you must excuse us. We have duties to perform," the major said to the *NKVD* officers and smartly saluting Galkovskiy, he nudged Larion and the two of them exited the tent.

"Sir, you must know what that means," Larion pleaded with his major. "We must do something. You know what that invitation means."

"Yes, Lieutenant, I know what it means and yes, we are going to do something about it. General Vinogradov is in camp right now and I want to inform him."

In the interim, Galkovskiy attempted to stall for time.

"Do you gentlemen have Comrade Stalin's invitation in writing?" he inquired politely.

The *NKVD* officers were confused by this query. Usually, their oral statement was accepted as sufficient and irrefutable. "There is no… No, we do not," replied the older of the two officers.

"No, Sir! We do not," Galkovskiy corrected him firmly. "After all, Captain, I am a Colonel and you are a Captain, and rank still counts."

"No, Sir! We do not," the elder *NKVD* officer corrected himself begrudgingly.

"Well, Comrades," Galkovskiy replied, "that shall not do. I have standing written orders from my general and I cannot permit them to be superseded by the word of a mere captain. If I were to accede to your uncorroborated request and disobey a direct written order from my commanding general, I could be subject to summary execution."

"And what do you think is waiting for you in Leningrad, Colonel?" Marchenko spat out sarcastically.

Just then, a group of officers entered the tent and a senior officer announced himself. "Excuse me, gentlemen!"

Everyone looked back at the new person who just entered Galkovskiy's tent. It was General Vinogradov. All of the men immediately executed a smart salute and clicked their heels. Larion, his company commander, the General's Adjutant, and personal guard were standing behind him. After being informed of the details, the general directed his attention at Marchenko.

"Comrade Commissar," he inquired politely. "Am I to believe that you have initiated this matter because you tried to argue that it was fit and glorious to die for the Motherland and the colonel corrected you by telling you that it was more fit and more glorious to have the other bastards die for their country? Do you disagree with the colonel's statement?"

"I do not have to explain myself to you, Comrade General Vinogradov," Marchenko spat out contemptuously.

"Now you are disagreeing with me, Comrade Commissioner," The General replied politely. "I am the commanding general of this division and I hold the power of life and death over everyone here, including you, Marchenko and even our most respected visitors."

Vinogradov turned to the two *NKVD* officers and said, "Comrade Captains, unfortunately, you have caught me at a most inconvenient time. I have standing Orders from my Army Command to advance northward to help relieve the Seventh Army. Colonel Galkovskiy is one of my most capable battalion commanders. I want both of you to know that under different circumstances, I would be more than pleased to accept you at your word and deliver Colonel Galkovskiy into your hands."

"But firstly, as I remember the regulations, you must present a written authorization duly executed by your commanding officer requesting me to comply. You do not have that document. Secondly, I would like you to consider whether the disagreement between the Comrade Commissar and Colonel Galkovskiy really warrants his removal to Leningrad at this moment. Would we be acting in the best interests of the Motherland or would you merely be acting to indulge the Comrade Commissar's petulance and personal dislike of Colonel Galkovskiy?"

The two NKVD officers looked at each other in confusion. They were not used to such treatment. The mere utterance of Comrade Stalin's name was usually more than sufficient to ensure compliance with their requests.

"This is most unusual, General Vinogradov. After all, we have our Orders," the elder officer finally replied.

"But you don't have those Orders with you, do you?" the general replied rhetorically.

"No, sir, we do not," the officer answered quietly. He was already thinking about how he would have to explain his predicament to his superiors when he returned to Leningrad. He also resented Marchenko for having placed him in such a position.

"Do you duty, you damned numb skulls!" Marchenko spat out at the two *NKVD* officers, who merely glared back at him silently.

"As for our Comrade Commissar," the general said, looking at Colonel Galkovskiy. "Are the casualty reports for this past week completed yet, Colonel?"

"Not quite, Comrade General," Galkovskiy replied knowingly.

The General turned to the two *NKVD* Captains.

"Comrade Captains," the general advised formally. "It is my duty to advise you that Comrade Commissioner Marchenko was unfortunately killed by a Finnish sniper two days ago. I believe his death resolves your problem and mine. Your complainant was deceased when you arrived and secondly, Colonel Galkovskiy had already advanced northward with his battalion to help relieve the Seventh Army."

"No, you cannot do this!" screamed Marchenko. "I speak with the voice of Comrade Stalin. My hands are his hands. My voice is his voice."

"Comrade Marchenko, you have probably never even met Comrade Stalin," General Vinogradov replied. "I have dined with him at his own table at the Kremlin."

Turning to the company commander and Larion, he directed them to take Marchenko away.

"Now Comrade Captains, is there anything I can do for you while you remain here or is there anything I can do to facilitate your return to Leningrad. I understand we were able to commander a couple of boats that can take you across Lake Lagoda much faster than you can travel overland."

"We would be most grateful for your accommodation, Sir," the elder officer replied and both officers smartly saluted and clicked their heels in unison before they left the tent.

"Allow me to express my gratitude, Alexei," Galkovskiy said to General Vinogradov.

"Well, Gregory," General Vinogradov replied, "before this war is over, there may come a day when we both receive an invitation to chat from Comrade Stalin."

*****

The *Winter War* ended on 13 March 1940. Of the original 450000 troops that invaded Finland on 30 November 1939, about 380000 became casualties; however, Stalin simply proceeded to replace them without a second thought. He did not care how many men or tanks were lost, so long as Finland ended up capitulating. Larion was also notified of his new redeployment to the Ukrainian front. Fortunately, his new assignment would take him through Belarus and give him an opportunity to see Tamara and his friends in Xhotimsk. But the uncertain length of the war and his possible survival were compelling him to make a drastic decision. Consequently, he decided to send Tamara a telegram to see if she was still in agreement.

Tamara, my love,

I have just been informed that I am being reassigned to the Ukrainian Front. That means I shall be passing through Belarus and my battalion commander, Colonel Galkovskiy, has granted me a three-week leave at my personal request. I have told my Colonel that I wish to get married.

If you will still marry me, Tamara...I shall be in Xhotimsk on 15 April 1940.

Do not try to answer this telegram for I am not sure that it will reach me before I leave. If you have changed your mind, I want you to know that I will understand and that I shall never bear you any resentment. I simply could never harbor any negative feelings against you. And I have been promoted to First Lieutenant. I know that it is still a long way away from becoming a general, but it is a step upward.

Louyna   *2 April 1940*

Chapter 13

Larion could not understand why the train schedule inevitably returned him home at midnight. That timing of his return always struck him as somewhat foreboding. As he deboarded the train and looked around, he was disappointed to find that there was no one there to greet him. His heart sank because he believed that Tamara had changed her mind. The promises they had exchanged just months ago were just fleeting words that dissipated into the air. Just as he reluctantly decided to reboard the train, he heard her anxious voice. "Louyna, Louyna!" Tamara shouted as she ran around the station building. "I am here. I am here."

Larion's spirits immediately lifted. Just as he turned to face her, Tamara jumped into his arms and commenced to smother him with kisses and questions. As he gazed over her shoulder, he saw her father, Dimitri, old Valodya and Boris Mikhailovich, the chief of police, also approaching.

His telegram had been delayed and only delivered to the *kolkhoz* that afternoon. Valodya greeted his young protégé with tears in his eyes, proudly smoking the pipe Larion had given him as a gift in his right hand. Its embers were glowing and Larion could smell the acrid smell of the Turkish tobacco.

"Greetings, Larion Daneelivich…or perhaps, I should say, greetings, my dear future son-in-law," bellowed Dimitri Aleksyevich Shanin as he gripped him tightly and lifted him off the ground. "You have put on weight, my son. The army must be feeding you well."

"Greetings, Larion Daneelivich," the police chief added and extended his hand in greeting and then pulled him into another bear hug that left Larion a bit breathless.

"And greetings to all of you, my dear friends…and mostly to you, Tamara…my one and only love," Larion spoke emotionally. He felt his whole body trembling and it seemed they all had tears of joy in their eyes.

Because it was so late, it was decided that they would all meet at the Shanin residence at the *kolkhoz* for dinner the following night.

When Larion arrived at the Shanin home, he was given the guest bedroom. He was so tired; he did not even get out of his uniform. He just collapsed on top of the bed and fell into a deep sleep. He did not hear Tamara enter the bedroom during the night and slip under the covers so that she could sleep beside him. In the morning, Dimitri looked for both of them, but they did not seem to be around. He quietly peered into the guest bedroom and saw his daughter chastely sleeping under the covers beside Larion, while he was sleeping on top of the covers, still dressed in his full uniform.

Dimitri quietly closed the bedroom door and smiled to himself. He could only envy them their innocent love. It brought back memories of the first time he shared a bed with Tamara's mother. It was a sweet memory that he remembered and savored on special occasions.

*****

The next evening, Tamara, with Larion's help, set the table for everyone. She had spent the whole day preparing the food they would consume and the table was overflowing with traditional *zakusti*. Old Valodya had contributed three small bottles of vodka to ensure appropriate sobriety. They exchanged introductory toasts to everyone's good health, happiness, and long life.

The last toast was solemnly made by Boris Mikhailovich. "*Me Boodim!*" (we persevere). Then they commenced to eat and share in traditional songs. Eventually, they began to question Larion incessantly about his adventures in Leningrad and in the *Winter War*.

Larion was suitably circumspect about his actual war experiences. He had killed numerous times in order to survive and to protect the members of his platoon, but it provided him with no joy or satisfaction. He just felt relief that he had actually survived three and a half months of hell. He thought about the fact that he did not only have to defend himself against the Finns, who fought bravely to defend their homeland, but he also had to defend himself against individuals such as Marchenko and his *NKVD* minions.

It reminded him of the Kertinskys and the way they manipulated the resettlement of his parents to Siberia. In his mind, he even compared the war to a poker game—fate was fickle and deceitful in both situations. In real life, he had experienced a fellow soldier being shot dead less than a meter away from himself. That bullet could have been intended to kill him instead of his companion, who was alive and well one moment, and then dead and gone the next.

Finally, the assembled group got around to the wedding plans Dimitri and Tamara had arranged. The wedding was to be a civil affair, followed by a modest feast and dance at the old converted church.

"And I will bring an extra bottle of vodka, Larion," Old Valodya stated proudly. "So that you can repeat your fiery *hopaka*."

"I do not think that I will be prepared to repeat that dance, Valodya," Larion replied. "I do not know how I survived the first time, but I know I do not want to press my luck."

"That's right," added Tamara. "Louyna and I shall dance together, as husband and wife, not like some drunken Cossacks falling off their horses."

"Oh, but it was such a sight to behold...those flickering flames on your boots, your trousers, your shirt..." Valodya reminisced. "And those scissor kicks over your head with the vodka flames licking at your boots and then that final flip up... I thought my heart was going to stop."

"You are neglecting to mention my burned boots, my burned trousers, my burned shirt, and my burned fingers," replied Larion, laughing at what he had endured and survived.

*****

After the wedding, the feast, and the dance, Dimitri made convenient excuses that he could not return to his home at the *kolkhoz* and that he would be spending the night at her godfather's home. Tamara did not say anything; she merely blushed.

Alone at the residence, the couple shyly went to the guest bedroom and looked at each other. Then they proceeded to undress slowly in the semi-darkness since the room was lit by a single candle, sequestered in a glass chamber to prevent it from being blown out by a draft. They examined each other with subdued awe, but there was a mutual emerging passion as well.

Once they were in bed, they kissed and explored each other with surprise and amazement.

"Louyna, have you been with another woman before?" Tamara asked quietly.

"No, I have not," Larion replied. "I know what they say about soldiers…and sailors, but I was never interested in being with another woman after I met you. I made up my mind that I was going to wait for you."

As they tried to be intimate, they laughed occasionally when they happened to fumble or stumble. Larion explored Tamara's firm breasts, kissing them as he ran his hands down her thighs and between her legs. Tamara caressed and explored Larion's firm body and then proceeded anxiously to guide him inside her. They loved each other tenderly, repeating their vows to be faithful. Larion promising to come back as soon as the war was over. Tamara promising to wait for his return.

The following two weeks passed quickly. There was no further letter from his parents and the police chief was not able to obtain additional information about their location or their welfare.

Tamara and Larion took long barefoot walks along the riverbank. They would lie down in each other's arms under the shade of a tree. They would make love each night slowly and tenderly before they would lapse into a deep tranquil sleep. Then it was time for Larion to leave and they were separated once again.

Tamara wrote to tell him that she was pregnant about three months later. Seven months after that letter, he received another letter announcing the fact that she had given birth to their son. In his absence, she decided to name him after her father. Their son's birth date was 5 May 1941.

Part 2
Struggle and Survival (1940-45)

Chapter 14

In 1936, Mussolini and Hitler had entered into a military pact and Mussolini coined the 'Rome-Berlin' military agreement as the 'Axis'. On 27 September 1940, Imperial Japan also joined. Subsequently, other fascist states in central Europe such as Romania, Bulgaria and Hungary also joined. Yugoslavia joined, however that decision resulted in a coup d'état which resulted in the subsequent Nazi invasion of Yugoslavia. The Yugoslav partisans would sustain 446000 casualties, exceeding those of the United States and of the United Kingdom. Finland joined the Axis in June, 1941, and it was termed the 'Continuation War' with Soviet Russia, after the Nazi Germany invaded Soviet Union.

Nazi Germany had previously approached Soviet Russia and hypocritically invited it to join as well. Though Stalin was agreeable, Nazi Germany was not prepared to accede to Stalin's request for assurances that his territorial 'sphere of influence' in Central Europe and in the Baltic would not be interfered with. That set the stage for Operation Barbarossa – Nazi Germany's invasion of Soviet Russia on 22 June 1941. In the interim, the Molotov-Ribbentrop Pact of 23 August 1939, gave Nazi Germany a free hand in Western Europe and Soviet Russia a free hand in the Baltic region.

The 'Battle of France' only lasted about forty-six days, even though military strength was approximately equal at about 3.4 million men each. However, Nazi Germany only sustained casualties of about 165000, while France sustained casualties of about 325000 and about 1.75 million French troops were taken captive. Winston Churchill was able to rescue about 340000 men from Dunkirk and he prophesied after the French surrender on 22 June 1940, that the Battle of France had ended, but that the Battle of Britain was about to begin.

As Soviet Russia consolidated its control over the Baltic States from November of 1939 through to March of 1940, Nazi Germany focused on subjugating England in the 'Battle of Britain', an air battle for supremacy over

English airspace. The battle between the Nazi Luftwaffe and the Royal Air Force lasted for three months and three weeks, from 10 July 1940 to 31 October 1940.

England, though outnumbered initially by 2600 planes to 2000 planes, lost 1750 planes while the Luftwaffe lost 2000 planes. The Luftwaffe also sustained pilot casualties of almost 3600 to England's pilot casualties of about 2000, which was critical to Nazi Germany's ultimate failure. Though England was victorious in maintaining control over its airspace, civilian casualties totaled about 35000 during the Battle of Britain.

Both Hitler and Stalin then made critical miscalculations about each other's military capability. Hitler was not impressed with Stalin's conduct of the Winter War with Finland, a minor country which exacted a horrendous toll on Soviet soldiers and material before being finally forced to sue for peace. Similarly, after Nazi Germany's quick defeat of France, its failure to win the Battle of Britain, a mere island nation, did not impress Stalin that Hitler posed a deadly threat to Russia.

Hitler was not impressed with Stalin's pyrrhic victory over Finland in the Winter War and Stalin was equally unimpressed with Hitler's failure to defeat England in the Battle of Britain. It was that Nazi failure which reassured Stalin that Nazi Germany would not attack Soviet Russia. Stalin's assumption proved to be drastically wrong and it resulted in horrendous Soviet casualties.

On 22 June 1941, Nazi Germany, with a total initial troop strength of about 3.8 million men, about 3800 tanks, and 5000 aircraft, attacked Soviet Russia along a 2900-kilometer front which was defended by about 2.9 million troops, 11000 tanks and 8000 aircraft. The initial invasion lasted about five and a half months, from 22 June 1941 to 5 December 1941. Nazi Germany's immediate casualties totaled about 900000, while Soviet Russia sustained immediate casualties of about two million. The attack was a three-pronged attack from the east focused on Leningrad in the north, Moscow in the center and ultimately, the City of Stalingrad in the south, since it was Hitler's nemesis' namesake.

The overwhelmed Soviet troops had three alternatives: fight to the death; retreat and be shot as deserters by the NKVD 'Rifle Divisions'; or infiltrate through the Nazi German frontlines and become partisans.

The vast majority of Soviet citizens in the occupied territories actually welcomed the Nazi troops as saviors from Stalin's oppressive regime. However, their initial infatuation dissipated fairly quickly because of their humiliating treatment by Hitler's Wehrmacht troops. Those troops were followed by the 'Einsatzgruppen', which were SS paramilitary 'death squads', charged with the responsibility of summarily eliminating all opposition: the intelligentsia, the priesthood, the cultural elite, political commissars, Jews, partisans, and all forms of real or imagined threats to the Nazi German presence in Soviet Russia. Neither age nor gender was a mitigating factor.

However, none of Hitler's strategic objectives were achieved in the end and after 1943, Nazi Germany was in retreat in the east, pursued by the Soviet Army; Mussolini was overthrown in Italy in July of 1943 and the Allies had commenced the Normandy Invasion of France in June of 1944. Hitler was then compelled to fight a war on three fronts: in the east, in the south, and in the west.

But Hitler's major error was his failure to appreciate the vast enormity of the Russian landmass.

Chapter 15

At the conclusion of the *Winter War* with Finland, General Vinogradov made sure that upon his transfer to the command of a division in the Sixth Army, which was deployed on the Ukrainian front, Colonel Galkovskiy and his battalion would follow him, and that included Larion's platoon. By the end of the Winter War, of the original fifty soldiers and the two non-commissioned officers he commanded, only thirty original soldiers and one non-commissioned officer remained. But they were battle-hardened and they had survived, notwithstanding the inept leadership of their three Soviet Army commanders and Stalin's sycophants: Meretshov, Voronshilov, and Timoshenko.

Meretshov had even been arrested by the NKVD shortly before the start of the Second World War and though he was released after a couple of months, that arrest had a profound effect on his confidence and decision making. Whether he chose to be bold or cautious, it inevitably turned out to be the wrong decision, which dramatically increased Soviet Russia's casualties. He was quickly replaced by Voronshilov.

Voronshilov, though one of the original five Marshals appointed by Stalin in 1935 and one of two who lived to survive the Second World War, was equally inept. His decisions were always an attempt to second guess '*what would Comrade Stalin have wanted him to do*'.

Voronshilov was quickly replaced by Timoshenko as overall commander of the combined eight armies which attacked Finland in 1939 and he was appointed a Marshal in May of 1940, after the pyrrhic conclusion to the Winter War. However, with the outbreak of Operation Barbarossa, which initiated the Nazi-Soviet portion of the Second World War in June of 1941, Timoshenko's initial defeats motivated Stalin to appoint General Georgy Zhukov to replace him.

Zhukov would successfully defend against the Nazi attack on Moscow and he would subsequently relieve the Nazi siege on Stalingrad. He also led the

Soviet armies into Germany to seize Berlin. He was aided throughout by General Konstantin Rokossovsky. He had been Zhukov's superior before being arrested by the *NKVD* after Marshall Tukhachevsky's arrest and execution. Rokssovsky was quickly reinstated after the Nazi invasion in 1941 and provided invaluable assistance to Zhukov throughout the balance of the war.

Zhukov was also instrumental in the arrest and execution of Lavrenty Beria after Stalin's death in March of 1953.

*****

As an experienced First Lieutenant, Larion was entrusted with an enhanced platoon of one hundred men and four non-commissioned officers. In the year following the end of the Winter War, matters were relatively quiet, though unstable, but Larion insured that his platoon was physically fit and ready. He had them practice organizing off-setting machine gun positions whereby each position, with the exception of the first and last, would be protected from an attack by having the companion machine-gun nests on either side provide covering fire against any direct attack on any one position. It proved to be very successful in live ammunition practices and he hoped it would be equally successful in the event of an outbreak of any war.

Though he was not really that interested in tanks or self-propelled artillery, Larion became seduced by the Katyusha rocket launcher. Though the basic concept went far back to ancient China and Leonardo da Vinci, Soviet General Kotskov modernized the concept. Basically, it was a multiple rocket launcher which was mounted on the back of ordinary trucks. It was composed of racks of parallel rails on which the rockets were mounted on a folding frame which would raise the rails to the desired angle, which determined their general launch distance and destination.

Each truck had a protective steel shield which would be lowered over the truck's windshield to protect it from the rocket's fiery discharge. Each truck could carry from fourteen to forty-eight one-meter rockets. Though they were not that accurate, a battery of twelve trucks firing simultaneously could discharge about five hundred rockets within two minutes for a maximum distance of about 5500 meters.

Consequently, they were very effective for a saturation bombardment. However, it took almost an hour to reload the launchers. Therefore, it was imperative to fire the *Katyusha* rockets and then move, reload, and fire again, before opposing artillery and mortars could be directed at their location.

The collective banshee screams of the *Katyusha* rockets exceeded that of the *JU-87* Stuka dive bombers in the *Luftwaffe*, whose *'Jericho'* sirens were fitted on the front of each of the two-wheel assemblies. Their screaming crescendo increased as the bombers dived down at their targets. The screeching saturation barrage of the *Katyusha* rockets had a similar effect. In fact, the primary goal of both the *Stuka* dive bomber and the *Katyusha* rocket was to instill fear in the opposing combatants.

The mobility of the rocket launcher was its second key advantage. A battery of launchers could be fired and the trucks could then be moved to a second location before the opposing artillery could hone onto their position and return artillery and mortar fire.

The Nazis nicknamed the rocket launchers *'Stalin's Organ'*, while the Soviets had them classified and they were only marked by the letter *'K'*. Consequently, the soldiers nicknamed the rocket launchers the *'Katyusha'*, a popular wartime song about a young girl named *Katya* who longs for her beloved who had gone away on military service to defend the *Rodina* (the Motherland).

Larion's platoon was designated to provide military support and defense for a *Katyusha* battery composed of ten trucks, each having a capacity to fire thirty rockets each, while they were stationed in his designated area. He loved the deafening sound of their shrill screams and he thought about how the Nazi troops would react to their collective shrieking sirens heralding their impending death. The drawback was that after the batteries released their rocket barrages, they had to withdraw and it was Larion's platoon which had to endure the return fire of the Axis artillery and mortar fire.

Larion's platoon was on active duty on Sunday, 22 June 1941, when all hell broke out as Hitler's Nazi troops initiated Operation Barbarossa. The combined Fascist forces totaled 3.8 million men who attacked simultaneously along a 2900-kilometer front which was defended by about 2.9 million Soviet troops. The attack commenced with an artillery fire of up to 23000 artillery pieces to disperse the opposing forces.

This was followed by an air attack by some 5000 assorted aircraft, which was followed by about 3500 tanks and the 3.8 million troops. Following closely behind were the seven battalions of 500 men each of the *Einsatzgruppen*, the *SS* death squads who massacred over 33000 Jews in two days at

BabiYar and another 25000 Jews in two days at Rumbula. Though separate and apart from the *Wehrmacht,* the regular combined German army, the *Wehrmacht* was still charged with giving the *Einsatzgruppen* appropriate logistical support.

The hellish cacophony of the attack was simply unending and unbelievable. It commenced with unending artillery shells whistling shrilly through the air and ending in horrendous explosions as they struck the ground. The explosions would throw up a dense clouds of dirt into the air and shrapnel in all directions. All one could do was hunker down in some hole or depression on the ground and hope or pray that the shells would not strike directly and that the shrapnel would not strike them, either.

The artillery barrage was coordinated by an air attack on the Soviet air bases. The *Stuka's* sirens added to the deafening noise as they dive bombed Soviet artillery positions and military airports. The *Luftwaffe's Messerschitt* and *Focke-Wulf* squadrons strafed anything which moved within the range of their gun sights and obliterated Soviet aircraft from the sky and on the ground. Nazi Germany lost approximately 2800 aircraft, while Soviet Russia lost over 21000.

The artillery and the air attacks were followed by the rapid advance of the Panzer Divisions which obliterated the mechanized defenses of Soviet Russia. Nazi Germany lost about 2700 tanks while Soviet Russia lost over 20000.

The tank attack was quickly followed by millions of Nazi soldiers who were augmented by troops from other fascist states such as Hungary, Slovenia, Croatia, Bulgaria, and Italy. Finland renewed its war with Soviet Russia on the Karelian Isthmus in the north—the Continuation War—in an attempt to re-cover the territory, it ceded at the end of the *Winter War* in March of 1940. Before the initial Nazi attack ground to a halt before the cities of Leningrad, Moscow, and Stalingrad some five months later, the Axis Powers would sustain over one million casualties, whereas Soviet Russia's initial casualties would total almost three million personnel.

*****

With the commencement of the attack, Larion implored the *Katyusha* bri-gade commander to fire half of his rockets in two separate barrages. In that way, there would be sufficient time to fire a third separate barrage of one hun-dred and fifty rockets for a total of four hundred and fifty rockets within one hour before the brigade would be obliged to move away to a new location. Larion hoped that the three separate barrages would disperse any attacking tanks and just leave opposing infantry to be met directly by his platoon and their machine gun batteries.

Fortunately, the three *Katyusha* barrages had the desired effect. The opposing Panzer tanks were deflected and circumvented his platoon's position to avoid unnecessary material losses. That left Larion's platoon to face only the oncoming German infantry and their Italian fascist allies.

Larion's platoon held for the first three days and two nights; however, he suffered a seventy percent casualty rate. Ammunition and food continued to arrive for his original compliment of one hundred men, but the desperate manpower shortage compelled Larion to seek a meeting with the battalion commander, Colonel Galkovskiy, to review their overall strategy and troop deployment.

*****

"Colonel Galkovskiy!" Larion announced. "First Lieutenant Sulupin reporting, sir."

"At ease, Lieutenant," Galkovskiy replied. "This is not the time to stand on formalities, Larion Daneelivich. Come and sit down beside me." Galkovskiy's Adjutant was a major who was standing beside Galkovskiy and drinking vodka from a half-empty bottle.

"Lieutenant, allow me to introduce myself. Major Dimitry Tynlenev, Adjutant to Colonel Galkovskiy, but at the moment, his stalwart drinking companion. Come join us, Lieutenant, or the good Colonel may decide to shoot both of us on grounds of cowardice," the major said half-seriously, as he handed the vodka bottle to Larion.

"Greetings, sir," Larion replied formally, still standing at attention.

"Lieutenant, I have ordered you to be at ease," Galkovskiy spoke quietly, but his baritone voice demanded immediate compliance. "Are you forcing me to have you summarily executed for disobeying my direct order?"

"No sir!" replied Larion, relaxing his stance. "Do I have permission to speak?"

"You do, once you have removed your hat, sat down, and shared a drink with me and the major," Galkovskiy replied wryly. "There is a time to love, a time to fight, and a time to die. At the present moment, I believe this is a time for a *payanka* (a drinking party). There are a couple of tins of salmon, some goat cheese, and some rye bread. We can eat, drink, and talk at the same time, my friend."

"By the way, I have heard how you persuaded the *Katyusha* brigade commander to fire his rockets in three salvos instead of one. He told me that it was your idea to try to persuade the opposing forces that his rocket brigade was more substantial than it was in order to try to turn away the advance of the Nazi panzers around your position.

"Good thinking, because it also permitted the remainder of my brigade to avoid a direct tank attack as well and that is why we have been able to hold out for three days. However, I fear that the next attack on our brigade will be successful, since we are not receiving any replacement troops. I hope that Comrade Stalin and his fellow geniuses in the Kremlin have finally seen the wisdom of a tactical retreat to permit us to fight on better terms on another day, but that revelation may come too late for us."

*****

The three officers then proceeded to assess the battalion's overall status. Their losses were horrific and though the brigade had been able to inflict greater losses on the enemy, the enemy had the advantage of a greater manpower reserve. Larion was shocked to hear that the remaining able-bodied troops which were left out of the original five-hundred-man complement, totaled less than one hundred.

Their brigade was not permitted to retreat at this point in time. They were ordered to stand their ground for at least another day to provide additional time for other retreating brigades. The issue which remained was whether to keep the remainder of their brigade scattered along the original perimeter or to consolidate them in one position. Either alternative posed severe handicaps.

Stretching out their remaining one hundred troops out along a one-kilometer line meant that those individual machine gun positions could be easily overrun. Consolidating them into a stronger one-hundred-meter perimeter would permit the opposing forces to outflank them on either side, while they were preoccupied with the main frontal attack. Either decision meant certain defeat and death.

*****

"So Larion Daneelivich, do you have any suggestions?" the adjutant asked in all seriousness, taking another long drink from the vodka bottle. "This war is almost the exact opposite of the First World War which we studied at the Military Academy," Larion replied. "That war involved reciprocal outflanking movements which resulted in a stationary line extending for hundreds of kilometers which lasted for over four years. Hitler's *blitzkrieg* is really a 'lighting war'. Their overwhelming strategy is to advance as quickly as possible. Perhaps we can try to utilize their strategy to our advantage."

"Please continue, my young friend," Galkovskiy interjected. "I like the way your young mind works. The Major and I are about twenty years older than you and it seems that we have a greater difficulty in being able to perceive new strategies in this new kind of warfare."

"Well, I believe that the Nazis primary objective is to break through our remaining line and continue their advance eastward," Larion replied thoughtfully. "Perhaps, just as my platoon was able to persuade the Nazis to deflect around our position with the three barrages of rocket fire by getting them to believe that the *Katyusha* brigade was more substantial than it was, we can persuade them that they have overrun us which would permit them to continue their advance, but leave the remnants of our brigade to live and fight another day."

"Humm? You mean to say that we just play dead?" the adjutant inquired; however, his facial expression was one of total disgust at that suggestion. He was more than prepared to die for the Motherland the next day.

"Not exactly, Major," Larion replied. "First, I suggest that we do not stretch out our remaining troops along our full kilometer line. That would just be suicidal, just as if we concentrated all or our forces in one position. However, if we spread our remaining troops in three positions along a three-hundred-meter line with about thirty troops at each location and at least three machine guns at each location, we should be able to make a forceful stand.

"If we can assemble three machine guns at each position, thirty troops should be sufficient to man each position. Those machine guns should give each group sufficient firing power to slow down any direct infantry attack. Each machine gun position would have ten men to operate those three machine guns and have twenty additional troops to provide supporting rifle fire. Their position would also be supported by fire from the adjacent machine gun positions to help stop any direct attack."

"I suggest that you, as brigade commander, position yourself in the central machine gun location, which would have supporting fire from both of the two flanking machine gun batteries. That should force the enemy to try to focus on either of the two outside batteries. Those troops should be under orders to maintain their position for a short time and then effect a strategic withdrawal to the central position."

"The opposing troops would assume that they have overrun the two flanking machine gun batteries and they would, in all probability, proceed eastward as quickly as possible. Finally, the fire from the central location should be reduced. Hopefully, the enemy would conclude that those remaining troops would not be worth the delay for final elimination which would hold up their advance."

"In that way, sir, we would have fulfilled our orders to delay the advance of the enemy without having to commit a group suicide. The remaining soldiers could then slip past the Nazis front line and continue to fight from their rear."

The two senior officers looked at each other thoughtfully and then back at Larion.

"Well, Major," Galkovskiy spoke first, "I do not have a better idea, so I am prepared to take a chance. At least it gives us an opportunity for survival and the opportunity to fight another day."

"I agree, Colonel," replied the adjutant.

*****

At dawn the next day, the attack proceeded exactly as Larion had anticipated. The withering fire from nine machine guns firing simultaneously encouraged the Axis troops to try to focus on the two flanking machine gun batteries. First the southern machine gun nest ceased firing all three machine guns sequentially. It only fired two machine guns and while the opposing troops were still five hundred meters away and then the final machine gun also ceased firing.

In the interim, whatever troops remained alive effected a tactical retreat from their original position and joined Colonel Galkovskiy's central position. Within a further fifteen minutes, Larion's troops, who were manning the northern machine gun nest, followed suit in the same fashion. However, the opposing enemy fire was relentless and the casualties were heavy.

Galkovskiy's central position, reinforced by additional machine guns, maintained a withering fire at any advancing troops, which then proceeded to advance on either flank. Gradually, there was only one machine gun which was firing and even that gun ceased firing after another five minutes. The Nazi troops proceeded to advance on either flank past the central position as quickly as they could. They displayed no interest in confirming that all Soviet troops were killed. They wanted to catch up with their fellow Axis troops in their accelerated advance towards Kiev, the capital of the Ukraine. They would leave the Soviet remnants to the *Einsatzgruppen* for a final clean up.

As dusk quickly darkened the June summer sky, what remained of Colonel Galkovskiy's battalion totaled only fifteen men. Galkovskiy, his adjutant, Larion, one senior sergeant, the Communist Commissar, Larion, and ten infantry soldiers. As dusk quickly turned to night, Galkovskiy assembled his men.

"Boys, there are only fifteen of us left," he announced in a hushed voice so that he would not be overheard by some lagging enemy troops who, for whatever reason, were not as inclined to proceed to the east with the same celerity as their fellow soldiers. "Now we have to decide what we should do."

"We have to fight, Comrade Colonel," the Communist Commissar replied. "We have to fight and die for the Motherland and for Stalin. There is nothing more to discuss."

"And just for clarification, Comrade Commissar," Galkovskiy inquired with a tired voice. "How many Nazis have you killed over the last three days and nights?"

"I do not keep count, Colonel," the Commissar replied smugly.

"Well, you did not operate any of the machine guns and I did not see you fire a rifle. All I saw you hold these last three days and nights was your Tokarev pistol and I am willing to bet that you did not even bother to fire it, since its effective range is only fifty meters and the Germans never got closer than two hundred meters. Give me your pistol, Comrade Commissar."

When the Communist Commissar balked at Galkovskiy's demand, Larion came up behind him and held him by both his elbows so that he could not draw his pistol. The adjutant quickly joined him and withdrew the commissar's pistol from his holster and handed the weapon to the colonel. Galkovskiy smelled the pistol and then checked its magazine. There was no acrid smell of spent gunpowder and the magazine contained its full chamber of eight rounds of ammunition.

"Now Comrade Commissar, I have to advise you that I am disappointed," Galkovskiy stated firmly in his hushed baritone whisper. "We have lost almost five hundred men in the last three days and nights of fighting and you have not even fired your pistol one fucking time. Do you call that fighting for the Motherland and for Stalin?"

"I am not answerable to you, Colonel," the Commissar spat out his words in contempt.

"Again, my dear Commissar, I am not inclined to agree," Galkovskiy replied. "I remember General Vinogradov in Finland about eighteen months ago in a similar situation and do you know what the good general had to say to another commissar?"

The commissar did not reply. He was not sure where Galkovskiy was going or what he intended to do, but he decided that it would be more prudent for him not to say anything.

"The General said: *that at this place and at this time, I have the power of life or death over everyone under my command*, or words to that effect in any case. Is that not a fact, Lieutenant Sulupin?"

"That is correct, Colonel," replied Larion.

"And since there are only fifteen of us left, Comrade Commissar, and now that we are behind enemy lines, what assurance do I have that you will fulfill your duty for our mutual safety…to kill as many Nazis as you can, since you have failed to kill one fucking Nazi so far. You sat back and hid behind a tree while almost five hundred of your fellow soldiers gave their lives for the Motherland…and even for Stalin?"

The Commissar glared at Galkovskiy, but he did not dare say a word.

"Since you have nothing to say for yourself," Galkovskiy replied rhetorically, "does anyone here object to a summary execution of our dear Comrade Commissar for gross dereliction of duty in the face of the enemy?"

No one uttered a word of objection, but all of the remaining men glared at the Commissar, whose knees suddenly weakened and he had to be held up by Larion.

"Since it would not be prudent to shoot you in the back of the head, which seems to be the preferable practice of your colleagues in the *NKVD*, I suggest that one of our soldiers volunteers to skewer this useless motherfucker with his bayonet."

Three of the soldiers immediately held up an arm to volunteer. Galkovskiy merely nodded his assent and the commissar was dragged out into the darkness.

Chapter 16

German troops were heavily indoctrinated into the German Empire's false capitulation at the end of the First World War and the inequitable Treaty of Versailles which further humiliated the German nation through the imposition of vast territorial concessions, punishing reparations, and the forfeiture of its naval, ground and air forces. That indoctrination paled in comparison to their indoctrination as to their 'racial Aryan superiority', which was coupled with an anti-Semitic, anti-Bolshevik and an anti-Slav ideology.

Hitler referred to Jews and Russian Slavs as *'Untermenschen'* (subhumans) and equated them to the 'Mongol hordes' which threatened Europe in the thirteenth and fourteenth centuries. Soviet Russia was said to be controlled by Jewish Bolshevik subhumans.

The Nazis even issued a ban on sexual relations between Germans and Slavs, however, it was only the Slav's who faced summary execution for breach of the ban. The Nazis 'recruited' about 38000 Russian women to fill brothels for the Wehrmacht troops, who were conveniently exempted from that ban.

Hitler described the war against Soviet Russia as a 'War of Annihilation' for the preservation of western European culture as exemplified by the German Aryan race. He said he had no intention of preserving the enemy in the current war only to have to fight that enemy again in thirty years. The *Einsatzgruppen* were to execute all Soviet functionaries, intellectuals, partisans and Jews. They obtained their preliminary experience in the systematic murder of Germans afflicted with physical and mental disabilities, as well as psychiatric patients in the fall of 1939. With the implementation of Operation Barbarossa, they comprised seven battalions of five hundred men each. The battalions were divided into five companies of one hundred men. The battalions were affiliated with five different Army Groups: 3rd Army, 4th Army, 8th Army, 10th Army, and the 14th Army. Any regular Wehrmacht officer who objected to their excesses was immediately demoted and removed from his command.

At the War's end, at least eighteen senior officers of the *Einsatzgruppen* were executed by hanging, but their battalions executed an estimated 1.3 million of the six million Jews, who were exterminated during the War and only about two hundred officers ever received any punishment.

As is in the nature of mankind, the Einsatzgruppen Kommandos found willing native collaborators in all of the Nazi conquered territories who enthusiastically assisted them in their indiscriminating slaughter of their fellow human beings.

Chapter 17

Galkovskiy decided that they should remain in place until the following night and then move west, initially, and then slowly turn to the north. He was hopeful that they would be able to meet up with other troops who survived that initial three-day Nazi onslaught. All of the men were ordered to scavenge as much ammunition as they could find, as well as provisions. He knew they needed food to survive and ammunition to defend themselves as best they could. They would only travel by night and communicate through hand signals and bird calls.

On the fourth day, they came across a village constructed in a clearing adjacent to a forest. It was not the first village they had come across, but unlike the other villages which had been burned to the ground, this one was still intact. Galkovskiy and his Adjutant, Major Tynlenev, peered through their binoculars towards the village. They had to make a decision whether to approach it in the daylight or wait until dusk. Their decision was made for him by a detachment of twenty troops bearing an unusual Nazi insignia.

"Dimitri, my friend," Galkovskiy asked, "can you identify those troops? They are obviously not regular *Wehrmacht*."

"When we invaded Poland in September of 1939, I came across troops bearing those kinds of patches," replied Tynlenev. "I believe that this is a detachment of the *Einsatzgruppen*. They are paramilitary execution squads. See how they are emptying the houses and rounding up the villagers. They will probably march them into the forest and execute them."

"Even the women and children?" Galkovskiy asked.

"That is what they do," Tynlenev replied. "They are too cowardly to fight on the front lines, but they have no scruples about executing ordinary unarmed civilians behind the lines."

"Lieutenant," Galkovskiy addressed Larion. "Here, take a look through my binoculars and give me your assessment of this situation."

Larion took the binoculars and focused them on the village about two hundred meters distant.

"I am not familiar with these troops, so I respectfully defer to Major Tynlenev's assessment," Larion replied quite somberly.

"Well boys," Galkovskiy addressed his small group of soldiers collectively. "What do we do?"

A young soldier spoke up first.

"With respect, sir," he replied earnestly. "We should do what we can to save as many villagers as possible and…kill as many as these pig fuckers as we can. Otherwise, why are we here?"

There was a general mummer of agreement.

"I agree, but let us see how this situation is going to unfold," Galkovskiy said. "We cannot shoot from here, because they will just summarily execute the villagers before we can mount any rescue."

"If they remain true to form, Colonel," Tynlenev replied. "They will have part of their detachment escort the villagers into the forest for execution, while the remainder will loot their homes and then burn them to the ground. But if they do that, then our odds will be more even."

*****

As Tynlenev predicted, approximately thirty villagers had been rounded up and the *Einsatzgruppen* detachment appeared to divide in half. One half proceeded to gesture to the villagers that they should walk towards the forest while the remainder separated and commenced to search the various residences.

"Alright, boys. We shall let them pass by to give the villagers a chance to scatter amongst the trees once the shooting starts. Each man is to pick two targets and each man is to let the others know which targets he has picked. No point in having fourteen men shoot at the same man."

As the villagers approached the forest, Larion could hear the muffled whimpers of the women and confused cries of the children. The elderly men walked stoically. They had lived their lives and they appeared willing to accept their inevitable fate.

There was one Nazi leading the procession with four soldiers walking parallel on either side of the villagers. The final soldier was carrying a machine pistol at the rear of the column. They were laughing at the fear they had in-stilled in the villagers and obviously looking forward to their execution.

Tynlenev agreed that he would take control of the front of the procession, while Galkovskiy would cover the rear. As they passed by Galkovskiy's position, he would wait until the last Nazi soldier walked by and then as he shot him, he would yell at the villagers to drop to the ground. Tynlenev would simultaneously take out the Nazi leading the procession and open up on the four Nazis on the right side.

Galkovskiy would open up on the four Nazis on the left side. His remaining troops would carefully aim at the four Nazi soldiers on either side of the column in the event the villagers panicked and did not drop down to the ground. Galkovskiy directed that one soldier take his binoculars and watch the village to observe what the remaining *Kommandos* did once the shooting started.

Galkovskiy thought that it was a simple plan which should work with a minimum of casualties. The unknown factors included how the villagers would react to the fire fight and secondly, how would the remaining *Einsatzgruppen Kommandos* in the village react to the shooting.

As Galkovskiy shot the Nazi protecting the rear of the procession, he yelled. "*smarte, lude.*" (watch out, people). The *Kommando* immediately crumpled to the ground as the pistol round shattered his spine. Simultaneously, Tynlenev shot the lead soldier in the side of his head, which exploded in a spattering of flesh and bone. Tynlenev then commenced to fire down the line of four soldiers on the right side with his pistol. The death squad troops were not used to being fired upon and it seemed that they panicked even more than the villagers.

The adult villagers dropped down to the ground and pulled some of the startled children down to the ground with them. The remaining eleven Soviet troops opened up on the *Kommandos*, each one methodically shooting at two separate soldiers, within seconds all of the ten Nazi death squad troops were lying dead on the ground. The villagers remained frozen, lying on the ground. Larion picked up two machine pistols and proceeded to shoot them in the air.

"What is happening in the village, soldier?" Galkovskiy asked the soldier peering through his binoculars.

"They were startled, but then the machine gun fire seemed to reassure them and they are just proceeding to search the homes, sir!" the soldier replied.

"Good thinking again, Lieutenant," Galkovskiy said. "Those bursts from the two machine pistols obviously reassured those bastards in the village that the execution was proceeding as usual. But we do not have much time. They shall expect their comrades to rejoin them fairly quickly."

Suddenly, shooting sprang up in the village and a couple of the remaining death squad soldiers dropped awkwardly to the ground, their weapons falling helplessly from their hands.

"It appears that we have some comrades, sir!" exclaimed Galkovskiy's lookout. "They must be partisans, because they are not wearing any uniforms."

*****

The remaining death squad soldiers were killed within a couple of minutes; however, there was one holdout in one home. He eventually came out of hiding, holding his hands high in the air. One partisan approached him and put his pistol under his chin and fired. The round blew out the top of the Nazi's head and lifted his helmet off his head. His lifeless body slumped down to the ground as his helmet fell down to earth with a bullet hole through its top.

*****

The partisans and Galkovskiy's men watched each other warily as they approached each other. Galkovskiy and Tynlenev had to shrug off the men and women who tried to kiss their hands in gratitude. The children merely stared up at the two tall officers in awe and reverence. Larion joined his two superior officers as they approached the partisan band of about a dozen men and a couple of women.

"Comrades. What are we going to do now?" A young woman from the village asked the trio as they continued to approach the partisans carefully.

"And who are you, my dear?" Galkovskiy asked with interest.

"Irina Karzhova," she replied. "I live in this village with my husband's parents. He is serving the Motherland in Belarus." Before Galkovskiy could continue the conversation, his group and the partisans finally joined up. There was one familiar face in the group which he recognized.

"Greetings, Gregory Andreivich, but I would like you to know that we have found that wearing military uniforms at this time is neither safe, nor convenient. And we also only address each other by our first names, not our rank."

"It is a pleasure to meet you again, my friend, Vasily Nikolaiovich Vinogradov. It appears we have both survived," Galkovskiy replied.

*****

Galkovskiy was relieved to meet up with his commanding general, but somewhat confused that the general had not been ordered away from the front line. It turned out that Vinogradov had to deal with another *'invitation from Stalin'* respecting another one of his junior officers, a Major, and once again he found the *NKVD*'s grounds and timing totally inappropriate. The *NKVD* officers were actually killed in action during the last Axis attack; however, Vinogradov decided that their *NKVD* superiors might find this event too coincidental to overlook.

Consequently, he, his Adjutant, and about ten of his remaining troops decided to infiltrate past the Nazi advance and continue to fight as partisans.

"Well, General, it is still a pleasure to see you again…and still breathing," Galkovskiy replied sincerely. "I must confess that I had a similar issue to deal with, but it was with a Communist Commissar. And you do remember my Adjutant and my First Lieutenant Sulupin?"

"Vaguely, Gregory," the general replied. "But we really have to get out of the habit of addressing ourselves by rank. If we get captured, our chances of survival and possible escape are substantially increased if we are deemed to be mere civilians."

"Comrades, I must insist on your clarification as to what we…the villagers are to do now?" a young woman asked.

The general looked at the young woman and Galkovskiy recognized her as Irina Karzhova, who had asked him the same question as they were leaving the forest.

"Your villagers are safe, Irina," Galkovskiy replied. "At least for now, so what is your concern?"

"You do realize that if any *Einsatzgruppen* detachment is attacked, their battalion will raze the village to the ground and the villagers shall be burned inside their homes," Irina explained passionately.

"Unfortunately, there is not much that they can do for themselves and we can only do less." Vinogradov replied, "We cannot stay here and there is no place for your villagers to go. They are surrounded by enemy troops and behind enemy lines. There is simply no escape. Their only hope is that the *Einsatzgruppen* battalion shall not have the opportunity to take punitive action against them. After all, they are growing crops and even the Nazis have to eat."

"But those death squads have already incinerated several villages and liquidated all of their inhabitants in this area."

"There is nothing that we can do," Galkovskiy replied. "And I sincerely regret to say that. We may have saved them today, but we shall not be able to save them tomorrow or next week or next month. We can help them bury the bodies deep in the forest and the villagers' only defense will be to deny any knowledge or dealings with the death squad. They are not to retain any souvenirs or weapons because if another squad finds them in their possession, being burnt to death may be a preferable way to die."

"In that case, comrades," Irina stated emphatically. "I insist that you permit me to join your partisan group. If I am going to die in any case, I prefer to die shooting Nazis."

"Can you cook, Irina?" Tynlenev inquired facetiously.

"I can cook and I can shoot a rifle," she replied seriously. "My husband taught me how to shoot. I can probably hit a Nazi in the head at three hundred meters."

"Well, Vasily," Galkovskiy asked. "Since you are our eldest leader, what do you say?"

"My practice is to permit the men to take a vote by majority, but in this case I believe I shall exercise my prerogative and approve her, if she can prove that she can hit a Nazi head at three hundred meters."

They proceeded to place three Nazi helmets on one-meter poles at a three-hundred-meter distance. Irina elected to fire one of the Soviet rifles, since she was more familiar with them. Her first shot struck the helmet and sent it flying.

"Probably, just a lucky shot," Tynlenev quipped.

"In that case, allow me to shoot a 'doublet' for the remaining two helmets," Irina replied confidently. She then fired two shots in quick succession and both helmets were sent flying off of their respective posts.

"It was a trick that my husband taught me. He even suggested that I apply for admission at the *Central Women's Sniper Training School*," Irina replied.

"And why would they bother to train women to be snipers?" Tynlenev asked, though he was quite surprised that she completed three hits out of three shots and that the last two shots were a 'doublet', a feat he was sure that he could not perform himself.

"I have been told that Comrade Stalin believes that women have more flexible limbs, and that they are more patient, more prudent, and even more cunning than most men."

"Well, if that is what Comrade Stalin says, how can we possibly argue with him," Vinogradov replied, ending the issue. "However, if the villagers are grateful, perhaps they can feed us and a little vodka would be appreciated as well. Also, could you arrange to have the villagers share some of their clothes so that my good friend, Gregory, and his colleagues could start looking more like civilians?"

Chapter 18

The former estates of the Russian nobility were not demarcated by straight lines identifying surveyed rectangular pieces of property which were owned by individuals. On the contrary, their estates were immeasurable with vast patches of forest which were deliberately reserved for hunting and for lumber. After the revolution, since all land holdings became vested in the State, the communists found no reason to alter that practice. Therefore, the land contained immense, thickly treed forests which were adjacent to pastures, grain fields and tracks of vegetable crops, with occasional apple and pear orchards.

These forests were a godsend to the partisans, who could hide in the forests and carry out their operations against the Nazi supply lines almost with impunity. They could also move fairly easily across the landscape, travelling from one forest to another. The forests were impenetrable to the Nazi tanks or other mechanized vehicles, consequently, the Nazi troops were obliged to enter on foot and the advantage swung to the partisans. The partisans were more familiar with their forests and had no problem moving through them, even on the darkest of nights.

Stalin's initial reaction was to treat all Russian partisans as deserters and a potential future threat to his Soviet state. However, by the end of July of 1941, he decided to utilize them in the interim and he even began to have them provisioned with food, weapons, ammunition and radio communication. These items would be air-dropped into those forests. The partisan's subversive actions however, were largely uncoordinated.

At times, the civilian population also had to worry about partisan punitive action if they were deemed to be too cooperative with the Nazi invaders. On the other hand, the civilian population had a never-ending concern with the *Einsatzgruppen* ethnic purges and punitive actions. This problem intensified once the Nazi invasion was halted in December of 1941, since the death squads had to expand their cleansing activities in the conquered territories to ensure the security of the *Wehrmacht*'s extended supply lines.

*****

Once the *Kommando* bodies were buried deep inside the forest, Galkovskiy agreed to follow Vinogradov's partisan group even deeper into the forest so that their group could meet up with the main partisan company, which was led by a Nikolai Pavlovskiy. Vinogradov's simple explanation and shrug was that he elected to defer to Pavlovskiy's leadership. They did not move through the forest in a single line, but were spread out like a fan. Vinogradov, who had executed the last death squad *Kommando*, assumed the central point of the fan. Other than hushed conversation with adjacent members, the partisans communicated by hand signals or by the snap of a tree branch being broken or a trunk of a tree being struck.

At that signal, they would immediately stop and there would be a brief conference. All decisions were relayed partisan to partisan by hushed voices and then they would continue to proceed cautiously through the forest.

Vinogradov, Galkovskiy, Tynlenev, and Larion advanced as a group. Irina Karzhova advanced closely behind them. After walking for hours, they reached their destination. There was a small clearing and an adjacent stream. The clearing was not large enough to attract attention from a plane, but it was sufficient to provide some sunlight into the surrounding dark forest. On the periphery of the clearing, but secluded in the trees, were improvised canvas tents which provided some relief from the summer rains and hopefully from the coming winter snow storms.

As the group entered the clearing, a single man came out of the gloom of the shadows of the trees and approached them. He was carrying a rifle across his chest, but Larion noticed that his right index finger was on the trigger and his left hand cradled the front part of the stock.

If they turned out to be combatants, he would be able to lower his rifle and get off at least two shots before he, himself, would go down. Larion assumed that once that happened, the remaining partisans would open up from the shelter of the trees and they would all be dead within a couple of minutes, if not sooner.

"Vinogradov, you old man," the stranger spoke calmly. "Who are the guests you have brought to us this afternoon?"

"Comrades," replied Vinogradov, as he turned to speak to Galkovskiy's group. "Allow me to introduce you to Comrade Nikolai Pavlovskiy, commander of our partisan company." Then he turned back to address Pavlovskiy. "We met by chance at the village of Zabinka. Our friends took care of half of the death squad detachment which took the villagers into the forest for execution. We took care of the rest in the village while they were looting the homes. I even had the privilege of executing one of the Nazi bastards. Shot him with my pistol under the chin to see if I could knock his helmet off."

"And did you?" Pavlovskiy asked.

Though the partisan continued to speak calmly, Larion could see that his rifle was still at the ready while his group held their weapons balanced in one hand and their barrels were pointed harmlessly at the ground to convey the fact that they did not pose any threat.

"Damn right I did," Vinogradov replied. "Blew out his brains and the helmet flew at least a meter over his head."

"That is pretty impressive, Vinogradov. You must possess the most powerful handgun in the Soviet Union. With a pistol that powerful, perhaps you do not have a need for a rifle. We can assign it to someone else."

"Well, perhaps it was only a half-meter above his head, Pavlovskiy," Vinogradov replied. "However, I believe I would prefer to keep both my pistol and my rifle…with all due respect, Commander."

It was obvious to Larion that Pavlovskiy was not aware of Vinogradov's military rank and that Vinogradov did not want the partisans to know his rank either. Finally, Pavlovskiy moved his rifle away from his chest and held it balanced with one hand, its barrel innocuously pointed at the ground.

"Gentlemen!" he asked firmly. "Who do I have the honor of addressing?"

As expected, Larion's officer group introduced themselves in order of rank, though no rank was identified.

"Gregory Galkovskiy!"

"Dimitri Tynlenev!"

"Larion Sulupin!"

As each man introduced himself, he was acknowledged by a curt nod from Pavlovskiy, as he attempted to put the man's name and his face in his own memory bank.

"And who is your attractive female companion?" Pavlovskiy inquired.

"My apologies," replied Vinogradov. "Allow me to introduce you to Irina Karzhova. She was one of the villagers and she asked if she could accompany us."

"Does she cook…or does she do something else?" Pavlovskiy inquired, his lascivious innuendo obvious to everyone.

"I am sure that she can cook…but better yet, she can shoot a Nazi head at three hundred meters. She even perfected a doublet on two helmets we had set up as targets," Vinogradov replied.

A woman came out of the forest and approached the group. She was smiling, but she held a sniper's rifle at the ready in any case.

"If she can shoot that well, then one of you men should be able to do the cooking for her."

"Allow me to introduce you to Tanya Akulich," Pavlovskiy interjected. "Tanya is our detachment's best shot and our designated sniper. Tanya, do you think that you can shoot a doublet at three hundred meters?"

"Of course. That would pose no hurdle for me," Tanya replied smugly. Then she turned to Larion and smiled at him with full lips and twinkling, mischievous grey eyes.

"And you, my handsome young man. Do you shoot?"

"Only when I have to, Comrade," Larion replied politely.

"Oh, Pavlovskiy," Tanya swooned. "I like him. May I have him?" She added teasingly, as she felt Larion's firm right biceps. "I really like this one."

Larion was surprised by Tanya's forward comments and initially, he was at a loss for words.

"Excuse me, Madam!" he replied. "But I am married."

"Oh, Comrade. Your wife is not here and the nights get cold…I promise not to tell her if you keep me warm for a couple of nights," Akulich replied flirtatiously.

Larion was not sure if she was just flirting with him or if she was serious. He decided, out of caution, to assume that it was the latter. It appeared to him that both Pavlovskiy and Akulich were equally amoral.

"You are a beautiful woman, madam, but I am married and I have sworn to be faithful to my wife," Larion replied apologetically. "I sincerely thank you, but I most respectfully decline."

"Sincerely? Most respectfully? Pavlovskiy, I must be losing my touch," Tanya replied, feigning hurt feelings with a frown.

"Dimitri Tynlenov, at your service, Madam!" Tynlenov stated authoritatively and positioned himself between Larion and Tanya. "I volunteer to keep you warm for as many nights as there are stars in the sky."

Tanya cast a last fleeting look at Larion and pursed her lips in disappointment. Then she looked up at Tynlenov and squeezed his biceps firmly and smiled again.

"Oh my, but you are so tall and so strong," Tanya bubbled in her newfound enthusiasm. "Shall we take a walk in the woods before dinner? They do the cooking in the late afternoon and keep the food warm by placing it on heated rocks. It is more discrete that lighting a cooking fire late at night."

"Excuse me, dear Comrades," Tynlenev replied. "But duty calls and I must answer that call."

After Tynlenev and Tanya left the group, Larion let out a sigh of relief, but his face was still flushed from a combination of embarrassment and shame. Tanya was a beautiful woman and saying no was not easy, but having declined her invitation, he felt exhilarated inside. Though he had harbored his own doubts from time to time, it felt good to be strong enough to resist the temptation which Tanya had presented. He was proud of himself and he truly felt good about it as well.

"Well, you ducked that bullet, Larion," Vinogradov observed.

"But be careful, my son," added Pavlovskiy jokingly. "I should warn you that Tanya is good at executing a 'doublet' as well. Do not be surprised if she propositioned you a second time before the night is over."

"Perhaps your sniper will find Tynlenev adequate for her needs," Galkovskiy suggested.

Larion blushed again and excused himself. Pavlovskiy and Vinogradov had matters to discuss between themselves. Galkovskiy turned to find that Irina was still standing close behind him.

"Irina, would you like to drink some cool stream water?" Galkovskiy asked boyishly, as he smiled at her seductively. "For whatever reason, my throat has just become extremely dry."

Irina merely looked up shyly at the tall, silver-haired man and smiled.

"I could use some cool stream water as well," she replied. "It may have something to do with all that walking we have done today or there may be something special in the air in this place."

*****

At dusk, the partisans were served their evening meal. It had been prepared on a couple of field ovens which were made out of modified fuel barrels. The tops of the barrels substituted for a stove top. A large square was cut out of one side to permit firewood to be placed inside. There was an improvised lid which could be lowered over that opening to maintain heat and minimize the escape of firelight from the burning wood. On the other side, four holes were cut in just below the top and just above the bottom of the steel drum, to facilitate air circulation.

The food was a simple thick stew made up of vegetables, mushrooms and a few pieces of shredded meat. There was a thick slice of rich rye bread and the meal was washed down with a rationed cup of vodka, which had been diluted by fresh water from the stream. If anyone was not inclined to drink his or her vodka ration, they could drink the cool stream water instead.

*****

"Pavlovskiy, I want to be candid with you," Vinogradov stated firmly. "I am General Vasily Vinogradov. I commanded a division in the 6th Soviet Army."

"I know, Vasily, and I want to be candid with you as well," Pavlovskiy replied just as firmly. "I am Colonel Nikolai Pavlovskiy. I commanded a battalion in Finland and I also commanded a battalion under you here in the Ukraine."

"My companions are: Colonel Gregory Galkovskiy, who was with me in Finland and recently in the Ukraine. Major Dimitri Tynlenev has been his Adjutant for the past three years. Our young companion is First Lieutenant Larion Sulupin—a capable lieutenant who has repeatedly proven himself in the hard fighting in Finland and here in the Ukraine. Do not underestimate his youth or his bravery."

"Well, since you are the senior officer—"

121

"No!" Vinogradov interrupted Pavlovskiy. "We shall not stand on rank here. Here you are the most experienced and knowledgeable partisan. I have no hesitation in following your command and I know that I speak for my other three officers as well. What we need from you is knowledge in how to survive and how to fight. Are we agreed?"

"Agreed!" Pavlovskiy replied somewhat reluctantly. "But I want you all to know that I welcome and encourage suggestions from everyone. But I agree we just address each other informally."

"We are agreed," Vinogradov replied. "What operations are you considering now, Vasily?"

"We have been focusing on interdicting the Nazi supply lines, especially the fuel supplies for their tanks and mechanized divisions. However, the *Einsatzgruppen* captured a ten-man group of our detachment last week and though we attempted to rescue them, the only thing which we were able to do was to watch them be shot by a firing squad into a trench which they were probably forced to dig. There were only ten of us and I counted at least thirty *Kommandos*."

"Had we arrived even ten minutes earlier we could have done something, regardless of the casualties we would have taken. But we arrived just when the shooting started. We watched as the men collapsed and crumpled. The velocity of the multiple rounds jerked their lifeless bodies backwards into that trench. Then some of the *Kommandos* went into the trench to bayonet the bodies to ensure that they were all dead."

"The ones who still showed any sign of life were rifle shot again in the head at close quarters. Then those sons-of-bitches got some elderly men and women from a village on the west side of the forest to cover them over with some dirt, but then they were shot as well. Their bodies were left to rot in the summer sun. Some of those *ublydki* (mongrel bastards) even proceeded to urinate and defecate into the trench. We must revenge them and let the *Einsatzgruppen* taste what it feels like to be executed like a rabid dog."

"Nikolai, I and my men are at your command," Vinogradov replied sadly. "Sometimes, revenge is the only option left to a man. We all shall die at some time, but I shall have no regret dying here and now if we are able to exact some revenge for the men you lost."

Pavlovskiy retrieved a small flask from the inside of his jacket and offered it to Vinogradov with the toast "*Me boodim*" (we shall persevere).

"*Me boodim*!" replied Vinogradov, as he took a deep drink and handed the flask back to Pavlovskiy.

Chapter 19

Pavlovskiy decided that the four senior officers in Larion's group would join six members of his own detachment. Tanya Akulich was also included in his group because of her sniper capability. The experience about to be afforded to the four officers would enable them to lead the remainder of their own group more effectively, if and when circumstances required it.

Their objective was to move eastward through the forest and then across the adjoining field at night and enter the next forest. They would then continue to the forest's northern boundary where another small village was located. Pavlovskiy was assuming that the village was a probable target for another *Einsatzgruppen* punitive action. If that did not materialize, there was an adjacent road which was being used to transport fuel to the Nazi German frontlines. If the death squad did not materialize, a fuel convey was a very probable alternative target.

They arrived at the edge of the forest midday. Vinogradov and Pavlovskiy used their binoculars to survey the Village. There was no sign of activity or life.

"Damn it!" Pavlovskiy swore quietly. "It seems that we may have arrived too late. The villagers must have been taken away to be shot, since there is no sign of any life in the village."

"Do you think they may have not been shot already?" Larion asked.

"They prefer to take the people to the forest for execution," Pavlovskiy explained. "In that way, they do not have to transport the bodies themselves and the forest helps to conceal their sins. But if the people had been executed, they would have razed all of the homes in the village before they moved on to their next objective. I believe that they have to be nearby because we have not heard any shots. They may be behind us, either to our left or to our right. We should send out a couple of our group to either side to reconnoiter and try to locate them."

"In the event they are located, how will that be communicated back to the rest of us?" Larion asked.

"There is only one way," Pavlovskiy replied. "A single shot in the air directed back to this location. That will help us identify whether to move to the right or to the left. To save time, we shall backtrack into the forest so that we can reach either location more quickly. Does anyone have any other questions or suggestions?"

"Won't that shot alert them, sir?" Larion asked again.

"Of course, it will, but if it is restricted to a single shot, they may probably assume that it is just a villager hunting in the woods. But there is no other way. The only other alternative would be to have our entire group try to guess which direction to take and if we guess wrong, we will not be able to save anyone…nor exact any revenge either."

"In that case, if I may offer a suggestion, Commander," Larion spoke respectfully. "Rather than sending just one member out in either direction, why not send two members? In the event unforeseen events arise, two members would be better able to defend themselves if they are attacked. That would also give us more time to come to their aid. That would still leave the remaining six members to take whatever action they may deem fit and appropriate, regardless of any developments."

"Vinogradov, what do you say?" Pavlovskiy asked.

"I am inclined to agree, but the final decision is yours."

Pavlovskiy considered the alternatives and then he quickly agreed with Larion's suggestion.

"To that extent, Sulupin, I want you and Tanya to advance to the right. And Tanya, if you are fortunate enough to find those bastards, you might as well take a sniper shot at their commanding officer, instead of just shooting in the air. Galkovskiy and I will advance to our left. Vinogradov, you direct the remainder of our squad back down the center."

The ten members of the squad proceeded to separate and re-enter the dark gloom of the forest.

To Larion's surprise, Tanya was totally focused on their objective. She moved her forefinger to her lips to silence Larion when he attempted to speak to her and gesturing with her hand, she indicated that he was to follow her.

After proceeding covertly in a crouched position for approximately a half hour, Tanya and Larion suddenly heard voices ahead of them and then a single shot rang out. They stopped immediately and then Tanya gestured that Larion keep to her right as she lowered herself to the ground and proceeded to crawl forward, holding her rifle in both hands in front of herself. Larion followed suit.

Ahead of them was a small clearing and about twenty-five individuals, including several children, were slowly stripping off their clothes. One uniformed individual seemed to stand out since he appeared to be issuing orders to the remaining men and the naked villagers as well. Without saying a word, Tanya raised her *Mosin-Nagant* rifle with its 3.5 x PU scope to her shoulder and aimed at the commanding officer. Within what seemed to be less than two seconds, she was able to get off two shots. The commanding officer crumpled to the ground, along with another *Kommando* who was standing behind him. All bedlam broke loose as the naked villagers started to scream and scatter into the forest. The remaining members of the death squad immediately lifted up their rifles and machine pistols, and surveyed the surrounding forest for any targets.

"Now that is how I shoot a 'doublet'!" she whispered proudly as she proceeded to shoot two more death squad soldiers.

Larion was not listening to her since he had started shooting as well. Within a few minutes, they heard shots coming from other parts of the forest while the remaining death squad soldiers scrambled for the safety of the trees themselves. A few of them picked the wrong direction and came under the direct fire of Vinogradov and his group of six partisans.

Fairly quickly thereafter, Larion could hear shots from farther left. It had to be Pavlovskiy and Galkovskiy joining the fray. Taking fire from three different directions, the remaining four members of the death squad threw down their arms and slowly re-entered the small clearing, holding their arms high in a sign of surrender. Vinogradov, Pavlovskiy, and their partisans then entered the clearing, their rifles pointed menacingly at the four unarmed prisoners. Tanya and Larion entered the clearing last. The remaining four *Einsatzgruppen Kommandos* were kneeling with their hands clasped together over their heads.

Pavlovskiy noticed that one of the prisoners was wearing a different uniform from the regular *Einsatzgruppen* troops. He was an 'auxiliary'. A native Belorussian who was either conscripted by the death squad or he had volunteered. In either case, he was the most heinous of traitors. A fellow countryman who was not only betraying his Motherland, but executing her people as well.

Pavlovskiy gestured at him to stand up, but to keep his hands clasped over his head. "I take it, comrade, that you understand Russian?" Pavlovskiy asked calmly.

"Yes! Yes, I understand Russian," the auxiliary replied anxiously, hoping that it might save him from certain execution.

"And I take it you probably understand some German as well!" Pavlovskiy asked, still keeping him voice calm, though he felt a rage of hatred slowly building inside himself.

"A little, comrade commander," the auxiliary replied in a tremulous, breaking voice.

"And what are you doing here, comrade?" Pavlovskiy asked.

"I…I'm just following orders."

"Just following orders?" Pavlovskiy asked rhetorically. "Well, if I were to give you an order, would you carry it out?" The auxiliary initially hesitated. He sensed that the partisan commander was playing with him, but then he decided that he had nothing to lose in agreeing.

"Yes, commander! You may order…and I shall obey."

Pavlovskiy finally looked at the bundle of the villagers' clothes and he noticed for the first time that two pre-teen boys had already been shot.

"Did you shoot those two boys, comrade?"

The auxiliary was not sure how long he may have been under the partisans' observation, so he decided to be truthful.

"Only with the greatest of regret, commander," the auxiliary replied, visibly shaking by this time. "They wanted to see if I could shoot both of them with one bullet. But I did not want them to suffer, so I made sure that my shot would be fatal to both of them. I really did not want them to just wound them, but I did not have any other choice."

"Really, you did not have any other choice?" Pavlovskiy asked, but his incredulity was unmistakable.

"Here is a Luger pistol with three bullets. I order you to go up to your three fellow *Kommandos* and you are to shoot them from under their chin up into their putrid skulls and make sure that their eyes are open. I want them to know what is about to happen to them."

Without hesitation, the auxiliary took the Luger pistol and approached the three kneeling prisoners. The first one attempted to close his eyes, but the auxiliary gouged him in one eye with his thumb and as soon as the prisoner opened the other eye, he shot him. Then he proceeded to the next prisoner, who was simply whimpering. He was shot in turn and the bullet pierced his helmet which was still strapped onto his head. Finally, he approached the third remaining prisoner.

"*Schnell!*" (quickly) The final *Kommando* spoke contemptuously. "*Schieben schnell, schweinhund.*" (Shoot quickly, pig-dog.)

The auxiliary shot him with obvious satisfaction. Clearly, he had suffered that *Kommando's* insults previously and killing him was an enjoyable act of revenge. After the prisoner had crumpled to the ground, the auxiliary turned to face Pavlovskiy and he handed the Luger back to him, butt end first.

"And there is another question I wish to ask you, dear comrade," Pavlovskiy continued to speak in a calm voice. "What was the purpose of having these villagers stripped of their clothes. They were only rags and of no possible use to your group."

"These pigs like to humiliate the people before they execute them. That is the only reason."

"In that case, comrade, I order you to take off all of your clothes," Commanded Pavlovskiy.

The auxiliary was truly frightened, but he assumed that if he willingly indulged the partisan commander, he might have a chance of surviving. He undressed quickly and optimistically folded his clothes neatly in a pile beside his feet so it would be easier to get redressed. His obese body was covered with dark hair, even his back. He truly resembled some form of primitive animal rather than a human being.

"Now I want you to kneel and close your eyes, comrade," Pavlovskiy ordered, as he placed his own Tokarev pistol under the auxiliary's chin. However, the auxiliary was unable to close his eyelids. All the muscles in his body had become frozen.

"In that case, comrade," Pavlovskiy spoke calmly, but the anger in his voice was unmistakable. "*Idi cherto!*" (Go to the devil)

As the shot went through his skull, the auxiliary's eyes opened up even wider and so did his mouth, but no sound emanated from his vile throat.

Pavlovskiy then called to the naked villagers in the forest and assured them that their tormentors had been killed and that it was safe to come out and get dressed. The first person to enter the clearing was a boy of about ten years of age. He sorted through the piles of discarded clothes until he found his own and then he got dressed. He approached the dead auxiliary soldier and started to kick him repeatedly in the head, cursing him with each kick until he finally broke down and cried. One of the two boys who were executed by the auxiliary was his older brother.

One by one the other villagers came out of hiding and dressed while they praised their survivors. Pavlovskiy explained his recommendation was that they should try to retreat eastward, travelling by night from forest to forest until they were able to reach the Soviet lines. Their chances were slim, but if they remained in their village, that would mean a certain cruel death. They would be incinerated in their burning homes by the remaining *Einsatzgruppen Kommandos* who would return to exact their own revenge.

*****

Pavlovskiy and Vinogradov decided that they should try to take advantage of attacking a fuel convey before they returned to their camp if they were able to find one using that solitary road. They placed a few mines on the road itself and then positioned themselves in the forest and waited. Several hours later a truck convoy of a dozen fuel trucks became visible in Galkovskiy's binoculars.

There was a *Schutzenpanzer* mechanized half-track troop carrier lumbering slowly down the heavily rutted dirt road in the front of the convoy and another one in the rear. They had to formulate a plan of attack quickly. The troop carriers were armed with fifty-seven-millimeter *Mauser* machine guns. Each troop carrier also carried at least a dozen soldiers.

"If the first troop carrier goes over one of our mines, then we should have a good chance of success," Pavlovskiy stated confidently. "It would incapacitate their machine guns and inflict some casualties. It would also block the road so that the tanker trucks would not be able to pass forward. If they left the road, their heavy weight would sink them into the soft soil and they would become immobilized. If the first troop carrier does not hit one of our mines, then we will have to decide whether we should proceed with the attack or withdraw to fight another day."

"Comrade Commander," Larion asked. "What if the troop carrier goes through, but one of the following tank trucks hits a mine? What should we do then?"

"If one of those tank trucks hits one of our mines, then you shall see the biggest explosion you have ever seen in your life. But our rifles are still no match for their machine guns. We would be cut to ribbons," Pavlovskiy replied.

"If Tanya can eliminate the gunners in the front troop carrier, then we should have a chance. We should be able to pick off the troops inside that carrier as they move out," Larion said in reply.

"If that happens," Pavlovskiy ordered. "Then I want you to shoot out the front tires on the half-track carriers and the tank trucks before you start shooting at the military escort. We do not have weapons to pierce the tanks themselves, but if can incapacitate the trucks, I would consider it to be a success."

*****

As fate would have it, the first half-track did not travel over any mine. However, the tank truck following it was not that fortunate. The initial explosion of the mine lifted the cab of the tank truck and before the wheels settled back on the ground some of its shrapnel pierced its fuel tank and the explosion which followed was truly horrendous. Yellow-red flames exploded, followed by an acrid-black smoke which billowed up into the sky. Within seconds, the heat from the exploding fuel could be felt by Larion and his fellow partisans who were hiding in the trees.

To his surprise, Tanya first shot the driver of the troop carrier and then focused on the two machine-gun gunners. She was not able to affect a 'doublet', but after three quick shots, both gunners were dead. In the interim, the remaining partisans opened up on the convoy's tires and then turned their attention to the soldiers who were exiting the first half-track and the tank trucks. They were trying to get away from the scorching flames from the exploding first tanker truck.

The remaining troop carrier was also half-track vehicle with regular wheels in the front and tank tracks in the rear. It attempted to get off the road and come to the assistance of the front of the line, but then another tank truck exploded from the heat of the original exploding vehicle. It spilled flaming gasoline on the troop carrier and it became ablaze as well. The troops were forced to exit their vehicle into the direct line of fire of the partisans. The attack proved to be a total success.

Chapter 20

It took the partisans a full day to return to their base camp. It was a time for some subdued rejoicing. Killing others was not the reason for the muted celebration. The reason was that they had engaged in two life-and-death struggles in one day and they had come out alive. Pavlovskiy directed that the vodka ration only be diluted by 50% that night.

Larion noticed that the relationship between Tanya Akulich and Tynlenev seemed to be blossoming as they walked back to their tent with Tynlenev draping his arm around Tanya's waist while she attempted to steady him. Obviously, he had consumed more than his vodka ration that night. Galkovskiy and Irina Karzhova also seemed to have become closer as well. Larion was initially annoyed by Irina's infidelity until Galkovskiy explained to him that though Irina had been married, her husband had been killed at the front. She merely maintained the pretense of being married to ward off unwanted suitors for her female companionship.

The following two months were extremely successful for Pavlovskiy's partisan group. They were successful in interdicting two additional fuel convoys, as well as exterminating two dozen *Einsatzgruppen Kommandos* and auxiliaries. That kind of success was guaranteed to attract unwanted attention by the *SS* and that increased attention was bound to increase the risk to Pavlovskiy's partisan company.

The *Wehrmacht* was obliged to provide logistic support to the *Einsatzgruppen* battalions and it was only a matter of time until they would be able to formulate a plan of attack to exterminate Pavlovskiy's vexatious partisan squad.

*****

Larion was fast asleep on his soiled military blanket when the mortar rounds started to explode all around the camp. They appeared to be coming from two principal directions—from the west and southwest. He immediately collected his rifle, water canteen, and his ration kit, and ran out into the clearing. Pavlovskiy was running around and shouting orders to his partisans that they were to immediately vacate the camp and proceed in the opposite direction from the direction of the incoming mortar fire. He was silenced immediately when a stray mortar round exploded close to him and he was killed by its shrapnel.

It was obvious that the *SS* and the *Kommandos* did not know the exact location of the camp, since the mortar rounds were spread out along a wide range; however, sufficient rounds were coming in close to the camp's position which insured substantial partisan casualties. The mortar barrage reminded Larion of the *Katyusha* rocket barrage; however, mortar rounds could be shot off every three seconds and if you had an array of twenty mortars, that would translate into about four hundred rounds within one minute.

The *Einsatzgruppen Kommandos* and the *SS* were not obliged to enter the forest. The mortar barrage would force the partisans out into the open fields. Larion decided that he should try to locate his colleagues, General Vinogradov, Colonel Galkovskiy, and Major Tynlenev.

The night had been pitch black and that darkness was accentuated by the density of the trees which obliterated even the moon and the stars, but the multiplicity of the exploding mortar rounds all around him made it almost as light as day. Though men were running around and screaming directions and orders, their screams became unintelligible because of the never-ending explosions.

Larion reached Tynlenev's tent. It had been ripped apart. As he peered inside, he could hear someone breathing fitfully. It was Tynlenev, but Tanya had obviously thrown her body on top of his to protect him from further injury until another mortar round exploded nearby and she was killed by shrapnel as well. Larion rolled her body off Tynlenev and then knelt down beside him. "Major," Larion implored him, "please lie still and try not to speak. I will try to help you up and get you away from here."

Tynlenev had to cough and spit out a mouthful of blood before he could answer. "No need to bother about me, Sulupin, my friend and colleague. I know when I am done for, but what a way to go. Tanya gave her life for me by trying to shield my body after I was wounded by that first round which came close to our tent. I had never known a woman who was prepared to sacrifice herself for

132

me. Unfortunately, fate would have it that we shall both die on this same spot. But she was all woman, Larion. All woman…"

Larion was still holding Tynlenev up by his shoulders, cradling his head in his left elbow as Tynlenev inhaled sharply one last time. As that last breath left his body, so did his life. Larion left him because there was nothing left for him to do. He resumed his search for Vinogradov and Galkovskiy. The mortar rounds kept raining onto the camp's position. The cacophony of their explosions deafened his hearing. All he could hear was this high-pitched shrill of the incoming rounds and the subsequent explosions ringing in his ears. He finally came across Galkovskiy and Irina. They were crouching and holding their rifles in front of them. Galkovskiy was leading and Irina was following close behind.

"Colonel!" Larion shouted so that he could be heard above the sound of the explosions which seemed to engulf the entire camp by this time. "Where is General Vinogradov? Vinogradov, where is he?"

"Sulupin, my friend. Vasily Vinogradov is dead. Dead, do you understand? We must leave now," Galkovskiy shouted in reply and then gestured to the northeast and proceeded to leave, pulling Irina along with him. When he noticed that Larion was still standing, he gestured that he should follow as well.

The three comrades-in-arms walked in a crouched position to the northeast, away from the incoming mortar fire until they could see the dawn slowly breaking before them. Then they finally stopped to rest and take a drink of water from their water flasks.

"What are we to do now, Gregory?" Irina asked quietly.

"We have to rejuvenate ourselves. We should try to rest and possibly go to sleep for a short period of time, if we are able. We shall need our strength and we shall need to be alert. But for now, we must rest. Tomorrow night, we shall travel by night to the nearby forests and see if we can join up with other partisan groups. The mortar attack came from the south and southwest, so their intention was to drive us north, where they are probably waiting for us with their machine guns and machine pistols. But these Nazis are impatient. If we stay here another day, they will probably disperse and we shall be able to travel in relative safety."

"With respect, sir," Larion replied. "I intend to go back home so that I can see my son, who will be almost one year old this coming Spring, or die trying.

I have fought enough for the Motherland. It is time for me to fight for my wife and my son, who I have yet to see."

"Irina, what would you like to do?" Galkovskiy asked as he looked onto her soiled face, which was streaked by the tears she had shed that night.

"We should stay together. If we separate, we would be weakened and made more vulnerable. If Larion Daneelivich wishes to try to reach his home to see his family, we should accompany him. We can still continue the struggle for the Motherland while we are in retreat. The Nazis shall never defeat Mother Russia." "The Mongol hordes tried and failed. Napoleon tried and failed. Hitler and his Nazis shall fail as well. But when that tide turns, the Soviet Army shall chase the Nazis back to their rat-holes in Berlin and this soil shall be bloodied again, but with Nazi blood."

Galkovskiy remained silent for a moment. At least Larion had a destination and a reason for going home. Irina's logic also made sense.

"Alright, since I am outvoted, we shall accompany Larion back to his home in Belarus. We can join up with partisan groups along the way and if fortune smiles upon us, we may be able to reach our destination…and hopefully kill a few Nazis along the way."

Chapter 21

Just as Hitler's blitzkrieg stalled by December of 1941, at the city gates of Leningrad, Moscow and subsequently Stalingrad in 1942, providence in the form of a harsh Russian winter interceded and exacerbated the Nazi German troops' fighting ability. The troops lacked suitable winter clothing to endure the thirty below Celsius temperatures. The lubricants for their mechanized equipment turned to tar in the excruciating cold temperatures and supplylines were stretched to the breaking point.

Notwithstanding the loss of millions of men, Stalin's Soviet Russia seemed to be able to draw upon her vast population and replenish those losses with relative ease. Factories had been moved to the east into the Ural Mountains and beyond the Volga river. Those factories were able to continue to replenish the vast losses of mechanized artillery, aircraft, and tanks, until the end of the war.

Nazi Germany, on the other hand, was not able to match Soviet Russia's recuperative powers.

Its blitzkrieg war philosophy was to attack and overwhelm the enemy quickly. But just as the Battle of Britain had demonstrated, Nazi Germany's failure to achieve a quick victory over its enemy doomed it to eventual defeat. It also eventually compelled Hitler to fight a war on three fronts.

Though Stalin's relocated factories could continue their production of armaments virtually unencumbered by enemy attacks, Hitler's production facilities became increasingly vulnerable and within the range of British and American bombers. This forced Albert Speer, as Reich Minister of Armaments and War Production, to transfer a lot of his armament production to underground facilities and his armament production also became increasingly dependent upon slave labor.

However, before Soviet Russia's general counterattack against its Nazi invaders in 1943, the Schutzstaffel (SS) and its subordinate Einsatzgruppen battalions, were still charged with the ethnic cleansing of the occupied lands and the implementation of the 'Final Solution to the Jewish Question', which, from a strictly military perspective, constituted an unnecessary distraction and misuse of troops and war material.

It also formed the cancer which would fatally infect the Nazi perception of themselves as 'ubermenchen' (super humans) and metastasize, resulting in its ultimate self-destruction. The Soviet Union would survive for a further forty-seven years before it, too, would die and fragment.

The critical battles, however, were yet to be fought. The battle for Stalingrad was to last from August of 1942 until February of 1943, with a loss of 850000 Axis casualties and one million Soviet casualties. The remaining Nazi troops commanded by Field Marshall Paulus would be taken into captivity and brought back to rebuild Stalingrad after the war ended. Of the 250000 captive troops, only about ten thousand would survive to eventually return to Germany.

The battle of Kursk, from 5 July 1943 to 23 August 1943, was the greatest tank battle of the war which took place after the successful defense of Moscow. Nazi Germany lost 200000 men and 500 tanks, while Soviet Russia lost almost 800000 men and 1500 tanks, but Soviet Russia was able to achieve another pyrrhic victory that would, thereafter, lay the foundation for its counteroffensive and result in Nazi Germany's retreat and eventual unconditional surrender in May of 1945.

The battle of Leningrad commenced within two months of Operation Barbarossa on 8 September 1941, but it lasted the longest, only ending on 27 January 1944. Though about 800000 civilians alone perished during the approximate 900 days of Nazi Germany's siege, Stalin's successful Winter War with Finland assured the continued provisioning of supplies across Lake Lagoda to the city and permitted the city to persevere.

Chapter 22

Larion's troika gradually moved their way northward to Belarus, joining other partisan groups whenever they could, but proceeding inexorably towards their final destination. Irina Karzhova was able to hone her sniper skills and Larion even taught her the lesson he had learned during the Winter War in Finland. Since the opposing Nazi snipers also preferred to position themselves up trees in the relatively flat terrain of northern Ukraine and southern Belarus, Irina was taught to advance at night and then conceal herself and watch the trees.

As the dawn rose and the rising sun silhouetted the snipers against the morning sky, they became easy targets. Galkovskiy and Larion would not permit her to advance alone, however, even though her accuracy surpassed both of them.

*****

Tamara looked upon her young son, Dimitri Larionovich Sulupin, sleeping peacefully beside her. He was to reach his first birthday within one month, yet she had not heard any news of Larion for almost a year. She did not know if he was alive or whether he had already died in the war without ever seeing his young son. She caressed the Orthodox cross that Larion had given her so long ago and still hung around her neck as she gently stroked her son's smooth cheek. She wanted to awaken him so that she could nurse him and then permit him to go back to sleep. He commenced to whimper softly and Tamara raised his lips to her breast and commenced to nurse.

Soon, even that intimacy would be ending between mother and child. She had chores to attend to and she knew that her father would rise before the dawn. He had to tread a careful line between appeasing the local *Waffen SS* commander, his *kolkhoz* workers, and the ever-present partisans, who would engage in sabotage by night and then innocently parade around the town by day, maintaining their pretense of being dumb, subhumans.

She had endured a lot of tragedy in the interim. Her godfather, Boris Mikhailovich Tunov, had been summarily executed along with the most of the local Soviet functionaries, since he was the police chief in their small city. Her adopted grandfather, Valodya, was also executed as being superfluous. He was deemed to be too old to be able to contribute and therefore, he was dispensable.

The Kertinskys had switched their loyalty from the *NKVD* to the *Waffen SS*, the military arm of the Nazi party which was under the direct command of *Reichsfuhrer SS* Heinrich Himmler. They had been instrumental in eliminating most of their perceived enemies, but the most prominent exception was her father, Dimitri Aleksyevich Shanin. As an efficient manager of the local *kolkhoz*, he was deemed to be essential for the continued food production which was required by the *Waffen SS*, as well as the regular *Wehrmacht* troops. Whatever food was not confiscated by the Nazi Germans was distributed by Shanin among the remaining Belorussian population as equitably as possible, but it was never enough.

Notwithstanding the Kertinskys' earnest attempts to have her father executed as well, those attempts had proven to be futile for the time being. The only factor which assured her father's continued existence was his ability to encourage his approximate two hundred workers to effectively maximize their food production. However, that same success earned him the enmity of the partisans, who only viewed him as a collaborator.

After she finished nursing her son, Tamara went out into the *kolkhoz* to look for her father and then she would assist the other women who were working in the dairy. To her surprise, she noticed that *Sturmbannfuhrer* (Major) Christof Gersdorff was already with her father, making another one of his surprise periodic inspections to ensure that no surplus food production was being diverted. As usual, he had arrived with a small platoon of *Waffen SS* troops.

Gersdorff was dressed in his black uniform with the *Totenkopf* (Death's head) prominently displayed on his headgear and on his uniform's collars, along with the ubiquitous *SS*. The regular *Wehrmacht* troops wore the 'eagle clutching the swastika' insignia on their green uniforms and on their headgear. His black boots glistened in the morning sunlight. Since she did not appreciate his lecherous stares, she decided to avoid him. She would have time to speak with her father after Major Gersdorff returned to the city.

Gersdorff was of average height, balding prematurely and myopic. However, in his *Waffen SS* uniform, he seemed to become enlarged beyond his obvious physical limitations. He literally had the power of life and death over everyone under his jurisdiction and he had repeatedly exercised that power since the town had been overrun in the initial Nazi German onslaught. He was the one who was responsible for having her godfather and her grandfather summarily executed. She knew that her father's life, her own life, and even her son's life relied upon his whim.

He permitted her father to continue to exist because he was performing a useful function for the Reich. The only reason why he permitted her and her son to continue to exist was because that was the sword he held over her father's head. Gersdorff knew quite well that her father would only work to maximize the *kolkhoz's* food production so long as his daughter's life and his grandson's welfare were assured. Her father was not afraid of death, but she was sure that he would not go peacefully to any ravine to simply be shot by the *Einsatzgruppen Kommandos* without fighting back in some way.

*****

"Tamara, my darling," Dimitri addressed his daughter affectionately. "I noticed that you wanted to speak to me while Gersdorff had me update him on our food production. He wants me to slaughter more cows so that he will be able to send more beef to their frontlines. He seems to take for granted that you cannot replace cows like you can potatoes, simply by planting them.

"Cows not only provide us with milk, but they also provide us butter, but he seems to think that all you have to do is order it and more cows will miraculously appear. I will be forced to have some of the older cows slaughtered in any case, since he has made a commitment to one of his generals. I seriously doubt if any of that meat will trickle down to the ordinary troops."

"Oh Father," Tamara replied, embracing him tightly. "Will this nightmare ever end? Some days when I look upon my son and I think of his father and of you, I wonder if our daily struggle is worth anything. It seems as if we are all going to die, so what is the point of enduring their humiliation and torture every day. Little Dimitri shall be one year old next month and neither he nor his father have been able to see each other, not even once. I do not even know if Louyna is alive or dead."

"Please do not speak like that. Do not even think like that," her father replied, clutching her close to himself. "We have to believe that this will end one day and because of that belief, we will have the hope to see us through this hell. After all, did you and Larion not promise each other that he will return...and that you will wait for him?"

"We did, Father," Tamara said softly, as she commenced to cry. "But sometimes it is so hard to believe. Sometimes I think that we merely exchanged empty promises and though they were well intended at the time, events and fate will never permit them to materialize."

"No!" her father exclaimed, pushing her away gently, yet holding on to her shoulders and gazing deep into her tear-filled eyes. "No! If we give up hope, then we might as well just kill ourselves and save ourselves from the daily torture we are obliged to endure. If we give up our hope, then we are really giving up on life."

"I know, Father," Tamara replied tearfully. "But it is not easy. I know what I promised Louyna the first time and the last time we parted. I promised that I would wait for him and I shall. I know when he promised that he would return to me, he will do everything in his power to fulfil that promise. I simply cannot betray the promise I made him, but Father, it is not easy."

"Each morning when I wake up and each night before I go to sleep, I repeat my promise to myself to give me the strength to make it through another day and to make it through another night. And when I look at our son, who seems so serene and oblivious to our hell, it does help give me the strength to go through another day and another night, but father, it is not easy."

"I know, my beloved daughter," her father replied. "I know that it is not easy, but we have no alternative but to hope and to endure...for the time being. You know that if it was not for you and my grandson... I would have left the *kolkhoz* a long time ago and joined the partisans. They forced me to watch as the *Einsatzgruppen Kommandos* executed Boris and Valodya, along with many others."

"They forced the victims to kneel in front of them above a ravine. I remember the inhuman look on the faces of the executioners. They were smiling, but their smiles were not of happiness. Their smiles were just not human. Their eyes were not human. They consider us to be subhuman, but they are the ones who are truly subhuman because how can one human being treat another human being in such a fashion."

"They jumped into the ravine to bayonet the bodies which were still alive and then they forced the rest of us to cover them with dirt. It was not easy for me, my dear daughter, but I endured it for you, for my grandson, and for my son-in-law, who I know shall return to you. If I was able to muster the strength to endure all of that, then you have to muster the strength to wait for Larion to return to us."

"Thank you, Father," Tamara replied softly. "I shall suffer, but I shall endure that suffering for my son's sake, for your sake, and for the sake of my husband and the life we promised each other we shall share."

Chapter 23

Tamara and her father took little Dimitri to town so that he could be checked out by their doctor. The doctor was a good man, but an alcoholic. He had once been a prominent surgeon, but his alcoholism made his hands shake so that he was no longer able to perform complicated surgeries unless he first consumed at least a half-liter of vodka. The alcohol seemed to pacify his body, but it did not instill much confidence in his potential patients.

Her son did not have any particular ailment, but her mother's anxiety compelled her to bring him to see Dr. Gerasimov periodically so that he could reassure her. Her father, however, would not permit her to travel alone and ensured that either he or one of his trusted workers would accompany her. Any one of Gersdorff's troops could rape her or kill her with impunity.

As they were leaving the doctor's small office, they were confronted by the Kertinskys.

"Get out of our way, you bloody bitch," Olga Kertinsky spat out at Tamara. "And get your bastard son out of my sight."

"There is no need for such insults," Dimitri Shanin replied.

"You better be careful, Shanin," Olga Kertinsky retorted loudly so that other people could hear her. "You are living on borrowed time and that time is running out!" Dimitri just shook his head and ushered his daughter and grandson away from the two Kertinskys.

"I believe it is time for me to have another chat with Major Gersdorff," Dimitri whispered to his daughter. "Let us go down to his office at the police station and see if he will do something to shut those two up. I would prefer it if you would wait outside with little Dimitri. You could sit on a park bench across the street from the station, but please do not engage in any conversation with any of the Nazi soldiers."

*****

142

"Major Gersdorff. May I have a brief word with you?" Dimitri enquired politely, deliberately refraining from crossing the threshold to the former police chief's office and holding his hat submissively in his hands until the Major nodded his approval. His dear friend's office had been appropriated by the *Sturnbannfuhrer* after he had the police chief summarily executed and dumped into that ravine.

Gersdorff had been reading some papers and his wire rim glasses were perched precariously near the end of his nose to improve their focus. He looked up at Dimitri's interruption with obvious annoyance.

"Yes, Shanin! What is it that you want?" he inquired petulantly.

"Could you do something about the Kertinskys, Major? Every time either I or my daughter come to town and we run into them, they attack us with verbal insults and threats."

"Would you like me to have them shot, perhaps?" Gersdorff facetiously inquired.

Dimitri paused for a moment before replying. He knew that Gersdorff, who had been a librarian in civilian life, relished the power of death that he now possessed. He did not think that Gersdorff would be receptive to his entreaty for help, so he decided to call the Major's bluff.

"If it would not be too much of an inconvenience, Major. I really do not see any other alternative. Before this war, they were informants for the NKVD, but you know that. I am surprised that you have permitted them to live this long," Dimitri replied solemnly.

"They have provided me with some useful information from time to time. Once they are no longer of any assistance, I would be happy to have them shot in the park before the entire populace."

"In that case, I shall pray that the day shall come sooner, rather than later, Major," Dimitri replied with appropriate deference. "I can also advise you that I had six cows slaughtered and dressed and your men can accept immediate delivery. After all, you did advise me that time was extremely critical to you."

"Thank you for being so expeditious in fulfilling my request, Shanin," the Major replied sincerely. "I am sure that the general will appreciate how quickly I have been able to fulfill his order and why don't you come in and sit down so we can share some *Jagermuster*."

Dimitri knew that it was an offer which he could not refuse. But perhaps this was an opportunity to engage Gersdorff in some other conversation.

Dimitri genuinely wanted to understand the Nazi's mind a bit better. In some ways, their thinking seemed to be similar to the communists. That blind adherence to an obviously flawed set of beliefs and though the communists held no more esteem for human life than the Nazis, he could not understand the racial hatred which seemed to pervade the Nazi soul, which clearly distinguished them from their communist counterparts.

"Major Gersdorff, if you do not mind, could you explain something for me?" Dimitri asked submissively, minimizing any eye contact with Gersdorff and looking down at the floor while he took a brief sip of the *Jagermuster*, which he truly detested for its bitter sweetness.

"You know, Shanin, *Jagermuster* was invented…perhaps it would be more accurate to characterize it as being 'created' in 1934. It contains fifty-six herbs, roots, and fruits which are soaked in alcohol and water until the mixture attains its unique flavor and a strength of 35%. After straining, it truly becomes a nectar of the gods. I am advised that our *Fuhrer* drinks it for purely medicinal purposes and so I have decided to follow his esteemed example. How do you like it?" the major inquired.

"It is truly unique…and quite medicinal, I am sure," Dimitri replied obsequiously.

"But what is it that you want me to explain to you, Shanin?" The Major asked, as he took a sip and slowly savored the flavor of the bitter potion.

"Soviet Russia and Germany signed a treaty in August of 1939. I believed that it would ensure peace between our two nations for my generation, but then Germany attacked our Motherland. I just do not understand why?"

"Self-defense, Shanin. Pure self-defense!"

"But Soviet Russia did not attack Germany. Soviet Russia did not even threaten to attack Germany," Dimitri observed politely.

"Ah…but our *Fuhrer* knew that Stalin would attack us, so we had to attack first in self-defense!" the major replied matter-of-factly. "Surely, you must understand that fact, Shanin. We had to attack Russia because we knew that Stalin would attack us. It was simply an act of self-defense. If you know that your enemy shall attack you, your only alternative is to attack them first. Doing nothing would just be the height of stupidity and *Herr* Hitler, our *Fuhrer*, is not a stupid man. He is a genius. A prophet for the modern age."

"Oh, I see," Dimitri lied, feigning his own revelation at the absurd rationale. "But there is another matter which I do not understand, Major Gersdorff. All

Soviet functionaries and Jews were eliminated from our city, but women and children were eliminated as well?"

"Shanin, if you were an educated man, you would understand," Gersdorff replied pedantically. "At the end of the Peloponnesian Wars between Athens and Sparta, some of Sparta's allies wanted to ensure that Athens would never attack again. They recommended that the entire Athenian population be either enslaved or all adult males be executed. Sparta then suggested that not only should all adult males be exterminated, but that the women and children be exterminated as well because in another thirty years, the children would become adults and the women would rear more children and then Athens would attack Sparta and its allies for revenge. Therefore, the logic is quite simple. You have to exterminate everyone...again for your own self-defense. If we exterminate all of the Jews now, they will not pose a threat to us Germans in the future."

"Oh, I see," Dimitri lied again.

He knew from his own studies that Sparta did proffer that false advice to its allies, who were truly appalled by that heinous suggestion since they were only contemplating executing all adult males. Sparta then suggested that an honorable peace at the end of the war was the best security for everyone's future.

Dimitri also remembered reading Jonathon Swift's treatise, *A Modest Proposal*, which was written in 1729, in which Swift proposed that impoverished Irish families breed Irish children as a source of food for wealthy Englishmen, thereby solving their poverty and helping control their own population, while providing a delicacy for the wealthy English. The fellow Englishmen, though reluctant to provide any assistance to the Irish who were starving to death, considered his 'modest proposal' to be totally repugnant.

Shanin also realized that an inherent human decency seemed to prevail on both of those occasions. That common sense of decency seemed to have escaped both the Nazi logic and Gersdorff.

"Thank you for your explanation, Major," Dimitri replied. "You have answered my questions in a most eloquent and informative fashion."

"You uneducated peasants should not worry about such things in any case, Shanin. Go home and plant your potatoes and milk your cows. Leave these heady thoughts to men like my *Fuhrer* and...like me."

As Dimitri crossed the street to pick up his daughter and grandson to escort them back to the *kolkhoz*, he realized that Gersdorff, albeit unintentionally, did reveal an aspect of the Nazi mindset to him. He finally understood that there was no limit to their moral depravity.

*****

As Tamara and Dimitri were finishing their evening meal, they heard a knock at their front door. Dimitri rose to see who their belated visitor might be while Tamara continued to playfully feed her son at the kitchen table. As Dimitri opened the door, he immediately recognized their nocturnal visitor.

'Larion! How in God's name—"

His question remained unfinished as Tamara came running up to the door with little Dimitri held tightly in her arms.

"Louyna! Louyna!" she cried out, as she brushed past her father. "You have come back! You truly have come back to me! Look…look at our beautiful son, my love."

Larion was gaunt from his reduced diet and extended travels, but he did feel an immense joy in his heart. He handed his rifle to his father-in-law and reached out to hold his son. He could see that the young child had inherited his mother's blond hair and blue eyes, but he knew that it was his son.

"Come in quickly, before someone notices you out here, Larion Daneelivich, my dear son-in-law," Shanin stated earnestly, quickly pulling Larion into his home.

"Thank you, Father, but I have two compatriots with me. We have walked all of the way from the Ukraine over these past several months. We are all hungry and thirsty. Can you provide them with some shelter as well?"

"Gregory! Irina!" Larion called out to them. "Come in quickly."

Galkovskiy and Irina came out of the shadows and into the light that was streaming out through the open doorway. They both looked lean, soiled, and haggard. Shanin quickly ushered them inside his home and then quickly drew all of the curtains closed so that anyone passing by would not be able to see who was inside.

"Gregory Andreivich Galkovskiy, at your service," Galkovskiy introduced himself to Dimitri. "And this is my…my very special companion, Irina Karzhova."

146

"Please come in and freshen up. We are just finishing eating, but Tamara has prepared a lot of food so you can have some borscht with meat, rye bread and some vodka to wash it down. Her *borscht* is so thick that your spoon will stand straight up all by itself."

"Father," Larion hastened to explain. "Gregory Andreivich was…is my battalion commander. He holds the rank of Colonel. Irina joined us shortly after the Nazi attack. She has been with us for almost the entire journey."

Shanin finally noticed that the two new visitors were also carrying *Mosin-Nagant* rifles and though they hesitated at first to lean the weapons against the wall, they were able to finally relax, wash their hands and faces in the basin Tamara presented them with, and sit down at the table to eat. Larion kept holding onto his infant son. He could not believe how delicate the child appeared to be. Little Dimitri, pleased with the attention he was receiving from this stranger, just smiled and gurgled even more. Tamara finally took him from Larion's reluctant arms so that he would be able to join the rest at the dinner table.

*****

Though all three were visibly ravenous, they ate slowly, savoring the hearty borscht and rye bread, which they dipped into the red beet broth. They took turns answering Dimitri's and Tamara's questions. They soon lost track of time and it was nearing midnight. Tamara remained unbelieving that Larion had come back to her…again. She also resolved that she would not permit him to leave her again. Wherever he decided to go, she and little Dimitri would follow.

*****

"I believe we all understand what has been happening behind our enemy's lines. They have been slaughtering everyone, it seems. The old, the infirmed, the communists, the intelligentsia, the Jews…and even women and children," Shanin stated sadly. "They executed Boris because he was the chief of police and they even executed old Valodya…because he was old and useless to them. If they suspect that you are a partisan or a partisan supporter, that is sufficient excuse for them to execute you on the spot. It is as if the world has been turned, not only upside down, but inside out."

"Father, would it be possible for you to arrange for accommodation and work for Gregory and Irina?" Larion asked.

"That shall not be a problem, but I will have to insist that he permit me to shear off that regal silver mane of his. It is bound to attract too much attention. Shorter hair will also make him look more humble. The *Einsatzgruppen Kommandos* have taken away three of my family workers, so there are three empty homes available. There are about two hundred workers on the *kolkhoz* right now, so it will not be difficult to have Gregory and Irina blend in, but it is imperative that they maintain a low profile."

"Why would they take away three of your families?" Larion asked.

"Our dear friends, the Kertinskys!" Dimitri replied with resignation. "Before the war, they were exposing our citizens to the *NKVD*, now they are betraying our citizens to the *Einsatzgruppen* and the *SS*.

"The head of the local *SS* company is a former librarian who has transformed himself into a fascist zealot who would not think twice about executing women and children. After all, the women would breed future enemies of the *Third Reich* and their children would grow up to become future enemy adults of the *Third Reich*. That is all the justification the Nazis need to strip and humiliate them, before executing them."

"I have to admit that I have wished and dreamed that if I was able to come back to Xhotimsk someday, the Kertinskys would both be dead and gone, like their damn son," Larion answered flatly. "I have seen a lot of good people die so far and yet these traitorous vermin continue to not only live but prosper."

"And what about the partisan activity in this area?" Galkovskiy asked.

"They are around...and they are active," Replied Dimitri wryly. "They continue to provide the *Einsatzgruppen Kommandos* their auxiliaries and the *SS*—with a never-ending justification for the Nazis' continued ethnic cleansing in this area and reprisals against the civilians."

"So, you will be able to assimilate Gregory and Irina within the *kolkhoz*, Father?" Larion asked.

"We will provide them with a small, but suitable home for them, which is close by. If Gregory can drive a tractor, I can assign him to ploughing and seeding the fields," Dimitri replied.

"I can drive a half-track and even a tank, so a tractor shall not be an obstacle to me."

"And Irina can help me in the dairy," interjected Tamara, who quickly looked back at Larion, still partially unbelieving that he had come back to her again. Larion still held his sleeping son, a bit unbelieving that he was partially responsible for creating this helpless little human being.

"So it is agreed," Dimitri said. "We do have a spare bedroom here, which Gregory and Irina can share tonight. Tomorrow, after everyone wakes up, I will show them their new assigned home. That only leaves the Kertinskys as our most immediate problem. If they discover, directly or indirectly, that you have returned, they shall disclose your status as a military college officer and that will be more than sufficient to justify your immediate execution and probably ours as well. The only reason why I am still alive is because they believe they need me to maintain the agricultural production on the *kolkhoz* to feed their troops, but I am sure that Gersdorff will find someone else."

*****

After washing up again, Larion retired to Tamara's bedroom that she shared with their sleeping son. As they both undressed and went to bed, Tamara dreamed of having her husband kiss her and caress her, and enter inside her, but those dreams would have to wait until morning. Larion was fast asleep as soon as he laid his head down on his pillow. Tamara merely clung on to him, intertwining her legs with his legs. She was simply too ecstatic to fall asleep right away. She had to hold on to him so that he would not disappear into the night once again.

149

Chapter 24

The following afternoon, Shanin arranged to meet with Galkovskiy and Larion to deal with the Kertinsky issue. He brought both men out to the river which flowed through the *kolkhoz* and they seated themselves in the shade of a large tree. The river flowed so slowly that Galkovskiy initially assumed that it was just a small lake.

"The anniversary of their son's death shall be next Tuesday," Shanin explained to the two men solemnly. "They have made it an annual pilgrimage to come to this spot with a luncheon basket to commemorate his death. This was the spot where we found his clothes all neatly folded and bundled up. They believe that he did not drown by accident, but that he was killed at this spot and his lifeless body was then thrown into the river."

Galkovskiy examined the surrounding terrain in all directions. It was obvious that the Kertinskys would have to be executed to preserve their own safety, including the safety of Tamara and little Dimitri. The fact that their death might also serve as recompense for the resettlement of Larion's parents and the execution of Shanin's friend—the police chief—and old Valodya seemed to be superfluous at this point in time. To kill to ensure your own survival was the primary objective.

"Well, it is very fortunate for us to know where they will be and when, don't you agree, Larion?" Galkovskiy asked. "It should simplify our task considerably."

"I agree, Gregory," answered Larion. "Though I would have loved to see the look in his eyes when I shot him and his bitch between the eyes. I would have told them both that this is in small recompense for sending my parents to Siberia and for their contribution to the execution of not only Boris Mikhailovich, but my dear old friend, Valodya, who tried his best to teach me some of the more important things in life."

"Revenge may feel good, Larion, but we have to treat this like a regular military operation. It would not be possible to approach them without being seen, therefore they have to be shot from a distance. We should use three shooters. One from the left, one from the right, and the third one from across the river—that would be the most difficult shot," Galkovskiy replied pensively, trying to anticipate what other unexpected elements may materialize to complicate their best laid plans.

"I can shoot, but I am not the best shooter on the *kolkhoz*," Shanin added. "But I am willing to participate and assist the two of you as best I can."

Larion and Galkovskiy exchanged a knowing look and then turned to address Shanin.

"Irina is the best shot of the three of us," Galkovskiy replied. "I think she should be positioned across the river for the two frontal shots. It is almost two hundred and fifty meters, but that is well within her range. Larion and I will deploy to either side of this tree so that in the event Irina does not hit both targets, we will be in a position for the final kill shot. There is suitable shrub coverage to conceal us and the distance is about one hundred to one hundred and fifty meters. That is well within our range."

"But how can I assist you?" Shanin pleaded.

"I think it would be best if you just made yourself conspicuous back at the *kolkhoz* when the shots ring out," Larion replied. "In case your Major Gersdorff chooses to conduct an investigation, you will have witnesses who will attest to the fact that you could not have had any involvement with this matter. I am confident that Gersdorff, who probably holds no affection for the Kertinskys in any case, will be inclined to assume that it was a partisan reprisal operation against two collaborators. But the most important thing is that there will be no attention or suspicion drawn to you, personally. You have helped immensely already, by identifying the time and the place. We will be able to handle the rest by ourselves."

"Dear friends," Shanin replied reluctantly. "It is agreed…but if either one of them is just wounded and requires a final disposition, I would appreciate it if you would advise that one that the final shot is in memory of my two dear friends, Boris Mikhailovich and old Valodya, who raised me as a child after my parents had been killed, and do not forget your own parents, Larion."

*****

151

Galkovskiy, Irina, and Larion left their homes before dawn and secreted themselves into their respective positions. Larion and Galkovskiy had to be careful that their respective lines of fire would not be at each other. Consequently, they positioned themselves in such a fashion that if they were obliged to shoot, they would be shooting at an angle away from each other. It had also been agreed that Irina would take the first shot. If she was unable to shoot both Kertinskys with a 'doublet', then depending upon the direction the remaining Kertinsky would take to try to escape, either Larion or Galkovskiy would take the next shot, but they had to take care not to shoot at each other.

Irina had positioned herself up a tree about three meters above the ground to afford her a better angle. The trees had suitably leafed out in the warm spring and their foliage helped disguise her position. Larion and Galkovskiy would have to shoot up while lying on the ground. Even if their shot was closer, their angle made their shot considerably more difficult.

*****

The Kertinskys arrived at the tree about noon. As they kneeled down and commenced to spread out a blanket for themselves, Irina took off the protective cap from her *3.5x PU* scope on her *Mosin-Nagant* sniper rifle. Tanya Akulich had given her the rifle and scope while they were with Pavlovskiy's partisans, which seemed so long ago. Irina was waiting until the Kertinskys separated so that she had a clear shot at both torsos. All she had to do was shoot them both. Larion and Gregory would complete the operation if either target was just wounded; however, she really wanted to affect a 'head shot' if possible.

In a split second, the Kertinskys separated and provided Irina with a clear double shot. She had prepared herself that once the opportunity presented itself, she would proceed without hesitation. She selected the male for the first shot, since he posed the more formidable threat. As soon as she pulled the trigger and the shell shot out of the barrel, she activated the bolt action to expel the shell to permit a replacement shell to lift up into the chamber as she aimed and fired almost immediately.

To Larion and Galkovskiy, it was as if both shots were merged together into one elongated double explosion, but before the Kertinskys could hear the first shot, the two bullets had reached their respective marks.

At the *kolkhoz*, the two shots were muffled by the distance the sound had to travel and it only warranted a fleeting curious look from Shanin and the two workers he was instructing on the appropriate maintenance of some farm equipment. Periodic shots were no longer that unusual since the war had commenced, so those shots did not warrant much consideration or discussion.

An ominous quiet then followed at the riverbank. Neither Irina, Larion or Galkovskiy moved from their positions. From their respective vantage points, they could see that both Kertinskys had been hit and were lying awkwardly prostrate on their blanket. Irina's scope, however, disclosed that though the male Kertinsky may have been fatally wounded, she could see that he was still coughing spasmodically. He had been hit in one of his lungs, since he was coughing up blood.

Larion finally got up and advanced on the Kertinskys' position. Galkovskiy also rose from his position once he saw that Larion was approaching the tree cautiously. As he looked across the placid river, he could see Irina lower herself down from her tree. She would have to travel a hundred meters farther north to a narrow pedestrian bridge that would permit her to cross the river and join them.

Larion could hear Kertinsky coughing. It was irregular, but strong. He may be dying, but he would live for a short time. Irina's shot had surprised him by the shocked look that had frozen on his face. His right eye seemed unbelieving. It was as if he knew what had happened to him, but he could not believe that anyone would have dared to do it. His body, arms, and legs were crumpled in a grotesque fashion as if he was just a broken wooden doll. His wife had sustained a head shot and died instantly.

As Larion leaned down by Kertinsky's body, Galkovskiy reached their position as well.

"The son-of-a-bitch is still alive," Galkovskiy observed. "Irina may be losing her touch."

"I doubt it, Gregory," Larion replied. "Which of the two would you have shot first?"

"I would have shot him, then his bitch," Galkovskiy replied.

"I would have done the same. But look at him. He was shot in the back and look at her, she was shot in the head, which is a much more difficult shot. He was shot first and she was shot second."

'Perhaps Irina wanted to save a part of him for you, Larion?"

Larion turned Kertinsky's body over onto his back. His right eye fluttered open and he recognized Larion. Even though he had been mortally wounded and in no position to fight back, the hatred in his face was unmistakable. He tried to utter a word, but he was unable to do so as his lungs continued to drown in his own blood.

Larion reached behind his back and pulled out his Tokarev pistol and pointed it at Kertinsky's forehead. He waited until Kertinsky opened his right eye again.

"I want you to know that the devil is probably fucking that bitch wife of yours right now, Kertinsky, but I also want you to know that when I shoot you in the head, it will be for my parents, Boris Mikhailovich, and for old Valodya. I want you to know that just as you had them killed and destroyed their lives, I am going to kill you right now. Your life is hardly worth any one of their lives, but it is the best that I can do to avenge your needless cruelty. May you burn in hell for eternity."

Larion pressed the end of the barrel in the middle of Kertinsky's forehead and pulled on the trigger slowly while Kertinsky's right eye was still watching his trigger finger. It seemed that at the very end Kertinsky did show some fear as he heard the soft click as the trigger was depressed and the hammer was released. Darkness enveloped Kertinsky and he did not even hear the sound of the shot.

Irina finally joined them and the three companions remained silent as they examined the two dead bodies.

"Should we throw them into the river?" Irina finally asked unemotionally.

"Instead of trying to hide their bodies, I think that it may be preferable to just leave them where they are. The local *SS* would be more likely to assume that they were killed by partisans. Partisans prefer to display their exploits in killing collaborators, instead of concealing their execution," Galkovskiy replied.

Chapter 25

It had been decided that Larion would simply move into the Shanin residence. Having the three adults and the young child live together would provide additional security and companionship for all of them. Shanin could assist in looking after his grandson when Tamara and Larion were performing their respective duties at the dairy, and Tamara, Larion, and little Dimitri would provide Shanin with some much-needed companionship as well.

Though a number of the female *kolkhoz* workers were aware of Larion and Tamara's true relationship, Shanin concluded that he could rely upon them maintaining that knowledge in confidence. They had all suffered some humiliation or abuse at the hands of the Nazi troops; consequently, they would not be inclined to expose Larion voluntarily.

The vast majority of his existing male workers had become employed subsequent to the outbreak of the war and had no prior knowledge of Larion. Most of the able-bodied men had either enlisted or been conscripted or had joined the partisans. The remaining male employees were either too elderly or unsuitable for any form of active military service or involvement with the partisans. A small risk remained, but Shanin and Larion had concluded that the risk was bearable.

However, the presence of Larion and Galkovskiy presented a new problem. Why would two relatively young adult males with no visible physical or mental disability be working on a collective farm while a war was raging all around them?

Galkovskiy decided to affect a fairly prominent limp, which he was able to achieve by placing a small, smooth stone in the heel of his right boot. Larion decided to become a mute who was also intellectually challenged as a result of some unknown wartime incident. Both disguises were thin and would probably not stand up under close scrutiny, but they would afford both men a convenient preliminary facade that would, hopefully, not attract that close scrutiny in the first place.

*****

As Tamara entered her home, she saw Larion and her father trying to teach little Dimitri how to learn to walk. Her father was providing balance and support by holding his grandson's hands up above his little head, while Larion was kneeling and encouraging his son to stumble towards his open arms. After little Dimitri, with the assistance of his grandfather, was able to take a couple of unsure steps towards his father, Shanin finally released his grip and little Dimitri stood unsteadily for a second and then bravely attempted to take another step forward, but quickly lost his balance. Larion reached forward and grabbed his son before he fell down. "Tamara, you have just witnessed your son take his first step," her father declared proudly. "Soon he will be running through the grounds and the fields and you will not be able to catch him."

"I think that I will be able to keep up to him for a few more years, but it certainly was a proud moment, though I am not sure that I would call it a successful 'first step'," Tamara replied. "Perhaps a successful first stumble would be more accurate."

Larion continued to hold his son proudly. He gently tossed him up into the air and then caught him. Little Dimitri found the exercise exhilarating and tried to encourage his father to repeat the exercise with smiles and extended arms.

"I do believe that you three men are going to wear me out. Who is responsible for dinner tonight?" Tamara asked, feigning disappointment.

"I came home early," replied her father, "and I have prepared a special treat. "It is cooking outside, so allow me to bring it in."

Shanin then brought in a ceramic pot which was charred by open flames. Then he placed it on the dinner table and lifted off the lid.

"Here is a geriatric chicken who has been unable to lay any eggs for a couple of weeks, but she decided to give her life for the Motherland and for us in particular."

"A chicken? A real roasted chicken?" Larion asked in surprise. "I have not tasted chicken for at least a couple of years."

"And it may be that you will not taste another one for another couple of years," Shanin replied. "Major Gersdorff has a special taste for chicken and we

156

only have a small bunch left. But let's eat and enjoy this old hen. Hopefully, her flesh shall not be too stringy or tough. She has been roasting slowly for about two hours. I have thrown in some small potatoes, onions, and carrots from our root cellar, so the fat from her skin should really improve the flavor of the vegetables."

*****

After their dinner, all three adults went to bed early since the next day was expected to be extra busy for all of them.

Tamara slowly nursed her son, who was suckling away in his sleep until his lips finally parted from his mother's nipple. Larion was laying on the bed, watching both of them proudly.

"Isn't life amazing some times?" he observed. "Look at our son. He is so small and so helpless and so dependent right now, but this evening he had taken his first step. Soon he shall be walking and then he shall begin speaking. Then he will transform into an inquisitive 'little person'. And then he will transform once again into a young man and go out and seek to make his own way in this world of ours."

"If only we can be sure that we shall all survive this horror and live to see it happen, Louyna," replied Tamara, as she gently placed their son in the little cradle her father had constructed and tucked him in with the hand-knitted wool blanket she had knitted herself. "All we can do is hope, believe, and survive, Tamara. But come to me now. Have I told you how much I have missed you today?"

Tamara just smiled coquettishly and confirmed that he had not spoken those words to her this day.

"In that case, allow me to demonstrate my love and affection for you, my dear, beautiful wife, who I love more than life, itself." They kissed and caressed each other tenderly and then they embraced and slowly united.

*****

Their slumber was rudely interrupted by Shanin knocking anxiously at their bedroom door just as the dawn was emerging from the gloom of the night over the eastern horizon.

"Larion! Larion! Wake up!" Shanin spoke with a quiet urgency. "Gersdorff and his *SS* are here. You have to go to the spare bedroom, as we had discussed before. Go quickly."

Sleepily, Larion pulled on his shorts and gathered up his clothes and went to the guest bedroom at the back of the residence.

"Tamara, my dear daughter. Please wake up. The *SS* are here. Please wake up and get dressed."

Just at that point, there was a sharp triple knock on the wooden front door.

"I am coming!" Shanin shouted. "I am coming!"

As he opened the front door, Major Gersdorff was standing demonically resplendent in his black *SS* uniform with his feet spread apart. The 'death head' emblem on his headgear was shining in the early morning sunlight. He was impatiently slapping his black-gloved hand with his black riding crop, though Shanin knew that he had never ridden a horse in his life.

"What took you so long, Shanin?" Gersdorff demanded rudely. "Are you getting too old for this kind of work? You should have been up hours ago!"

"With all due respect, *Herr* Major, I am up now," Shanin replied. "What can I do for you, *Herr Sturmbannfuhrer* Gersdorff?" Shanin added obsequiously for the benefit of Gersdorff's *SS* troops.

"Have you seen the Kertinskys? They were supposed to attend at my offices yesterday afternoon, but they never showed up and when I sent my soldiers to their residence, there was no sign of them. They had promised me some very important information."

"With respect, *Sturmbannfuhrer* Gersdorff," Shanin replied formally. "No, I have not seen them. I can think of no reason why they would come out to our *kolkhoz*."

But Shanin had learned in his various dealings with Gersdorff that a partial truthful admission was preferable to an outright denial or lie. "But let me think…oh yes. They do come out each year on the anniversary of their son's drowning. They come each year and share a small meal by the river. There is a large tree where we located their son's clothes, all neatly folded and awaiting his return. We found his body a couple of kilometers downstream, close to town. Something had happened and he had drowned. The police had investigated and a post mortem was conducted, which confirmed the presence of water in his lungs. The formal decision was that he had accidentally drowned after coming down to the river to meet with some of his friends to go fishing."

"Take us down to this tree by the river! *Schnell!*" Gersdorff commanded.

*****

Shanin had not bothered to inspect the site again after he had shown it to Larion and to Galkovskiy a few days earlier. It appeared that the two bodies lay sprawled in the same position in which they had been shot. Olga Kertinsky was face down, her body partially laying on the blanket and partially on the grass. When one of Gersdorff's soldiers rolled her over on her back, the exit wound had obliterated a good portion of the right upper side of her face, confirming that she was shot from behind. Ivan Kertinsky had been shot twice. Once in his back, with a final kill shot to the middle of his forehead.

"*Sturmbannfuhrer* Gersdorff," Shanin volunteered. "I do recall hearing a couple of shots yesterday, shortly after noon, while I was instructing a couple of *kolkhoz* workers on the proper maintenance of one of our tractors. But hearing shots is a fairly common occurrence of late."

Shanin decided to embellish his story in the hope that his opinion would assist Gersdorff in coming to the appropriate conclusion.

"It had to be the work of those goddamn partisans, Major," he concluded. "They shoot at anything they come across. My workers, your soldiers, everyone… Look, they had to have wounded Kertinsky and then they shot him in the forehead."

"Why would you say that, Shanin?" Gersdorff asked suspiciously.

"If they had shot him in the forehead first, there would be no need to shoot him again in his back. He would already be dead, like his wife."

Shanin decided to stop talking. He had tried to plant a seed in Gersdorff's mind and now he had to give it time to nurture and grow. Gersdorff, with his self-avowed superior intellect, would have to convince himself.

"Shanin, you know our protocol. If we even suspect that anyone on your *kolkhoz* had a part in this killing, my men would have to take appropriate reprisal action against some of your workers," Gersdorff replied smugly.

"All of my male workers are either old or infirmed or both. There are two new male workers, but one is severely crippled and not too bright. The other one has sustained some sort of shock, because he has lost his power of speech. He is not too bright either. You have to hold him by the hand and show him what he is to do. But they are both strong and they can do heavy work that the other old men are not capable of doing. The rest are just women who have trouble even milking a cow." "

Well, Shanin, you are not all that intelligent either, so when you tell me that these two new men are not that bright, they must be retarded," Gersdorff replied rudely. "But I want to see them when we return to your home and I shall make up my own mind. You know that our *Fuhrer* has directed that all such defective human beings should be put out of their misery, since they cannot truly appreciate life."

"I shall arrange for it immediately, *Sturnbannfuhrer* Gersdorff," Shanin replied, obediently. "But we do need their strength to carry out the heavy work here. We do not need them for their minds. As I have said, the rest of the men who are working here now are either old or infirmed or both. I need their strength to maintain our food production."

Shanin instructed one of his workers to run to the main *kolkhoz* compound and arrange for Larion and Galkovskiy to attend at his residence so that Gersdorff could assess them both, personally.

When they arrived back at the compound, Larion came out of Shanin's residence shabbily dressed and suitably submissive, not attempting any eye contract with Gersdorff.

"*Kommen sie her! Schnell!*" Gersdorff ordered.

Larion merely maintained a confused countenance and gestured with his hands that he did not understand, looking to Shanin for some assistance.

"Come here, Larion. Do not be afraid. Just come here," Shanin spoke gently in Russian.

Larion attempted to affect a vacant look by focusing on Gersdorff's glistening 'death's head' on his officer's headgear. He followed Shanin's instructions and came forward slowly. His shabby clothes disguised his physical build quite effectively and Gersdorff dismissed him from any further consideration.

"*Rouse! Du hurensohn!*" (Leave, you son-of-a-bitch)

"And where is the second man?" Gersdorff asked as he turned back to Shanin.

"Here he comes. He is driving that tractor. Though he is lame, he is quite handy, mechanically. He services most of our farm equipment, as well as our tractors." Shanin gestured to Galkovskiy to get off of his tractor and to come forward. Galkovskiy dismounted the tractor and placed his right foot gingerly down onto the ground and then came forward with a pronounced limp.

"As I have said, *Sturnbannfuhrer* Gersdorff," Shanin continued to address him obsequiously. "He is so lame that if he were a horse, we would have him shot. But he is indispensable to me for his mechanical ability."

As Galkovskiy approached Gersdorff, he also affected a submissive facial expression and physical posture. His shabby clothes also disguised his physical condition, but it was Shanin's butchered haircut which made Galkovskiy resemble a shabby scarecrow in the field. The haircut was uneven, with straying tufts of hair protruding in all directions. His physical appearance made even Gersdorff laugh.

Galkovskiy maintained a confused visage, nervously rubbing his hands together and tugging at his oversized trousers which were slowly slipping down his narrow hips.

"*Rouse! Du luschel*!" (Leave, you useless jerk) Gersdorff commanded, totally disgusted with both of these lower forms of life. "*Rouse!*"

Gersdorff turned to Shanin to commiserate with him in respect of the obviously inferior manpower which the *kolkhoz* manager had to deal with.

"I must say I pity you, Shanin. How you are able to function with these subhumans is almost beyond even my superior intellect."

"I have to cope with what I have, *Herr Sturmbannfuhrer*," Shanin replied apologetically. "But allow me to make amends. I had my daughter prepare a chicken for you. It is all dressed and ready to be cooked. I was going to come into town today myself and deliver it personally to you. Allow me to get it for you."

"I would prefer it you had your daughter come out and give it to me, personally," Gersdorff replied, as he licked his lips lasciviously. "Since she has prepared the chicken especially for me, I would like to thank her…personally."

After being summoned by her father, Tamara exited their home with the chicken carefully wrapped in a clean piece of white cloth.

"*Danke, meine liebling*," (Thank you, my darling) Gersdorff thanked her flirtatiously.

Tamara merely nodded her head in a polite acknowledgement at Gersdorff, but remained silent.

"In that case, Shanin, I must be off," Gersdorff announced in his perfunctory fashion. "Please dispose of the bodies as you deem fit. The Kertinskys are of no further use to me."

*****

As Gersdorff and his *SS* troops boarded their truck transport and left the farm compound, Galkovskiy reciprocated Gersdorff's insults by directing his own farewell in German.

"*Fick dich, dummkopf!*" (Fuck you, you idiot!)

Chapter 26

That evening, Galkovskiy approached Irina as she was washing their dinner dishes and placed both hands on either side of her waist and gently moved them down to her hips and then slowly back to her waist again.

"Gregory, I am sure you can wait for another couple of minutes to give me a chance to finish cleaning our dinner plates before I permit you to have your way with me...again. You are surprisingly virile for being such an old *luschel*...isn't that what did Gersdorff called you?" Irina asked facetiously, as she turned her head over her shoulder so that she could look at him while she finished the dishes.

Galkovskiy merely ran his hands up Irina's sides and gently cupped her firm breasts and nuzzled the nape of her neck.

"I must confess that I do not seem to get enough of you, Irina Karzhova," Galkovskiy replied. "You have put me under your spell. You would not be a witch which slowly draws the essence of a man's soul and then simply lets him wither and die?"

"Well, I am finished with the dishes, so why don't we go to bed. It is much more comfortable in the bedroom, than in the kitchen. And you need not worry about my supernatural powers. I am merely a woman who adores and cherishes the man she has fallen in love with. Rest assured, I shall not permit you to wither or die," Irina replied smugly, kissing him tenderly on his lips.

"But there is one serious matter which I would like to discuss with you, before we love each other...again," Galkovskiy replied seriously.

His sudden change in attitude surprised her, so Irina remained silent to afford Galkovskiy an opportunity to explain his serious matter. "Larion came here for a purpose. He wanted to see his wife and his infant son. He seems to be content to remain in that role until the war ends. I am not. I am restless. We have had an ample opportunity to relax and become reinvigorated, but I cannot spend the rest of the war simply driving a tractor and repairing farm equipment

163

while the Nazis bleed the Motherland to death," Galkovskiy replied solemnly. "I need to fight and kill our enemies."

"I understand, Gregory," Irina answered solemnly in reply. "I left my husband's village to avenge his death after I discovered that he had been killed on the front defending Minsk during the initial Nazi onslaught in late 1941. I also needed time to recuperate and I do not want to spend the rest of the war milking cows, not when there are more Nazis and *Einsatzgruppen Kommandos* to kill. But what do you propose to do?"

"I have been able to make contact with a local partisan group which is led by a 'Vishlova'," Galkovskiy replied quickly.

"Vishlova?" Irina asked. "The partisans are being led by a woman?"

"Yes. Her name or at least the name she chooses to go by is 'Natalia Vishlova'. Her partisans operate with Stalin's blessing and he supplies them with all of the war material they require. They alternate between the three forests which surround Xhotimsk," Galkovskiy explained excitedly. \

"Are they the ones who have been responsible for the recent attacks on the *Einsatzgruppen Kommandos* and the local *SS*?"

"Yes. They are the only partisan group which is left in this area. There was another group of about one hundred partisans, but they got caught in a trap and the remaining captives were executed by a firing squad which was commanded by Gersdorff, himself. That occurred about two months ago.

"Vishlova wants to take a major reprisal action against Gersdorff in the near future, but she has not shared her plans with me since she has not yet decided to trust me completely."

"But then, Gersdorff shall take reprisal action against not only the town's inhabitants, but against Shanin's *kolkhoz* as well," Irina replied with obvious concern. "Their reprisals will not only be extreme, but random as well. A lot of innocent people will be executed by Gersdorff's *SS*."

"I agree, Irina," Galkovskiy replied. "But a lot of innocent people have already died and a lot more shall die before this nightmare ends. We have seen the mass executions and killings, as well as the burnt-out villages and towns as we made our journey from the Ukraine to Belarus and that was when the Germans were victorious as they marched eastward. Try to imagine the horror they shall inflict if Soviet Russia is able to stop their advance and then force them to retreat. They will show no mercy. If I am going to die in any case, I would prefer to die fighting."

"I will support you in any decision you choose to make, Gregory. Fate has deemed fit to throw us together and I am prepared to face anything which fate shall confront us with in the future," Irina replied with total dedication and sincerity. "But we must discuss this with Larion and Shanin in the morning…but I want to make love to you tonight. Who knows if and when we shall have the opportunity to share our love again?"

*****

Irina and Galkovskiy went to the Shanin residence at dawn the next morning. Irina left for the dairy with Tamara, while Galkovskiy stayed behind to inform Shanin and Larion of his plan to join the partisans. "Gentlemen…no, that is not the correct way to address you two this solemn day," Galkovskiy spoke emotionally in his deep voice. "Dear friends…"

Galkovskiy proceeded to inform Larion and Shanin of the discussions he had with Natalia Vishlova and with Irina the night before. Neither Shanin nor Larion spoke one word until Galkovskiy had finished.

"Well, dear friends, is there anything you would like to say to me at this point?"

"Gregory," Larion spoke first, "I understand your frustration and if it were not for my wife and my son, I would follow you again without hesitation. I did not have to ask Tamara to marry me just when this war was starting, but I did. We did not have to have a child, but we did. I, too, want to defend the Motherland against its invaders, even though our communist governors leave a lot to be desired, but I must stay and protect my wife and my son…but I shall try to kill as many Nazis as I can."

"Colonel Galkovskiy," Shanin added, "I was a soldier once as well, so I fully understand your desire to fulfil your duty to the Motherland. I agree, Vishlova's actions shall result in serious reprisals against the people in town, as well as my workers…possibly even me, personally. But I also understand that this is a total war and either we destroy the enemy or the enemy shall inevitably destroy all of us."

"After all, they consider us to be subhuman and not deserving of life, but my primary duty is to protect my workers as much as I can and to continue our food production so that we can feed out fellow citizens. But Gregory, I want you to know that I support your decision with all of my heart and soul. Russia's

165

history seems to have been one of enduring hard kisses and bitter tears, but we can hope for a better life in the future. For that hope I, too, am prepared to lay down my life, but like Larion, I believe that my workers, my daughter, and my grandson should have a chance to continue to live. My duty is to protect them as best I can."

"Then we are agreed," Galkovskiy replied. "Irina and I shall proceed to join the partisans and we shall not return to work at the *kolkhoz*. But that will make the risk of reprisal against the *kolkhoz* that much greater if we happen to be caught or killed, and they are able to link us to you."

The three compatriots then rose in unison and embraced each other. Each one had tears flowing freely from his eyes as they exchanged kisses on each other's cheeks. Each one knew that they may not meet again in the future. Each one knew that they were all doing what they believed they had an obligation to do, not only for themselves, but for their eternal Motherland.

*****

With dusk, Galkovskiy and Irina stole out of the *kolkhoz* under the darking cover of night to join the Vishlova partisans. Galkovskiy was not sure that he would be able to locate them immediately, but he was fairly certain that Vishlova had provided him with appropriate clues in their last discussion. He was certain that she was testing his intelligence as well as his loyalty. If he remembered her clues correctly, he would be able to locate them within a day or two.

*****

They had proceeded deep into the forest and continued to be guided by the faint light of the moon which was occasionally obscured by passing clouds. After several hours, Galkovskiy and Irina paused to rest and eat. They had brought ample provisions of salted meat, rye bread, and cheese, and both had their personal canteen filled with water.

"Irina, why don't you go to sleep for an hour or two, while I stand watch," Galkovskiy suggested gallantly. "Then we can switch and proceed through the forest in the morning."

Irina gladly agreed. She was exhausted and needed to rest. She dozed off within minutes. Her dreams were the same…first her deceased husband's face would loom out of the darkness and it seemed as if he wanted to speak to her. Though his lips were moving and his eyes seemed earnest, she could hear no sound. Then Gregory's face would loom into view and she could hear his deep baritone voice whisper words of love…she wanted to reach out and hold him in her arms, but when she would reach out, he seemed to drift back out of her reach. Suddenly, she felt someone shaking her vigorously, commanding her to awaken.

"Irina! Irina! Wake up," Galkovskiy spoke to her with a quiet earnestness. "Our friends are here. Please wake up, my darling."

Irina slowly came out of her stupor and she tried to adjust her eyes to the diminished light of the night. She could feel Galkovskiy support her as she tried to rise up.

"Is it my watch, Gregory?" she asked sleepily. "Just give me a moment and then you may rest."

"It is not time for anyone to rest right now, comrades," a female voice commanded her. "We have a long journey to complete before the sun rises. Allow me to introduce myself, comrades. Commander Natalia Vishlova at your service. I command this company of partisans."

*****

The platoon of about twenty men and women reached the southern edge of the forest by dawn. Vishlova decided that they would rest until dusk and then proceed to cross the open fields at night and then enter the next forest which was located immediately to the south of the town.

They were eating a cold meal since a fire would involve an unnecessary risk. The platoon had broken up into four separate groups. Irina, Galkovskiy, and Vishlova were part of one group.

"So, comrade Vishlova," Galkovskiy asked politely between mouthfuls of cheese and rye bread. "Are you prepared to share your plan on how you intend to exact revenge against Gersdorff?"

"I must know you two a bit better before I share that kind of information," Vishlova replied.

Galkovskiy estimated her to be in her late twenties. Average height and average build, but she exuded confidence and authority. Irrespective of her gender, he could understand why men would be prepared to follow her command. It was also obvious that she was a doctrinaire communist.

"What would you like to know about me, comrade Vishlova?" he inquired.

"Everything, comrade Galkovskiy," she replied tersely as she continued to eat her cheese and rye bread.

"I am thirty-nine years old, single, no children. I have been a soldier in the Soviet army for almost twenty years. I held the rank of colonel and commanded a battalion in the Winter War with Finland and on the Ukrainian front under General Vinogradov. My battalion was practically wiped out in the first few days of the Nazi invasion.

"I and some compatriots, knowing that we were facing complete destruction, infiltrated the enemy lines and we were able to join up with a partisan company commanded by an individual named Pavlovskiy. We fought with him for a few months and we were quite successful in interdicting enemy fuel supplies, but our success also spelled our doom. The Nazis were able to track us to our forest and during the night, they bombed the forest with a large battery of mortars."

"I estimate that our position sustained about five hundred mortar rounds over an hour. Those rounds effectively destroyed the entire company with the exception of me, Irina, and a couple of others. After that, we decided to head north and we have collaborated with a number of partisan groups until we were able to reach your town of Xhotimsk, where we decided to recuperate for a short time and then try to join up with another partisan group."

"And what about you, comrade?" Vishlova asked Irina a bit contemptuously.

"I am a widow. My husband was killed at the front defending our capital, Minsk. The *Einsatzgruppen Kommandos* were conducting a reprisal against my husband's village, but we were saved by Pavlovskiy's partisans. That was when I met Gregory."

Vishlova was not impressed and that was obvious from her disdainful facial expression. She assumed that Irina was just Galkovskiy's mistress or lover and that she would not be able to contribute effectively to any military operation. But Galkovskiy was a colonel and had commanded two battalions. He definitely had promise on both a military level and perhaps on a more personal level as well. As commander, her men had to be prepared to serve her on both levels. She considered herself to be the 'she-wolf' of her pack. That gave her first choice in respect of all matters at all times.

Galkovskiy sensed Vishlova's disappointment and decided to intercede on Irina's behalf.

"Irina has been acting as a sniper with every partisan group we have fought with so far. I believe that she has seventeen confirmed kills and some of those were while she was under heavy mortar and machine gun fire. So do not be deluded by her calm demeanor, comrade Vishlova."

Vishlova preferred to remain dismissive until Karzhova could prove otherwise. Besides, if what Galkovskiy said was true, Irina may prove to be a more formidable opponent than she had assumed and Vishlova was not interested in being forced to compete with another woman when she decided that she wanted a particular man.

"We shall see how good a shot she is tomorrow," Vishlova replied. "My plan, Galkovskiy, is to have your mistress assassinate a couple of Gersdorff's officers. That should force him to take a reprisal action. When he takes his reprisal action, we shall take him."

"Sounds simple, comrade Vishlova," Galkovskiy replied skeptically. "Almost too simple, perhaps. Where are we going to hit him and where do you think he will try effect his reprisal?"

"That is for me to know for the moment," Vishlova stated ambiguously and then proceeded to assert her authority and dismiss Irina. "Karzhova, why don't you go to your assigned tent while Galkovskiy and I discuss the plans for tomorrow. He can join you later."

Irina and Galkovskiy exchanged a quick, knowing look. Galkovskiy could see the smoldering hatred in Irina's eyes; however, he was surprised that she could still manage an innocuous smile as she slowly rose and walked away. As Irina walked away, her grip on her rifle had stiffened. She was fantasizing a 'head shot' at three hundred meters and it was Vishlova's head which manifested itself in her mind's eye. She could feel the sensation of slowly pulling back on the trigger, hearing the simultaneous explosion in the chamber and feeling the recoil of the stock into her shoulder. Then she could visualize Vishlova's head explode in the distance as her body became limp and slowly crumpled to the ground.

"Come, my dear colonel," Vishlova whispered to Galkovskiy. "I shall show you the way."

Galkovskiy was aware of the intent behind Vishlova's possessive expression. He had become 'her' dear colonel. Listening to her speak and observing her behavior caused him to revise his initial assessment of her. In addition to being confident and able to lead her men, she was also a firm dogmatic communist to whom doctrinal purity came before military prudence.

But this woman was also not averse to abusing her authority for her own personal benefit. That kind of personal indulgence made her dangerous since she seemed oblivious to the fact that her conduct could alienate her company's confidence in her being able to lead them effectively. He also recognized that she was a potential threat to both himself and Irina. He remained hopeful that Irina would understand.

Vishlova pulled back the entrance flap to her tent and beckoned Galkovskiy to enter, quickly pulling it shut behind her as she followed him in.

"Well, I have never had a colonel before, Galkovskiy," Vishlova stated firmly, but her voice became a bit hoarse from her rising passion. "Come here, my colonel!" she commanded and spun him around so that they would be facing each other.

"I think colonels basically do it the same way as everyone else…but perhaps a bit better. After all, we are colonels," Galkovskiy replied jokingly.

"Oh, shut your mouth and kiss me, Galkovskiy!" Vishlova commanded as she pressed her lips fiercely against his lips.

Galkovskiy could feel her tongue push past his lips and explore his mouth. Then she proceeded to bite his tongue, causing him to retract it defensively. She held his right hand up to her breast and then she guided it inside the front of her uniform jacket so that he could feel her full, warm, naked breast. His cold hand caused her nipple to dimple. She then placed her left hand on his crotch and started to stroke him. Though Galkovskiy tried to maintain control of his emotions, Vishlova was obviously experienced in arousing a man. He decided that since she was not giving him any choice, he would copulate with her vigorously and painfully. He lifted up her military issue skirt over her waist and then pushed her back onto her cot. Soon he was inside her and he had her knees positioned over his shoulders. If she wanted to know how it was to be fucked by a colonel, he would oblige her.

*****

As Galkovskiy made his way back to his own tent, he was hopeful that Irina would be fast asleep; however, he knew that he was just being fanciful. As he opened the entrance flap to their tent, he imagined he saw three demonic glowing red lights, but it was only Irina smoking a cigarette and he knew that she was not pleased.

"Did you fuck her well?" Irina asked calmly, though obviously disgusted with his behavior.

"I did what I had to do, my love," Galkovskiy replied tenderly. "I assure you that it held no pleasure for me."

He sat down on the bed beside her and attempted to caress her cheek.

"I would suggest that you do not touch me tonight, Gregory, if you want to retain your fingers or your love organ."

"I did what I had to do, Irina. Try to understand that fact. That bitch is a dangerous woman and I do not understand how she has been able to survive this long because of the unnecessary risks she is prepared to take, but we need her at this moment."

"I may have to shoot her in the head, Gregory. So do not get too attached to her, my dear. I am going to sleep now, but I do not believe there is room for you to lay beside me tonight."

Irina turned her back to him as she rolled over so that she would not have to look at him. Galkovskiy remained seated on the side of her cot, but he knew that Irina was not prepared to indulge him further this night and that it was best if he could try go to sleep rolled up in his blanket on the cold, hard ground.

He has not wanted to copulate with Vishlova, but he had to submit to get her to trust him. He needed to know her plan so he would be able to analyze its strengths and, more importantly, its weaknesses. Those weaknesses meant success or failure, casualties and death.

Though Irina had feigned that she had gone to sleep, she remained motionless on her cot until she could hear Gregory commence to breathe heavily. It was only when she was certain that he had finally drifted off to sleep that she permitted herself to fall asleep as well. She had never hated a woman as much as she hated Vishlova. Her impudence in brazenly taking away the man she loved in her own presence was not going to remain unanswered.

Chapter 27

The Waffen SS was composed of five divisions at the outbreak of Operation Barbarossa in June of 1941. It was initially composed of the cream of the German army, but as the war dragged on, casualties had to be replaced by non-German 'Aryan-looking' soldiers from other countries. Consequently, the SS uniform was amended to identify 'German' and 'Non-German' soldiers and officers.

The 'SS' runes patch on the right collar of the uniform identified that soldier to be of pure German stock and only pure German soldiers could wear that SS patch. Other nationalities had to use other collar insignia.

The 'Totenkopf' (death's head) insignia, which was worn on the officer's headgear, had been resurrected by the Nazis from former Prussian Hussar uniforms. It initially signified the commitment to die for one's regiment and country, but its Nazi significance was that the wearer of the Totenkopf had the arbitrary power of life and death over all subjugated people. As the war waged on and the Nazi advance was initially halted, then slowly reversed before turning into a complete rout which would end at the entrance to Hitler's Fuhrerbunker in Berlin, the Waffen SS and the Soviet armies both adopted the protocol of not taking prisoners. Prisoners had to be guarded and fed, and that delayed any advance or retreat. It was preferable that both sides fought to the death. In the event any soldiers on either side elected to surrender, they were merely delaying their inevitable execution. Both sides knew that no quarter was to be afforded by either side.

The Wehrmacht (the regular German Army) and the Waffen SS (the Nazi Divisions), adopted a scorched-earth policy in their retreat, hoping that it would delay the on-coming Soviet troops after 1943. It was a policy which the Soviet troops had initially adopted when they were forced to retreat in 1941. As the Soviet armies advanced westward towards Nazi Germany after 1943, it was a time for Soviet retribution for the Nazi atrocities inflicted upon the

Soviet citizens and soldiers, however, the Soviet Russians did not herd German citizens into churches and barns, and then proceed to incinerate the occupants while they were still alive. They were satisfied by merely raping the women and executing the men. Stalin sanctioned this conduct by characterizing it as "...the boys are entitled to a little fun".

On 8 February 1942, Hitler appointed his favorite architect, Albert Speer, as Reich Minister of Armaments and War Production. Speer's former accomplishments included the reconstruction of the Reich Chancellery, which Hitler had deliberately destroyed and then used as a pretext to seize dictatorial power; the Nuremberg Nazi party stadium; as well as numerous concentration camps.

Speer was initially praised for the miracle he was able to achieve in increasing armaments production through the initial use of forced Jewish labor and then 'slave labor' generally. The Wehrmacht and the Waffen SS were both directed to collect available slave labor in the subjugated territories and herd those people back to Germany's factories. Military trucks would scour the towns and the cities, randomly collecting males, females and even families for deportation to Germany. Anyone who refused or resisted was executed on the spot.

The 'miracle' in armaments production was diminished substantially by the summer of 1943 as a direct result of the extended range of Allied bombing capability. This compelled Speer to transfer a lot of the armaments production to underground facilities in southern Germany to avoid that vulnerability and actual armaments production peaked in the summer of 1944. However, a shortage of fuel which resulted from the Allied bombing of Romanian oilfields, coupled with a shortage of soldiers which resulted from the series of catastrophic defeats on the eastern front, left a lot of this increased armaments production under utilized.

Chapter 28

Though *Sturnbannfuhrer* (major) Gersdorff was the master of his domain, his immediate superior was *Oberst* (Colonel) Elias Schalburg, whose headquarters were at the provincial capital of Mogilev. Whenever *Oberst* Schalburg felt the inclination to criticize or chastise Gersdorff for his sundry acts of omission or commission, that criticism would not stop with him. Gersdorff considered it his duty to pass on *Oberst* Schalburg's displeasure to his subordinate officers, *Hauptmann* (Captain) Bochmann and *Oberleutenant* (First Lieutenant) Weidinger.

"Herr *Sturnbannfuhrer* Gersdorff," *Oberleutenant* Weidinger respectfully addressed Gersdorff. "You were requested to report to Herr *Oberst* Schalburg by nine hundred hours this morning. I have him on the line for you."

Weidinger submissively passed the telephone to Gersdorff and then stepped back to afford the Major some privacy. He knew that Gersdorff was extremely sensitive to his commanding colonel's criticism and that confidentiality was of utmost importance to him.

"*Oberst* Schalburg, mien Herr," Gersdorff spoke obsequiously. "What may I do for you?"

"You may explain how a convoy of slave laborers was ambushed in your sector, Gersdorff," Schalburg replied rudely. "And you can explain what you have done about it. You know that we are under the direct Orders of the Reich Minister of War Production to deliver a certain quota of labor to the Reich and you have been consistently short on meeting your quotas for the preceding two months. Furthermore, it seems that your sector also appears to be extremely vulnerable to partisan incursions and interruptions."

"Sir, I respectfully protest," Gersdorff sputtered indignantly. "We have just wiped out one partisan company last month and I have plans to wipe out the remaining partisan company before the end of this month."

"So, you say, Gersdorff. So, you say!" Schalburg replied impatiently. "However, what are you going to do about filling your sector's labor quota for this month?"

"That too shall be fulfilled, without question, Herr *Oberst!*"

"Then see to it!" Schalburg replied loudly. "I do not want to have to speak to you about these matters again."

"*Heil Hitler, mein Herr Oberst Schalburg*!" Gersdorff replied, however, he knew that Schalburg had already hung up the line at his end.

"Weidinger! Find Bochmann and bring him to my office immediately," Gersdorff commanded.

Within moments, Weidinger and Bochmann presented themselves to Gersdorff. They knew from his agitated state that Schalburg had probably verbally criticized him, again, and they knew that Gersdorff was going to pass that criticism on down the line. They remained standing at attention while Gersdorff continued to pace back and forth in his black *SS* dress uniform, slashing his riding crop repeatedly against his right boot.

"Bochmann, what are you doing about that partisan bitch who attacked that slave labor convoy the other week?" Gersdorff's high-pitched voice seemed even higher when he was excited or upset. "*Oberst* Schalburg demands an immediate explanation and an immediate reprisal!"

"As you are aware, Herr *Sturmbannfuhrer* Gersdorff," Bochmann replied calmly. "The partisans attacked the convey, killing twelve soldiers and twenty foreign workers. The remaining forty foreign workers escaped. We believe that we know which forest harbors the partisan's current camp and we have requested that the local *Wehrmacht* battalion provide us with forty to fifty mortars so that we can affect a barrage on that forest and drive the partisans out into the open. We are just waiting for the *Wehrmacht* to accommodate our request because we do not have that capacity ourselves. It seems that they are giving priority to supporting the *Einsatzgruppen Kommandos.*"

"I do not want excuses, Bochmann!" Gersdorff shouted. "I want action! *Oberst* Schalburg wants action. Do you understand? Do what you have to do, but I do not want any further excuses. Advise the *Einsatzgruppen* commander that he operates under my authority and my order is to locate and exterminate that remaining partisan company. Secondly, you are to affect an immediate reprisal action against the town and the *kolkhoz.* I want these subhumans to know that if they give any aid or sustenance to the partisans, they will pay a heavy price."

Bochmann and Weidinger remained standing at attention. After all, Gersdorff did not advise them to stand at ease and he had not dismissed them.

"Why are you still standing here?" Gersdorff shouted. "You are dismissed. Get out of my sight."

*****

Vishlova was standing by the improvised camp stove, getting her early morning ration of a thick vegetable stew as Irina and Galkovskiy approached her. She noticed that Irina's facial expression was neutral, while Galkovskiy appeared to be uncomfortable.

"Morning comrades. I trust you both slept well," Vishlova addressed them snidely, trying to provoke some reaction from Irina. "I know I slept like a babe in her mother's arms."

"Good morning, comrade Vishlova," Irina replied politely, ignoring her mocking tone. "I slept like a babe in her mother's arms as well…but then, at least I knew my mother."

Irina looked at Vishlova and smiled innocently. Though Vishlova knew that she had just been deliberately insulted, she was taken aback and unable to respond immediately. She was not used to being the recipient of sarcasm or insults from the people under her command.

"If anyone cares to know, I actually did not sleep well at all," Galkovskiy added quickly and apologetically to try to distract Vishlova from Irina's veiled insult.

"And why is that, Colonel?" Vishlova finally replied. "I would have thought that you would have slept the sleep of the angels…"

Irina did not bother to respond to Vishlova's rude jibe. She knew that her innocent smile would bother Vishlova even more.

"I would like to be informed of your plans, comrade Vishlova," Galkovskiy replied seriously. "After all, this is not a game which we are playing."

"I disagree, Colonel," Vishlova replied. "It is a game, albeit a serious game of life and death. And please call me Natalia, since I would like us to become close friends, as well as comrades-in-arms."

176

Irina decided to take her morning ration and walk away to another area of the camp where a couple of men and women were eating and talking casually. She knew that she would find it increasingly difficult to maintain her composure if Vishlova continued to needle her. As Irina walked away from them, Galkovskiy decided to press Vishlova on her plans.

"Let us find a quiet spot in the sunlight somewhere and perhaps you can explain matters to me in more detail."

Galkovskiy picked up his morning ration and proceeded to walk away from Vishlova, forcing her to follow him. He hoped that by remaining with her in the open sunlight that it might assuage Irina's feelings and help restore her trust in him.

"You said that you wanted to assassinate a couple of Gersdorff's officers. Exactly how do you hope to accomplish that feat?"

"We have already given Gersdorff good reason to take a reprisal action, Galkovskiy," Vishlova replied as she tried to consume her steaming hot breakfast ration. "Last week, we attacked a convoy of traitors who the Nazis were taking back to Germany to man their factories. We were successful in killing a number of soldiers who were escorting those traitors, as well as a number of traitors as well. However, a large number of them also were able to escape while we were preoccupied with eliminating that escort. Gersdorff will have to act and we have our contacts in town who shall advise us when and where Gersdorff will attempt to proceed." "But what can you do to prevent him taking a reprisal action against some of the townspeople?"

"We all have to make sacrifices for the Motherland and for comrade Stalin, if we are going to be victorious over the Nazis."

"And do you really consider those people who the Nazis had rounded up like cattle and who are being forced to go to Germany against their will...to be traitors, comrade Vishlova? Do you believe that they are acting out of their own free will?"

"Please...Gregory," Vishlova implored him sweetly. "After last night, I would prefer you to address me as Natalia...or even 'Natusha'...at least when we are alone. And I would die before I would perform labor for my Motherland's enemy! Those traitors had the same choice. When they chose to betray the Motherland...they forfeited their lives."

"And do not forget about their betrayal of comrade Stalin...Natalia," interjected Galkovskiy.

Vishlova looked into Galkovskiy's eyes to see if she could discern his real intent, but his eyes did not disclose that he was merely needling her at that moment.

"Comrade Stalin is the Motherland's savior, Galkovskiy," Vishlova replied slowly, watching his face closely so that she could detect his true frame of mind. "He is a prophet who fate has sent to the Russian people to save them from themselves. He intends to make Russia a great nation that other nations shall fear and respect."

"Yes, I agree, Natalia," Galkovskiy replied directly and then quickly proceeded to change the subject back to his issue of prime concern. "Since you have already successfully attacked that labor convoy, then you have already given Gersdorff more than enough reason to take a severe reprisal action, so why did you say that you wanted Irina to assassinate a couple of his officers?"

"I just wanted to see if she would flinch!" Vishlova spat the words out. "But she is a cold fish, that one. She did not even blink!" Galkovskiy realized that his current position was between two women who were both jealous of each other and there was not much he could do to remedy that situation. He also realized that the only prudent action he should take would be to ensure that he did not do anything to exacerbate it.

"The *Wehrmacht* and even most of the *Waffen SS* are fighting the brave Soviet soldiers at the front. The *Einsatzgruppen Kommandos* and their auxiliaries are too cowardly to enter the forest to fight us directly. Since they will not come to us, we have to go to them," Vishlova concluded.

"If I may make a suggestion, Natalia," Galkovskiy spoke respectfully. "When we were with Pavlovskiy's partisans a few months ago, the *SS* and *Einsatzgruppen Kommandos* also did not want to enter the forest where their superior numbers were more of a handicap, than an advantage. However, they bombarded the forest with about five hundred mortar shells in a couple of hours and the partisans who were not killed by that mortar barrage, were forced out into the open fields and then they were slaughtered by machine gun fire. Gersdorff may try the same tactic with you."

"So, what would you suggest?"

"We have to know if Gersdorff will adopt the same tactic and where. I suggest that you assign two partisans to position themselves at the four corners of your forest. Whoever notices a military buildup of a battery of mortars will immediately report back to you. Then, instead of remaining in the middle of the forest, we should advance on their battery position. Gersdorff will be bound to have assigned his remaining troops around the forest to kill anyone who tries to leave with his machine guns. However, they would not expect a frontal attack on their mortar battery position. They would expect us to go in the opposite direction."

"Hummm! That makes sense, Galkovskiy, but after all, you are a colonel while I am just a lowly partisan commander," Vishlova replied in a self-deprecating manner.

Chapter 29

Larion decided to take Tamara down to the river for a brief respite from their respective duties at the *kolkhoz*. Her father, Dimitri Shanin, volunteered to stay and watch over his grandson.

The sun was warm and the grass and trees were resplendently verdant. The birds were singing and chirping joyously. For a brief moment beneath the shade of a tree by a slowly flowing river it was difficult to believe that millions of soldiers were ardently attempting to annihilate each other.

"Louyna…will this nightmare ever end?" Tamara asked quietly. "Look at how peaceful life can be."

"It has to end, my love," Larion replied tenderly. "It has to end. We just have to endure until it does end. We have each other. We have our first-born son. We have your father. Thank God for what we still have."

"But you have not heard from your parents, Louyna. You do not know if they are alive or dead, yet you seem to be so calm." "No, I do not know how they are, but considering their position, I can only hope that they remain safe and alive. At least they are not directly exposed to this war, but I am happy what I do have. That is you, our son, and your father."

They held each other closely and then kissed. Larion could not believe that in the poignant midst of the horror of the war that they could share such a tender moment. He fantasized that they were floating slowly in a rowboat on the river, their bodies gently warmed by the summer sun.

"*HANDE HOCH!*" (Hands up)

The German scream jolted them both out of their revery. Larion sat up to see two *SS* troopers standing over them with their rifles pointed directly at him. Their *SS* insignia clearly displayed on their right collar. Larion immediately complied with their demand and raised both of his arms in submission.

"Please do not panic and just follow my example," Larion implored Tamara.

The two troopers focused on Larion since they did not consider Tamara to pose any threat. They gestured for him to stand up.

"*HANDE AUF DEN KOPF!*" (Hands on your head) ordered the older trooper.

"*BIST DU EIN JUDE?*" (Are you a Jew) demanded the younger trooper.

"*Nien, mien herr,*" (No sir) replied Larion calmly.

"*DANN BIST DU EIN COMMUNIST!*" (Then you are a communist) said the younger trooper.

"*Nien, mien herr,*" replied Larion calmly.

"*DANN BIST DU EIN PARTISAN!*" (Then you are a partisan) said the older trooper.

"*Nien, mien herr,*" replied Larion again, denying their accusation.

"*SEHAU DIN DIESE SAFTIGE SCHLAMPE AN*" (Look at that juicy bitch) interjected the younger trooper.

"*WIR KONNEN SIE GLEICHZEITIG FICKEN,*" (We can fuck her at the same time) added the older trooper. "*ABER WIR MUSSEN IHN ZUERST HIN-RICH TEN.*" (We have to execute him first).

The two *SS* troopers gestured to Larion to stand up against the tree and gestured to Tamara to stand aside. Tamara was crying hysterically and had her arms wrapped around herself; however, she was unable to move so the younger trooper used the barrel of his rifle to move her away. As she finally moved, he caressed her breasts with his rifle barrel. Larion remained motionless since the other trooper was still aiming his rifle at his chest.

"Please do what they ask, Tamara, or they will just shoot both of us," Larion begged.

"*HALT DIE KLAPPE!*" (Shut your mouth) ordered the older trooper.

"*Mein herr, darf ich bitte eine zigarette haben?*" (Gentlemen, may I have a cigarette, please?) Larion asked politely, hoping that the two troopers would grant him this small last concession.

The two troopers chortled at what they took to be a dying last request. The younger trooper retrieved a package of cigarettes from his uniform breast pocket and extended a cigarette to Larion.

"*Bitte zunde meine zigarette an,*" (Please light my cigarette) Larion asked politely.

The younger trooper, smirking in anticipation of executing this low-life Slav and then fucking his girlfriend, held his rifle in one hand and then flipped his lighter on and extended it. Larion lowered his head down to accept the light and cupped his left hand over the cigarette to protect it from being blown out.

At that moment, the younger trooper looked over to his companion in satisfaction; however, he had placed his body between his fellow trooper and Larion. Larion immediately headbutted the younger trooper beneath his chin, causing him to drop his rifle and fall backwards. Before the elder trooper could recover, Larion reached behind his back and pulled out his Tokarev pistol and shot him twice in his chest. The older trooper dropped his rifle and fell backwards, rolling into the river face down in the water and slowly drifting away with the current.

The younger trooper tried to recover, but his mouth was filled with blood since the head butt had caused him to bite through his tongue. His effort was hampered by the fact that he was choking on his own blood; however, he knew that he had to react or he was going to die. As he rolled and scrambled towards his rifle, Larion cursed and shot him twice as well. Once in the chest and once in his head.

"*Fich dich du hosenscheiber*!" (Fuck you, you pant-shitter) Larion exclaimed in disgust. Tamara remained frozen in shock. She had never seen someone killed before her very eyes and she remained transfixed on the dead young trooper's facial expression. His eyes were wide open in disbelief, his mouth was agape, the blood still flowing freely from his severed tongue. That flow would soon cease since his heart was no longer functioning.

Larion rolled his body into the river so that he could join his companion, but he knew that the two soldiers would be missed by their platoon once they had failed to report and the two bodies would eventually flow down to the town in any case. Their deaths would be noted quite quickly and that also meant that Gersdorff would exact an immediate reprisal on the workers on the *kolkhoz*. They had to get back to the collective farm and inform his father-in-law, Dimitri Shanin.

"Come, Tamara," Larion pleaded with her as he placed his arm around her shoulders. "We have to get back and warn your father. I do not think he will be able to convince Gersdorff that the partisans executed two of his soldiers this time."

*****

182

When they got back, Larion informed his father-in-law about what had transpired by the river.

Dimitri Shanin remained quiet and listened carefully. He realized that sometimes in life, matters go astray and that there was not much that one could do to avoid the inevitable consequences.

Tamara remained in a partial shock at the events she had witnessed. Though, on the one hand she was extremely relieved that she and Larion came out unscathed, witnessing her husband kill two other human beings, even though it was in self-defense, remained a traumatic event and she continued to tremble as if it was a cold winter day instead of a warm summer afternoon. It was only when she heard her young son crying from the bedroom that she was able to collect herself and go to him.

"What action do you think Gersdorff shall take, Dimitri?" Larion asked, even though he was fairly sure what the inevitable answer would be.

'He will conduct a severe reprisal, Larion," Shanin replied. "I have seen him execute ten civilians for every soldier he has lost to the partisans. If he cannot execute a partisan, he will randomly select and execute at least twenty of my employees as soon as he learns that his soldiers died on the *kolkhoz* grounds."

*****

The next morning, Gersdorff and thirty *SS* troopers arrived in two military transport vehicles.

As soon as the two trucks stopped in front of Shanin's residence, Gersdorff, *Oberleutenant* Weidinger and *Hauptmann* Bochmann exited the two vehicles and approached Shanin's front door. The thirty SS troopers exited the back of the two trucks and assembled themselves in three equal groups, holding their bayoneted rifles and machine pistols across their chests, ready to fire upon command.

"Shanin, you old fart," Gersdorff swore. "Get your fat ass out here at once or I shall burn your home down around your ears with that slut daughter of yours and your bastard grandson."

Shanin quickly stumbled out of his front door, trying to tuck his shirt into his trousers.

"*Herr Sturnbannfuhrer* Gersdorff," Shanin addressed him submissively. "What is the problem? What can I do for you?"

"What can you do for me, Shanin?" Gersdorff echoed sarcastically. "Well, you will not be able to buy me off with another dressed chicken this time. Someone on your *kolkhoz* murdered two of my troopers yesterday and do not even try to convince me that it was the partisans again. Even if it was the partisans, it happened on your territory and I hold you personally responsible."

"*Herr Sturnbannfuhrer* Gersdorff," Captain Bochmann addressed Gersdorff formally, clicking his heels as he addressed his commanding officer. "How many persons do you wish to have punished?"

"Round up twenty, Bochmann!" Gersdorff commanded. "Ten men and ten women. *Schnell*!"

Bochmann directed Lieutenant Weidinger to take ten troopers and round up the ten women. He proceeded to take another ten troopers to round up the ordered compliment of ten men. The remaining ten soldiers remained with Gersdorff to provide him with his own security.

Shanin remained stoic. He knew that there was no reasoning with Gersdorff this time. He knew that regardless of how submissive or fawning he may attempt to be, Gersdorff was going to have twenty of his workers killed.

Within thirty minutes, the Lieutenant and Captain returned with their respective victims. The elderly men remained stoic and resigned to their fate. The ten young women were crying hysterically and begging for mercy. They were young and they had not had an opportunity to live their lives, yet.

"I want all of them stripped!" Gersdorff ordered, and the Lieutenant and Captain ordered their respective soldiers to put that order into effect.

"I appreciate that punishment must be meted out, *Herr Sturnbannfuhrer* Gersdorff," Shanin said as he attempted to intercede. "However, you know that the punishment you are about to mete out to these people is not warranted to the extent that they had not committed this crime. Can you find it in your heart to afford these poor wretches some personal dignity and allow them to die fully clothed?"

Gersdorff found Shanin's insubordination in front of his officers and his troops intolerable. He felt that he had to act decisively and without mercy, otherwise his men would think that he was weak.

"For your insolent defiance, Shanin, you can join these subhuman wretches and you can strip naked as well."

Shanin dutifully complied and urged his workers to follow his example. He did not fully understand why he chose to comply, but he thought it might ameliorate their execution in some way. The *SS* troopers might be persuaded to shoot to kill, rather than just simply to main, which would then require further action.

He also noticed through the kitchen window that Larion had his hand over Tamara's mouth and that he was trying to pull her away from the window to the relative safety of the interior of their home, for which he was grateful. He knew that Larion could not do anything to help him and he only hoped that his son-in-law would be able to protect Tamara and his young grandson and namesake.

The *SS* soldiers marched the twenty-one victims to a nearby ravine and ordered them to stand at its edge, but facing their executioners. All thirty soldiers had their rifles and machine pistols at the ready and on Gersdorff's command, they commenced to strafe their victims. Upon being struck with the initial volley of shots, most of the victims crumpled and collapsed backward into the ravine. A couple of the young girls were not hit by the initial rounds, but they were then struck by multiple shots each as all of the soldiers aimed at the last two survivors. Those multiple rounds lifted their bodies off their feet and threw them on top of the crumpled bodies who were already in the ravine.

"Captain Bochmann, Lieutenant Weidinger!" Gersdorff screeched in his high-pitched voice. "Order your men to bayonet all of those bodies. I do not want anyone crawling out after we leave."

*****

It took Larion hours to console Tamara after Gersdorff and his men left. He had to arrange to have the bodies buried, but their bodies had to remain in that mass grave. Fortunately, little Dimitri went to sleep after he had his dinner, unaware of what had transpired earlier in the day. Larion was able to take Tamara to bed, but she was unable to go to sleep until she finally passed out due to total emotional exhaustion. It was only then that Larion was able to leave her and go back to the kitchen and try to decide how they should proceed from this point in time.

While he was lost in thought, there was a subdued knocking at the front door and a familiar hushed voice asking entry. As he opened the door, it was

Gregory Galkovskiy and Irina Karzhova, both were carrying their rifles and they had their fingers on their triggers.

"Gregory, please come in quickly and close the door. We have had a massacre today. The *SS*, under Major Gersdorff, carried out a reprisal and they even executed Dimitri Shanin," Larion explained as he ushered his visitors into the Shanin home and quickly pulled the curtains closed over the windows.

"We heard the shooting, but we were not able to get here in time, Larion. I apologize," Galkovskiy replied.

"There was not much you could have done in any case, Gregory," Larion answered quietly. "Sometimes fate does not provide you with any alternatives. But why are you here now?"

Galkovskiy explained to Larion what had transpired with Natalia Vishlova's partisans and the anticipated action they expected Gersdorff to initiate against them in the forest located immediately to the south of the town.

"Remember what happened to Pavlovskiy's partisans, Larion?" Galkovskiy asked. "The *Einsatzgruppen Kommandos* would not enter the forest, but they initiated that mortar barrage which wiped out practically the entire partisan company and the surviving partisans were driven out of the forest right into the direct fire of the Nazi machine guns.

"It appears that Vishlova has also irritated Gersdorff by interdicting a slave labor convoy which was heading to Germany a couple of weeks ago. Her partisans killed a number of soldiers and workers, but most of the workers were able to escape. Vishlova is fairly confident that Gersdorff intends to take a reprisal action against her partisans. Though she has succeeded in provoking him, she has no plan how to defend against the expected reprisal. Her plan is to simply get into a shooting contest with the Nazis, hoping that the forest shall provide her partisans with sufficient cover to even out the odds. Her plan is basically a decision to commit mass suicide."

"But what are you doing here, Gregory?" Larion inquired. "I thought you and Irina were gone and that you would not be returning before the war ended."

Galkovskiy explained the delicate situation which Vishlova had placed him in and explained that he needed his assistance. He believed that her continued command of this partisan group would result in their eventual annihilation, which he anticipated would come sooner, rather than later.

"She is a doctrinal communist who believes that Stalin is a prophet and the savior of the Motherland. She is prepared to abandon all caution in the name of communism and Stalin, and sacrifice her company and even herself for that cause. I have two objectives which I hope to accomplish with your assistance, if you are able and willing, Larion."

"And what are those objectives, Gregory," Larion replied. "You know that I will do what I can, but I do not know if I can leave Tamara and little Dimitri in light of what happened to her father today."

"Firstly, it may provide you with an opportunity to exact some revenge for the murder of your father-in-law and possibly against Gersdorff, personally. Secondly, I need to eliminate Vishlova before she gets her partisans to commit a deadly operational blunder. I have Irina to support me, but I do not know all of her partisans that well and some of them may be averse to a change in their leadership. I need you to provide me with that additional support and I need you to look out for Irina's safety, because I have reason to believe that Vishlova may take some personal action against her once the fighting commences."

After Galkovskiy finished speaking, he knew that Larion had a very difficult decision to make. Though only a few minutes passed in silence, the time seemed interminable.

"Gregory...and I say this from my heart and my soul," Larion finally replied. "I just cannot leave Tamara and my son right now. Tamara witnessed the humiliation of her father and then his execution. After they shot the victims, Gersdorff ordered them to be individually bayoneted. It took me hours to console her and she has just been able to fall asleep finally out of total emotional exhaustion."

"No, Larion, you must go. I want you to go!" Tamara spoke with a soft determination as she stood in the doorway to the kitchen. "Gregory and Irina need your help, but more importantly, you must avenge the execution of my father, your father-in-law, and the paternal grandfather of your firstborn son. You need not be fretful as to whether I will be able to cope, myself, and look after our son. I may not have been able to show that strength today, but my father's death has strengthened me. It is as if his soul left his body and permeated my own. And I know it is taught that a person should forgive his or her tormentors, but there must be exceptions to that rule. I believe that this is just one such occasion. Just as Gersdorff had humiliated my father and those other twenty people today, I believe that he is deserving of equal punishment in this life. If there is a God, he can punish all of us in the next life."

Larion had remained silent while Tamara was speaking, but when she finished and stood trembling, leaning against the wall for support, he embraced her tightly and kissed her fiercely. Both had tears streaming down their cheeks.

Then Gregory Galkovskiy and Irina Karzhova rose and all four companions embraced and exchanged some bitter tears and hard kisses.

Chapter 30

Shortly before dawn the following morning, Larion, Irina, and Galkovskiy left the collective farm and proceeded to join Vishlova's partisan group. Just as the sun was setting, they were finally able to arrive at the camp. Galkovskiy was relieved to confirm that Vishlova had at least followed his suggestion in strategically posting a couple of partisan guards at the four sides of their forest sanctuary. The two partisans who were stationed at the west side even greeted them as they entered the forest and confirmed that there was no evidence of a deployment of mortars in their sector.

Since the forest was located immediately to the south of the town, Galkovskiy anticipated that Gersdorff's *SS* and the *Einsatzgruppen Kommandos* and Auxiliaries would initiate the mortar barrage from the northern side of the forest. It was the most convenient location as it was adjacent to the town itself. It did not make sense that Gersdorff would move the mortars from the armory, which was located at his headquarters in the former police detachment, then attempt to circumvent the forest so that the barrage would be initiated from the south side of the forest. The west side also involved an increased distance to transport those armaments. The east side was a possibility, but the most convenient location remained the north side.

Galkovskiy concluded that most, if not all of the partisans should be deployed to the northern sector of the forest. This would increase their safety by removing them from the center of the forest which was the expected main target of the barrage. His proposed deployment of manpower would also increase their strength when the partisans launched their counterattack against the mortar batteries, themselves.

Gersdorff and his officers would, presumably, be stationed at that location as well. Furthermore, Gersdorff would have to thin out his manpower to surround the entire forest to prevent the escape of any partisans from their current sanctuary to some other adjacent forest. His actual weakest position was where the mortars were located because the troops would be preoccupied with manning the mortars, as opposed to attacking escaping partisans.

The only remaining issue Galkovskiy had to resolve was to convince Vishlova that his analysis was prudent and his proposed deployment was sound.

*****

As the troika entered the partisan camp, Vishlova immediately approached them with two of her senior aides. They were all armed, but they were carrying their rifles in a neutral position.

"My dearest Gregory," Vishlova greeted Galkovskiy in a very familiar fashion which was solely intended to exacerbate Irina's feelings. "Greetings, comrade. It appears that you have returned just in time. We have just been notified by our comrades who were deployed to the northern sector of our forest that the Nazis have moved in several transport trucks carrying dozens…yes, dozens of mortars and hundreds of mortar shells. So the anticipated mortar barrage shall come from the north. Gersdorff is also deploying at least fifty machine guns batteries along the eastern, southern and western sectors." "I believe they anticipate that whoever is not killed in the barrage will try to escape to the south."

Vishlova finally looked at Larion and scrutinized him in the same lascivious fashion she had evaluated Galkovskiy when she met him for the first time.

"And are you going to introduce me to your young friend, Gregory?" Vishlova asked.

"Larion Daneelivich Sulupin, comrade Vishlova. A First Lieutenant under my command in the Winter War with Finland and on the Ukrainian Front. He was one of the partisans who was able to escape the slaughter of Pavlovskiy's company in the Ukraine, which I had previously told you about."

"Alas, only a First Lieutenant?" Vishlova replied with exaggerated disappointment. "Such a pity."

"He is an experienced junior officer and an experienced partisan. I would trust him with my life," Galkovskiy replied firmly. "I specifically went back to recruit him to join your partisan group because he will be able to provide us with invaluable support."

Vishlova carefully examined Larion one last time with obvious regret. Larion was not sure if it was because of the fact that copulating with a lowly First

Lieutenant, after successfully copulating with a Colonel, would diminish her stature in some fashion or for some other reason; however, he was gratefully relieved in any case.

"Let's adjourn to my tent and decide how we shall proceed tomorrow morning, comrades," Vishlova replied and proceeded to walk away, flanked by her two senior aides.

*****

The six individuals sat around a small makeshift table in Vishlova's tent with chairs improvised from small tree trunks. Vishlova had spread out a hand-drawn map of the forest so that all parties would be able to visualize matters a bit better.

"This is where they are deploying their mortars," Vishlova announced, pointing to a specific location on the map. "And this is where we are right now. I suggest that we get some rest and then move out at dawn to attack."

"Comrade Vishlova, I really believe that we should move into position now, not next morning," Galkovskiy replied. "The attack on Pavlovskiy's camp took place in the middle of the night when most of the partisans were asleep. The attack caught everyone by surprise and caused a lot of initial disorientation. We were on the defensive from the start and we were not able to recover. If Gersdorff has already delivered the mortars and the mortar shells to this location, then we should move into our position immediately before the mortar attack commences…which may occur tonight."

"And what if there is no attack tonight, comrade Galkovskiy?" Vishlova asked, somewhat annoyed that Galkovskiy was second-guessing her proposed strategy.

"If there is no attack tonight, we will have lost absolutely nothing," Galkovskiy replied in all seriousness. "We would still be in a position to counterattack in the morning. However, if they do attack tonight, we will be militarily castrated. We will be preoccupied with defending ourselves and trying to survive, while the mortar shells and the shrapnel will be cutting us to ribbons, we would not be able to move into our offensive position to be able to counterattack."

"I do not believe that Gersdorff is that clever," Vishlova responded dismissively.

"And I have learned that even stupid people can make smart decisions from time to time," Galkovskiy replied, raising his baritone voice and furrowing his dark eyebrows to emphasize his point.

"If Gersdorff's men can launch a mortar barrage tonight, why would he wait until morning? To give us a better fighting chance?" Galkovskiy's rhetorical sarcasm was palpable.

Vishlova merely scowled at Galkovskiy for continuing to disagree with her proposed strategy; however, one of her senior aides attempted to break the impasse between the two leaders. "Comrade Vishlova, comrade Galkovskiy's assessment seems to be sound and minimizes the risk to our company. I believe it has merit. I, for one, do not expect the Nazis to be accommodating when they are intent on annihilating us."

His companion quickly followed suit.

"Comrade Vishlova, I must concur. Comrade Galkovskiy's strategy minimizes our risk and maximizes our chances for success. Sleeping in our tents tonight does not make much sense. We can move into position now and even get some sleep until morning if the Nazis hold back their attack until then."

"Well, it seems that I am outnumbered," Vishlova admitted reluctantly. "Alright, we shall proceed accordingly. We shall break camp now and move into position to the north. If Gersdorff commences his mortar attack tonight, we shall counterattack immediately."

Vishlova then turned her attention to Irina. She intended to salvage some of her command authority and who better to exercise it against except Galkovskiy's mistress.

"Comrade Karzhova. I want you to position yourself no further than one hundred meters from the mortar batteries and I want you to do that tonight. In the event Gersdorff commences his attack tonight, I want you to locate and eliminate as many officers which you may be able to identify. Is that understood?"

"Understood, comrade Vishlova!" Irina replied tersely. "However, may I assume that I shall be permitted to eliminate any troops who are operating the mortars in the event I am unable to identify any officers?"

Vishlova was aware of Irina's underlying contempt, but she deliberately decided to ignore it.

"Galkovskiy has sung your virtues as a sniper, madam. You do not need my permission. You are at liberty to exercise your discretion as you may deem fit and proper."

"There is still one additional factor which we should resolve," Galkovskiy added almost apologetically. "Are you going to deploy all of the partisans to the north or are you still intent on a more dispersed deployment?"

"We should hold back some men as reserves...if for nothing else but to prevent an attack from our rear or our flanks."

Fortunately, Galkovskiy was not obliged to man the vanguard of the opposition to Vishlova on this strategy since both of her senior aides immediately assessed and voiced their positions in direct disagreement with their company commander.

"I cannot see any *SS* or *Einsatzgruppen Kommandos* and auxiliaries entering the forest while the mortar barrage is in effect, so there will be little risk of an attack on our flanks or from our rear."

"Exactly!" continued the second senior aide. "We shall be outgunned and outmanned when we attack the mortar batteries in any case. We will need every man and woman we have. I see no reason for anyone to be held in reserve. If our counterattack is not successful, then we will all end up being killed. I see no sense in holding critical manpower back at all!" Before Vishlova had an opportunity to voice her disagreement, Galkovskiy, Irina, and Larion all concurred with Vishlova's own senior aides.

"Well, I seem to have been outnumbered again, dear comrades," Vishlova replied, attempting to concede defeat graciously, but her contempt for both Galkovskiy and Irina was quite obvious. "Alright, let's break camp...now! Galkovskiy, you may select ten of my men to your command. That shall mean that your complement shall be thirteen, including Karzhova. Try not to get them killed needlessly."

As Vishlova marched away in disgust, her two senior aides remained behind with the Galkovskiy troika.

"Comrade Galkovskiy, I and my friend would appreciate it greatly if you would select the two of us to your company. If we are going to get killed tonight or tomorrow, I believe that if we are fighting with you, we shall not die needlessly."

"My friends," Galkovskiy replied sincerely. "In my experience, I have always found it preferable to fight with volunteers, as opposed to conscripts.

Consider yourselves selected. Furthermore, to show my trust in both of you, your first duty is to select the other eight men to complete our complement."

*****

Larion, Irina, and Galkovskiy were left alone as the two senior aides left to complete their selections. Irina could not resist the opportunity of exacting some small revenge on Galkovskiy.

"Larion, did you notice that Vishlova initially addressed my lover as 'My dearest Gregory', then it was just plain 'Gregory', then it was 'Comrade Galkovskiy' and finally it was just plain 'Galkovskiy'." Turning her attention to Galkovskiy. "I do not think you can expect a second invitation to warm her bed, my love, by that conversation."

"And I am most thankful that I will not be afforded an opportunity to decline any such invitation," Galkovskiy replied with a smirk, provoking Irina to jab her elbow into his ribs playfully.

"But I have to admit that I feared for my young friend here," Galkovskiy continued. "He certainly came close to becoming another notch on her bed post…assuming she has one."

"You are not the only one who harbored that fear, Gregory," replied Larion half seriously.

*****

As Vishlova walked away, she was extremely upset at having her strategic proposals being countermanded, in effect, by Galkovskiy. She knew that her senior aides would not have questioned her decisions if Galkovskiy had not criticized them in the first instance, irrespective of whether or not that criticism had merit. She recognized that Galkovskiy posed a potential threat to her continued command of her partisan company and she concluded that he should not survive the coming battle.

If he was not killed by the *SS* or the *Einsatzgruppen*, then she would have to ensure his death herself.

Chapter 31

Sturmbannfuhrer Gersdorff could hardly contain himself. By 0200 hours, the men manning the machine guns surrounding the forest would be in place and he would issue the command to initiate the mortar barrage. His instructions were that the barrage would commence in the center of the forest and then gradually spread out, driving the partisans who were not killed to the periphery of the forest and out into the open fields where they would be cut down mercilessly by his machine gun batteries.

By dawn, the last partisan company in his district would be wiped out. He could hardly wait to inform *Oberst* Schalburg of his accomplishment. Not only had he carried out reprisals at the *kolkhoz*, but in the town as well; most importantly he had eliminated the final partisan company which was still operating in the Xhotimsk district. Those accomplishments might even elevate him to *Oberst* status as well and then he would no longer have to endure the slights and insults of his commanding colonel, since he would be a colonel as well.

"*Hauptmann* Bochmann, can you confirm that our machine gun batteries are in place?" Gersdorff excitedly asked his *SS* captain. "I specifically ordered that everyone be in place by 0200 hours."

"*Herr Sturmbannfuhrer*, I can confirm that all machine gun batteries have reported in except one and that one will be in place in time," Captain Bochmann replied formally. "It appears that their transport suffered a blown tire and it had to be replaced. They assure me that they will be in place before 0200 hours."

"*Oberleutnant* Weidinger, can you confirm that our mortar batteries are in position and ready to fire?"

"Yes, *Herr Sturmbannfuher*," replied Lieutenant Weidinger. "They are arrayed along a one-hundred-meter line. They have instructions to commence fire on your command. They will each fire twenty shells to the center and then gradually alter the trajectory every ten minutes so that the barrage will move away from the center." "Excellent! Excellent!" Gersdorff squealed, as he proceeded to strut around, slashing his black polished boots with his riding crop.

*****

Irina had moved ahead of Galkovskiy and his company of ten partisans. Soon she could hear the enemy troops' muffled conversations in the near distance. Obviously, they had not expected the partisans' counter tactic and they were not concerned about maintaining absolute silence. The quiet of the night permitted sound to carry a bit further than usual. She continued to advance closer. Positioning herself at less than seventy meters from the edge of the forest, she had a clear line of sight across a sufficient horizontal range. She would have preferred to position herself closer to the edge of the forest, but she could not locate a suitable tree so that she would have the benefit of an elevated position.

The forest was a remnant of a primeval forest which once covered thousands of hectares and it was composed of birch, larch, spruce and even oak trees, which ranged in age up to eighty and even two hundred and fifty years old. Irina tried to locate a mature oak tree which was close enough to the edge of the forest to afford her a suitable height and a sufficient broad spectrum.

Once she found it, she scaled up approximately five meters and shrouded herself in its leaves and branches. In the stillness of the night, she could barely hear Galkovskiy and his ten partisans approaching her position. She was tempted to disclose herself, but her intuition held her back. Perhaps it was better that Gregory and his group, not to mention Vishlova, were not aware of her position.

As she peered through her 3.5x PU scope, she could see Gersdorff addressing two subordinate officers. He appeared to be excited, walking back and forth, lashing his riding crop against his leg.

It was apparent to her that Galkovskiy's premonition had been correct. Gersdorff's *SS* and *Einsatzgruppen Kommandos* were not going to wait until dawn to attack. Their attack was imminent.

She resisted the temptation to call out to Gregory as he and his partisans proceeded beneath her position. They were going to station themselves at the very edge of the open field where several transports had been herded together.

It appeared to be the Nazi command center since the mortar batteries were arrayed to either side of those parked military transports.

A few minutes later, she heard Vishlova and her complement of fifteen men deploying themselves about fifty meters immediately behind Galkovskiy's group. That deployment struck Irina as unusual. It had been agreed that the various compliments of partisans would spread out as evenly as possible. Irina could not understand why Vishlova would position herself behind Gregory and his men, but she assumed that Vishlova just wanted to have Galkovskiy and his men bear the brunt of any initial counteroffensive the Nazis might launch. However, if Vishlova and her group intended to participate in the coming battle, they would be firing directly through Gregory's position.

Irina peered through her scope at Vishlova. The subdued light of the full moon disclosed that she was gesturing to her men to spread out and conceal themselves behind Gregory's men. They were less than twenty meters in front of her position.

*****

Gersdorff pulled back his black left glove so that he could ascertain the exact time. He then proceeded to count down the seconds to the stipulated 0200-hour deadline. As the second hand approached the numeral twelve, he raised his riding crop. As the second hand reached that number, he dropped his right hand and yelled the command to commence firing.

"Beginnen sie jetzt dun angriff! Beginen sie jetzt dun angriff!" (Commence to fire)

Bochmann and Weidinger each ran towards the respective sides of the parked transports, repeating Gersdorff's command.

"Beginensie jetzt dun angriff! Beginnen sie jetzt dun angriff!"

Almost immediately, the nearest mortar batteries commenced to launch the mortar rockets into the dark night sky and that mortar fire spread down the line in both directions like two burning fuses. Each mortar battery was composed of three men and the mortar rockets were dropped down the tubes within five seconds of each other. Almost immediately, the night's darkness and silence became displaced by the thundering fire of the mortar rockets screaming high into the night. Within seconds, their distant explosions also disturbed the night like ominous echoes.

As soon as the multiple launches of the mortar rockets commenced, the partisans opened fire on the mortar batteries. The three-man crews immediately ceased firing the mortars and grabbed their rifles and machine pistols to return the partisan fire, which was coming from the edge of the forest.

Irina continued to watch Vishlova and her partisans. Though her complement remained concealed and did not participate in attacking the mortar batteries, Irina observed Vishlova go to the back of her own partisans and then stand up and aim at Galkovskiy's partisans. Before she was able to get off a single shot, Irina shot her through the back of her head. At that point, Vishlova's partisans were startled to see that their own leader had been killed. They immediately looked back in the direction the single shot came from.

"You sons-of-bitches better move up to the frontline and assist your colleagues or I will shoot every one of you!" Irina screamed to the confused men.

Though the partisans could hear her and they knew that she was close, they were unable to see her position in the confusion of the ongoing battle and the blackness of the night which was interrupted by the never-ending scattered bursts of rifle fire from both sides. One of Vishlova's men immediately moved ahead to join Galkovskiy's group and the remaining partisans quickly followed.

Irina then proceeded to focus on the soldiers in the mortar battery positions. She would aim, fire, eject the spent shell, and repeat that process again and again. Once in a while, she would scan the transports and she believed that she saw Gersdorff attempt to shield himself beneath one of them, but she returned her concentration to the *SS* and the *Einsatzgruppen Kommandos* who were returning fire to her partisan colleagues.

In the confusion of firing and taking returning fire, there were ceaseless, fleeting flashes as the bullets exited their rifle barrels on both sides. The simultaneous cacophony seemed to go on endlessly for a while. However, soon the returning fire from the Nazis diminished and then it finally stopped. As the return fire ended, Galkovskiy rose and advanced in a crouched position towards the Nazi center of command. He yelled at the surviving partisans to hold their fire and advance on the enemy position.

"Kill all wounded!" he commanded. "We are not going to take any prisoners today. And that includes anyone who attempts to surrender. Remember, they would not give us any quarter and we shall do the same. Advance carefully, my friends."

He was followed quickly by Larion, who was watching for any movement. If he saw any movement ahead of himself, he was going to shoot first.

Irina slid down her oak tree and proceeded carefully to join Gregory and Larion who were standing near the transports. In the distant, she could hear her partisan colleagues curse and shoot any survivors. When they were satisfied that Gersdorff's troops had been completely eliminated, they congregated around Galkovskiy and Larion by the transports.

"How many casualties did we take, boys?" Galkovskiy asked anxiously.

"What you see is what is left of us," Vishlova's senior aide replied. "I would estimate that we took losses close to fifty percent, but the Nazis took one hundred percent."

"And what about comrade Vishlova?" Galkovskiy asked.

"She took a round to the back of her head just before she opened fire on you, my love," Irina interjected, smiling with satisfaction. "That bitch had her men position themselves behind you and I believe that she wanted to eliminate you, Gregory."

Irina then looked at the two senior aides who had volunteered to join Galkovskiy's complement.

"And probably your two new friends, as well."

The two former senior aides both cursed their dead commander under their breath, but they were grateful for the decision they had made to leave Vishlova and join Galkovskiy.

Galkovskiy ordered some men to check to see if they could locate any Nazi officers who were commanding the enemy troops. The *SS* Captain and the *SS* Lieutenant were quickly identified. Both apparently had died in the battle.

"Has anyone found Gersdorff?" Larion asked anxiously. "I saw him by the trucks before the fighting started, but I do want to know if he got killed or not."

There was no immediate reply to Larion's question, until Irina spoke up.

"I believe I saw him take refuge under one of the transports when the shooting started, Larion."

The partisans immediately commenced to search under the transports. Almost immediately, one of the partisans located Gersdorff hiding under one truck. Gersdorff refused to crawl out voluntarily, so the partisan pulled him out from under the truck by his black boots. Larion looked at Galkovskiy and both understood what had to be done. Galkovskiy merely nodded his head to confirm that Larion could proceed as he deemed fit.

"Since you are not taking any prisoners, I demand to be executed by firing squad like a true soldier of the Third Reich!" Gersdorff demanded, once he was able to collect himself, hoping that his bravado would impress these subhumans.

"Well, *Herr Sturmbannfuhrer* Gersdorff," Larion replied. "We shall be happy to indulge you, but there are certain formalities which have to be observed first."

"Formalities? What formalities?" Gersdorff asked, genuinely confused.

"Well, I believe that the *SS* and the *Einsatzgruppen* have a protocol that the individuals who are about to be executed have to disrobe first," Larion replied calmly, as he removed his Tokarev pistol from his jacket pocket.

"I object! I am an officer of the Third Reich…" Gersdorff tried to argue strenuously, however, his fear was parching his throat and impeding his ability to speak.

"Gersdorff, do you remember having Dimitri Shanin executed at the *kolkhoz*? I remember the man pleading with you to permit his men and women to die with some dignity; however, you ordered them to be stripped. Killing them was not enough for you…you had to humiliate them as well."

Gersdorff was not able to reply. His only hope was that these subhumans would just shoot him dead. He knew that he was going to die in any case, but he just did not want to suffer physically and he did not want to be humiliated in the process. After all, he held himself in considerable self-esteem.

"Gersdorff, take off your clothes…or I promise you that you will suffer, but you will end up being naked one way or the other," Larion commanded.

When Gersdorff refused to respond in any fashion, Larion proceeded to shoot him in his right foot, which evoked an animal-like scream and caused him to jump up and down on his left leg, protecting his right foot.

"Gersdorff, you are to take off your clothes or I am going to shoot you in the left foot as well and then I intend to shoot you in both your knees. My pistol has seven additional shots before I will be forced to reload and it is important for me that you not only die, but that you suffer accordingly. How much you suffer shall depend solely on how quickly you follow my commands."

Gersdorff proceeded to take off his tunic jacket and then his shirt.

"I cannot take off my trousers because I cannot take off my right boot, since you shot me," Gersdorff replied. "You will have to shoot me with my trousers on."

"On second thought, perhaps I should just shoot you in your genitals, Gersdorff?" Larion asked rhetorically. "After all, you probably have not had much use for them in any case...and what do you prefer? *"Fick schafe oder schweine?"* (Fuck sheep or pigs)

Gersdorff decided that if he did not comply with Larion's demands, there was a possibility that they would just tire of trying to humiliate him and then they would just kill him quickly, so he decided to neither respond, nor comply. Consequently, Larion proceeded to shoot him in his left foot as well, which caused him to collapse on the ground and writhe around in pain.

"Now, you son-of-a-bitch, get up or I will proceed to shoot out both your kneecaps, which I understand will be even more painful," Larion commanded.

Gersdorff did not want to find out if Larion was bluffing or not. He positioned himself on his hands and knees and then gingerly attempted to rise up, but the shattered bones in both feet cut against his nerves and the pain radiated like lightning bolts throughout his body. However, he was able to rise and he was even proud of his accomplishment.

"Comrades," Larion addressed his fellow partisans. "Could one or two of you assist *Strumbannfuhrer* Gresdorff to take off his boots, trousers, and shorts so that we can proceed to let him give his life for his beloved *Fuhrer* in the appropriate manner?"

Three partisans immediately leaped upon Gersdorff and while one restrained him, the other two proceeded to pull off his black boots, his trousers, and his shorts.

"Well, stand up, Gersdorff! Stand up!" Larion commanded.

"*Mein Herr*, I beg you. Just shoot me. I know that I am going to die, but please afford me this last little dignity," Gersdorff begged between sobs as he remained kneeling on the ground in pain.

"But *Mein Herr*," Larion replied formally. "You did not give my father-in-law any last little dignity before you had him shot and bayoneted."

"Your father-in-law?" Gersdorff asked, clearly uncertain to whom Larion could be referring.

"Yes, my father-in-law!" Larion answered calmly. 'Dimitri Aleksyevich Shanin. And that is the last name you are going to hear as you plummet down to hell. Now stand up or the next shot will be at your genitals."

Gersdorff slowly rose to his feet. The other partisans proceeded to mock his small penis and some were even making wagers as to whether or not he had two testicles or one testicle or no testicles at all. Notwithstanding the fact that he did feel degraded and disgraced, Gersdorff decided that the last two words which would pass his lips would be shouted in homage to his Fuhrer. Though his stance on two wounded feet made him unsteady, he proceeded to raise his right arm in the traditional *Nazi* salute, but all he could utter was the word '*Seig*'...

The next shot from Larion's Tokarev pistol struck Gersdorff in the middle of his temple and his nude body crumpled to the ground. He did not have a chance to complete his final salute.

*****

After Galkovskiy's partisans collected as much material and armament that they could reasonably carry, the decision was made to retreat to the next proximate forest that was even larger in area than the one which housed their current camp.

"We must leave now, for the other *SS* and *Einsatzgruppen* troops will have realized that Gersdorff's plan failed," Galkovskiy explained to his remaining partisans. "We do not even have the time to bury our own dead. That shall have to wait for another day. Fortunately for us, all of the transports were congregated in this spot, so I want each engine to be incapacitated to the extent that they will have to be replaced before they become operational. That should give us sufficient time to get away safely, but after this night, the *SS* and the *Einsatzgruppen* shall exact a heavy reprisal action against the citizens of Xhotimsk.

"Gregory, I want to thank you for the opportunity to avenge my father-in-law's execution," Larion spoke emotionally as his body began to tremble before he was able to will it into submission. "But now I must go back to my wife and my son."

"Go, my dear friend, but perhaps fate shall will it that we shall meet again sometime…somewhere," Galkovskiy replied, his baritone voice vibrating with emotion.

Irina came up to Larion and gently whispered into his ear, "Go, dear friend. Go! Go to your wife and to your son."

Then she kissed him tenderly on his cheek and she could taste the salt of his perspiration and his tears.

Chapter 32

It took Larion two weeks before he was able to return to the *kolkhoz* so that he would be able to see his wife and son again. The successful partisan action resulted in increased *SS* and *Einsatzgruppen* patrols searching for partisans. That meant that he had to take additional precautions, which translated into a cautious journey home. However, as he approached the Shanin residence, he noticed that there were lights on in the home though it was past ten o'clock in the evening.

He proceeded up the steps to the front door and attempted to listen and determine if there was anyone visiting Tamara, but he could not hear any voices. Cautiously, he knocked on the front door three times and in a quiet voice called out to Tamara, but there was no response. Finding the front door unlocked, he opened it cautiously and quietly entered the front room, holding his rifle in his right hand.

"Tamara! Tamara!" Larion whispered. "It is me. Are you here?"

Tamara slowly opened the bedroom door and peered out, holding her father's ancient heavy pistol in both hands. She slowly opened the door and pointed the pistol at the stranger who had entered her home.

"Put up your hands or I shall shoot you!" she said with a nervous voice.

"Tamara!" Larion replied softly. "It is me. Larion. I really would prefer that you do not shoot me. If not for my benefit, then for yours, because I am reasonably confident that the relic you are holding will probably blow up and then you might kill us both."

Tamara dropped her right hand and lowered the pistol. Though she had not recognized Larion at first sight because of the condition of his facial appearance and his clothes, she finally recognized his voice. She placed the pistol on the kitchen table and rushed into his arms.

"I have to confess that I have not had the opportunity to either wash or shave since I left you two weeks ago," Larion confessed. "And I find it difficult to believe that you would embrace me so passionately when I am so obviously odious."

Tamara continued to cling to him tightly.

"Well, now that you mention it, you definitely do not smell as sweet as the first time we danced together so long ago. I believe you told me that your mother shared her homemade lotion to make you more appealing," Tamara responded laughingly, so grateful that he had returned home to her again.

"Quickly, get out of these filthy clothes while I boil some water for you so that you can wash and shave. I am not looking forward to making love to you while you scratch my face with your bristles."

Larion commenced to undress while Tamara put a pot of water on the stove to bring it to a boil. Her intention was to mix the boiling water with some cold water to ensure that Larion had enough hot water to shave and warm water to wash with.

"And why are you still up so late? Is Dimitri feeling unwell?" Larion asked as he shed his soiled clothes which Tamara immediately placed outside on the front porch because the stench of a couple of weeks' accumulated stale perspiration was gradually overwhelming even her reserves.

"Your young son is fine and sleeping peacefully in the bedroom. However, he was not willing to go to sleep at his usual time this evening, so I decided to serenade him with some of the songs my father used to sing to me when I was a young girl after my mother died. I am not sure though, if my songs lulled him to sleep or if he went to sleep because of total exhaustion. Why don't you look in on him while I wait until your water comes to a boil?"

Larion went to their bedroom which they still shared with their son. Little Dimitri was laying on his back, his head turned to his left, sleeping serenely in the cradle his grandfather had built for him. It was obvious that he was outgrowing it quickly and Larion would have to build a bigger replacement fairly soon. He was amazed at how quickly his son was maturing. Soon he would be not only walking, but talking and asking endless, inquisitive questions about the world around him.

On the one hand, Larion was eagerly looking forward to trying to answer those queries, but on the other hand, how could anyone explain the war to an innocent child.

After washing himself thoroughly in the warm water which Tamara had placed in a basin, he then proceeded to shave for the first time in two weeks with the scalding hot water she had reserved for that special purpose. Then they retired to their bedroom and made love tenderly to each other, restraining their mutual exuberance in the fear that they might awaken their son.

*****

Tamara commenced to question Larion on the events which had transpired over the preceding two weeks. Though Larion attempted to provide just the basic facts, Tamara kept pestering him for further details until there was nothing further to be said.

"I am ashamed to confess that I am not displeased with how you exacted revenge against Gersdorff for executing my father," Tamara spoke guiltily. "Perhaps that is not the most accurate way to describe my true feelings…it is not that I am not displeased, it would be more correct to say that I am satisfied that my father's death has been duly avenged. He was a good man and he did not deserve to die in that fashion, but I still feel ashamed for feeling the way I do. My father read the entire Bible a couple of times and he said that the moral teachings it contained were proper and correct. For example, that we should do onto others as we would have them do onto us. That is such a simple statement, but it carries such profound common sense."

"I have to admit, Tamara, that in hindsight I also feel some guilt and shame for what I had done, however, at the time it did seem right and appropriate to me. I have been forced to kill on many occasions since this war has commenced, but it was always because you either kill or be killed. This was different. I did not have to kill Gersdorff because my life was in jeopardy, but I felt that I had to kill him because of the manner in which he executed your father.

"Killing your father was not enough. Gersdorff had to humiliate him and all of the other innocents he had killed that day. That is why I decided that he should also feel that kind of humiliation before he died. Now I have to admit that perhaps I should not have lowered myself to his level. Perhaps there is just no God and he is just a myth which our parents and the church have taught us to believe in."

"No, Larion. Please do not say that," Tamara implored. "My father was a communist, but he still believed in the teachings of the Bible. He believed that the two could be reconciled."

"Alright, we shall save this discussion for another day," Larion replied gently. He did not want his comments to disturb her sleep. "Close your eyes, my love, and dream about how you want our lives to be like in the future."

"Kiss me and hold me tightly and I shall dream that dream," Tamara replied slowly, as she drifted off to sleep.

*****

Subsequent to Gersdorff's debacle at Xhotimsk, *Oberst* Schalburg received orders to report and take command at Xhotimsk and rectify the situation on a forthwith basis.

Schalburg had served in the Imperial Germany army as an eighteen-year-old cadet in the last year of that war. Subsequently, he had enlisted as an *Oberleutnant* (first lieutenant) in the Weimar Republic's *Wehrmacht,* which subsequently became Nazi Germany's *Wehrmacht* after 1933. Because of his *'Aryan'* appearance: tall, blond hair, blue eyes and an arrogant aquiline nose, Himmler had selected him to apply to join the *SS* since his physical appearance exemplified Himmler's perception of 'Aryan' perfection. Inasmuch as Schalburg did not believe that he was in a position to refuse the *Reich Fuhrer SS,* he acceded to that direction and he was quickly promoted through the ranks to his current position as *Oberst SS* (colonel).

However, some of his superiors began to question his committed adherence to *SS* dogma. Rumors commenced to circulate that his adherence was more 'in form', rather than 'in substance' and just as quickly as he had been elevated within the *SS*, his ascent was just as quickly halted. Now that he was approaching his mid-forties, he felt that his career was at a standstill.

Schalburg was undeniably a competent commander who had repeatedly demonstrated his bravery in battle, however, the shadow over his *SS* orthodoxy had relegated him to mere administrative duties behind the front lines. He knew that if he failed to live up to his superiors' expectations in respect of his current assignment, his future in the *SS* and the *Wehrmacht* was in extreme jeopardy.

Schalburg held no personal animosity towards either the Jews or the Slavs, but he was a soldier and soldiers follow orders. He personally felt that the bulk of *SS* dogma relating to ethnic superiority and need for ethnic cleansing was fallacious at best and that it was a needless distraction from winning the war against Stalin's Soviet Russia.

He personally believed that Hitler and Himmler were more preoccupied with ethnic cleansing in exterminating the Jews, Slavs and other undesirables, than they were in winning the war, itself. Schalburg felt that it was just a waste of resources and manpower. Most importantly, it was an unnecessary distraction from what should have been Germany's primary goal—victory over Communist Russia.

He, however, was not prepared to make a moral judgment on the propriety of those Nazi policy objectives. He merely considered himself a soldier who fulfilled his assigned duties and followed orders. He had tried to offer his sincere advice and recommendations to his superiors previously and on all of those occasions his advice was consistently rebuffed. Some even considered him to be delusional to hold such distasteful contrary notions.

He also recognized that his current position was delicate, at best and definitely uncertain, at worst. Though he did not believe that implementing a policy of ever-increasing ferocity of reprisals ('collective actions' as the *SS* preferred to call them) against the civilian population was either necessary or effective, his superiors believed to the contrary. He believed that reprisals only tended to harden the resolve of the civilian population to continue to oppose Germany's occupation and rule.

However, his immediate concern was to correct Gersdorff's failures and shortcomings, and he knew that his *SS* superiors would have their collective eyes on what he was about to do or not do. After arriving at Xhotimsk by plane at the small rural grass field which acted as their airport runway, he concluded that he had no option but to act quickly and viciously. It was obvious that his superiors had mistaken his practical logic for weakness. Schalburg did not consider himself to be weak.

*****

"*Sturmbannfuhrer* Kampfe, the following are our immediate priorities," Schalburg announced formally to his adjutant. "Firstly, I want you to direct the *Einsatzgruppen Kommandos* and their auxiliaries to round up two hundred citizens and march them to the location where Gersdorff and his soldiers were killed. I also want them to round up at least another one hundred citizens who are to witness their mass execution. It will be convenient to have this second group to bury those bodies afterwards as well."

"*Jawohl, herr Oberst Schalburg*!" Major Kampfe replied, clicking his heels in affirmation.

"Secondly, Gersdorff has been consistently short on fulfilling his quota of foreign workers for our dear Reich Minister for Armaments and War Production. After the execution is completed, I want the *Einsatzgruppen* to arrange for the transport of that second hundred back to Germany to fulfill Gersdorff's current quota shortfall.

"Reich Minister Speer has decided to prioritize tank production and he is in dire need of additional manpower. We must fulfill our quota without delay. Having these hundred witnesses, the executions should make them more compliant and submissive for they should realize that either they obey the Reich or they will die.

"However, if our esteemed Reich Minister did not force the workers to work ten to twelve hours a day, seven days a week and if he afforded them better rations, his ceaseless need for additional replacement workers would not be so dire. However, I am obliged to accede to my superiors' general attitude that these foreign workers are disposable and replaceable. It is not for me or for you to second guess them."

"Consider it done, *Herr Oberst* Schalburg!"

"Finally, we have to deal with these partisans, Kampfe," Schalburg concluded. "I want you to give this last issue considerable thought and provide me with some alternative proposals, but this can wait until after the first two matters have been duly fulfilled."

"*Jawohl, Herr Oberst* Schalburg!" Kampfe replied for the last time, clicking his heels in affirmation of his receipt of his orders. He then spun around and strode quickly out of Schalburg's office to implement his orders without further delay.

Chapter 33

Mogilev, the capital city of the Mogilev oblast (province) in eastern Belarus, had a population of about one hundred thousand people prior to the outbreak of the Second World War, of which sixteen thousand were Jews. It was located approximately two hundred and fifty kilometers west of Xhotimsk. The Romanov's had built their 'Summer Palace' in the city on the bluff overlooking the Dnieper river valley. Nicholas II also made it his headquarters after he assumed responsibility for directing the First World War against Germany and Austria-Hungary. Minsk, the capital of Belarus, was located a further two hundred and fifty kilometers to the west of Mogilev.

SS Obergruppenfuhrer (senior group leader) Erich von Zelewski set up his headquarters in Mogilev and he was the senior SS commanding officer for the Mogilev oblast after the Wehrmacht occupied the city after a three-week siege in July of 1941. The Soviet army was only able to recover the city on 28 June 1944. It was subsequently used a prisoner of war camp for Wehrmacht prisoners who were forced to help rebuild the city.

Though von Zelewski was primarily responsible for murdering the entire Belarussian Jewish population and for brutally suppressing the Warsaw Uprising in October of 1944, he was never convicted of any war crimes. He was convicted of a couple of murders of fellow Nazis during the pre-war struggle between the 'Brown Shirts' of the SA and the 'Black Shirts' of the SS, for which he served a few years in prison after the Nuremburg trials, which ended in the fall of 1946.

His orders to the Jewish population of Mogilev to collect their belongings and travel to the city center for resettlement, were generally followed willingly by the optimistic Jews who showed up with their meagre belongings carefully tied up in bed sheets which they carried over their shoulders. They remained hopeful that the Nazi representations were true. In fact, it was just a pretext to initially ghettoize the Jews of the city and then proceed with their systematic extermination.

Einstazkommand 8, part of Einsatzgruppen B, claimed responsibility for executing over 45000 Jews in Mogilev by June of 1944, when the Soviet Russians were able to retake the city.

However, Hitler's blitzkrieg had begun to sputter out by 20 April 1942, when the Soviet army was able to halt the siege on Moscow and commence to drive the Nazi Wehrmacht back. The siege of Stalingrad was lifted on 2 February 1943, and finally, the siege of Leningrad was lifted on 27 January 1944. By the end of 1943, the 'blitzkrieg' had become a 'zeitlupen ruckzug' (slowmotion retreat).

Chapter 34

Larion wanted to maintain a low profile on the *kolkhoz* for a couple of days, but the shortage of manpower on the collective farm made that impossible. The workers attempted to carry out their respective tasks as best they could, but they lacked coordinated direction. Consequently, Larion was obliged to provide whatever leadership he was able to give to the remaining workers. Tamara assisted in the management of the dairy, but the land holdings were vast and varied.

Larion quickly realized exactly how complicated running a large collective farm actually was. Not only had the work force diminished by about seventy people, most of the remaining men were very elderly and were simply not capable of performing the more strenuous physical work by themselves. Fortunately, they realized that though they could not do everything themselves, working together they were able to succeed in most tasks.

In any case, the food production continued to diminish while the local *SS's* demands for meat, grain and vegetables continued to increase. The fact that Gersdorff had executed twenty of them did not make management of the farm any easier. Larion sensed that a lot of the workers may have been deliberately decreasing the food production in retaliation for that reprisal action.

*****

"Louyna, could you take me into town today?" Tamara asked. "It is little Dimitri's regular appointment with Dr. Gerasimov."

"Of course," Larion replied, handing his son to his wife as he stood up. "I will hitch up the old mare to the wagon and if we travel slowly, she should be able to make it to town and back."

*****

As they entered Xhotimsk, Larion noticed that the *SS* and the *Einsatzkommandos* seemed to be making elaborate preparations for some kind of action, but he tried to avoid all eye contact as he drove by them. Tamara simply held her son even tighter as if one of them might decide to pull Dimitri out of her arms. As they approached Dr. Gerasimov's office, they noticed that he was standing on his porch, watching the military activity.

"Tamara, Larion Daneelivich," he greeted them kindly. "Please come in, it is much cooler inside. And how is that beautiful son of yours?"

After they entered the doctor's office, he offered them some black tea which he sweetened with some honey and added a small slice of lemon. Larion was tempted to ask how he came into possession of such precious commodities, but he had learned that sometimes it was better not to know. However, though the doctor was elderly and frail in appearance, his mind was still perceptive and he noticed Larion's unspoken curiosity in respect of the honey and the small lemon slices.

"Larion, I have a friend who keeps a couple of beehives in the forest and he provides me with a jar of honey from time to time. His friend has an apple tree in his backyard, but he also tried to nurture a miniature lemon tree in his home from a seed and he succeeded. He keeps it adequately exposed to the sunlight and kept warm through our cold winters. They provide me with the honey and the lemon, and I reciprocate by providing them with some modest medical services in return."

"I admit I was curious, Dr. Gerasimov," Larion confessed. "But I thought it would be rude to inquire."

"I remember your mother and father well, Larion. They were good people, but we seem to have lost a lot of good people since these troubles have arisen once again. Your parents were both educated and well mannered, and it is obvious that they passed those characteristics on to their son."

"Dr. Gerasimov," Tamara interjected. "Dimitri seems to be in good health, but lately he does not want to go to sleep at the proper time. I literally have to sing to him for half an hour before he finally surrenders and decides to doze off."

"Let me see your young son, Tamara," the elderly doctor requested politely as he reached for Dimitri with arms which seemed to be trembling in unison. "My, but he is growing quickly. It must be that Cossack blood that he inherited from his handsome father."

Larion noticed that the doctor's overall physical condition was gaunt. His arms were thin and his fingers were long and slender, like those of a musician. Perhaps a violinist or a pianist, but he seemed to possess an inner strength. He lifted Dimitri up effortlessly and then the old man and the young boy stared at each other, exchanging cheerful smiles.

"You must be feeding your son very well, Tamara. I swear that I will not be able to pick him up in a few months," Dr. Gerasimov observed quite proudly and then he addressed Dimitri personally. "Well, young man, allow me to examine you."

The examination appeared to be quite thorough to Larion. He checked his lungs and his heart with an ancient stethoscope. He held two fingers over his wrist to check his pulse. He pried a small, thin wooden spoon in Dimitri's mouth to examine his throat. After approximately fifteen minutes, the doctor pronounced Dimitri Larionovich Sulupin to be in excellent health.

"Thank you, Dr. Gerasimov," Tamara replied.

"And do not worry about him preferring to stay up a bit longer on occasion. You have a very healthy young boy. I assure you that there is no need for you to worry about anything."

Tamara had brought in a small parcel which was wrapped in a white linen towel.

"Please accept this small gift. I baked a loaf of rye bread for you and there is also some cheese and butter. And I was even able to borrow a couple of eggs as well. I am sure that the chickens will not miss them. Unfortunately, the *SS* have confiscated most of our meat, but Larion wants to butcher an old sow and once I make some preserves, I will have Larion bring you some.

"You are much too generous, Tamara, but I shall gratefully accept your gifts."

"Dr. Gerasimov, we noticed a lot of activity with the *SS* and *Einsatzkommandos* as we drove by the police headquarters. Are you aware of what they may be up to?" Larion inquired politely as he looked out the window and observed a procession of a number of military transports passing by the doctor's home.

"Whenever they are busy like that, it usually means that they are up to no good, Larion," the old doctor replied solemnly. "It seems that Gersdorff has been replaced by a colonel who has been sent down from Mogilev to straighten matters out. I understand that the colonel has been ordered to take appropriate 'collective action' in reprisal for the partisan attack which killed Gersdorff and his subordinate officers and men. The Nazi reprisals seem to be getting more vicious all the time, so I expect that a lot of our citizens shall be dying in the next day or two in repayment. I believe that the *SS* and the *Einsatzkommandos* are going out to round up their victims."

Larion remained silent. There was nothing that he could say. It was just one vicious cycle that seemed to have no end. The Nazis would punish the civilians as a reprisal for any partisan attack on their forces. The partisans would then retaliate against the Nazis, who would then carry out a further reprisal against other civilians.

"But this colonel…I think they address him as *Herr Oberst Schalburg*. He is much smarter than Gersdorff and I believe that he is up to something very dramatic. I do not know if you are aware of it or not, but Hitler has failed to take Moscow and then there was a great tank battle at Kursk and Stalin's forces were successful. The Nazi armies are commencing to retreat, but they are still laying siege against Stalingrad and Leningrad…but I sense that the tide of this war is starting to turn in our favor, though a lot of people shall still continue to die on both sides for a while longer."

"And how would an old doctor in a small town on the Russian border come to know such things?" Larion asked inquisitively.

"You have to keep your ears open and your mouth shut when other people are talking," Dr. Gerasimov replied with a sly smile. "Did you know that I was fortunate enough to take some advanced medical training in Germany…but that was before the Nazis came to power in 1933…but my listening vocabulary in German is pretty proficient, though I do not speak it well at all. So you hear things…and you think and then you are able to come to some conclusions, Larion. It is not that difficult, my son."

"Well, that is good news, Doctor," Larion replied. "But be careful, you are not the only one who is probably listening and watching and thinking. Some of our own people would be prepared to betray you for fifty grams of salt and pepper."

"I am just a helpless old former alcoholic doctor…but I am not as stupid as some of these Germans and even some of my fellow comrade citizens may think. I have also heard something else, but I would like to confirm it before I share it with you. By the way, how did you enjoy the *Frunze Military Academy* in Moscow?"

Larion smiled at the old man, who maintained his own inquisitive sly smile in silent reply.

"So, you have not forgotten that I was fortunate to attend the Academy?"

"No, my young First Lieutenant, I have not forgotten too much. I have not forgotten what happened to your parents and how your father-in-law and the chief of police were able to get you out of Belarus to safety. I have not forgotten how the Kertenskys' useless son drowned in the river or how his parents were subsequently slain at the *kolkhoz* by partisans for being informers. I also remember that two *SS* troopers were slain on the *kolkhoz* as well which resulted in Tamara's father being executed. But the partisan attack on Gersdorff was something special. That kind of attack would require special military training and experience. It will be deserving of a vile reprisal by Schalburg's *SS* and *Einsatzkommandos*."

What Dr. Gerasimov had stated and what he implied were equally significant and important. Larion sensed that he was telling him that he believed that Larion may have been involved in some, if not all of those matters. But he was also suggesting that he may have some important information that Larion may be able to pass on to the partisans. Information which may have to do with a possible reprisal action by the newly assigned *SS* colonel.

"Sometimes timing in these kinds of matters is very critical, my old friend," Larion replied somewhat ambiguously.

"Never fear, Larion," Dr. Gerasimov replied. "If the information materializes, I will find a way to get it to you as swiftly as possible."

"If you two conspirators are finished for now," Tamara interjected civilly. "Perhaps it is time for us to return to the *kolkhoz* and permit Dr. Gerasimov to return to his medical practice."

*****

Sturmbannfuhrer Kampfe had no difficulty with advising the *Einsatzkommandos* of *Oberst* Schalburg's initial instruction that there was to be a collective action against two hundred citizens of the town. Rounding up a further one hundred was not going to be a serious issue either; however, transporting three hundred people to the northern edge of the forest where Gersdorff was killed was another matter. Kampfe had to arrange for sufficient transportation and it was simply not available. He had also given considerable thought to the final matter which pertained to eradicating that last partisan company and he believed that he had come up with a possible solution. He was confident that if he presented his proposals to Schalburg effectively, both of the issues would be resolved.

*****

"*Herr Oberst Schalburg*," Kampfe addressed his commanding colonel formally as he entered his office, but then he stood at attention, waiting for permission to speak.

"*Kampfe*, don't just keep standing there keeping me in suspense," Schalburg addressed him impatiently. "Out with it, man. What do you have to tell me?"

"Firstly, *Herr Oberst*, we have a problem with a transport shortage. Considering the transports which Gersdorff succeeded in losing, I am only able to muster enough trucks to transport two hundred civilians and a small company of twenty *Einsatzkommandos*. If you are not willing to reduce the reprisal group to one hundred, then we will have to march the three hundred civilians to the execution point, but that will require at least fifty additional *kommandos* and *auxiliaries*."

Schalburg did not bother to respond immediately to this news. He was considering whether his superiors in Mogilev would be sufficiently impressed with a mass execution of just one hundred, as opposed to two hundred. He was confident that higher numbers mattered.

"Kampfe, do you think my superiors would be more impressed if the reprisal involved two hundred civilians or do you think they would be more impressed with a paltry one hundred civilians? After all, they stripped an SS Major and then executed him. They also killed two other officers and about a couple of dozen or so SS troops. So, my response to your proposal is a definite NO! The reprisal has to involve at least two hundred civilians."

"Very well, *Herr Oberst,* but I believe that I have come up with a possible alternate plan which may solve both of your pressing issues, the reprisal and the annihilation of the partisans. We can even use our transport shortage to give us more credibility in respect of my plan to lure the partisans to come to us."

Schalburg did not bother to respond, but his interest was piqued. He merely glanced up at Kampfe, who was still standing at attention before his desk, and indicated with a nod that he should proceed with his proposal.

"Gersdorff located the partisans in that particular forest and his plan was simply to direct an intensive mortar barrage to the center of the forest to drive the partisans out into the direct line of fire of his machine gun batteries which surrounded the forest. Obviously, the partisans became aware of the deployment of the armament and troops, and they attacked him at his most vulnerable position. They attacked at the point where the mortars were deployed, instead of being herded into the direct fire of the machine gun batteries."

"We can both agree that is what probably happened, so we cannot attempt the same scheme a second time. Furthermore, since it did not work the first time, it would probably fail again," Schalburg replied, his disappointment in his adjutant was becoming increasingly evident.

"I agree, *Herr Oberst*! They tried to force them out of the forest and it did not work, but I suggest that this time we attempt to lure them out!" Kampfe responded ambiguously.

"And how do you propose we attempt to lure them out? Offer them vodka or whores or both?"

"Here is how I believe we can lure them out."

"At ease, Kampfe, and be seated. You are finally starting to interest me," Schalburg replied.

"Since we only have transports to convey two hundred civilians, I suggest that you effect your desired reprisal action against the two hundred civilians, but in two separate slices. We take out two hundred and we have the *Einsatzkommandos* proceed to execute one hundred, with the remaining hundred witnessing it. You then make an announcement that a second hundred shall be executed because of *von Zeleski's* outrage at the partisans' execution of three SS officers and the other *SS* troops and the same hundred shall have to witness it again.

"However, instead of transporting a second one hundred civilians for execution, those additional transports shall be filled with one hundred *SS* troops and *Einsatzkommandos* and auxiliaries armed with machine pistols. We should also be able to have fifty-millimeter machine guns positioned in each transport as well. The partisans will be forced to take action against us in retribution for

218

the execution of the first hundred civilians and they will be forced attempt to save the second hundred at the same time.

"The lure, *Mien Herr Oberst*, shall be the second hundred civilians. Once the partisans attack, our superior numbers and armament should carry the day. The one hundred witnesses will then be transported to Germany to fill Gersdorff's foreign worker shortfall and then we can proceed to execute the second hundred civilians."

Schalburg did not reply immediately because he was reviewing the proposal in his mind. Finally, he rose and slapped Kampfe on his shoulder as a sign of congratulations. "*Wunder voll!* (Wonderful) *Ausgezeichnet!* (Excellent)" Schalburg shouted as he jumped up. "I believe it will work!"

Chapter 35

Larion learned about the *SS* reprisal a day later. One hundred citizens, comprised of men, women, and even children, had been executed at the same spot where he and his partisans had executed Gersdorff and his fifty men a few weeks earlier. Though he was saddened at the news of the death of those one hundred innocents, he found himself hardened to the reality that he knew that someone was going to have to pay for what he and the other partisans had done. And he knew that fact when he had executed Gersdorff that day.

He was equally positive that Galkovskiy would proceed to reciprocate with another attack to avenge those who had been executed by Schalburg. However, before that inevitable response occurred, only to be followed by a further more horrendous reprisal, there may be a brief tranquil respite from the ongoing bloodshed. But Larion was also aware of the fact that Schalburg had announced at the end of that execution that it was only a first installment and it was going to be followed by the execution of a further one hundred people.

His announcement had been disseminated quickly throughout the town by the hundred witnesses. The citizens were living in dire fear that fate may select them for the second mass execution, however, that uncertainty, coupled with the unknown timing of the promised second execution, was starting to have the desired effect of alienating some of the civilian population against the partisans.

*****

Tamara was just preparing to serve a hearty potato soup for lunch when they heard an anxious knocking at their front door. Larion rose to answer it while Tamara looked on apprehensively. A young boy in his early teens stood anxiously in the doorway as Larion inquired who he was and what did he want?

"I am Andre….Dr. Gerasimov is my *dzedushka* (grandfather) and I have memorized a message which I am supposed to only pass on to Larion Daneelivich Sulupin," he spoke breathlessly.

"I am Larion Daneelivich," Larion replied calmly. "Please come in. You look as if you ran all the way from the town. Come in quickly and sit down. Tamara was about to serve lunch and you are more than welcome to share."

"I could use a glass of cool water," the boy replied. "I could not run all of the way…but I tried to run most of the way. My grandfather told me it was important that I get this message to you as quickly as possible. I ran as much as I could."

"Here is a glass of cool water, young man," Tamara spoke consolingly. "Once you have given your message to my husband, I insist that you have a bowl of soup and some rye bread. You are also welcome to have a glass of milk as well."

The young man turned to Larion and he closed his eyes to focus his concentration. Then he commenced to anxiously recite the message which his grandfather made him memorize.

"My *dzedushka* (grandfather) instructed me to tell you as follows:

The colonel intends to carry out the second execution in three days at the same place. This has already been announced in town. The announcement is to draw the partisans out of the forest; however, it shall be a trap. Instead of transporting another one hundred victims, the transports shall be carrying SS and kommandos. When the partisans attempt to rescue the victims, the Nazis shall open fire on them.

"That is what my *dzedushka* instructed me to tell you. I think I better repeat it again in case I forgot something."

Larion and Tamara listened carefully as the young boy closed his eyes and repeated the message exactly the same.

"You have done well, young man," Larion replied. "Your grandfather should be very proud of you. Your message is very important and delivering it to me was very dangerous, so you are a very brave young man. Now, I want you to rest and eat, and when you return to the town, I do not want you to run because it may attract attention. Some other people may want to ask you why you are in such a hurry and your grandfather's message is a very important secret. Only your grandfather, you, and I should know of it. Do you understand?"

The young man looked at Larion seriously. Though he did not fully understand the significance of the message, he understood that it was to remain a secret.

"And in the event you are stopped on your way back to town, you should have a reason for coming out to the *kolkhoz* in the first place," Tamara spoke soothingly to try to reassure the young man. "Your grandfather examined our young son a few days ago, so I am going to send you back with some eggs, cheese, and bread. If anyone stops you and asks you why you came out here, you can just tell them that you came to pick up the payment for your grandfather's services. But the less you say, the better."

"I think I understand. Because this is our secret. We have to fool other people so that they do not discover our secret. Is that correct?" the young boy asked hesitantly.

"That is exactly correct, young man," Larion agreed.

After Dr. Gerasimov's grandson ate and left, Larion looked anxiously at Tamara.

"You know what I have to do now, Tamara," he spoke quietly and reluctantly.

"Yes, I know and I understand, but that does not make it any easier for me to see you leave us once again, my love," Tamara answered sadly. "But I understand that you have to do what you have to do…and little Dimitri and I are obliged to endure it."

Larion embraced her tightly and kissed her forehead lovingly. Tamara kept her head bowed so that he would not be able to see her tears. How she wished that she would be less emotional and more resolute. She believed that the more emotional she became, the more anxious Larion would become, which would only increase his danger. "I have to go to Galkovskiy and warn him. A lot of good people will die if I am not able to pass on Dr. Gerasimov's message in time. The significance of the message is underscored by the fact that the good doctor was prepared to risk the welfare and life of his own grandson. The least I can do is try to warm my friend and comrade-in-arms."

"Louyna…I told you that I understand that you have a duty and an obligation…but that does not mean that I have to like the fact that you are going to place your own life in jeopardy once again.

"But I do not want to say anything to you which you may deem unkind at this time...I just do not want you to worry needlessly about me and little Dimitri. I started to become stronger after witnessing my father's execution and I believe that I am becoming stronger every day. I will look after myself and our son while you are away again...just promise me that you shall return...and I promise you that I shall wait for that moment once again."

"You have always been stronger than you may have thought, my love," Larion answered haltingly. He was so proud of his wife. "And I promise you that I shall return."

*****

It took Larion a full day to locate Galkovskiy and his partisans. Fortunately, they had set up their new camp and remained in the same forest to which they had retreated after the Gersdorff debacle.

"*Privyet, moy brat* (Greetings, my dear brother)," Galkovskiy said. "It is my most sincere, though unexpected pleasure to see you so soon. But I must confess that your presence today probably indicates that you are the bearer of sad news."

Larion embraced his superior officer and comrade-in-arms. He noticed that his silver white mane had grown back, but was neatly trimmed. Galkovskiy noticed Larion's preoccupation with his hair and just laughed.

"It seems that my Irina is a woman of several talents and skills...besides being an excellent sniper," Galkovskiy preened as he ran his right hand through his long silver locks. "It seems that she is more than a competent barber as well. Have I regained my former regal personage when women would throw themselves at my feet and implore me to make love to them?"

"If you persist in fantasizing, my love, I may have to restore that peasant cut you were wearing during our time at the *kolkhoz*," Irina interjected jokingly. "And if I see another woman prostrating herself before you, I may be obliged to shoot her as well."

Irina then turned her attention to Larion.

"And it is an unexpected pleasure to see you again, Larion, and so soon. However, like Gregory, I suspect that your presence here today is more of a harbinger of some dark news?"

Irina, Larion, Galkovskiy, and his two senior aides retired to Galkovskiy's tent where Larion relayed Dr. Gerasimov's portentous message.

"We heard about the execution of the hundred civilians, but it was only after it had already occurred," Galkovskiy explained. "In fact, for the past week we have been considering various reprisal actions of our own and it appears that comrade Stalin has come to appreciate the contributions which the various partisan groups are making to the cause. It appears that the Nazi dream of being able to subjugate Mother Russia was just a delusion in Hitler's twisted mind.

"Our forces have ended the siege of Moscow and there was a tremendous tank battle near the city of Kursk, involving literally thousands of battle tanks on both sides. The casualties and losses were horrendous, as in the Winter War with Finland, which apparently allayed itself with the Nazis when they attacked us on 22 June 1941. A decision which I am sure they come regret someday."

"But to return to comrade Stalin, it seems that he has come to appreciate the contributions the partisans have been able to make in interdicting the Nazis supply lines to the front. Most especially, comrade Stalin has issued directives to the partisans that we are to focus on disrupting their train transports and fuel deliveries."

"It is reassuring to hear that comrade Stalin has had this epiphany, Gregory," Larion replied.

"Perhaps it will mean that we shall be treated honorably at the end of the war, instead of being jailed at hard labor for twenty-five years or shot as traitors and deserters."

"After observing comrade Stalin over the preceding twenty years, the only thing we can be certain of is his 'uncertainty'," Galkovskiy concluded sadly. "But let us turn to the matter at hand, do any of you have any suggestions as to how we should respond?"

"Larion, you should know that as a result of comrade Stalin's change of attitude, his air force has been able to provide us with some radio communication and additional weapons," the older senior aide replied. "This permits us to coordinate and execute our actions more effectively. Our primary directive is to interrupt the Nazis supply lines, especially their rail transport to the front and deny them the opportunity to exploit the Motherland's existing resources, thereby making the Nazis even more dependent upon being supplied from Germany. This has become really imperative since there are signs that their *blitzkrieg* has stalled and that their retreat is eminent."

"I assume that you were able to scavenge some heavier weapons from Gersdorff's men? Is that correct?" Larion asked hopefully.

"You are correct, but they are heavy and difficult to transport," Galkovskiy replied. "We were able to obtain two functional *MG-42 Mauser* 57 mm machine guns and their tripods. However, they fire about 1200 rounds a minute. So, though the machine gun is not that heavy, the required ammunition is extremely heavy considering how quickly it is used up. Their muzzle velocity is about 800 meters per second, but at the distance of about 100 meters, they can literally shred the enemy and their transports—that is until the ammunition runs out."

"Were you able to scavenge any of Gersdorff's mortars and mortar shells?" Larion asked. "How do they compare?"

"We have six operational *Granatwerfer 34* mortars. Each one weighs almost sixty kilos and the mortar rounds weigh about 3.5 kilos each," Gresha, Galkovskiy's younger senior aide, replied. "We should be able to fire up to ten mortars a minute, if we practice."

"When I was a student at the Academy, one of our non-commissioned instructors kept recommending that we keep an open mind and try to adapt to a changing situation," Larion replied. "He kept stressing that a changing situation demands an altered response, because the traditional response may no longer be viable most of the time. Can those mortars be fired horizontally?"

"They are capable of being fired in the transverse position at a minimum elevation of ten degrees with an effective range of about four hundred meters," the senior aide replied.

"So what are you suggesting, Larion?" Galkovskiy asked.

"The *SS* and *Einsatzkommandos* are going to be heavily armed because they will be able to transport their machine guns and ammunition by truck transport. We, on the other hand, shall be obliged to carry those machine guns, mortars and ammunition over open ground and we have to be in place within the next day and a half, or we shall be out of time."

"However, if we can synchronize the use of the machine guns and utilize the mortars in the transverse position, we may be able to neutralize the Nazi advantage. We will not be able to surprise them this time because they shall be expecting us to attack. Our only element of surprise is how we will attack them," Larion replied. "I do not think they will not expect us to attack them from the field with horizontal mortar fire."

"Considering the time we have and the distance we have to transport our heavy armament, the problem I see is that we will only be able to transport sufficient ammunition for the two machine guns and the mortars for approximately two to three minutes, maximum," Galkovskiy replied. "Furthermore, if we are going to position the two machine guns in the forest and perhaps four mortars in the field, we have to ensure that we do not end up firing on ourselves. But go on, my young friend," Galkovskiy implored Larion. "Just what have you dreamed up in that fertile mind of yours?"

"Once the Nazis are in position, they will expect us to attack from the forest. I would recommend that we commence our attack by the mortars being aimed at the transport vehicles from the field. Four mortars should be sufficient if we can fire them at a minimum of six rounds per minute, since we would have to ensure that they remain aligned appropriately after each round.

"The Nazis will have to be shocked to suffer a mortar barrage from an open field. If we are lucky and some of those mortars strike their transports, the advantage shall be ours. Once they focus on the mortar fire from the field, you can open up with the two Mauser machine guns. If you are able to transport sufficient ammunition for even two or three minutes, that should be sufficient to distract them from the mortars. In the interim, the remaining partisans should be able to pick off the disoriented *SS* and *Einsatzkommandos* exiting the transports at will."

Galkovskiy and his two senior aides conferred briefly and agreed that the proposed plan was feasible, though synchronization of the utilization of the mortars and the machine guns was critical to the plan's success. Galkovskiy then instructed his two senior aides accordingly.

"I suggest that we immediately direct some of our men to commence the transport of the two *Mauser MG 42* machine guns, four mortars and sufficient ammunition," Galkovskiy concluded. "We will position the Mausers appropriately at the edge of the forest where we had attacked Gersdorff. Secondly, we position and camouflage the mortars in the field at approximately at one hundred meters. from the target site. We have to ensure that the mortars and the machine guns shall be firing at an angle away from each other.

"If we can hit some of those transports with some mortar rounds, the *SS* and *Einsatzkommandos* will scramble out of the back of those transports and then we will open up on them with our heavy machine guns from the forest and the remaining transports. The bulk of our partisans will be in the forest as well, armed with machine pistols and rifles. We should be able to not only surprise them, but annihilate them as we had done with Gersdorff's men."

The five companions remained quiet for a moment. Each one was reviewing the proposed plan of attack and it seemed to be sound, but they all knew that unexpected events would probably arise in any case.

"Ivan," Galkovskiy addressed the younger senior aide, "select ten men and proceed to have them transport the Mausers and the ammunition to the forest. I am counting on you to make the appropriate decision in respect of positioning both machine guns. Ensure that each position shall be capable of providing supporting fire to the other position in the event the Nazis attempt to overrun one position.

"This is a critical requirement. It is imperative that you position the two machine guns so that each can support the other, otherwise you shall not be optimizing the use of our limited firing power. I expect that we shall only have two minutes to utilize them. In the event we do not take out all of transports, our men shall be on the receiving end of their return machine gun fire."

"Understood, commander," the younger aide replied and immediately stood up and walked away to carry out his orders.

"Gresha," Galkovskiy addressed the older senior aide, "I want you and Larion to test fire a mortar in the horizontal position. I want you to fire a couple of rounds—no more than three at most, to determine what the most appropriate trajectory should be to strike a target at about one hundred yards. I am only giving you a couple of hours because we shall have to commence to transport that armament and still have time to position and camouflage them appropriately. As I said before, we do not want to end up firing the mortars or the machine guns at ourselves."

Larion and Gresha rose up and proceeded to walk away to fulfill their task. Though Larion had come up with the plan, he was not sure if it was really practical. However, the mortars seemed to be the most effective weapon the partisans possessed which would give them the element of surprise over the Nazis.

The logic seemed simple. All you had to do to fire the mortar was to slide the mortar shell down the tube. Four mortars firing a mortar shell every ten seconds would result in a barrage of forty-eight shells in the first two minutes. Two minutes would probably seem like an eternity once the firing started. Then the two Mausers would be able to fire 2400 rounds in the following two minutes.

Though his cursory logic made sense to him, he and Gresha had to test that logic to see if it was possible to affect a successful mortar strike on a transport at one hundred meters when the mortar was aligned in the minimum transverse position of ten degrees.

Irina had remained quiet during the discussion between the four men. Now that she was alone with Galkovskiy, she felt it was an appropriate time to speak up.

"Am I going to be deployed with the other partisans in the forest, Gregory?"

Galkovskiy's pause in replying confirmed Irina's worst fear. He was not going to permit her to participate in this proposed action.

"Gregory! I want to fight with you and…I am prepared to die with you," Irina stated emphatically.

"My love, you shall fight with me and if we die together, so be it," Galkovskiy replied. "But not this time."

"But why?" Irina implored. "We have fought together for almost two years and we have survived. You do not have to protect me."

"I want you to go to Tamara at the *kolkhoz*," Galkovskiy replied, his baritone voice breaking with emotion. "I do not understand why exactly, but that is what I want you to do this time. If everything goes well, I shall join you in a few days. But I am making this an order."

Chapter 36

Galkovskiy and the remaining partisans deployed themselves in the forest between the two machine gun batteries to maximize their combined firing power and provide themselves with the additional defensive support from the two Mausers being positioned on either side.

Galkovskiy had directed that each of the four mortars be manned by three partisans. One was to aim that mortar; one was to arm and load it and the third partisan was to check the line of flight and advise the first partisan of any required correction. Once they ran out of shells, they were to advance on the transports and provide assistance to their fellow partisans who would be firing from the forest. Larion and Gresha were instructed to initiate the mortar barrage since they had the most experience. It was agreed that they would target the last transport. If it was struck, it would hinder the escape of the remaining transports.

The two partisans were pleasantly surprised that firing a mortar in the transverse position was very similar to firing a rifle and at one hundred yards, there was little need for any substantial adjustments. However, once a round was fired, it was imperative to reset the mortar's alignment with the intended target before firing again for the recoil of the mortar shell was sufficient to shift its position.

They passed that information on to their somewhat skeptical fellow partisans who would be manning the other three mortar batteries

*****

Schalburg rode in the front passenger seat of a half-track armored carrier nicknamed the '*Hanomag*'. It had light-angled armor on all sides which was an adequate defense against standard rifle and machine gun fire. It had a two-man crew: a driver and a gunner who manned a *MG 34* machine gun which was mounted above and behind the driver's compartment. It also accommodated ten additional passengers.

As soon as it stopped, Schalburg exited his passenger seat. Kampfe and nine *SS* troopers exited the passenger compartment. The *SS* troopers were to deploy around the civilians to ensure that they would not try to escape, while the other soldiers would remain hidden.

The half-track led a convoy of ten transport vehicles. The first four transports were crammed with twenty-five civilians each and the remaining six vehicles were crammed with the *SS* soldiers and *Einsatzkommandos*. As luck would have it, Schalburg had the vehicles stop a bit further west of the original Gersdorff location, which enhanced the angles for both the mortars in the field and the two Mauser machine guns positioned in the forest. Both would be firing farther away from each other.

The civilians in the first four transports were ordered to exit their vehicles and assemble in one group in front of Schalburg's vehicle. The people were fearful for they were not sure if they were simply going to be spectators or victims that day. They just followed their orders compliantly, silently resigned to their fate. After Schalburg and Kampfe exited their armored carrier, they positioned themselves so that the armored carrier would shield them from the anticipated partisan rifle fire from the forest.

Once the civilians had exited the first four transports, the four mortar batteries focused on the remaining six transports which remained stationary and inactive.

*****

Larion exhaled slowly and gave Gresha the signal to slide the mortar shell into its tube.

"*Davai, Brati.*" (Let's do it, my brothers)

Almost instantaneously, the rocket roared out of the tube and struck the last transport near its fuel tank which exploded and lifted the front of the transport off the ground. Immediately after Larion's initial mortar shot, the remaining three mortar batteries fired sequentially as well. The roar of the mortar shells coming from the field and the subsequent explosions caught Schalburg and Kampfe by complete surprise.

Once they realized what was happening, they immediately sought shelter on the other side of their armored carrier. Though only two transports were destroyed in the initial barrage, a couple of shells did tear through the tarpaulin canopy on the back of two other transports. Both officers were screaming at their troops to raise the canopies on the remaining transports so that they could return fire.

Shortly after the initial mortar attack on the Nazi transports, the assembled civilians panicked and ran for the safety of the forest since their *SS* guards became preoccupied with the incoming mortar rounds. That was a relief to Galkovskiy, since he wanted to try to minimize collateral casualties.

Just as the four remaining transports commenced their machine gun fire at the mortar batteries in the field, Galkovskiy decided to initiate his two Mauser machine guns. It was imperative that his men provide immediate covering fire from the forest since the Nazis were commencing to fire their machine guns at his mortar positions. As the two Mausers commenced to spit out their 57 mm shells at 1200 rounds per minute, another round of mortars struck the transports which resulted in an additional two direct strikes. In the interim, the Mausers were successful in disabling the remaining two transports carrying the *SS* soldiers and the *Einsatzkommandos*.

As anticipated, both able and injured Nazi troops proceeded to exit or crawl out of the various transports only to be met by a hail of fire from the remaining partisans positioned in the forest. Soon the machine gun and mortar fire ceased. The twelve partisans manning the mortar batteries proceeded to advance in a crouched position towards the transports. The *SS* and *Einsatzkommandos* who succeeded in exiting their transports attempted to use the remnants of their vehicles as cover as they laid down on the ground, exchanging fire with the unseen partisans in the forest and the approaching twelve partisans from the field.

As Larion and the other partisans approached the convoy, he could see that they were exposed and extremely vulnerable. As soon as he saw two of his fellow partisans get hit, including Gresha, he yelled at the remaining partisans to drop down and return fire from a prone position.

Kampfe, realizing that their position was hopeless, re-entered the armored personnel carrier and ordered the driver to leave the battlefield with all haste. Schalburg quickly followed. Some of their *SS* escort also succeeded in re-entering the *Hanomag*. The gunner was firing his Mauser at everyone in sight as he directed his fire from the partisans in the field to the partisans in the forest, including even firing upon his own soldiers who were trapped in between the other two groups.

Galkovskiy watched Schalburg escape with disappointment, but he did not have the means to stop him. He would have loved to have one additional mortar shell to fire at Schalburg's escape vehicle as it left the field of battle.

*****

Kampfe, who was seated in the passenger compartment with another six *SS* soldiers, could hear Schalburg cursing from the front passenger seat. It was understandable. Kampfe's grand plan had become a fiasco because he failed to anticipate the partisan's possible retaliatory response. If only the partisans had reacted as he had predicted, his plan would have been a huge success. Now, just as Schalburg's superiors at Mogilev would hold him personally responsible for the loss of about one hundred soldiers and ten transports, not to mention the escape of the one hundred civilians who were destined to be transported to Germany to fill *Reich* Minister's Speer's foreign worker quota, Schalburg would hold him personally responsible for this debacle as well.

When they returned to their headquarters in town, Schalburg ordered Kampfe to report to him in his private office.

"Kampfe, you idiot!" Schalburg screamed. "Can you explain what just happened and why you permitted it to happen?"

"I sincerely and deeply apologize, *Mien Herr Oberst Schalburg*," Kampfe replied obsequiously. "Their utilization of traverse mortar fire was simply totally unforeseeable. I take full responsibility and I am prepared to accept whatever punishment you may deem fit to meet out."

"Your fucking apology will not restore my lost men or my lost equipment, you fucking idiot!"

Schalburg continued to scream at Kampfe, "Why is it that I am surrounded by such idiocy?" He asked rhetorically, "Those idiots in Mogilev are more preoccupied with their 'ethnic cleansing' than they are in defeating Stalin's communists. They have no fucking idea what is going to happen if Germany loses this war. The Versailles Treaty will seem like a godsend by comparison."

"All I can say is that I sincerely apologize, *Herr Oberst*!" Kampfe replied quietly.

"I should have you taken outside into the courtyard and shot by a firing squad for your insipid idiocy!" Schalburg continued to scream.

Kampfe remained silent. He finally realized that nothing he could say would ameliorate his position to any degree at that moment. He decided that he would let his commanding officer rant and rave until he became exhausted and dismissed him. Kampfe knew that his former special status with Schalburg was irretrievably destroyed and his only option would be to apply for an immediate transfer to another battalion.

He would use Schalburg's defamatory comments about his own superiors in Mogilev to facilitate that transfer and possibly even effect Schalburg's own summary execution for gross insubordination. He would embellish his report by confirming that the rumors about Schalburg's possible pro-Semitic leanings were accurate and true.

Suddenly, Schalburg stopped pacing and withdrew his luger pistol from its holster and pointed it at Kampfe.

"*Herr Sturnbannfuhrer* Kampfe!" Schalburg addressed him formally in a restrained voice. "I am placing you under arrest and ordering your immediate execution by firing squad."

As Kampfe proceeded to protest and requested clarification of his colonel's reasons for the imposition of such a drastic punishment, Schalburg summoned a couple of non-commissioned officers to enter his office and take Kampfe into custody. He ordered them to arrange for his immediate summary execution by a firing squad.

"But what crime have I committed, *Herr Oberst*?" Kampfe pleaded.

"For gross incompetence which has resulted in the death of almost one hundred soldiers, the loss of ten transports, the escape of one hundred foreign workers, and for cowardly behavior in the face of the enemy," Schalburg replied sarcastically. "I believe the foregoing are more than sufficient, but I may add additional grounds in my subsequent formal report. However, your most glaring offence is your unbelievable, arrogant stupidity."

Schalburg turned to the two non-commissioned officers and ordered them to proceed to carry out his orders immediately.

Within fifteen minutes, Kampfe was placed against a cement wall in the courtyard, with his hands tied behind his back and a black blindfold covering his eyes. The non-commissioned officers had arranged for a six-man firing squad who were armed with rifles. Schalburg ordered the *SS* soldiers to aim and fire on his command. As he dropped his right hand, the six rifles angrily spat out their bullets which struck Kampfe simultaneously in his chest. Schalburg then withdrew his pistol and approached Kampfe's lifeless body and discharged a final shot to his lifeless head.

That last shot seemed to satiate his desire for retribution and revenge against a subordinate officer who had placed his career and possibly his own life in supreme jeopardy.

Executing Kampfe also permitted Schalburg to eliminate the most credible opposing witness at his own possible court martial; however, he knew that it was imperative that he complete the reprisal action and fulfill Gersdorff's foreign worker shortfall immediately.

Chapter 37

Within the following week, Schalburg proceeded to have a further two hundred Xhotimsk citizens executed in the courtyard of his headquarters. He was not about to risk another symbolic execution at the site of Gersdorff's assassination. Those victims were mostly male, but included some women and even children who were unfortunate enough to be in the vicinity when the various roundups occurred.

He then ordered other townsmen to transport those corpses to the forest for cremation and burial. His *SS* superiors had initiated these new directives which seemed intended to ensure that evidence of such reprisal atrocities would be minimized and not that easily discovered. Perhaps his superiors were not as stupid as he had assumed and that they, too, were concerned about their own personal consequences if Germany ended up losing the war.

Schalburg had informed *SS Obergrupenfuhrer* von Zeleski in Mogilev of the disaster which had occurred under the command and direction of *Sturn-bannfuhrer* Kampfe and the extreme action he was obliged to take against Kampfe personally, and the remedial 'collective action' he ordered against three hundred civilians.

His formal report did not mention the fact that he was personally present and that he had had ultimate command over that operation. Since there was no conflicting evidence from the remaining *SS* officers and troops in his battalion, his report was accepted at face value for the time being, but only because von Zeleski was becoming preoccupied with the increasing partisan interruption of rail transportation of armament and supplies through Poland and Belarus.

That partisan activity brought von Zeleski under increasing criticism from the Generals and the Field Marshals who were commanding the various divisions and armies on the eastern front. Stalin seemed to be able to replenish losses of men in the hundreds of thousands, as well as destroyed armament and lost material, almost at will.

Hitler, on the other hand, continued to undermine the command of his frontline generals and field marshals by insisting that there be no retreat in the face of overwhelming opposing forces. Nazi Germany's losses of hundreds of thousands of men, such as at the siege of Stalingrad, could not be as easily replaced, but Hitler irrationally held on to his belief of the inevitable invincibility of his *blitzkrieg* and the racial superiority of his Aryan race.

The orders which Schalburg received from von Zeleski had two priorities: firstly, Speer's demands for 'foreign workers' had to be expedited by the increasing shortfall of workers in Germany's armament factories; and secondly, Schalburg was to take whatever measures he deemed appropriate to decrease the partisan's sabotage of Nazi Germany's supply lines to the eastern front.

It was because of those orders from von Zeleski that Schalburg and his *SS* company showed up the Shanin *kolkhoz* the following week. His transport trucks were not filled to capacity and he assumed that he could obtain additional men from the collective farm.

Immediately upon arrival, he ordered that all workers on the collective farm assemble before the manager's residence so that his subordinate officers could select the most suitable workers. Once they were assembled, he was not impressed. Of the men, he was only prepared to accept ten older men who seemed to be in relatively sound physical condition. The one younger man who stood out was Larion.

"You!" Schalburg commanded, pointing to Larion, who was standing beside Tamara and their young son. "Step forward. Why are you not fighting at the front or with the partisans?"

"*Herr Oberst*," Larion replied obediently, "I have a young wife and a young son. Furthermore, my father-in-law was the former manager of this collective farm. After he died, someone had to manage the farm to ensure continued food production. In any case, I was not prepared to fight for Stalin."

"So, you are not a communist or a communist supporter!" Schalburg responded with satisfaction.

"No, sir," Larion replied. "Stalin had my parents arrested for no reason and sent to Siberia. That is why I would not fight for him."

"In that case, you are going to go to Germany to help build Tiger tanks so that we will be able to defeat Stalin and his fellow Semite-communists."

"No!" Tamara cried out in anguish. "You cannot take him away from me and my son. We need him."

"I assure you that the Fatherland needs him even more; however, since you appear to be so dedicated to your husband, you and your son shall accompany him to Germany. I am sure that they will be able to find something suitable for you to do."

Schalburg then proceeded to select a further fifteen women who struck him as sturdy peasant stock who would be able to perform support services for the men which he had selected. He then advised all of the selected 'foreign workers' that they were to travel by truck transport back to town where they would board a train to travel first to the provincial capital at Mogilev, then across Belarus and Poland, and their final destination would be the city of Kassel in central Germany.

He then afforded his new selections fifteen minutes to gather some personal belongings, food, and drink for the road; however, he also advised them that if they did not return within that allotted time, he would order his men to locate them and execute them summarily.

*****

As Larion helped Tamara and little Dimitri board the back of one transport, a thin arm reached out to assist Tamara who was holding her son in her right arm. The arm felt strong and firm, even though it was trembling.

"*Privyet* (hello), my pretty young one," Dr. Gerasimov greeted Tamara politely as he helped her board the back of the transport.

"Dr. Gerasimov, what are you doing here?" Tamara asked in surprise as she happily accepted his assistance. "Surely you are too old to work in the German factories."

"It seems that the commanding colonel decided that a doctor…any kind of doctor…even *a piyanitsa* (drinker) like me may be helpful on our long journey to Germany," the doctor replied with resignation. "So, he suggested that I volunteer."

Larion jumped up into the back of the transport and he was equally surprised to see Dr. Gerasimov with his enigmatic smile.

"Well, at least I shall not be making this journey alone," the doctor observed happily. "I shall have my *drov* (male friend), my beautiful *padroha* (female friend), and their little *malchik* (son) as my travelling companions."

237

At the train station in Xhotimsk, the four companions boarded the train and were fortunate enough to be able to share one small compartment. A large number of their fellow travelers were relegated to sharing cramped livestock cars and baggage cars. As the train commenced to pull out of the station, Larion could see that Dr. Gerasimov looked longingly at the small town where he had lived the bulk of his life. He could also see him silently mouth some words.

"Dr. Gerasimov, if I am not being overly intrusive, can you tell me what you just said?" Larion asked respectfully.

Dr. Gerasimov's eyes were tearful. "I said *das vidaniya* (until we meet again) Xhotimsk. Though I appreciate that I may be overly optimistic in that farewell, but we shall see. It does not hurt to remain hopeful for the best, even in the most trying of times."

As their train headed west, it made several stops along its journey and at each stop, additional 'foreign workers' were crowded on board. Soon Larion, Tamara, with Dimitri sleeping in her arms, and Dr. Gerasimov, were relegated to share one wooden bench in the compartment and the other bench was occupied by three other young males in their mid-twenties. Gradually, the gentle swaying of the carriage car and the rhythmic click of the wheels rolling over the rail-joints induced an uncomfortable sleep in all of the travelers sharing that small compartment.

Suddenly, they were all awakened by screeching steel wheels grinding against the iron rails. The train was braking severely and quickly coming to an unanticipated stop.

As soon as the train came to a complete stop, *Wehrmacht* soldiers started to run up and down the aisles, cursing and exchanging conflicting instructions. An officer opened up the door to their compartment and indicated that Larion and the three new male companions were being ordered out to affect some repairs to the track.

When Larion and the other young men exited their carriage, they were directed under armed guard with several other men to the front of the train. Even in the gloom of the night, faintly illuminated by the engine's faint light, he could see that some rails had been splayed away from their wooden ties. Upon closer inspection, the fasteners had been removed which permitted the rails to be separated from the ties and each other.

Fortunately, the engineer had noticed some anomaly on the track and engaged the brakes so that the train was brought to a safe stop. Had the train not come to a complete stop, the engine would have gone off the rails into a deep ravine, pulling a large number of the following carriages after itself.

The railway workers were obviously experienced in dealing with such emergencies and they immediately took control over effecting the necessary repairs. The *Wehrmacht* guards merely insured that none of the foreign workers would attempt an escape. The repairs themselves required extensive labor to restore the rails to the ties and then to replace fasteners to connect the rails to each other.

The railway workers were Slavs and spoke either Polish, Belorussian, or Ukrainian. They kept cursing the partisans who they held responsible for the attempted sabotage. A couple of the workers did acknowledge that they were fairly fortunate in that the partisans had not used any explosives, which were usually detonated as the engine was passing over the mined area. If that had happened, it would have resulted in a major disaster and the loss of many lives. Gradually, as the repairs were being completed, their attitude focused on their good fortune that no explosives were involved.

When the repairs were finished, Larion and the other three young men rejoined Tamara and Dr. Gerasimov in their passenger compartment. Larion shared their meager rations of bread, cheese, and water. Gradually, everyone returned to a fitful sleep once again.

*****

Larion was the first in the group to awaken. In his exhausted sleep, he felt the train slowing down and then coming to a complete stop just as dawn was breaking to the east. They had arrived at Mogilev. He understood that they would be changing trains, so when the *Wehrmacht* troops ordered everyone to exit the train, it was not a surprise. What was a surprise was the row of gallows which had been set up parallel to the train tracks. What was even more surprising were the eight bodies which were hanging stoically from eight nooses, their respective heads angled awkwardly from their vertical bodies. The

239

commanding officer proceeded to explain that it was an example of how the *Reich* dealt with partisan saboteurs who attempted to sabotage the rail network.

Larion noticed the regal long white hair first and he quickly turned Tamara away from the gruesome sight. He recognized that it was Galkovskiy, and hanging beside him, was Irina. He also noticed that both bodies bore bloodstains, confirming that they had been shot. He cautioned her so that she would not show any sign of recognition of their two good friends.

"Tamara, my love," Larion implored her softly under his breath, "when you look upon those hanging bodies, do not show any sign of recognition or emotion. It appears that Galkovskiy and Irina have finally run out of luck, but they died together. Hopefully, they died before they were hung up for display. Please be strong and do not look up at their faces in case you break down."

As Tamara, Larion, and Dr. Gerasimov were marched past the hanging bodies, Tamara heeded Larion's advice and kept her line of sight low. Though Dimitri was still sleeping, she made sure that his face was buried in her left breast in case he awakened as they were passing by. Though she yearned to look onto the faces of their two good friends one last time, she realized that she may lose control and reveal that Galkovskiy and Irina were known to her.

"*Das vidaniya, brati,*" (Until we meet again, my brothers) Larion addressed his two comrades-in-arms in a hushed voice one final time. Though Irina was a woman, she had fought like a man and he felt no shame in calling her a brother.

*****

There were no travelling compartments or carriages on the new train. It had a powerful engine and an ample supply of coal, but all of the passengers were relegated to closed baggage cars which were devoid of windows; however, open vents in the ceiling afforded a flow of fresh air which lessened the repulsive body odor which permeated the car.

There was a tank of drinking water in the center of the car, with a dangling tin cup which was attached to the tank itself by a metal chain. The water was replenished periodically at the various stops when the train's water supply had to be replenished. There were also four large latrine buckets which were distributed throughout the car. The passengers were also provided with some meager rations which would ensure that they would survive until they reached their next scheduled stop. Those periodic stops also afforded the passengers an opportunity to empty the latrine buckets; however, the smell inside the carriage became increasingly more abhorrent.

However, they had to change trains again once they crossed the Polish border. Their new train did not have any travelling compartments or carriages and it was also devoid of any baggage cars as well. All of the cars were simply livestock cars which reeked of human urine, excrement, and body odor. None of the passengers were aware of the fact that these trains were returning from the various concentration camps which had been mostly designed by *Reich Minister* Speer before he became the Minister of Armaments and War Production. Those camps were being used to systematically exterminate approximately six million Jews and another three million undesirable Slavs, Romanis, and others, who the Nazi ideologues deemed were not fit to live. Finally, their train reached its final destination at the city of Kassel, Germany.

Chapter 38

Kassel was an industrial city with a population of about 236000 in 1939, which was located in central Germany in the state of Hesse, approximately 379 kilometers south of Berlin. The Brothers Grimm lived in Kassel in the early nineteenth century and composed some of their 'Tales' there.

Georg Christian Carl Henschel founded 'Henschel & Son' in 1810 and the company developed into a major manufacturer of locomotives. Early in 1935, it commenced to manufacture Panzer I tanks. After 1939, it began the large-scale production of the Panzer III tanks and became the sole manufacturer of the Tiger I tank. During World War II, it also branched out into the manufacture of a variety of fighter and bomber aircraft, as well as rocket powered missiles and rocket powered glide bombs.

By 1945, Henschel & Sons had about 8000 workers, working in two shifts of twelve hours each, seven days a week. The majority of those workers were 'forced laborers'. Nazi Germany would abduct approximately twelve million people from about twenty European countries, two thirds of whom came from Eastern Europe and approximately 2.8 million were Soviet workers. The 'forced labor' work force comprised twenty per cent of the total Nazi German work force.

The unconditional defeat of Nazi Germany in 1945 confronted the Allies with the repatriation of about eleven million 'forced workers' and 'prisoners of war', who were collectively categorized as 'displaced persons' or pejoratively referred to as 'DP's'.

The foreign workers were categorized in three basic groups. The 'Gastarbeitnehmer' (guest workers) came from Germanic and Scandinavian countries, as well as Nazi Germany's allies. The 'Zwangsarbeiter' (forced workers) included military internees or prisoners of war which totaled about 2 million by 1944.

The second category of 'forced workers' were civilian workers, who primarily came from Poland and totaled a further two million by 1944. They had to live under severe personal restrictions and bear the letter "P" on their clothes to identify them as such. The final category was the 'Ostarbeiter' (eastern workers) who had to bear the letters "OST" on their clothing and they had to live in barracks located in barb wired camps and under armed guard.

Though the Polish 'forced workers' were paid, it was less than one half of what was paid to the 'guest workers'. The 'eastern workers' were not paid at all. Millions of Jews were 'forced workers' before they were shipped off to extermination camps.

Racial consciousness and purity ('Volkstum') were regulated strictly through the prohibition of sexual relations between Germans and the foreign workers. Germans were continuously reminded that such propagation constituted a threat to the purity of their Aryan blood. Foreign female workers were subject to imprisonment or execution for breach of this prohibition. Foreign male workers were simply executed. The soldiers in the SS and in the Wehrmacht were exempted from this general prohibition.

Nazi Germany even had contingent plans for the deportation and enslavement of the British male population in the event Britain was defeated.

However, the dire working conditions and living conditions of Henschel & Son's foreign workers, was exacerbated by the Allies' forty bombing raids on Kassel from 17 February 1942, until March 21, 1945, which were necessitated because of the significant armament production being carried on in the city. Of particular significance was the 22-23 October 1943 raid by 569 Allied bombers which dropped more than 1800 tons of bombs, as well as magnesium fire sticks, on the city center, notwithstanding the fact that the factories were mostly located in the suburbs. It is estimated that more than 10000 citizens perished in that one raid and that 150000 citizens had been 'bombed out'. By 3 April 1945, there were only 50000 inhabitants left in the city when Patton's Third Army was able to gain final control of the city.

Though Hitler's blitzkrieg in the Battle of France seemed to glorify the superiority of the German Panzer III tanks, their actual combat performance against the French 'SOMUA S35' and 'Char B1' heavy tank, as well as the British 'Matilda II' infantry tank, underscored the need to make Nazi Germany's tanks better armed and better armored. This need was further exemplified in the Panzer III's inferior performance during Operation Barbarossa in

June of 1941, against the Soviet T-34 which incorporated an innovated 'sloped armor' design which helped deflect direct frontal hits and appeared to be superior in overall performance and maintenance.

Accordingly, the Tiger I prototype (heavy tank) had enhanced armor which increased its weight to over forty-five tons and increased its gun caliber to 88 mm. It was set for a due date of 20 April 1942, Hitler's 53rd birthday. The Tiger I design did not incorporate the 'sloped armor' innovation which the Soviet T-34 had introduced. Per unit cost was 250800 Reichsmarks (or about $1.9 million US in current funds).

Henschel & Sons obtained a monopoly on the manufacture of the Tiger I and shared the manufacture of the Tiger II with Porsche.

Chapter 39

Upon their arrival at Kassel in early October of 1943, since they were designated 'eastern workers', Larion and his group of forced workers were taken to a camp which was enclosed by a barbed-wire fence with armed guards. It was adjacent to their designated factory which facilitated the commute between the camp and the factory. The camp was composed of twenty barrack units which were designed to hold approximately forty workers per barrack. Since the forced workers were scheduled to work in the Henschel factories in alternating twelve-hour shifts, each barrack actually accommodated double that number. When one shift was working, the other shift was resting and sharing those available bunks.

The barracks were designed to be self-supporting. Each barrack had two enclosed bathrooms and several latrine buckets. Each barrack also had two improvised communal kitchens. Though some women were also assigned specific tasks in the factory, they were able to organize themselves so that they could ensure appropriate child oversight when women with children were assigned to work in the factory. Their primary task, however, was to prepare the two meals a day which the male workers consumed at the commencement and at the conclusion of each shift.

All of the men were assigned to specific tasks in the factory. Workers who were deemed guilty of undue absenteeism, poor performance or sabotage, were summarily punished by being transferred to the various proximate concentration camps for extermination.

Poor rations, overwork and the twelve hour shifts quickly exhausted even the most physically fit. At the end of a shift male workers were barely able to consume the standard staple of boiled potato skins or the rinds of carrots and beets, with some occasional stale bread and rancid meat. After consuming their meager ration, they would fall into a fitful sleep from exhaustion, only to be roused again too soon to repeat that daily grind again and again.

Larion, Tamara, and Dimitri were obliged to share their two threadbare blankets on one bunk. They used one blanket as a makeshift mattress and the other blanket to cover themselves. On a cold night or day, they would huddle together for warmth with Dimitri sheltered between them.

Fortunately, Dr. Gerasimov was assigned a separate bunk with one blanket for himself. The various maladies and sicknesses which manifested themselves in the barracks kept him busy for more than twelve hours per day, since he had to make himself available to both shifts. Though he was becoming more gaunt with each passing week, Tamara tried to ensure that he was eating as much as she could set aside for him. She also tried to ensure that he obtained as much sleep as possible. His general welfare had a direct effect on the eighty occupants of their barracks, but her primary concern was for his own general health. He was an elderly man in declining health. He was also their dear friend who was able to maintain a positive attitude notwithstanding their dire surroundings.

*****

Tamara and Larion lay huddled together with little Dimitri sheltered between them. Though it was still October, the night was unusually cold. The two kitchen stoves were simply not adequate to provide sufficient heat for the entire barracks.

In the distance, even in his exhausted slumber, Larion imagined that he was hearing the distant rumble of lightening rousing him from his sleep. He slowly willed himself to consciousness and observed that Tamara and his son were still asleep. Then he saw the flashes in the distance through the dirty barracks windows. He realized that it was not lighting, but another Allied bombing of the city. The flashes of the exploding shells continued and were quickly followed by the cacophony of their explosions. Tamara soon awoke as well. Dimitri, fortunately, remained oblivious to the intermittent bursts of light and the continuing harsh dissonance of the distant bombs.

"Larion…is this a storm?" she asked him sleepily.

"No, my love. It is not a storm, but another Allied bombing. However, it appears to be directed at the city center and not at our suburbs or at our factory," he replied.

Larion's assessment turned out to be an understatement. He subsequently learned that more than 550 allied bombers made a concerted attempt to bomb the city of Kassel into oblivion. Wave after wave of bombers continued to fly over the city for approximately the next fourteen hours, dropping almost 2000 tons of bombs and magnesium flares which were intended to initiate a conflagration of any buildings which were not destroyed by the bomb blasts, themselves.

Subsequent to the October 23rd and 24th bombing raid, some 150000 of the Kassel residents became homeless and a further 10000 civilians were killed either by the bombs or the subsequent fire which raged through the downtown core of the city.

So great was the destruction that the Henschel factory had to shut down for the next week. This afforded the workers a welcome respite, but that halt also caused a serious disruption in the manufacturing schedule which the workers would be obliged to make up so that the Tiger I tanks could be completed and placed on rail transport for immediate deployment to the eastern front.

*****

"Larion, I am not sure how long I shall be able to endure this hardship. I thought that the war in Belarus was difficult to bear, but the war here is totally unbearable," Tamara confessed tearfully.

"I am trying to be strong for you and for Dimitri…but there are times when I just pray that I can go to sleep and not wake up. I yearn to see my mother and father again. I want them to hold me and shelter me again. I want them to assure me that this madness shall end."

"Tamara, my love," Larion replied in a gently reassuring voice. "I am trying to be strong for you and for Dimitri as well. I also yearn to see my parents one day. But we have to be strong for our son. After all, we brought him into this world and he is our primary responsibility. You have to remember that there was a life we shared before this war and I know that there shall be a life…a better life after this madness ends. All I can promise you is that this madness shall end, but we have to endure until that time. There may be a time for both of us to meet our parents again, either in this life or the next, but we must focus on living right now…for our son."

Larion looked at Tamara in the dim light of the barracks and he could see that she was crying softly and that her whole body was trembling with emotion as she looked upon their son who was sleeping blissfully between them. Larion reached over and kissed his wife on her cheek as she looked up at him and tried to smile back reassuringly.

"Larion, I shall try my best…for our son and for us…but I shall need to rely upon you from time to time," Tamara replied with resignation and in recognition that her choices in life were truly inevitable. She had…they both had to persevere for their son. That was their only hope of salvation.

*****

A week later, Larion returned to the barracks after completing a particularly difficult shift. As he entered the barracks, he noticed that there was a commotion in the vicinity of their bunk. He quickly hastened his tired stride out of concern that something may have befallen his wife or his son.

As he reached their bunk, he noticed that Tamara was clutching her hands together as if she was praying in church. Dr. Gerasimov was leaning over their bunk. He could not see his son.

"What is the matter?" Larion asked anxiously. Seeing Dimitri laying on his back with his eyes closed, he became anxious about his son's welfare. "Is there something the matter with Dimitri?" he asked as he kneeled down by the bunk, looking at his immobile son.

"He was just jumping up and down on our bunk," Tamara replied. "He was so happy; I did not have the heart to caution him to stop. There is so little for him and the other children to do. But he jumped too close to the edge of the bunk and lost his balance and he fell, landing on the back of the right side of his little head. Though he was crying after the fall, he seemed to be alright, but he wanted to lay down. Shortly after he laid down, he became unconscious and I was not able to rouse him, so I asked Dr. Gerasimov to examine him."

"Dr. Gerasimov?" Larion asked anxiously. "What is the matter? Will Dimitri be alright?"

Dr. Gerasimov was seated on the bunk beside Dimitri. Instead of responding to Larion's question, he instructed him what he would like him to do.

"Larion, I am going to pull back Dimitri's eyelids and I would like you to compare his two pupils and advise me if they seem the same to you or if they appear to be different."

Gently, he drew back the left eyelid and then he drew back the right eyelid. Larion watched his son carefully and compared the two pupils. They were not the same.

"I believe that the left pupil seemed to contract as you drew back that eyelid, but the right eyelid remained more open," Larion replied anxiously.

"The left pupil contracted when it became exposed to more light, while the right pupil remained dilated. It remained more open because the ocular neurons were not signaling the oculomotor to contract the pupil, even though the amount of light which is entering that eye is the same as the other eye," Dr. Gerasimov explained quietly.

"But what does that mean, Dr. Gerasimov?" Tamara asked, wringing her two hands in concern. "Will he be alright?"

"I am inclined to assume that Dimitri has sustained a *hematoma* when his head struck the wooden floor. *Hematoma* means that he has bleeding and fluid leakage within his skull which is displacing his brain within the skull cavity. As the blood and fluid continues to build up, it will continue to place even more pressure on the brain. You cannot compress a fluid, whereas the brain is malleable and it is susceptible to compression within the skull. That will cause inevitable brain damage at the very least and eventually death."

"It has already affected his oculomotor neurons as you noticed with his right pupil failing to contract like the left pupil when I lifted those eye lids. The failure of the right pupil to contract normally confirms two things. Firstly, it confirms that he sustained an injury to the right side of his skull as Tamara had described."

"Secondly, the internal bleeding has commenced as evidenced by the fact that the pressure is already compressing the right oculomotor neurons. The brain is encased in a membrane called the *dura*. If the bleeding and fluid buildup is occurring between the *dura* and the skull, it is called an 'epidural hematoma'. If that fluid buildup is occurring between the dura and the brain, it is called a 'subdural hematoma'.

"I believe that Dimitri has sustained an *epidural hematoma*. That, fortunately, reduces some of the contingent risks, however, that pressure has to be relieved…but it is a delicate operation. You have to drill a tiny hole through Dimitri's skull so that the blood and fluid can escape and the pressure can be relieved, but look at these useless limbs of mine."

Dr. Gerasimov shamefully extended his two arms…they were trembling in unison as usual.

"My arms have to be absolutely calm and motionless. I cannot perform the operation if they are going to continue to tremble," Dr. Gerasimov replied apologetically.

"And what shall happen if there is no operation?" Larion asked.

"He will remain comatose, become increasingly more brain damaged…and he shall eventually die."

Larion and Tamara exchanged anxious glances and then looked down at their helpless young son.

"If there is anything which you can do, Dr. Gerasimov?" Tamara asked tearfully. "I beg you to try."

Dr. Gerasimov was aware that the only available solution to calm his hands might mean that he would destroy himself in the process. He was a heavy drinker in his youth, as were most Russian men. Drinking was as natural as breathing. His drinking had previously brought him to the brink of his own death. It was only the love and encouragement he received from his departed wife and his only surviving daughter, the mother of his only grandson, which saved him. However, he knew that he had caused irreparable damage to his liver and that if he drank again, he may not survive.

He was able to stop drinking, but the consequence of being able to save himself was that it destroyed his ability to perform the operations which he was once able to perform. His colleagues and his patients described him as possessing *zolotaya rukee* (golden hands) which were capable of performing medical miracles.

But he knew that the only way he would be able to stabilize his arms, hands, and fingers in order to perform the delicate operation would be to satiate his body's long-suppressed addiction to alcohol. It was an overwhelming desire which he had been able to fend off for the preceding decade, but the only way he would be able to still the trembling in his hands would be to succumb into that addition, very possibly for the last time if his damaged liver was not able to cope with the ingested alcohol.

"There is something we can try, but you need to obtain certain items for me. I will need at least a liter of vodka and the finest thin-steel drill bit you can find at the factory. I will also need a small drill which can be operated manually by a circular crank," the good doctor replied with a determined resignation.

250

When he saw the apprehensive look in Tamara's eyes, he tried to reassure her quickly.

"I need the vodka to sterilize the drill bit, my hands and we have to sterilize the location of the injury where I shall have to drill," he replied. "Tamara, while Larion is locating the bit and the drill, I shall also need you to shave your son's skull where I will have to operate."

Tamara commenced to gently shave the location which Dr. Gerasimov had selected on Dimitri's skull, just above and behind his right ear.

Larion was able to locate an extremely fine drill bit and he was also able to locate a hand operated drill in the factory workshop, but the most difficult request to fulfill was Dr. Gerasimov's request for the vodka. They were finally obliged to exchange Tamara's gold crucifix for the alcohol which had been brewed in an adjoining barracks by another forced worker. They tested it by lighting it and it burst into a light blue flame.

In the interim, Dr. Gerasimov got Tamara and one of the other women in the barracks to boil some water in which he dropped the drill bit so that it could be sterilized with boiling water first, then he carefully drenched it with the vodka. The drill bit had to be carefully and firmly inserted inside the hand drill, but he was not able to tighten it to his satisfaction so he asked Larion to tighten the bit as much as he could. Finally, he turned Dimitri over on his stomach and turned his head to the right to optimize his access to the injured skull.

"Larion, I want you to hold Dimitri's head in this position. It is imperative that you do not permit him to move at all. A mere millimeter may mean the difference between success or failure."

Dr. Gerasimov then proceeded with his delicate operation on the three-year-old child who had sustained a serious head injury and who was laying comatose before him. Larion and Tamara were so preoccupied with their son's welfare that they did not even notice that Dr. Gerasimov's former tremulous hands had become calm and still. Once he had positioned the drill bit against Dimitri's skull, he proceeded in a deft fashion.

His right hand turned the manual control like a virtuoso while his left hand maintained a vise-like grip on the drill as the bit slowly turned and started to exude first flesh, then fine shavings of bone. Dr. Gerasimov remained motionless with the exception of his right hand turning the drill's circular control evenly until a reddish-white fluid squirted from the drill bit's entry cavity. Then he immediately stopped and withdrew the drill bit and exhaled. He had been holding his breath during the entire procedure.

"Tamara, please douse a clean cloth with the vodka and dab that area which you had previously shaved," Dr. Gerasimov spoke confidently. "And place some long strips of cloth inside that pot which is still boiling. I want to be sure that Dimitri's bandages are sterile as well. Wait for them to cool down before you tie them around his little head. Make sure that the hole remains open until the seepage stops. Also, ensure that the opening does not get contaminated." He paused for a moment. "Now I have to leave you all for a little while."

It was only when Dr. Gerasimov rose to walk away from the bunk that Larion noticed for the first time that the vodka bottle was nearly half empty as Dr. Gerasimov carried it away with him, but he did not give that matter a second thought.

Tamara and Larion slept in shifts that night so that one of them would be able to watch and care for their little son. The bandages which they had initially applied had quickly become stained with the blood which continued to ooze from the drill hole, but gradually the bleeding abated over the course of the night.

When Dr. Gerasimov did not come back to examine Dimitri in the morning, Tamara went looking for him as Larion departed to the Henschel factory to perform his daily shift. She found Dr. Gerasimov on his bunk, cradling the empty vodka bottle against his chest with both of his arms.

"Dr. Gerasimov," Tamara spoke softly as she tried to awaken him so that she could assure herself that he was alright and so that she could thank him again for what he had done the previous night.

However, she was unable to rouse him. In fact, the good doctor had diagnosed himself quite accurately. He had to drink a copious amount of vodka prior to conducting the operation so that the alcohol would calm the tremors in his hands. Then he had to operate quickly and efficiently before the alcohol affected his senses. But after tasting that hypnotic liquid again, he was unable to resist his addiction and he proceeded to empty the bottle quickly after he left his companions. Unfortunately, it was too much for his severely damaged liver to cope with and his body went into shock and then his heart stopped.

Though no one else would ever be aware of the act, the last cogent thought which floated through his mind was that his fatal decision had hopefully saved the life of a three-year-old innocent child. He, himself, was satisfied that he had lived long enough and that his life was well spent.

Though Larion, Tamara, and several other 'forced OST workers' attempted to arrange for a modest funeral and burial for their good friend, their requests were denied. Dr. Gerasimov's gaunt body was thrown unceremoniously on the back of a transport with several other deceased 'forced workers' for final disposition at the nearest concentration camp crematorium.

Chapter 40

After Dr. Gerasimov's death, Tamara assumed primary responsibility for the care of their young son. She was relieved that the following morning she was roused from her fitful sleep by the gentle movement of his small body. It was the first voluntary motion she noticed since he fell into unconsciousness after his fall.

"Dimitri…Dimitri, my dear son," she spoke to him endearingly, however there was no response. He merely fidgeted in her arms, attempting to become more comfortable, however, his actions did come as a relief to her.

Tamara carefully removed his head bandage and examined the tiny drill hole in his skull. It remained open as it was still slowly oozing that reddish-yellow fluid. She assumed that it was a good sign since it must mean that the fluid was not building up inside her son's head and exerting pressure on his little brain. She replaced it with another clean strip of sterilized cloth and she continued to watch him and wait.

*****

"Uhummm! Uhummm!"

Tamara quickly awakened at the sound of her son's muffled voice. She watched him and it seemed as if he was trying to open his eyes since his eyelids were both fluttering. Then he opened his left eye and then his right. When his mother's face came into view, he gave her a radiant smile in recognition.

"Mama! Mama!"

"Are you alright, Dimitri?" Tamara asked anxiously. "How do you feel?"

"Hummm! I think my head hurts," Dimitri replied as he tried to reach up and touch his injured skull.

"Do not worry. You hurt yourself when you were jumping on the bunk and you fell off," Tamara explained. "But Dr. Gerasimov has made you well again, but it will take some time before you start running all over the place again. You will have to be careful so that you will heal quickly. You promise me?"

"I promise, Mama, but my head hurts…but just a little bit."

"Well, Dr. Gerasimov had to make a little hole in your head, Dimitri," Tamara explained.

"I have a hole in my head! Really, Mama?" Dimitri asked incredulously. "Can I show my friends my hole in my head?"

"You will have lots of time to do that, but you have to be very careful," Tamara replied, her relief was increasing with every comment her young son made. "And you do not remove your bandage. Only I or your father shall do that for you."

"Do you have a hole in your head, Mama?"

"No," Tamara replied. "Fortunately, you have the only hole in our family. But as you heal, it shall close and then the hole will disappear forever."

"Oh, it will disappear?" Dimitri asked disappointedly.

"Yes, my dear, young son," Tamara replied. "Then the three of us shall be the same again."

Dimitri did not seem to be fully satisfied with his mother's reassuring words. He thought that having a hole in one's head made him special and that the other young children in the barracks would be envious. He was sure that they would want similar holes as well. While Dimitri was pondering his circumstances, Tamara carefully watched her son's pupils. Both pupils seemed to contract and dilate equally as she slowly moved him in and out of the sunlight streaming through the soiled barracks' window.

"Mama. I think I am hungry now," Dimitri announced.

Tamara had squashed the vegetable rinds in the simmering pot on the kitchen stove as much as possible and slowly fed her son with the warm, tasty broth until he slowly closed his eyes and went to sleep again.

*****

As Dimitri recovered quickly from his fall and his surgery, Tamara commenced to try to educate him and another couple of young children. She commenced with the recognition of numerals and Cyrillic letters, then simple addition, subtraction, and short words by rote memory. She was able to accomplish this by the 'teaching cards' which Larion was able to create for her. She would hold the cards up and the children would compete as to who could answer correctly first. Those lessons were a welcome distraction not only for the young children but for Tamara as well.

Larion also attempted to teach his son and Tamara how to speak some rudimentary German because he knew that they would not be able to return to the Soviet Union. Comrade Stalin may have forgiven him for not dying in the initial attack and then fighting with the partisans behind enemy lines, but he knew that their vindictive leader would never forgive him for becoming a 'slave laborer' in a German munitions factory that manufactured weapons which were then used to kill other Soviet soldiers. That act was a clear act of treason and beyond redemption.

Even as a captive young junior officer, he would face either a minimum twenty-five-year sentence at hard labor in the *Gulag* (acronym for *Glavnoe Upralenie Lagerie*—Political Labor Centers initiated by Stalin in 1930) or summary execution. Therefore, if they were to remain in Germany after the war, knowledge of the German language should help them all adapt and survive.

Otherwise, their lives remained a never-ending, mind-numbing routine that was repeated day after day after day.

*****

The October 23/24 heavy-bombing raid and the subsequent fifteen Allied bombing raids on Kassel, which took place from 18 March 1944 through to 21 March 1945, continued to interrupt Henschel & Son's manufacturing schedule for the Tiger tanks. The Tiger I production was to be phased out by August of 1944 and replaced by the manufacture of the heavier Tiger II tanks, which continued until 30 March 1945.

The Tiger I tank had been rushed into production in 1942 and that necessitated ongoing changes to its design throughout its production run. Those ongoing changes required ongoing modifications to the instructions which the production line workers required. Breakdowns in communication in respect of these ever-changing instructions resulted in increased accusations of attempted sabotage by those workers.

They were subject to arbitrary discipline by the other superior 'guest workers', their German civilian supervisors, and the paramilitary guards. Larion was able to keep his own errors to a minimum and his engaging manner usually made his apologetic explanations palpable to even the most ardent anti-Slav superiors.

However, the dynamics of the Second World War had changed dramatically by January of 1944. The *blitzkrieg* attacks on Moscow, Stalingrad, and Leningrad had stalled and then been lifted. The *Wehrmacht* and *SS* armies on the eastern front were in retreat. Montgomery had defeated and pushed Rommel out of northern Africa. From Africa, Montgomery and Patton's armies were pushing the Nazi German armies back up through Sicily and Italy.

By June of 1944, the Allies had successfully staged the Normandy invasion in northern France, opening up the third front which Nazi Germany had to defend.

Stalin's Marshall Zhukov and his armies were advancing from the east, while Roosevelt's General Eisenhower and his armies were advancing from the west.

Larion's primary concern was to hope that it was the Allies' armies which would liberate Kassel and not the unforgiving Soviets.

*****

By March of 1945, General Patton's Third Army had been able to cross the Rhine near Mainz on 22 March 1945. Then Patton pushed northeast and reached Frankfurt by 26 March 1945. By 30 March 1945, he directed elements of his Third Army towards Kassel. In anticipation of the forthcoming attack on Kassel, the Allies had conducted a further four bombing raids from 2 March through 21 March 1945, including a heavy raid involving 176 aircraft on 8 and 9 March 1945, to soften the Nazi German defenses of the city.

At the Henschel factory complex, Larion and the other 'eastern OST workers' were ordered to complete the construction of the final thirteen Tiger II tanks, which were immediately turned over to two of the *Wehrmacht's* Heavy Tank Battalions stationed in Kassel and they were duly transferred on 30 March 1945.

Thereafter, a four-day battle ensued between General Patton's forces and the remaining elements of Kassel's defenses which were under the command of *Generalmajor* Johannes Erxleben. Though Erxleben had limited battle experience, Hitler declared the city of Kassel a *Festung* (a fortress) which obligated Erxleben to fight to the last round, notwithstanding the overwhelming American military supremacy.

As the thirteenth Tiger II tank rolled off of the assembly line, the German factory supervisors and paramilitary guards abandoned the factory and attempted to become assimilated within the German civilian population. Larion and his other fellow 'eastern OST workers' also abandoned the Henschel factory for the last time and proceeded immediately back to the camp. Upon reaching the camp, they discovered that the camp guards had also abandoned their posts and disappeared.

Larion went into his barracks to try to locate Tamara and little Dimitri. Tamara was conducting a math class by holding up cards which indicated numerals which were either to be added or subtracted before a rapt audience of five pupils, including Dimitri. She was holding up a card indicating that four was to be subtracted from seven, when she saw Larion enter the barracks and approach her. "And what is the answer to this riddle, children?" Tamara asked politely.

"Hummm! I think it is three, Mama," Dimitri replied, smiling proudly as he saw his father nod his head in affirmation that it was the correct response.

"Tamara, I think it is time to end this class and send the other children back to their mothers," Larion spoke quietly with restrained excitement.

"Why are you back so early, Larion?" Tamara asked, somewhat surprised by Larion's premature return, since she did not expect him to finish his daily schedule for several hours.

"It seems that the end may have finally begun, my love," Larion explained. "The Americans are here and though there will be a fight, it should be over fairly quickly. I believe that the beginning of the end of our nightmare has finally arrived."

*****

Though those final thirteen Tiger II tanks constituted a formidable addition to Erxleben's forces, their 88-mm guns were no match to Patton's 155-mm artillery. The American artillery's higher caliber and longer range was able to shred several Tiger II tanks before the tanks were able to come into their own range. By 4 April 1945, Erxleben surrendered unconditionally, along with about 1300 remaining regular forces. That effectively ended the Battle of

Kassel and the nightmare the Sulupins had to endure for the preceding five years of war.

Chapter 41

Western Europe first experienced a major displacement of civilians at the end of the First World War. Consequently, on 9 November 1943, at President Roosevelt's suggestion and encouragement, forty-four nations signed a charter entitled the 'United Nations Relief and Rehabilitation Administration' ('UNRRA'), which was charged with the responsibility of providing economic relief to the displaced people in the areas which the 'United Nations' were going to liberate.

Roosevelt initially coined the expression 'United Nations' in 1942, after the United States had entered the war in the Pacific and in Europe in reference to the 'Allies' who were fighting Germany in Europe and Japan in the Pacific. The United Nations organization was not established until 24 October 1945, after the end of the Second World War, at which time the UNRRA became part of the United Nations.

At the end of the Second World War, about eleven million people had been displaced from their home countries with about seven million located in Allied-occupied Germany. They included surviving prisoners of war, released slave laborers, and both Jewish and non-Jewish survivors of the Nazi concentration camps.

These refugees were collectively categorized as 'Displaced Persons' and usually referred to by the acronym, 'DPs', more often than naught in a pejorative sense. This general categorization was further segregated into a number of sub-classifications to facilitate administration; however, the final category was that of being a 'stateless person'. The UNRRA assumed responsibility for the care of these DPs from the military and commenced to deal with their care and resettlement.

The primary plan was to try to repatriate as many refugees to their respective countries of origin as quickly as possible, however, that posed special problems in some cases. The 'Allies' initially tended to manage the refugees who were located within their particular 'Occupation Zone'; however, many refugees attempted to migrate from one Zone to another, with the primary exception of the Soviet Zone.

Though about six million of the original eleven million refugees had been repatriated by the end of 1945, the various Allies implemented cutoff dates in their respective Zones to terminate this on-going internal migration from Zone to Zone, to help facilitate the administration and resettlement of the remaining refugees. The British authorities set the date of 30 June 1946. The American authorities ceased accepting additional migrating refugees on 21 April 1947.

Nearly all of the refugees were malnourished or ill or dying. They were in dire need of food, medicine, clothing and shelter. Since the refugees' initial contact was not with the UNRRA, but with the occupying military, the initial support came from those military personnel sharing their own supplies of food, medicine and clothing. As for shelter, the refugees were obliged to continue to use their prior barracks; however, even some German castles were commandeered for this purpose. By 1 October 1945, the UNRRA undertook the management and administration of approximately eight hundred such camps. Living conditions improved, rudimentary schools were established and even sport teams were set up while the on-going process of resettlement of the remaining refugees was dealt with. However, a large number of the refugees also suffered psychological problems such as depression which resulted from enduring years of trauma and they were distrustful of the authorities and not that cooperative at all material times.

Though many refugees were anxious to return to their country of origin and reunite with family and friends, voluntary repatriation in a number of cases posed a special problem. Stalin's general attitude was that all Soviet prisoners of war were traitors and that all Soviet slave laborers were also traitors, and that both groups were deserving of punishment in the Gulag.

Jewish survivors were also reluctant to return to their countries of origin because of the previous prejudice they had experienced and the loss of their former businesses and homes which had been expropriated, they generally expressed a preference to migrate to Palestine in fulfilment of the Balfour Declaration of 2 November 1917.

Palestine had remained a British Mandate from 1920, however, the British Government imposed severe restraints on the number of Jews who were approved to migrate. Consequently, many surviving European Jews commenced an underground movement to migrate to Palestine in any case and by any means.

In 1947, the United Nations proposed a partition of Britain's 'Palestine Mandate' into a Jewish state and a Muslim state. When the Muslims rejected the proposal, it forced the Jews in Palestine to declare the creation of the State of Israel on 14 May 1948. That declaration resulted in the end of the British Mandate and the outbreak of the first Arab-Israeli War in 1948.

In respect of the Soviet issue, at the Yalta Conference in the Crimea which was hosted by Stalin from 4 February through 11, 1945, Stalin was able to obtain a commitment from both a frail Roosevelt, who would die within a couple of months, and from a naive Churchill, who proposed an 'influence sharing' agreement between England and the Soviet Union in the Eastern European countries liberated by the Soviets, for an agreement that England and the United States would implement a policy of 'forced repatriation' of all former Soviet citizens located in their respective Occupation Zones back to the Soviet Union.

At the subsequent Potsdam Conference which was held in Germany from 17 July through to 2 August 1945, a more robust and confident President Truman took a harder stance with Stalin in respect of forced repatriation. Though the primary purpose of the conference was to define the terms of surrender of the Japanese Empire, Truman's confidence was infused with the American success in the development of the atomic bomb and he even hinted to Stalin that the United States was in possession of a very powerful 'super weapon' in an attempt to intimidate.

In fact, after the Japanese Empire declined to accept the initial American terms of unconditional surrender, Truman authorized the use of the atomic bomb on Hiroshima on 6 August 1945, and subsequently on Nagasaki on 9 August 1945, which ended the war in the Pacific.

By 1946, Stalin's duplicity was quite evident to Stalin's former 'Allies' and it was epitomized in Churchill's 'Iron Curtain' speech in Missouri on 5 March 1946, which heralded the commencement of the 'Cold War': "From Stettin in the Baltic to Trieste in the Adriatic, an Iron Curtain has descended across the continent."

Truman's subsequent declaration of the 'Truman Doctrine' on 12 March 1947, that the United States intended to initially 'contain' the Soviet Union and then communism in general, was a de facto declaration of the Cold War and the commencement of the nuclear arms race.

The emergence of the Cold War underscored the necessity for the accelerated reconstruction of Japan and Germany to help facilitate the containment of Stalin's Soviet Union and Mao's Communist China. This reconstruction was basically financed by America through the 'Marshall Plan'. In 1947, Truman's Secretary of State, George C. Marshall, former General and Chief of Staff, proposed the 'European Recovery Plan' which was implemented in 1948 and totaled about $13 billion US (approximately $235 billion US in current value). The aid was economical and it was of mutual benefit to Europe and the United States, since the relief was purchased from America and even had to be transported to Europe in American ships. Marshall was awarded the Nobel Peace Prize in 1953.

The resolution of the issue of the 'non-repatriables' also remained a problem, but between 1947 and 1952, a number of countries implemented policies of large-scale immigration. Belgium accepted 22000 refugees; the United Kingdom accepted over 200000 refugees, Canada accepted almost 160000 refugees; Australia accepted about 182000 refugees; Israel accepted about 650000 Jewish refugees; and other countries accepted a smaller quota. The United States accepted about 450000 refugees, of whom about 137000 were European Jews.

Part 3
Regenesis – 1945

Chapter 42

The Sulupins' camp was located near the small village of *Furstenwald*, which was located about eleven kilometers from downtown Kassel or approximately two kilometers northwest of Kassel's city limits. There were two additional camps located in adjacent villages of *Monchehof* and *Rothwesten*. *Monchehof* was the biggest camp and it turned out to be the last *'Displaced Persons Camp'* in Germany which only ceased operations in 1957.

*****

After Larion had explained what had transpired that day and why the camp guards had left, they both remained speechless. It was initially difficult to accept that their ordeal may have commenced to end, however that incredulity was quickly followed by their mutual concern as to what they were going to do now. Their lives had been totally controlled for the past two years. Their anticipation of having that burden finally removed from their shoulders was quickly replaced by a new apprehension as to what they were going to do now.

"Louyna, I must confess that I find this turn of events almost unbelievable," Tamara finally admitted, almost regretfully. "But what are we to do now?"

"It is difficult to believe, is it not?" Larion replied. "But we have to make some plans, my love. I am not sure what is going to happen to us from this moment on, but I do know what we have to avoid at all costs."

"And what is that?" Tamara asked quietly, since she noticed that Dimitri had fallen asleep. It appeared to her that since his accident and his surgery, he rested and slept more frequently, but he did seem to be improving with each passing week.

"We cannot return to Belarus, for one thing," Larion replied sadly.

"But why not?" Tamara asked anxiously. "If the war is finally over, why cannot we go back?"

"We cannot go back because of the fate which will certainly be awaiting me and possibly even you and Dimitri. Stalin may forgive me for not dying on the day of the Nazi attack back in June of 1941, but he will never forgive either me or you for becoming 'forced workers' working for the Nazi German war machine. At a minimum, they will imprison me for twenty-five years at hard labor in the Gulag or they may be inclined to just execute me. Individual human life has very little meaning for Stalin and his sycophants. But they believe in collective guilt and collective punishment, so you may be resettled in Siberia like my parents, if you are fortunate, but they may decide to send you and our son to the Gulag as well."

"Then what shall we do? Where shall we go?" Tamara asked earnestly. "I really do not want to remain in Germany after what they have done to us."

"You cannot blame the entire German race for the actions of Hitler and his Nazis, Tamara," Larion reasoned. "No more than we can blame the entire Russian race for the actions of Stalin and his communists. I know that it will not be easy, but it is important that we recognize that fact and try to mold our attitudes accordingly, otherwise the cycle of hatred will not end. It will merely continue into the next generation. I would like to think of a future world where we and the Germans will recognize and accept each other as fellow human beings. After all, we share the same basic needs, desires and fears."

"But what shall we do now?" Tamara asked.

"For now, we shall stay here for a few days and see what happens," Larion replied. "I have a feeling that future events will help us decide what we should do."

*****

Six days later, Larion heard the approach of several motorized vehicles enter their camp. As he rose and peered through the grime on the window, he recognized that their visitors appeared to be American soldiers who had arrived with a couple of jeeps and two transport vehicles. Gradually, some of the other 'forced workers' cautiously exited their barracks and stared in amazement at the young exuberant American soldiers who cheerfully beckoned and encouraged them to come out.

"Come Tamara. Do not be afraid," Larion tried to coax his wife. "Let us go out and greet our visitors."

As they approached timidly, a young smiling officer saluted them and then quickly greeted them with a beaming smile, even though he noticed that the two adults and the young child were soiled and dressed in filthy thread-bare rags.

"Lieutenant James Thornton, at your service," he proudly announced. "Do any of you speak English?"

An elderly voice behind Larion spoke up and confirmed that he was able to speak some rudimentary English. Larion looked behind at the person who spoke up and though he recognized him, he realized that he had never had an opportunity to speak with him before.

"I speak some English," the elderly voice replied. "I apologize my English not good."

"Are you kidding me, man?" the young lieutenant replied thankfully. "Some English is better than no English at all. I will speak slowly and I would like you to translate what I say to these people, but please tell them that the Germans have surrendered in Kassel and that they should not worry. They have nothing to fear from us. We have brought some food, medicine, and some clothes, and by the look of all of you, it appears that you can use it all."

The announcements by the American lieutenant were duly translated to the assembled camp workers and a sense of relief gradually pervaded them and they even dared to approach closer. Some of the camp workers were tempted to reach out and touch the young, smiling soldiers to verify that they actually existed and that they posed no threat, but they also became aware of the disparity in their respective appearance once the translator explained that the Americans had brought them replacement clothes. For the first time in a long time, they became self-conscious of their personal decrepit appearance and they felt embarrassment and shame.

The young American lieutenant explained that they were there to help them. He wanted them to select replacement clothing from the supplies they had brought and then to bathe themselves. Their old clothes were to be burnt as soon as those clothes were removed. They would have to heat their water on their kitchen stoves.

Anyone requiring medical attention was to identify themselves and he would direct one of the attending medics to examine those people. He finally advised them that they had also brought food supplies, but he cautioned them to divide those supplies equitably and that they should try to restrain their appetites until they became more accustomed to a more nutritious diet.

Finally, he advised that they would have to remain in their current accommodations, however, his men would assist the male camp workers to clean and sanitize the barracks. They would also be provided with clean, standard military replacement blankets. Personal hygiene was to be a priority for everyone.

When the advisement about possible medical treatment was mentioned, Tamara immediately requested their translator to ask that a medic examine Dimitri.

"Well, little guy," the medic happily addressed Dimitri. "And what is your name?"

Not understanding what the soldier with the red cross sewn onto his uniform had said, Dimitri was unable to respond. He merely furrowed his brow in his confusion. Once the translator quickly explained, Dimitri immediately responded, "Dimitri Larionovich Sulupin!" he replied proudly.

"Dimitri?" the medic inquired quizzically, as he slowly untied the linen bandage from his head so that he could examine the injury.

"Dimitri Larionovich Sulupin!" Dimitri repeated his name proudly, beaming at the young medic who was now engrossed with inspecting the wound and merely smiled back at him.

"Tell his mother that I am just going to clean and sterilize the wound," the medic announced, affecting a more serious note. "Could you have his mother explain what happened to him?"

Tamara complied dutifully once the translator conveyed the medic's request. The young medic nodded his understanding. His examination and her explanation verified his initial conclusion. Under the circumstances, the successful operation was nothing less than miraculous.

"Well, please tell her that the wound is healing nicely. It does not seem to be oozing much fluid or blood, but she should try to keep it open a bit longer. I shall sterilize the entry and the surrounding area and provide her with some additional clean replacement bandages. But please assure her that she has looked after him very well and I am sure that he will recover soon."

As the translator completed his translation, the medic reached into his pocket and extracted a small Babe Ruth chocolate bar and handed it to Dimitri. Dimitri looked to his parents for permission to accept this unknown gift from this stranger and upon receiving their respective nods of approval, he gleefully accepted the gift and enthusiastically embraced the young, kneeling soldier in gratitude. The young medic rose smiling and indicated that he appreciated Dimitri's thanks. Then the medic proceeded to go and attend to the other camp workers' medical needs.

"Sir?" Larion inquired respectfully, addressing his query to the elderly translator. "I have a favor to ask of you, if you do not mind."

"A favor?" the translator replied. "I am not sure that there is much, if anything, which I can do for you, but if I am able…of course I shall do what I can."

"Since we shall no longer be working at the factory, I would greatly appreciate it if you could teach me some English," Larion explained. "It may be a language which would be important to know."

"Well, at least you asked me for something which I am both able and willing to do, Larion Daneelivich Sulupin," the elderly translator replied, somewhat relieved. "My name is Andre…we can speak again tomorrow."

The translator then proceeded to follow the American lieutenant to another group of camp workers who were waiting patiently, eager to ask their own questions of their American benefactors.

*****

"Father, can you help me open my gift?" Dimitri implored his father. "I just cannot do it myself. Do you know what it is?"

"I believe it is chocolate," Larion replied. "It is like a candy…a very special treat. But be sure to share it with your mother for I do not believe she has ever tried it before. But now let us go to the transport and select some new clothing and blankets. Then we shall go to our barracks and bathe ourselves as best we can and then we shall put on our new, clean clothes. After we have eaten, I will open your chocolate treat and you may share it with your mother as a dessert."

"I will share my chocolate with you as well, Father."

"Do not worry about me, my young son. I have tasted chocolate when I was in Moscow at the military academy. It is exquisitely delicious. Just share it with your mother, but do not eat the whole thing at one time."

"Listen to your father, Dimitri," Tamara interjected. "But let us go and select some new clothes and blankets and then we can bathe and eat."

*****

After selecting some clothes and shoes, Tamara and some of the other women proceeded to boil some water on the stoves which they then diluted with cold water. After arranging some of their new blankets to afford them some privacy, the women tried to scrub themselves clean with bars of coarse military soap before they put on their new clothes. The men and the remaining soldiers attempted to clean the barracks as best they could and then the men took their turn at scrubbing themselves while the women attempted to prepare a meal from the food provided by the Americans. Most of the fo,odstuffs were familiar, but the quality was substantially better than what they were used to; however, some of the packaged goods were totally foreign and mysterious to them. Those goods were left for another day.

Finally, they were able to retire on their freshly cleaned bunks and their three new military blankets. For the first time in a long time Larion reached out to embrace Tamara. He could not remember how long it was since they had been intimate. But he held her close to him and kissed her tenderly, and she responded in kind. They explored each other, but they refrained from attempting to consummate their passion.

With Dimitri lying beside them and the proximity of some of the other camp workers, it just did not seem appropriate to make love. They would have to be satisfied in embracing each other and remembering those past moments when they were able to be intimate.

"You know, Louyna, my father told me that when a young man went courting, he would bring his sweetheart flowers, chocolates and champagne, as proof of his affection," Tamara spoke teasingly. "You know, I do not remember you ever doing that for me, well at least not yet."

Larion prudently chose not to reply. Finally, they surrendered themselves to a deep peaceful slumber, still clinging tenderly to each other. For the first time that they could remember, they eagerly awaited the dawning of the next day.

Chapter 43

The following morning, Larion sought out the elderly translator. He did not want to waste any time in commencing to learn the English language. In some ways Andre reminded him of his old friend, Valodya, when he was a volunteer worker helping to complete the spring planting on the collective farm. Seeing Andre shuffle out of an adjoining barracks, he hailed and approached him.

"*Privet tsebe, tovarish* (Greetings to you, comrade)," Larion greeted the elderly man. "Do you have time to speak with me?"

"Of course, my young friend," Andre answered happily. "So, you want to learn how to speak English?"

"I would like to learn how to read and write English as well, but learning how to speak the language first makes sense to me," Larion replied. "Is it a difficult language to learn? I can speak some German since I studied it at a Military College and I had to use it the past two years working in the factory. The German supervisors were certainly not going bother to learn to speak Russian."

"That shows that you may have an aptitude for learning languages," Andre replied. "So it may be easier for you than it was for me. I was an upper school instructor in Minsk before the war and I was teaching English as a second language, even though I was trying to learn it myself at the same time. However, I am pleased that you are so motivated. Let us go see Lieutenant Thornton and see if he can provide us with some English books. It should be constructive for both of us."

"But what can I do for you in return for your instruction?" Larion inquired politely.

"No need to discuss that at this time. We both know that neither one of us has much to barter with," Andre replied. "Perhaps you may be able to do me a favor sometime in the future, but let us go see Lieutenant Thornton."

They proceeded to the former camp commandant's office, which was appropriated by the Americans as their headquarters. To their surprise, there were three Soviet soldiers in the office as well. Larion recognized that they included a captain and two non-commissioned officers.

Thornton acknowledged them as they entered and he directed them to be seated by the front door where several spare chairs had been arranged along the wall. After speaking with the Soviets through an interpreter, he merely stood up and exchanged a crisp salute and escorted them to the front door. The Soviet captain stopped in front of Andre and Larion, examining them both closely.

"*A ve govorist po Ruski* (Do you two speak Russian)?" he asked contemptuously. "*Vy sukiny deti* (You sons-of-bitches)!

Andre did not respond. He had learned to endure verbal and physical intimidation for the preceding two years he had been a forced worker, even though he was no longer obliged to wear the OST insignia sewn onto his jacket. The insult spat out by the Soviet captain reminded him that remaining timid and silent was the best course of action to adopt in such circumstances. Larion, on the other hand, was not prepared to endure such a gratuitous personal insult.

He rose up in front of the offending officer and looked him directly into his eyes. He wanted him to know that he did not fear him and he did not respect him.

"*Trakhni tebya* (Fuck you)," Larion replied firmly. "*Ty ponimayesh moy Russkiy* (Do you understand my Russian), *Vy bespdeznyy kusok der'ma* (you useless piece of shit)?"

The Soviet officer immediately reached to withdraw his pistol. Thornton, however, placed a firm hand on his forearm and indicated that he was not going to tolerate any such conduct on the part of his Soviet visitors, even though they were still technically allies in the war against the Nazis. The two other American soldiers in the office immediately rose up as well in case their commanding officer required any assistance.

"Please advise my dear comrades that they should leave this compound. After all, we liberated it and it is officially designated part of the 'American Zone'. They have no authority here," Thornton instructed his Russian translator to advise his Soviet guests accordingly.

The offended Soviet officer left his pistol in its holster and gradually lowered his arm, however he continued to glare at Larion. His intuition had been correct. Both of these camp workers were Russian and he understood that regardless of the Zone any *displaced persons* may be located in, the respective Allied leaders had agreed that the primary directive was that all such persons were to be repatriated to their original countries of origin, voluntarily or involuntarily. He intended to ensure that when Larion was forced to be repatriated to the Soviet Union, he was going to be present and take personal charge of him.

"I shall be seeing you again, comrade," he addressed Larion tersely. "And I assure you that it shall be under different circumstances and it shall also end differently as well." Then he and his fellow soldiers turned on their heel and marched out in unison into the camp yard.

Thornton looked at Larion with mixed feelings. Though he admired the camp worker's nerve in standing up to the Soviet officer and he knew that both of them had exchanged insults, he also wanted to avoid further complications. His responsibility in attempting to physically rehabilitate the people under his command was his first priority, however, he was also obligated to initiate the background documentation for them as well. He, too, was familiar with the agreed protocol that all *displaced persons* were to be repatriated as quickly as possible to their original countries of origin.

"Well…Andre?" Thornton asked apologetically. "I hope I remembered your name correctly. What can I do for you and your argumentative friend?"

Andre proceeded to explain Larion's request and his need for an English text of some sort, as well as a couple of pencils and some writing paper. Thornton directed one of his attendants to see that the request was fulfilled on a forthwith basis. However, he decided to also share his understanding of the repatriation protocol, as he understood it.

"Andre, I would like you to explain to your friend that our respective leaders have agreed that the primary protocol in dealing with the millions of displaced persons currently residing in Germany is to repatriate them back to their original countries of origin."

Andre duly translated the message and Thornton noticed that Larion's body had stiffened slightly when the message was completed, though his facial expression remained impassive.

"I would also like you to explain to your friend that there are certain exceptions to that general protocol. For example, if your friend is Jewish who was discriminated against in his country of origin or if he lost his business or his home or he is concerned about continued discrimination, I am not obliged to repatriate him."

Andre duly translated the message and Thornton noticed that Larion had indicated to Andre that he was not Jewish.

"I would also like you to explain to your friend that there are some other exceptions. For example, the boundaries of many countries in central and eastern Europe and even the Soviet Union have been changed. Lithuania, Estonia, and Latvia seem to have disappeared. If your friend originated in one of those countries, then I can exercise my discretion and refuse to forcibly repatriate him if his country no longer exists, albeit technically. Please explain this exception carefully, Andre."

As Andre proceeded to translate Thornton's last statement, Thornton watched Larion closely. Once again, he saw Larion nod his head in obvious confirmation that he understood what Andre had told him, but there was no indication that Larion also understood the subliminal message which Thornton was trying to convey. He had remembered the young man as the husband of the attractive young woman whose son had suffered some sort of head injury. He remembered directing one of his medic's attend to the child's injury. Considering the hardships, the family had probably endured to this point in time, he was prepared to do what he could to minimize any further hardships which may confront them while they remained in his custody and under his control.

"Andre, please advise Lieutenant Thornton that I, Tamara, and our son, Dimitri, are Belorussian; however, we were residents of Lithuania when the war broke out. However, it seems that our homeland no longer exists, thanks to comrade Stalin," Larion replied quickly and then addressed Andre. "And I believe, my friend, that Lithuania was also your homeland as well, was it not?"

Andre appreciated Larion's attempt to save him from a forced repatriation as well, however, his position was substantially different. He was elderly and his only relatives, if they were still living, resided in Belarus. He explained to Larion that he was too old to start a whole new life in another country. He was prepared to return, irrespective of the fate which may await him. If he was to be punished by banishment to the Gulag, he was certain that his punishment would not be long because his health was very frail. Alternatively, if he was reunited with his family, that was his best expectation. If his family was no longer living, then he was prepared to accept probable resettlement in Siberia.

At least his teaching skills could be utilized for whatever remaining time he may have left.

Thornton watched closely as Larion and Andre completed their conversation. He waited with quiet anticipation to hear what the two camp workers would have to say in reply.

"Lieutenant Thornton," Andre addressed the American officer formally in his fractured syntax. "My colleague, Larion Daneelivich Sulupin, advises that though his family are Belorussian, they were living in Lithuania when war came. Since Lithuania no more, Larion Daneelivich believe family qualify for exemption from repatriation. Lithuania now Soviet Union. I, too, Belorussian, but I living and working in the capital, Minsk, when war come. I teaching English, so Belarus my country of origin."

"Are you sure, Andre?" Thornton asked again, hopeful that he may be able to persuade Andre to modify his position so that he would be able to assist him as well.

"I positive, Lieutenant," Andre replied solemnly. "Besides, if my family alive, they be in Belarus. If they not alive, I too old, too tired to start new life in new country. But I like thank you, sincerely, for you try help me. I insulted, threatened, and beaten many times by many people. You, your soldiers, first people who treat me as fellow man. It rests my soul. Mankind have hope in future, maybe, long as people like you treat us people with kindness, with respect. Not cruel and not contempt."

"Advise Mr. Sulupin that I would like to have him attend tomorrow morning at 0900 hours so that I can initiate the preparation of their identity papers," Thornton replied. "Also advise him that it would be extremely helpful if he could come up with a city or town or an address in Lithuania as well. That is a requirement for their identity and travel papers."

The following morning the Sulupin family was up early to make themselves as presentable as possible. Larion and Tamara even combed their hair for the first time in months. Dimitri's hair was carefully combed so not to disturb his fresh bandage, but Larion was obliged to apply some of his saliva to keep a wayward lock from drooping over his son's forehead.

Tamara had rubbed her cheeks a rosy red in her attempt to remove the last vestiges of grime. They then examined themselves in the dull reflection of the barracks' window. Though the faces that peered back at them seemed a bit pitiful, they believed that they were reasonably presentable, dressed in their new clothes.

Andre came to their barracks to accompany them to Lieutenant Thornton's office to assist them in their official processing.

Larion entered the office casually, while Tamara entered with an innocent shyness. Little Dimitri entered confidently and immediately proceeded to introduce himself.

"Dimitri Daneelivich Sulupin!" he announced proudly, adding an American salute he had observed the American soldiers exchanging on the camp grounds.

Dimitri's innocent antics brought a smile to Thornton's face. Then proceeding efficiently through Andre, he invited them to be seated and he initiated his formal interview so that he would be able to provide them with their respective papers, without which they were basically captives.

He proceeded to have his subordinate type in the date and place of the interview, their full names, gender, and place of birth. He also recorded their respective parents' names and their habitual place of residence. Fortunately, Larion, when he had previously been assigned to Leningrad, was able to recall the names of some of the cities proximate to the Soviet border. He decided to select the capital of Lithuania—the city of Vilnius, as their residence and place of birth.

Once the identity forms were completed, he had another subordinate take their respective photographs. He was able to persuade Tamara to remove Dimitri's bandage and his photograph was taken in profile from his left side. The one thing which stuck out in Thornton's mind was that all three individuals adopted a solemn, almost a sad demeanor when their photographs were taken.

It seemed odd to Thornton when he thought of the standard practice in the United States. Photographed individuals would beam radiant smiles at the camera, not frown. However, being photographed in the United States was usually a happy event, whereas being photographed in Germany at the conclusion of a war was a solemn event, especially when one was not sure of his or her future.

Thornton left Andre's application for last, hoping that he would have a change of heart; however, Andre remained resolute in his decision to be repatriated back to Belarus.

"Andre, please advise your friends that they now will have to be examined by our doctor and nurse. X-rays will also be taken to ensure that they are not infected with tuberculosis. Tell them that we should have the photographs processed today and they can come by and pick up their identity papers tomorrow morning. Tell them this is the first step in the commencement of their new lives.

"Their papers shall entitle them to leave and return to this camp as they may deem fit. Indeed, they shall be permitted to travel throughout Germany. Mr. Sulupin shall be entitled to go into the city to find employment and Mrs. Sulupin shall be entitled to go into the city to do some shopping, once they have earned some money.

"In fact, management of the Henschel factory have approached me about possibly hiring some of their former forced labor workers to come back to work for them again, but now they shall be paid."

"Lieutenant Thornton, assistance appreciated much, but past two years, we 'OST' workers not pay. 'German workers' and 'guest workers' pay. Maybe you suggest Henschel pay OST workers, then OST workers work again?"

"I will make that suggestion to Henschel, Andre," Thornton replied. "It certainly seems fair to me. There will be a lot of available work rebuilding Kassel, which shall start soon, so labor should be at a premium, especially for experienced factory workers. And you may tell Mr. Sulupin that I shall insist on a prepayment of three months wages…as sort of a signing bonus. Henschel is going back to building locomotives. They will not be building tanks or rockets for quite a while."

"*Dobra* (Excellent)!" Andre replied, quickly translating the message back to Larion, who smiled for the first time since he had met Lieutenant Thornton.

"But you, Andre, I would like you to help set up a school for the approximate twenty children currently living in this camp. Please recruit a couple of women who may be interested. I would like to have the education program started as quickly as possible. Tell me what your immediate needs are and I shall try to fulfill them as quickly as I can, but it is time to get the children's lives back on track as well. You and the other teachers will also receive a modest salary."

*****

As the four friends walked away from Thornton's office, they were so elated at their quickly changing circumstances. They felt they were floating above the walkway and their feet were not touching the ground. It was as if they had just been literally reborn.

Chapter 44

Hitler, to appear 'selfless', elected to waive his 'salary', but when advised that he was substantially in arrears on his taxes, he was made retroactively 'tax exempt'.

Henschel offered Larion the total sum of 150 *RM*. His future monthly salary was to be 50 *RM*. Furthermore, Lieutenant Thornton assured him that if he was not satisfied with his payment or his salary or his working conditions, he was not obliged to return to work. Larion accepted the 150 *RM*, since he reasoned that it was in payment for services he had already rendered, but he was not prepared to go back to work for even ten hours a day, six days a week at monthly salary of 50 *RM* a month. With his 150 *RM* in his pocket, Larion walked to Kassel and attempted to spend his newfound wealth; however, what he was confronted with was a devastated city core. There were very few operating stores and those stores barely had any inventory left and what inventory there was, was exorbitantly priced. After searching for hours for a suitable gift for Tamara and Dimitri, he was prepared to give up. The 150 *RM* were basically useless pieces of paper. Finally, he approached a fountain which was still working in one of the remaining city parks to quench his throat and consider what he should do. Larion did not notice a young German in his mid-twenties watching him from the shade of an adjacent tree.

"*Hallo, mein freund* (Hello, my friend)," the young German called out to him. "*Wie Gehts* (How are you)?" He had curly brown hair, sparkling blue eyes, and a bemused smile on his thin lips. Larion looked around to see who was speaking and then the young German rose from the grass, brushed off his pants, and proceeded to approach him, his hands casually tucked inside his trouser pockets. Larion examined him cautiously. He was not used to having the freedom to roam around the city and he was unsure why the young German decided to hail him in the first place. "*Was ist dein problem* (What is your problem)?

Kann ich dir helfen (May I help you)? *Deutsch verstehen* (Do you understand German)?"

"*Ein wenig* (A little)," Larion replied as the young German extended his right hand for a handshake.

"If you are able to sell me a small bottle of champagne and some chocolates," Larion replied, curious as to how the young man would respond. "Then perhaps you may be of some assistance."

The young German was sincerely surprised. The last response he expected to elicit in the bombed-out city core of Kassel was a young foreigner looking for champagne and chocolates.

"My friend, you may be asking for too much," he replied. "Look around you. Does this look like Berlin, Paris, or London? Perhaps we should forget about Berlin," he added jokingly.

Larion took the extended hand and squeezed it firmly, quickly releasing it in case his new friend's intentions were not totally honorable. He didn't want to be disadvantaged holding his hand.

"Helmut Seiz, at your service!" he replied, bowing slightly. "And you are…?"

"Larion Sulupin…at your service," Larion mimicked his reply. "I have been a 'guest' at your Henschel factory for the past couple of years. They finally paid me 150 *RM* and I have nothing to spend the money on. But seriously, I am looking to purchase some champagne and chocolate, but it appears no one has any to sell."

"You must have been one of our Russian 'guests', *nein*?"

"I was one of your Russian 'guests', *ja*!" Larion replied. Seiz may be a German, but he obviously had a sense of humor, so Larion decided to reciprocate.

"My friend, if you really want something or you really need something, I assure you that it is still available…even in Kassel at this time. But of all of the things a man could possibly ask for, why would you be asking for champagne and chocolate? They are not the necessities of life."

Larion was not sure if he wanted to continue this conversation, but the young German suddenly had an epiphany.

"It has to be a beautiful *fraulein, nein*?"

"*Ja!* It is a very beautiful *fraulein*…my wife. The mother of my young son. She reminded me recently that I never brought her any champagne, chocolate, or flowers, when I was courting her. I would like to be able to fulfil those obligations."

"She must be very beautiful, *mein herr*. I envy you," the young German responded. "But perhaps I may be of some assistance. Are you familiar with the *Schwarzmarkt*?"

The 'black market'?" Larion asked.

"*Ja! Der Schwarzmarkt!*" he replied with a mischievous grin. "All you need is to know someone…who knows someone."

"But that is my problem. I do not know 'someone'," Larion replied.

"*Mein freund!*" Seiz exclaimed with satisfaction. "You know me! I am your 'someone'!"

"Well, *mein freund!*" Larion replied. "How much will it cost me?"

"That is the problem, my dear friend. The commodities you seek are available, but they are pretty scarce. I believe you may purchase a bottle of French champagne and a box of Swiss chocolates for 500 *RM*."

"But, *mein freund*," Larion replied, "I have already told you that I only have 150 *RM*."

"No problem, *mein herr*," Seiz replied dismissively, then asked. "*Glucksspiel – mann* (Are you a gambling man)? *Karten spielen* (Do you play cards)?"

Larion simply smiled at his would-be, self-professed, newfound friend. He was not sure if he was about to be taken advantage of or whether this young German could be a friend. However, the *150 RM* he had in his pocket seemed to be worthless in any case, consequently, he decided to take a chance.

"I have played on occasion, but not for a while," Larion replied.

"*Ich verstehen, mein freund* (I understand, my friend)."

$$*****$$

Helmut Seiz then proceeded to make Larion a proposal which he hoped that the Russian would accept. He would introduce him to a group of card players and if he was successful, he would introduce him to some black marketeers who would sell him a bottle of French champagne and a box of Swiss chocolates for 500 *RM*. When Larion inquired about the flowers, Seiz casually pointed to the flowers in the park and suggested that he could take as many as he wanted without any cost.

However, when Seiz got back to the matter of gambling, he cautioned Larion that the group of card players were all German and that he should be prepared that they would play as a team against him, even for a relatively paltry sum of 150 *RM.* He was relieved that Larion's ability in the German language was much better than what Larion had initially claimed. He suggested that he keep his true ability in German to himself.

Larion finally asked Seiz what was in it for him. He was surprised by Seiz's response.

"I will simply make the introductions and I intend to watch you carefully and decide if I would really like to have you as a friend," Seiz confessed. "Someone who I can rely upon and someone who I can trust. Someone who I deem to be worthy of my friendship. That is all!"

"And I would like you to know that my expectations of you are the same, *mein freund*!" Larion replied.

*****

The card game was a variation of American 'stud'. Each player received five cards and then there was an initial bet before anyone could draw some replacement cards. Then each player put his cards in the order he wanted to reveal them and after the first card was disclosed by all of the players, there was a second bet. If any player elected to just 'call', he was precluded from raising another player's bet. After four of the five cards were disclosed, there was a final raise. High hand won.

Larion tried to remember the lessons old Valodya had tried to teach him years ago. The most important lesson was that he had to pay attention to the flow of the cards. At times, fortune seemed to smile on a particular player in that the winning cards would simply end up in that player's hand for a while. However, he was also taught to remember that luck was deceitful and fickle…it could change in a heartbeat.

He was also taught that if luck was not running in his direction, he had the choice of either slowly bleeding to death by simply continuing to surrender his 'ante' (participation bet) each hand or he could simply walk away or he could bet his entire bankroll on one hand if he had that indescribable premonition that luck was about to change and smile upon him.

But old Valodya had taught him other rules of engagement as well. He should never permit any player to draw new cards for free. If a player was going to discard some cards, he should be obligated to pay for the new cards. A small initial bet from all of the participants increased the pot and encouraged higher bets at the end of the game. He also advised that he should learn to keep the opposing players uncertain.

This was accomplished by revealing his last card, on occasion, to show that the last bet was a bluff and that his draw did not perfect his hand, after the remaining players folded. But it was equally important to disclose the last card, on occasion, to show that he had perfected his hand. The final overriding rule was that he had to be inconsistent and not reveal his last card every time the other players folded. It was important to keep his opponents guessing.

*****

The game had continued for about two hours before Larion lost the last of his 150 *Reich Marks*. He was about to rise from the table and leave when Seiz withdrew a thick roll of *Reich Marks* and deposited a further 1000 *RM* in front of Larion.

"Alright, *mein freund*," he announced confidently. "I believe that you have toyed with these gentlemen long enough. Let us play some serious poker now!"

Larion looked at Seiz, who returned his stare with an enigmatic smile. Seiz then winked at Larion as if to say that the preliminaries were over and that Larion should go for the other players' jugulars and their scrotums. There was to be no mercy!

*****

Within another two hours, Larion succeeded in winning a further 3000 *RM*. A couple of the other players then indicated that they were going to leave after one last game if they lost, but if they won, they reserved the right to keep on playing. To be fair, Larion announced that the next hand was going to be his last hand, win or lose. If they wanted to win back their money, they were going to have to play hard against him.

Larion's initial hand contained three hearts, including the ace of hearts, the deuce and the five. The remaining two cards were discarded. His drawn cards included the three of clubs and the four of spades. He had succeeded in completing an inside straight. He was confident that it was probably a winning hand, but having a winning hand did not guarantee that you would win a big pot.

The strategy now was how to arrange the cards so that the other players would assume that he was bluffing a strong hand and stay in the hand to the bitter end. If one player continued to play, he would double his bankroll to 8000 *RM*. If two players stayed, he might be able to win 12000 *RM*. Whatever the end result, it certainly beat working two hundred and fifty hours for 50 *RM* a month.

Larion decided to reveal the ace of hearts first. He anticipated that the other players would become confused by him revealing such a strong card at the outset, instead of concealing it to the end. He hoped that most of the players would assume that he intended to bluff and that the two cards which he had drawn did not help his hand.

The next two cards he played were the other two hearts. Basically, he hoped that the other players would assume that he was trying to bluff an ace-high heart flush; however, they would have to call two more times to see his entire hand. Two of the players decided to call his third bet. The fourth card which Larion disclosed was the four of spades. At that point, Larion was no longer showing a potential heart flush which was interrupted by the spade. Therefore, his best possible hand was a straight—the ace through to the five, if his two drawn cards completed it. His second-best possible hand was that he may have picked up a second Ace. Any other player at the table who had two of kind or three of a kind or better, would have the better hand.

Larion proceeded to raise the final 1500 *RM* he had in front of him and he slowly pushed those bills into the center of the round poker table. The remaining two players would have to call this final bet to protect the 2500 *RM* investment each of them had made to that point in time. The first player threw his cards down in disgust.

He was certain that Larion had two aces, which beat the two kings which he was showing. His hole card was totally useless. He had attempted to disclose the two kings as his third and fourth reveals to bluff a potential three kings, but he had convinced himself that Larion's strategy was to disclose one ace at the outset and the second ace was his hole card. Otherwise, why would the Russian make such a bet against his two kings? Two aces always beat two kings.

The remaining player had disclosed a pair of tens as his third and fourth reveals. He was more confident than the preceding player who just folded his hand in disgust. His hole card was a third ten. Three tens always beat two aces. He also assumed that Larion was trying to fill a heart flush and that was why he had retained the deuce and five of hearts. But, both of his drawn cards would have to fit in between the ace and five of hearts.

It was extremely difficult to fill an 'inside' straight with one card. If his assumption was correct, Larion would have had to have drawn two cards to complete his inside straight, which he deemed was statistically next to impossible. He also assumed that Larion may have assumed that he was bluffing and that he did not have the third ten.

He called Larion's final bet and pushed his 1500 *RM* into the pot and waited for Larion to concede defeat. To his utter surprise, Larion merely reached for his final hole card and flipped it over to reveal the three of clubs. Larion's straight beat his three tens. There was no reason for him to even bother revealing his third ten. He turned his revealed cards face down, conceding defeat. He had been positive that he had succeeded in inducing Larion to believe that he only had two tens so that Larion would make that final bet, only to discover that he was the one who had been trapped.

"*Danke, mein herr*," Larion said politely as he reached over to collect his winnings, but he was on his guard. He was also oblivious to Seiz casually moving his right hand inside his jacket pocket. At times, disgruntled players took exception to luck turning against them. After all, there was over 11000 *RM* in the center of the table. But if there was a displeased player at this table, he would have to guess whether or not Seiz was holding a concealed pistol or whether he was just bluffing. Considering Larion's last turn of luck in filling an inside straight with a two-card draw, no one seemed inclined to see if Seiz might be bluffing. The losing player just continued to stare at the small straight in disbelief.

*****

After the other players left, Larion counted out his original 150 *RM* and Seiz's 1000 *RM*.

"I believe we get to share a profit of 5000 *RM* each, *mein freund*," Larion announced with a smile, handing Seiz his share. "Now, you promised me that you would get me some French champagne and Swiss chocolates for my beautiful *fraulein*, who will probably not be too pleased with me since I shall be two hours late for dinner."

"If we're going to be friends, it is time we started addressing ourselves by our respective first names, Larion. My black marketeers are just around the corner and I believe that I better arrange safe transport back to the camp for you. In that way, you shall not be two hours late and you will be safe. And if you wish to join me in my little enterprises, I would be more than pleased to discuss having you as my partner. But I hope this afternoon has demonstrated that you can sweat for Henschel for 50 *RM* a month or you can earn 5000 *RM* in one day with me."

*****

Tamara was initially concerned about Larion's tardiness, but as she watched him approach their barracks through the now clean window, her concern turned to first relief that he was safe, then to disappointment that he could be so irresponsible.

"Tamara, my love," Larion beseeched her. "I beg you to forgive me for returning late."

Then he pulled his right hand from behind his back to reveal a beautiful bouquet of flowers.

The surprise flustered Tamara momentarily, while little Dimitri went running happily up to greet his father, grabbing him around his left thigh.

"Humm!" Tamara stammered. "The flowers are nice. In fact, they are beautiful, but your dinner is ruined. It is cold. I shall have to reheat it and it probably will not be the same. Lieutenant Thornton showed me and some of the other ladies how to make this Italian dish—it is called 'pasta'.

"I really truly apologize and I beg your forgiveness, my love," Larion pleaded, feigning sincerity, but Tamara detected a mischievous smirk. Then Larion pulled out a bottle of champagne from the inside of his jacket pocket.

"What is this?" Tamara asked. "A bottle of wine?"

"It is champagne, my love," Larion replied, still attempting to appear contrite. "You criticized me for not bringing you flowers and champagne when I was courting you, so I worked very hard today and I was able to locate some flowers and some champagne—just for you."

"What is the matter with you, Louyna?" Tamara asked indignantly. "First, you are late for dinner. Then you show up with flowers and a bottle of champagne. I am surprised that you have not brought me chocolates, as well."

"Well, I must confess, my love, that I was also able to find you some chocolates. But not just any chocolates, Swiss chocolates. I am told that they are the best chocolates in the world!"

With that confession, Larion reached into his jacket again and pulled out a small box of chocolates.

"Will you forgive me now, my love?" Larion asked forlornly.

"*Oh, ty glupyy prestupnik* (Oh, you silly delinquent)!" Tamara replied, but her disappointment was dissipating quickly as she recalled admonishing Larion for his acts of omission during their courtship.

"Mother," little Dimitri announced with concern as he stepped between his parents. "You are being much too harsh with father. Look at the *podarki* (presents) he has brought you.

"Yes, Tamara, my love," Larion added a bit insincerely. "Just look at your presents."

Tamara looked down at her son and she could only shake her head in a motherly disbelief.

"Here I have carried you inside of me for nine months; I have nursed you; I have cared for you. And now that your father and I have a disagreement, you abandon me and defend him."

"No, mother," Dimitri replied emotionally. "I love you both, but I do not want you to argue with each other, that is all."

"And I love you both as well, my dear, protective, little son," Tamara replied, then she gently tousled Dimitri's bandaged head and reached up to passionately kiss her prodigal husband.

*****

While Larion ate his reheated meal, Tamara sipped her small portion of champagne from a chipped ceramic mug. Dimitri yearned for one of the chocolates, but he was taught to be patient and wait to be offered a treat, since it was rude to ask. He simply stared silently at the chocolates in the ornate colored box, occasionally looking up at his mother to remind her that it was impolite of her not to offer him one.

"Alright, young man," Tamara said, finally yielding. "Dimitri, why don't you select one of the chocolates for yourself."

*****

After Larion finished his meal and Dimitri was put to sleep in their bunk, Tamara offered to share some of her champagne with her husband. Larion took a sip, but he was unimpressed.

"I do not understand why women are so enamored with *champagnski*," he said. "It is a bit sweet and it does not have much of a kick to it."

"Perhaps it is because women prefer to drink in a more refined fashion. We are not interested in racing to see who gets drunk first. And those bubbles make the drink more refreshing."

Larion chose not to respond. He merely watched his attractive, young wife taste one of the chocolates and take a sip of her champagne from her ceramic mug. He had made her happy and that was all that mattered. He would discuss the recent change in their finances tomorrow morning and discuss Seiz's proposal for a business partnership. In his mind, he had decided that working in the Henschel factory for the preceding two years was enough to last him a lifetime.

Chapter 45

The following morning, Tamara awakened Dimitri early so that she could take him to Lieutenant Thornton's office to pick up their identity papers and then go to his first day of classes. Andre was waiting for her outside her barracks, but he did not notice her come out initially since he was watching three Soviet soldiers who had arrived in a military vehicle and parked outside of Thornton's office. They were the same soldiers with whom Larion had exchanged insults the previous day. He decided that he would keep that information to himself because he did not want Tamara to be unduly concerned.

"Good morning, Andre," Tamara greeted their new friend happily.

Larion's surprise gifts had pleased her immensely, but she was hopeful that they would receive some new accommodations which could provide them with more privacy. The lack of any personal privacy in the barracks for the preceding two years seemed bearable before, but no longer.

As they approached Thornton's office, the Soviet captain called out to Dimitri. "*Debroye utra malenkiy malchik* (Good morning, little boy). *Vy pomimayete po-russki* (Do you understand Russian)?"

Tamara felt an instant chill run down her spine as she clutched Dimitri's hand firmly and dragged him away from the soldier's vehicle.

"But mother," Dimitri explained. "We are being rude to these strangers."

"Dimitri, come, we have to go inside and get our papers," she replied anxiously.

"*Ne perezhivay, suka* (Do not worry, bitch). *Tvoy synok nechego boyatsya nas* (Your son need not fear us). *Ve otichiye ot vas, vash syn nevinoven* (Unlike you, he is innocent)." Then they burst into a cruel laughter when they saw that they had succeeded in scaring her.

Andre proceeded to open the office door and quickly ushered Tamara and Dimitri away from the three soldiers. Tamara's former joy had been quickly replaced by her fear that the Soviet soldiers would attempt to apprehend her son and take him away from her. As they entered the office, Lieutenant Thornton, ever pleasant and accommodating, approached them carrying some documents.

"Please come in. Your documents have just been delivered. Andre, please explain to Mrs. Sulupin that their X-rays were clean. No sign of tuberculosis."

Tamara examined the two Identity Certificates, which were on a regular-sized page of yellow paper. Dimitri and his photograph had been added to her *Identity Certificate*.

International Refugee Organization
U.S. Zone of Germany
Serial No. 2G-7085
Certificate of Identify for the Purpose of Travel and Immigration

1.   *The holder of this Certificate is the concern of the International Refugee Organization.*

2.   *This Certificate is issued by the International Refugee Organization to Refugees and Displaced Persons qualified for emigration to* **Canada.** *It is issued without prejudice to and in no way affects the Holder's nationality.*

3.   *This Certificate is NOT valid for travel unless it bears the signature of the I.R.O. Officer.*

Exit Visa (reverse side) and the appropriate Military Permit has been granted.

FAMILY	*CHRISTIAN NAME*
Sulupina	Tamara
MAIDEN NAME	Shanina
DATE OF BIRTH	06 March 1920 *Sex* F
DP No. 584552	

(PHOTO)

PLACE AND COUNTRY OF BIRTH Vilnius, Lithuania
NATIONALITY	Stateless Person
OCCUPATION	Farm Worker
FATHER'S NAME	Dimitri Shanin

MOTHER'S MAIDEN NAME   Josephina Dorokuna
Height 160 cm **Weight** 52 kg
Nose Straight **Shape of Face** Oval
Special Characteristics None *(PHOTO)*

Children up to 16 years accompanying Holder
Hair Blonde **Name**   **Sex Place and Date of Birth**
Eyes Blue/ Sulupin, Dimitri M Vilnius 05 May 1941
(SIGNATURE)
Resettlement Officer (signature and position)
Date 2 May 1945 *(VISA OVER)*   **Place** Furstenwald DP Camp
(Kassel)

Tamara also examined Larion's *Identity Certificate*. Though they shared the same *DP* No, Larion's Serial No. was sequential and it came first: *2-G 7084.*

Thornton proceeded to explain, through Andre, that he had included their common place of birth as Vilnius, Lithuania, as it was related to him by her husband. Inasmuch as the Soviet Union had absorbed Lithuania and the other two Baltic states in June of 1940, Lithuania ceased to exist. To that extent, he had stipulated that her nationality, along with that of her son and her husband, were that of 'Stateless Persons'. The significance of that stipulation was that it gave him the discretion to exempt them from the 'forced repatriation' protocol.

"As you can see, Andre," Thornton explained, pointing to same three Soviet soldiers sitting in their military vehicle. "Our Soviet allies seem to be very anxious to get me to forcibly transfer the Sulupins to them for repatriation to the Soviet Union. But I am only acting as a temporary *I.R.O.* officer and I shall be transferring that authority as soon as the official *UNRR* official arrives in a couple of weeks.

"He is a Canadian and acting on his authority, I have even approved the Sulupin family to emigrate to Canada, but there are a couple of additional formalities which they will have to resolve with Mr. Lionel Balmelle, the *I.R.O* officer personally.

"I should be able to fend off the Soviet's demands for summary repatriation until then, but please explain to both Mr. and Mrs. Sulupin, that these Identity and Travel Certificates should be utilized as soon as possible. I strongly recommend that they move to another DP Camp as soon as possible. So long as our Soviet friends know that they are here, they will continue to press for their forced return."

*****

When Tamara returned to their barracks at about noon, she was pleasantly surprised to find that Larion had prepared a light lunch for all of them.

"Larion, Lieutenant Thornton gave me our Identity and Travel Certificates, but he also strongly recommended that we move to another DP Camp as soon as possible," Tamara explained, giving Larion his papers. "There were three Soviet officers who were pressing the Americans to turn us over to them. They insulted and scared me. I was afraid that they might try to snatch Dimitri out of my arms."

"I understand, Tamara," Larion replied. "They were probably the same Soviets that I ran into with Andre. I had asked Andre to try to teach me some English and we went to the Lieutenant's office to obtain an English book and some writing material. But apparently, five years of bloodshed and killing has not been enough for those Russians. But I have some good news for you in any case."

*****

Larion proceeded to relate the events of the previous day and his gambling success. Tamara remained somewhat incredulous until Larion showed her his remaining 4500 *RM.*

"So, what is it you propose to do?" Tamara asked apprehensively.

"Even if we were able to stay here, I had decided that I was not going to work at the Henschel factory for 50 *RM* per month (before taxes)," Larion explained. "They have squeezed two years of free labor out of me and then they only paid me 150 *RM.* I know that I cannot provide for you and Dimitri on the salary they are offering me now. Let them find some Germans to work for that kind of money. The war is ended and hundreds of thousands of *Wehrmacht* soldiers are returning home and they will be looking for work."

"So, what is it that you propose to do?" Tamara repeated her question.

"I have told you about this Helmut Seiz. He is about my age and I believe that I may be able to make some money with him. There are risks, but we would share those risks," Larion replied.

"Are you speaking about 'illegal matters' or the *chernyy rynok* (black market)?" Tamara asked. "If you get involved in illegal matters and you are arrested by the Americans, they may have to send you back to the Soviet Union. If the German authorities arrest you, you may just go to prison here in Germany. If that happens, then what am I and Dimitri going to do?"

"There are risks in all facets of life right now, Tamara," Larion replied. "At the Henschel factory, men were being crippled and killed on a weekly basis. Their work might be legal, but the money they are offering to pay me is not sufficient when you consider our cost of living and those risks. What if I am crippled or killed in a factory accident? What would you do then?"

Tamara remained silent as she listened to Larion's explanation, but if he thought that he was allaying her concerns, he was sadly mistaken. If anything, his explanations only increased her anxiety and her concern, not only for herself and their son, but for him as well. She could not conceive of a life without her son…or without her husband.

"I believe I understand, Larion…at least a little bit," Tamara replied solemnly. "But I want you to understand me as well. If you get yourself arrested…or imprisoned…or God forbid… killed…! I shall never be able to forgive you!"

Larion simply looked at his wife helplessly. How could he possibly rebut that kind of innocent logic or argument? It only made him adore her even more.

"My love…" Larion replied solemnly, "I love you and Dimitri with all of my heart and soul. I shall be obliged to take some risks over the next couple of weeks…I will not lie to you and tell you otherwise. But I promise you that any risks which I may be obliged to take shall be measured carefully. If matters work out the way I hope they will, we should have the finances for a better life, whether we decide to stay in Europe or emigrate to this…*Canada*. I promise you solemnly on the memory of your father, old Valodya, and my parents."

Tears commenced to well up in Tamara's eyes and little Dimitri noticed that his mother was starting to cry. He could not understand why, because his parents were not arguing, but he could not understand their conversation either.

"Mother! Please do not be sad. Do not cry…for I may become sad and cry too and then I know that you will just become sadder and cry even more."

"Come here, both of you!" Tamara commanded, between her intermittent sobs. "I want to hold both of you…tightly so that neither one of you shall ever leave me. Please hold me close."

*****

After lunch, Tamara and Dimitri went back to their makeshift classroom which Andre had been able to plaster together. Tamara and two of the other young camp women, who also had children of their own, had volunteered help Andre to set up a simple educational program for approximately twenty children aged four to ten. After enduring years of inactivity, all of the children were enthusiastic about learning…practically anything.

As Larion was attempting to think out his own alternatives, a young American soldier—but to be truthful, they all seemed so young to him even though he was only twenty-seven himself—advised him that he had a visitor waiting for him at the camp office. His name was Helmut Seiz.

*****

"*Guten tag,* Helmut, *mein freund*!" Larion addressed him as Seiz spun around and smiled upon seeing Larion.

"Larion, *mein freund*!" Seiz replied enthusiastically. "It is good to see you again. Are you ready to make some more money?"

Seiz proceeded to explain to Larion that the card-playing companions wanted an opportunity to win back some of their lost funds, if he was so inclined. Larion assured him that he was more than willing to give them another opportunity, but hopefully for them to lose, not win. Seiz then explained that there may be a couple of new players as well. Larion responded that he could not see how that would be a problem, but there was one remaining issue to resolve between themselves.

"And how is our partnership going to work this time, Helmut?" Larion inquired.

"We shall both contribute 2500 *RM* and share any winnings or losses equally," Seiz explained. "Would that be satisfactory to you?"

"It sounds fair to me, Helmut," Larion replied. "Although I do the playing, you make the arrangements for the game and you also trust me with your

296

money, which permits me to bet more and hopefully win more. I believe it is fair to both of us. Are we agreed?"

"So agreed!" Seiz replied.

"But I am a bit apprehensive to ask you when this game is going to be held," Larion confessed.

"Later this afternoon," Seiz replied. "We shall be obligated to play until curfew at 1100 hours or when we run out of money, whichever comes first. They have that rule because some winners like to run away quickly if they are winning, but they want everyone to play forever when they are losing. After the first curfew deadline, play is optional for whoever may want to continue to play."

"I was afraid that it might be today," Larion confessed. "My wife and I had a long conversation at noon today and I was hoping that I would not do anything else today, to stress her more."

"The players shall be bringing a lot of money, Larion, but I shall leave it up to you," Seiz replied. "I do not want to be held responsible for upsetting your *fraulein*. Sometimes the value of a good woman cannot be compared to a possible monetary gain—at least, that is what my mother told me one time."

"Well, I better go see her in any case," Larion replied. "I should inform her of the change of plans. By the way, you were in the military during the war, correct? I only ask since you said 1100 hours instead of nine o'clock."

"I have done a lot of things during this war, Larion," Seiz replied equivocally. "And I may have even spent a couple of years in the *Wehrmacht* as well."

*****

Tamara was not pleased at the new development in Larion's plans for the day, but she assured him that she was conditionally resigned to his new way of life. However, she reminded him of her condition that he be careful and he assured her that he had not forgotten.

Seiz was also extremely polite and courteous when Larion introduced him to Tamara and to Dimitri. He did not want to say or do anything which might contribute to any increased anxiety which Tamara may be feeling. He knew that trying to deny all possible risks would neither be honest nor truthful. He merely assured her that they would take all reasonable precautions.

"Larion, until I met you, I had never met a man who was prepared to spend 500 *RM* on a bottle of sparkling wine and a small box of chocolates, but after meeting your beautiful wife, I can understand why you would do such a thing," Seiz confessed. "*Mein freund*, I salute you."

"You mean to say that you have never done such a thing?" Larion asked, somewhat surprised at Seiz's admission.

"Not for 500 *RM*," Seiz replied laughingly. 'Perhaps 250 *RM*, but never 500 *RM*. If I ever meet a woman for whom I would be prepared to pay that kind of money for a bottle of sparkling wine and a box of chocolates, I would propose to her on the spot and ask her to bear my children as well."

"Remember, Helmut," Larion chided his new friend, "it was a bottle of French champagne, not just a bottle of sparkling wine and it was a box of Swiss chocolates. The best chocolates in the world."

"You are right, *mein freund*," Seiz replied with a smirk. "But here is a present for you, just in case things get difficult today."

He reached inside his jacket pocket and pulled out a small pistol. It was a *Walther PPK* (*PolizeiPistole Kriminal*). It had a sleek modern design with a seven-cartridge magazine. Seiz explained that it was originally manufactured in 1929.

He would not recommend it for war; however, within the close confines of a poker room, it had distinct advantages. It was discreet and easily concealed. It was also deadly at close quarters, but he did recommend a double shot in the event Larion was obliged to shoot anyone. Just to be certain.

"The last time you played, I believe there were two players at the table who were contemplating stripping you of your winnings; however, all I had to do was reach into my jacket pocket and they had a change of heart. That is the reason why I decided to arrange for your transportation back to the Camp. Greed motivates stupid people to do stupid things from time to time. But even stupid people can get lucky once in a while. I trust you know how to use it?"

"*Danke, mein freund*," Larion replied. "I will know how before we get to our destination."

Chapter 46

The Soviet captain and his two non-commissioned officers were watching the people and the vehicles which were entering and exiting the Camp. Since their American allies were being difficult in acceding to their demands for the forced repatriation of the insolent Belorussian and his family, he was hopeful that an opportunity would present itself whereby they take custody of him in any case. The Belorussian was not that important, in himself, but the Soviet Captain was not inclined to permit anyone to insult him and escape unscathed. In fact, he was contemplating not even repatriating him back to the Soviet Union and simply exacting his revenge, personally.

But Germany had been divided into four independent Zones. The Soviet Zone occupied the north eastern third of the country, while the British Zone was immediately to the west of the Soviet Zone. The American Zone occupied the south eastern third of the country, immediately to the south of the British Zone. The final and smallest Zone was a narrow strip of land along the western boundary of the British Zone and the American Zone, which was allocated to the French as a token gesture, since it was bounded by France immediately to the west.

The Soviet Captain's plan was to apprehend Sulupin as he was either leaving or returning to the camp. Then the intention was that he would be transported north to the Soviet Zone for final disposition. Either summary execution or forced repatriation to Belarus.

They initially noticed a decrepit Volkswagen enter the compound and then, shortly thereafter, it exited the camp and they noticed that the rude Belorussian was seated in the front passenger seat. The vehicle was moving quickly and there was substantial traffic on the road, so the decision was made that they would move farther away from the Camp and attempt to interdict him on his return. After all, it was reasonable to assume that since that vehicle had come to the camp to pick him up, it would also return him to the camp as well. All they had to do was be patient and wait.

What irritated the Soviet Captain almost as much was the young, sanctimonious American Lieutenant when he advised him that he had just issued *Identity and Travel Certificates* for the family. The American was obviously hoping that it would dissuade him from pursuing Sulupin. The Sulupin family could travel or be transferred to another DP Camp in the American Zone and they would lose track of him, so time was critical.

*****

When Helmut and Larion arrived at the poker game in Kassel, the other five players had already arrived and were anxious to commence play, though they did not bother to commence play between themselves. One of the five German players was the individual who had lost the final hand to Larion. They were waiting for the lucky Belorussian who was able to pull a proverbial rabbit out of a hat. They could not bring themselves to believe that a Slav had the intelligence and the guile to outwit them. A Jew, perhaps, but never a subhuman Slav. They had agreed that they would play as a team and focus solely on defeating him.

By agreement, all players placed 5000 *RM* in front of them to qualify to play. No money was to be removed from the table until the initial deadline, the 1100-hour curfew. No player was permitted to leave before that deadline, on penalty of forfeiting the funds he had on the table.

If a player was wiped out, he was permitted to advance himself not less than another 5000 *RM* stake. After the first curfew deadline, any player could leave of his own volition. Extensions in play after that deadline would be in one-hour increments and subject to the same rules.

It quickly became obvious to Larion that the Germans would only play if they had a reasonable hand. Furthermore, they were all reluctant in initiating bets, since they expected Larion to make those preliminary bets to build up the pots as he did the first time he played with them. Finally, they would not play against each other if Larion folded his hand. One or the other player would simply concede the hand to the other player.

However, old Valodya had also cautioned Larion that when circumstances change, your poker strategy had to change as well.

Consequently, Larion decided that he would not initiate any raises, which forced the other players to eventually raise instead. Secondly, if he was not reasonably confident that he had a winning hand, he would simply fold his hand as soon as possible. He wanted to convey to the other players that he had no intention of bluffing this day. However, he was reasonably successful in catching a couple of the other players when they attempted to bluff him.

Finally, he decided that he would not disclose his final 'hole' card under any circumstances. If they wanted to see his last card, they would have to call his bet. This changed strategy eventually forced his opponents to initiate the betting themselves and even play against each other. Larion would simply fold his hand, sit back, and observe their play.

Since it became obvious that Larion was not going to play aggressively this day, the other players finally became more cannibalistic and they commenced to turn on each other. If they could not win against Larion, they would at least try to win against each other.

After a few hours, Larion examined the stake which lay in front of him and he estimated that he was ahead approximately 1500 *RM*. Though some of the other players would count out their respective stakes once in a while, old Valodya had taught him that it was unprofessional and totally inappropriate. Valodya told him that a 'counter' differentiated a dilettante from a professional gambler.

Finally, there were only twenty minutes left before the first curfew deadline. It was also apparent that Larion's new strategy had resulted in some of the other players developing bruised egos. Some players were down substantially to the other players and they were resentful. Their collegial alliance was breaking down.

*****

Larion examined his hand. It contained three deuces and two face cards. He decided to initiate the betting for the first time and he threw away his two face cards. Probability indicated to him that his chances were better in retaining the three deuces and attempting to improve his hand from that position, rather than throwing away his 'Three of a Kind'.

When he was dealt his two replacement cards, he deliberately did not bother to examine them and he tried to ensure that the other players noticed that decision. He merely shuffled his five cards face down for a few seconds and then he placed his hand down in an obvious random order. He turned over the first card. It was one of his original deuces—a deuce of hearts.

Larion did not have to initiate the next bet since all five of the remaining players had revealed a higher card. His second revealed card was a deuce of diamonds. His pair was not the highest pair on the table since another player was showing a pair of jacks and he had the privilege of making the initial bet.

Larion then proceeded to double it with a raise. Three of the other players decided to fold and observe developments. This time the player with the high pair chose not to bet and Larion proceeded to make the initial small bet. After all, he had drawn two cards and he was just showing a pair of deuces and he had not even bothered to examine his two-card draw. He knew that he was holding three of a kind—three deuces—even though he did not know how they would be revealed.

One player at the table was showing a potential flush, while the other player, who he had beaten in the last hand the previous game, was showing a pair of Jacks. However, both of these other players knew exactly what remaining cards they held, since they had examined the cards they had drawn.

Larion's third revealed card showed a king of spades. He was showing a pair of deuces with a king. The one player who was showing a potential flush disclosed another matching suited card, so he was showing a three-card flush and he had only drawn one card. The other player who was showing a pair of Jacks, revealed an eight of hearts.

Larion had 2500 *DM* left in front of him and when the other two players elected not to bet, he decided to bet 1000 *DM.* Both of the opposing players proceeded to call his bet, but they were precluded from raising since neither one had bothered to bet in the first instance. That was a potential error on their part, but Larion concluded that both players had playable hands.

Larion then proceeded to reveal his fourth card, which was a deuce of clubs. He was now showing three deuces and his best hand was potentially four of a kind, if he was lucky enough to have drawn the fourth deuce or possibly, a full house, if his hole card was another king.

However, the player showing a potential flush who had only discarded one card remained confident. His discard happened to be the fourth deuce. The critical point was that both of his opponents believed that Larion did not know what his last card was going to be. If the one opponent's last card was another

Jack, then his three Jacks would beat Larion's three deuces. If the other player was able to get a lucky draw and complete his flush, his hand would be the overall winner.

The issue at this point was which player was going to 'blink' first. Since Larion had the technical high hand showing three deuces, it was his bet. Larion proceeded to bet only 100 *RM*. The player showing the two Jacks proceeded to call and then the player showing a potential flush raised the bet to a total 500 *RM*.

Larion finally looked at his hole card and then increased the bet to 1500 *RM*. Since he had made an initial 100 *RM* bet, he was entitled to raise under their rules.

The new critical factor was that he had looked at his hole card for the first time before he made that final bet. All three players had invested heavily into this pot, but the two German players had to figure out why Larion only made an initial 100 *RM* bet, which he subsequently increased to 1500 *RM* after he finally examined his hole card. Logic and probability would dictate that Larion had the three deuces when he made his two-card draw.

The player showing the two jacks reluctantly decided to fold his hand, even though he had a third jack as his hole card. He was sure that he had the better hand against Larion this time; however, he was confident that his colleague had completed his flush.

Finally, the remaining player quickly called Larion's bet and triumphantly turned over his hole card revealing that his one card draw was successful and that he was playing a flush—five cards of the same suit. It would take a full house or four of a kind to beat him and he knew that Larion did not hold the fourth deuce.

Larion revealed his hole card. It was a king of clubs. He had a full house, which defeated his opponent's flush.

The German player who was holding three jacks and who had lost to Larion the last time, breathed a sigh of relief and dramatically wiped his forehead. He had a losing hand against both opponents and he was relieved that his judgment, which had failed him the last time, prevailed this time.

"*MUTTER FICKER* (Motherfucker)!" the remaining German screamed in disgust. "*VERDAMMTER BETRUGER* (Goddam cheater)!"

Helmut proceeded to slowly place his right hand inside of his jacket pocket again, but Larion remained silent and he made no attempt to reach into the pot and commence gathering his winnings. He did not want such an action to be interpreted as a taunt to the losing player, which might provoke a violent reaction. He wanted to give the loser an opportunity to calm down.

"*Meine Herren! Ich erwarte dass sie alle gute. Gewinner und gute Verlierer sind* (Gentlemen, I expect you to be good winners and good losers). *Verstehst du* (Do you understand)?"

The words were spoken by a man who was standing behind Larion, but when he came into view, it was a man who he had met before. Schalburg, the *SS* colonel who had executed over three hundred civilians in Xhotimsk and who probably had Galkovskiy and Irina shot and hanged. Apparently, he was operating the poker game for a five percent slice of the money which was wagered in every pot. He was holding his Luger pistol; however, he was just pointing the barrel innocuously up at the ceiling as he limped around the table and positioned himself in front of the only door.

"*Er die karten verteiite nicht* (He did not deal the cards). *Er sehaute nicht einmal auf seine zwei gezogenen karten bis zum letzten einsatz* (He did not even look at his two drawn cards until the last wager). *Gutes spiel und viel gluck* (It was just good play and good luck). *Verstehst du* (Do you understand)?"

Schalburg directed his rhetorical question at the German who had just lost over 5000 *RM* on that last game.

"*Ja! Ich verstehst* (Yes, I understand)," the loser replied reluctantly and rose to leave the room.

Schalburg then looked over at Seiz.

"*Helmut, mein freund*! When you withdraw your hand from your jacket pocket, I trust that your hand will be empty.

"Of course, *Herr* Schalburg," Seiz replied reassuringly. "Things got so excited for a moment that I thought I was going to experience a heart attack. That is all."

Schalburg finally looked at Larion, who deliberately attempted to be as calm as possible, notwithstanding the fact that the man who had probably executed his mentor and military comrade was standing a mere meter away from him. His *PPK* had been inside his left trouser pocket, but he now held it in his left hand, albeit under the poker table. He also calculated that any attempt to kill Schalburg would not be successful since Schalburg's weapon was already drawn and in his right hand. "*Kenne ich dich* (Do I know you)?" Schalburg asked, directing the question to Larion, who remained silent. *"Kennen wir uns* (Have we met before)?"

"Xhotimsk!" Larion finally replied without emotion.

Now it was Schalburg's turn to observe Larion more closely and search his memory.

"Xhotimsk! *Ja. Ich erinnere mich gut* (Yes, I remember well)," he finally replied knowingly.

Turning to the remaining German players, Schalburg announced that the game was over for the evening. He asked them to take their remaining funds and leave…except Seiz and his friend from Xhotimsk.

"I would like to speak with both of you."

*****

Once the other players had left, Schalburg suggested that Seiz divide their winnings while he brought them a bottle of brandy and three glasses. Seiz proceeded to collect, count, and divide their winnings. They had won 5500 *RM* each.

Larion remained seated, his right hand still on the table and his left hand still on his lap beneath the table. He just continued to watch Schalburg carefully. Schalburg, though he moved casually throughout the room, continued to watch Larion with care as well…and he continued to hold his Luger pistol. He brought out a sealed bottle of *Wilthener Weinbrande*, which he placed on the poker table. Then he got three glasses and placed them on the table. It was only then that he finally placed his Luger on the table on its left side, when he sat down. The Luger remained easily accessible to his right hand and remained directly pointed at Larion.

"So, *mein herr*, is our war over or are we still going to fight?" Schalburg asked Larion casually, as he proceeded to unseal the brandy and commence to pour it into the three glasses with his left hand.

"Did you have anything to do with hanging any partisans at the train depot in Mogilev a couple of years ago?" Larion inquired solemnly as he raised his glass of brandy with his right hand. His left hand remained on his lap beneath the table. He had been holding the PPK in his left hand since the losing player's obscene outburst. However, it would be too risky to try to shoot under the table, since it had a central pedestal and Schalburg was seated directly opposite to him. Larion would have to raise his left hand above the table if he was going to try to kill Schalburg. Schalburg still held the advantage.

"I had to execute many partisans from time to time, since they were causing us great havoc with our supply lines," Schalburg replied. "But no, I was never involved in hanging any partisans in Mogilev, which I believe was about two hundred and fifty kilometers away, if I remember correctly."

Schalburg casually picked up his glass with his left hand and took a short sip. His right hand remained on the table mere centimeters away from his Luger. All he had to do was to grasp it quickly and shoot.

Seiz could sense that the conversation was going to be bilateral and he concluded that the less he said, the better. Consequently, he concentrated on just sipping his brandy and observing the other two men.

"But allow me to ask you another question. How did you end up here in Kassel?" Schalburg inquired politely.

"If anyone is responsible for my presence in Germany, it is you, Herr Schalburg. I had the misfortune of being at the *kolkhoz* when you rounded up me and my family and had us transported to Kassel," Larion replied evenly, his voice betraying no emotion. "And how did you end up here, since the war just ended in the last two months?"

"A partisan sniper shot me from about four hundred meters and shattered my right leg. I have to regretfully admit that it was an excellent shot. I was sent back to Kassel to recuperate since my family lived here. Unfortunately, I was not deemed fit to return to service, so I started up this little enterprise about a year ago. Even though I am not a gambler myself. I provide the amenities and ensure security…for all of the players, for a modest five percent of each pot. "

The trio lapsed into an uncomfortable silence for a few minutes, finally, Larion felt obliged to ask another question.

"Why did you ask me if our war was over or whether we were still going to fight?"

"I sensed that possibly you and I were former antagonists and that…perhaps you still harbored a desire for retribution for whatever reason," Schalburg replied evenly.

"I remember you killed a number of innocent civilians in that small town, Herr Schalburg."

"Perhaps you should know that both of my parents and my young sister were killed in the Allied bombing of Kassel. They were a just a small part of the 10000 innocent civilians who were killed in two days of the bombing of the city core, even though the factories which were manufacturing munitions were all located out in the suburbs. But they are dead and there is nothing which I can do to bring them back. However, I do not believe that seeking revenge will give me any solace or satisfaction," Schalburg replied. "I even believe that my parents and young sister would not want me to try to avenge their unnecessary deaths. The killing and cruelty have to stop at some point so that we can learn to begin to respect each other as fellow human beings, don't you agree?"

"Do your miss your family?" Larion asked in reply, declining to answer his question.

"I miss them every hour of every day and I have no other family...except this illegitimate rascal," Schalburg replied, turning to acknowledge Seiz. "Helmut assures me that we are distant cousins...probably 'very distant'. But I have to ask you again, is our war over or are we going to continue to fight?"

Larion analyzed his situation thoughtfully. Trying to engage in a shootout with Schalburg did not make sense, because the tactical advantage was in his favor. Furthermore, even if he was successful, he had to consider the potential consequences to himself and his family. If he was able to kill Schalburg in revenge, his risk of arrest was substantial. There were numerous witnesses who could attest to his presence and the fact that Schalburg was alive when they left that evening. Seiz was also a witness.

If he was arrested, the Americans could change their mind and forcibly repatriate him back to the Soviet Union or allow the nascent German civilian authorities to imprison him. If that occurred, what would Tamara and Dimitri do? Would they survive? Finally, he made his decision.

"Though I may personally believe that you deserve to die, if not for killing my comrades, then for that reprisal execution of those three hundred innocent civilians," Larion replied calmly. "I am no longer on the winning side of this war. I am deemed to be a deserter and a traitor by my own country. I do not have the right to judge you, pronounce sentence, and execute that sentence. I do have a son who has just turned four years of age and who has endured years of hell. I also have a wife who I love dearly and who has waited patiently for me," Larion then paused briefly. "I must confess that when I saw you again, the first thought in my mind was to avenge all of my friends who were killed in the war by killing you, but revenge only breeds further retribution.

"We all did what we had to do to survive and there are a lot of things which I regret in hindsight. Perhaps there are others out there who may be seeking to exact revenge against me. Finally, you are not worth the consequences that I and my family would have to face if I killed you. But just as all things have a beginning, they should also have an end. So, to answer your question—no! Insofar as you and I may be concerned, Herr Schalburg, I have no desire to continue to fight."

"Then *Prost* (cheers!)" Schalburg replied solemnly, draining his brandy. "Perhaps you can put away that Walther *PPK* which you have been holding in your left hand under the table."

Finally, Seiz excitedly decided to join the conversation.

"Larion, it was my dear cousin here who gave me the *PPK* and suggested that I give it to you in the event you won again and the losers were less forgiving. I told him that you were my *guter freund.*

"By the way, Belorussian," Schalburg inquired, as he replaced his Luger in his belt holster and Larion replaced his *PPK* in his jacket pocket. "What did you estimate your likely chances of success to be if you decided to try to kill me? I ask merely out of curiosity."

"I believed the odds were about even," Larion replied, taking another sip of his brandy. "You held the initial advantage because you left your pistol on the table and all you would have to do was to merely grasp it and shoot. I had the disadvantage because I could not fire my pistol under the table, but you knew that. I would have to raise it above the table in order to shoot.

"Your advantage was lessened by the fact that you decided to place the Luger on the table and it was further evened out by the fact that you had decided to let me decide if I was going to try to kill you or not. Though unforeseen events may had distracted you for a split second which would have given me the advantage, as I have already told you—even if I was successful, the consequences of killing you simply were not worth it and I did promise my dear wife that I would not take unnecessary chances."

"That is right," Seiz interjected again. "We both promised his beautiful wife that we would not take unnecessary chances.'

Schalburg merely furrowed his brow and smiled at his alleged distant cousin, and doubted that they could be actually related.

"Though I know I was not that analytical in my own decision making, it is what I had hoped would happen," Schalburg replied imperturbably. "I, too, have become tired of killing. However, self-preservation is a strong emotion. I decided that if you wished to exact revenge against me, the least I could do was give you a reasonable opportunity to try and hope that you would decide against it. However, I believe that I retained a small advantage at all times. But I am relieved that I did not make your wife a widow and your son an orphan. Perhaps one day, if we meet again, we may be able to consider each other to be *Freundes* and share some *Wilthener Weinbrande* without my Luger lying on the table in front of me and without you holding a *PPK* on your lap."

Chapter 47

As Seiz drove Larion back to the Camp, he was elated while Larion was subdued. He knew that the decision he had made in respect of Schalburg was correct, but somehow, he still felt unfulfilled.

"Just think about it, *mein freund*," Seiz said. "In just a matter of a few days, we have won about 10000 *RM* each. And I must admit that your style of play is simply amazing. How do you do it?"

"When one cannot afford to lose, it usually heightens one's senses or compels you to make potentially disastrous decisions," Larion replied obliquely.

"In any event, at this rate we shall both be rich!" Seiz exclaimed. "We shall be rich!"

"No matter how well you may play, everything becomes dependent on fate at certain times," Larion replied. "You cannot expect to win every time you play. Besides that, if you continue to play with the same players, they shall start to revise their play to counter your play. So, my friend, I have to tell you that I have no intention of gambling again. I have won enough for my family's safety and comfort, and more importantly, I have promised my wife."

"That is most unfortunate," Seiz replied sadly. "If we could win another 20000 *RM*, then we would have the capital to enter the *Schwarzmarkt* in a big way. The black market is where you can make the big money and set yourself up for the rest of your life. You could have decided to work for Henschel for 50 *RM* a month, but you have won two hundred times that sum in less than a week. Remember how much you had paid for that bottle of champagne and that small box of chocolates. You would have had to work a year at Henschel just to save up that sum."

"But you can assume the risk of being imprisoned for a few years, I simply cannot," Larion explained. "Perhaps if I did not have a wife and a son, I would be prepared to continue to take such risks, but my circumstances are entirely different from yours, my friend."

Larion offered to return the *PPK*, but Seiz declined to accept it, suggesting that Larion probably needed it more for his own protection and for the protection of his family.

Seiz finally became resigned to Larion's decision to retire from gambling, but his furtive mind was already formulating alternate plans for his own future. As they were approaching the Camp, they were overtaken by a couple of American jeeps who were also returning to the *Furstenwald* DP Camp, filled with several inebriated American soldiers.

It was a fortuitous event, though no one was aware of that fact at the time, since the three Soviet officers had been waiting patiently for hours for Seiz's Volkswagen to return. Just as they saw it approaching their position, their plan was stymied by the chance appearance of the two American jeeps which proceeded to pass the Volkswagen at their precise interception point. The chance appearance of the American jeeps passing Seiz's vehicle prevented the Soviets from acting. The Soviet captain merely cursed and became even more obsessed with capturing the Belorussian who had insulted him.

He desperately wanted to punish him.

*****

Larion tried to enter his barracks quietly, but Tamara was still awake. She could not go to sleep until she was sure that he had returned safely.

"Louyna, you have finally returned, thank God," she spoke quietly so as to not awaken their son. "You cannot believe how much anguish you are causing me. It even makes me question whether you still love me or not."

"Well, my love. I promise you that I shall not cause you any more anguish," Larion replied soothingly, gently caressing her cheek. "I was fortunate enough to win again and I believe we have enough financial security for a while, so I promise you that I shall not gamble again. Now let us both get some sleep."

*****

After breakfast, Larion gave Tamara the bulk of his winnings, which totaled about 10000 *RM*, for safekeeping. He only retained 1000 *RM* which he wanted to use to purchase her and Dimitri some better shoes. As Tamara and Dimitri proceeded to go to the makeshift school, he went to see Lieutenant

Thornton to advise him that he was going to walk to Kassel and see if he could make those purchases. Then he proceeded to exit the Camp and walk the approximate two kilometers to Kassel.

A military gray-green vehicle swooped out of the trees and commenced to bear down on him from behind. Before he could see the Soviet Red Star insignia on its hood and on its doors, the vehicle swerved in front of him and two gloating Soviet soldiers jumped out with their Tokarev pistols aimed directly at him. There was no need for them to say anything. Larion merely raised his arms in surrender. It was the same Soviet captain with whom he had exchanged words in Thornton's office and his non-commissioned officers.

"Well, we meet again, you useless son-of-a-bitch," the captain swore and then spat at him. "Put your hands behind your back so that we can tie them up."

After they had restrained Larion, they put him in the back of their vehicle seated beside one of the sergeants. The Soviet captain was seated in the front passenger seat and his other sergeant was driving. Just at that moment an American jeep proceeded to pass by the Soviet vehicle on its way to the Camp.

The sergeant seated beside Larion attempted to shove him down into the seat so he would not be seen, however, the young American corporal did glimpse him briefly. Since they were in the American Zone, the presence of a Soviet military car was unusual. What attracted the American's attention was that the activity in the vehicle also seemed suspicious. He was tempted to stop and investigate, however, the Soviet vehicle quickly sped away.

"Those American bastards will not be able to save you today," the captain sneered and ordered his driver to drive even faster. "We need to get to the Soviet Zone as soon as possible. Then we shall have all the time in the world to continue our discussion with our quick-witted comrade."

*****

When Tamara returned to their barracks for lunch, she had expected to find Larion to have prepared a light lunch for the family and she was initially surprised to find that he was not there. Slowly, she started to develop a growing anxiety as she fed Dimitri. On their return to Andre's school, she asked him to accompany her to Lieutenant Thornton's office so that she could make appropriate inquiries.

Lieutenant Thornton advised them that he had a conversation with Larion earlier that morning and he advised her of Larion's decision to walk to Kassel to hopefully purchase some shoes. Thornton tried to assure her that there was nothing to worry about and that she should be patient. The young American Corporal who happened to pass the Soviet military vehicle that morning overheard their conversation and it piqued his interest.

After Tamara and Andre left, he approached Thornton to share his information. He had been in the office during the initial verbal altercation between Larion and the Soviet captain, and he was also aware of the Soviet's persistent demands that Larion and his family be turned over to them.

"Corporal, are you certain that you saw the Soviets pick up Sulupin this morning?"

"Sir, I cannot say that I am positive, since I merely caught a fleeting glimpse as they shoved him down onto the seat as my jeep passed by, but I can say that I recognized the Soviet captain and the two 'non-coms' who had argued with Sulupin," the Corporal replied briskly. "Those Soviets have been pretty persistent in trying to get us to agree to repatriate him. You advised his wife that you had a conversation with him this morning and then he proceeded to leave the Camp to walk to Kassel. That timing coincides with my arrival and the Soviet behavior on the road this morning was very unusual. Since they do not have any authority to conduct any such apprehensions in our Zone, I would be very surprised if they had not abducted Sulupin this morning."

"Very well, Corporal," Thornton replied and then proceeded to examine an enlarged military map of the local region.

The various Military Zones had been demarcated by different colors. Red for the Soviet Zone; Orange for the American Zone, Green for the British Zone and Blue for the French Zone. The map also identified the roads between Kassel and the British and the Soviet Zones. Kassel was located at the juncture of the British, Soviet and American Zones in the north eastern portion of the American Zone.

Geographically, Kassel was close to the British Zone and the Soviet Zone, however, Thornton focused on the available road accesses from Kassel to the Soviet Zone. He quickly decided that if the Soviets had kidnapped Sulupin, it would not make sense for them to travel north because they would have to enter and travel through the British Zone before the roads would permit them to turn east towards the Soviet Zone. They would also have to first pass through

British Zone security. Furthermore, they would have to travel north for about one hundred kilometers through the British Zone before they could access a road which would take them in an easterly direction into the Soviet Zone.

It was fortunate that there was no direct easterly road from Kassel to the Soviet Zone. He then examined the only other viable alternative. There was a convenient southbound road which connected with an easterly road which would be able to take them directly from the American Zone into the southern portion of the Soviet Zone.

It compelled Thornton to conclude that the Soviets would have taken this southern route. They were already in the American Zone and they would not have to cross over into another Allied Zone.

They could travel south and then east to cross directly into the Soviet Zone.

"Corporal, please radio all of our military police installations along this route and advise them that we believe a Soviet vehicle is carrying a kidnapped victim who is under American jurisdiction and our responsibility," Thornton ordered. "Advise them that this is just another arrogant act being perpetrated by the Soviets which is in strict contravention of the *Displaced Persons Repatriation Protocol*. In fact, it is also a criminal act and an insult to American sovereign governance in our Zone of responsibility. It may not hurt to mention the humanitarian issue involved here in that the father is being forcibly separated from his wife and four-year-old son."

"Yes sir!" the corporal replied.

"And Corporal, I want you to notify our military police manning this border crossing into the Soviet Zone," Thornton added anxiously. "It appears to be the nearest exit point from our Zone into the Soviet Zone. Advise them to stop any Soviet military vehicle leaving our Zone today and advise them to search the vehicle carefully and check the occupants' identification papers."

"Yes sir!" the corporal quickly replied and ran to the radio communications office so that he could relay his orders.

*****

The Soviet captain eventually instructed his driver to decelerate and not to attract attention by excessive speeding. He was reasonably confident that they were safe and secure. All they had to do was to cross over into their own Zone. Though he contemplated simply stopping their vehicle and summarily executing their insolent passenger, he dismissed that idea because a passing American military vehicle could stop to investigate and force them to surrender their captive.

More importantly, he decided that he wanted their captive to suffer, whether it was at his own hands or by being deported back to the Soviet Union for further appropriate disposition. If he happened to be a former soldier, that meant either execution or a quarter century of hard labor in the *Gulag*. His thirst for retribution was going to be fulfilled. It was only a matter of another couple of hours and less than a hundred kilometers and they would be back safely in their own Zone.

The captain also attempted to engage Larion with insults and threats, however, Larion simply remained non-responsive. Even when he was struck repeatedly in the right side of his face by the non-commissioned officer seated beside him, he continued to maintain his silence.

"Soon, you son-of-a-bitch, you will be squealing like a stuffed pig roasting on a spit," the captain sneered. "You will be squealing like those *Deutsche schampen* (German sluts) we have fucked over and over again. They raped our innocent women, so we had to avenge their loss of chastity by letting their *shiyukhi* (whores) experience what it feels like as well. Perhaps, if one of my boys is so inclined, I may even permit him to rape you as well. Which hole do you prefer or perhaps, we can fill all of your holes, you traitorous bastard."

Finally, the captain lit his cigarette and ignored him. Larion feigned that he had passed out after the non-commissioned officer struck him again one last time in his face. He deliberately collapsed awkwardly in the rear footwell of the vehicle with his back to the door so that he could try to untie his hands. He had his *Walther PPK* pistol in his left trouser pocket.

All he had to do was loosen his restraint so that he could reach and pull out his gun. He decided that if he was successful, he would shoot the coward who had repeatedly struck him in the face, first. Then he would shoot the captain, but he would spare the driver so that their vehicle would not crash.

Larion quietly strained at the thin coarse rope which bound his wrists together until he felt a wetness. He knew his wrists were bleeding, but he hoped that the moisture would gradually saturate the rope fibers and loosen them so that he could pull stretch the rope binding. Finally, he was able to slowly draw out his left hand. He opened up his left eyelid slightly so that he could observe his riding companion. He noticed that the sergeant was dozing, the captain in

315

the front passenger seat was smoking and facing forward. The driver, seated immediately in front of him, seemed focused on his driving.

He had never fired the *PPK*, so its muffled 'pop' came as a surprise to him as much as it did to his fellow passengers. Following Seiz's advice, he quickly got off two quick shots at the sergeant's head. The first shot entered his left cheek, spinning his head to his right. The second shot entered the back of his head, even though he was probably dead after the first shot.

The first shot caught the Soviet captain by surprise, however, in a split second he was able to recover and he desperately tried to reach for his Tokarev pistol which was in his belt holster on his left side. The driver was also alerted by that first shot, but he was only able to observe his fellow sergeant get shot by the second round.

He commenced to swerve his vehicle from side to side to frustrate Larion's aim; however, it was more frustrating for his Captain whose pistol was still holstered. That permitted Larion an extra moment to shoot for the third time from his left hip as he slowly rose up from the back footwell of the vehicle. The shot struck the Soviet captain in the left side of his face. His fourth shot missed and went over the Captain's head as he slumped down into the seat, but that bullet shattered the right passenger window.

Larion finally transferred his pistol to his right hand and commanded the driver to bring the vehicle to an immediate stop or his brains would be splattered against the windshield. The driver duly complied and commenced to beg for mercy.

"*Tovarish*!" the sergeant pleaded. "Please spare my life. I have survived three years of war and I do not want to die by a roadside in Germany after the war has already ended. I have a wife and a daughter back home. Please spare me. It was not my wish to force you to be repatriated. It was not me who assaulted you when you were bound up. It was the Captain's decision. I am merely a sergeant and I am obliged to obey or be shot."

Though Larion was still partially disoriented from the beating he had sustained, he decided that the more prudent course of action was that he would attempt to drive their vehicle back to the Camp himself. If the remaining sergeant drove, he would remain a continuing threat. The sergeant might decide to deliberately crash the vehicle or he might decide to overwhelm him at an opportune moment.

Larion ordered the sergeant to exit the vehicle slowly as he opened up the left rear passenger door and stepped outside the vehicle as well. He ordered the sergeant to remove his pistol with his right thumb and forefinger, and then to drop his weapon on the road. He was to step away from the car with his hands on his head.

As soon as Larion heard the pistol hit the pavement, he felt a wave of nausea well up inside him. He could not prevent himself from vomiting the bile which rose up his esophagus and exuded from his mouth. The sergeant sensed his weakness and dropped his hands. Then he attempted to rush Larion and knock him down to the pavement.

Larion's PPK recoiled twice in his right hand as he shot it. The first shot struck the sergeant just below his sternum. As the sergeant doubled over, the second shot struck him in the top of his head and he fell lifeless at Larion's feet.

He regretted killing the second sergeant. It was his intention to spare his life so that he could return to his wife and daughter, just as he wanted to return to Tamara and Dimitri. But he knew that the sergeant would have killed him, if he did not kill him first. As Schalburg said, self-preservation is a very strong emotion.

After removing the two bodies from the vehicle and rolling the third body off the road, Larion got behind the steering wheel of the Soviet vehicle and turned it back north. He took a couple of breaks to rest when he felt that he was going to lose consciousness, but eventually, he had to pull over so that he could sleep.

*****

Larion was dreaming that he was swimming underwater and that he was desperate to refresh his lungs with fresh air, but he seemed unable to break the surface of the water which seemed to be just beyond his reach. He also attempted to bring himself back into consciousness, but he was not quite able to achieve that objective either. Voices, strange voices seemed to hover around him. Then he thought he saw blurred faces through his unfocussed eyes…just before he lost consciousness again.

*****

317

Someone was speaking to him…gently…sweetly. They were washing his face with a moist cloth. For a moment he sensed that he was back in that water…slowly, helplessly sinking down into its cold, dark depths…

"Louyna…can you hear me, my dearest?"

The voice was both familiar and yet…unrecognizable. He tried again to bring himself out of that mental pool of water which seemed intent on drowning him. He tried again to bring himself back to consciousness.

"Father…Father."

He could hear a young voice. It was a boy's voice…he was able to recognize this voice. It was his son. He knew that he had to be alive…now, if he could only force his eyes open. For some reason, he could not open his right eye…it had been swollen shut by the numerous blows it had sustained. He was able to open his left eyelid to permit some light in…he was able to see Tamara gently sponging his face. He could see his young son looking at him anxiously…tears had welled up in his son's eyes and were gently spilling down his round, rosy cheeks.

Larion finally knew that he was alive and that somehow, he had made it back to the Camp. He had returned to Tamara one more time.

Chapter 48

Larion was still lying motionless on his bunk as he slowly regained consciousness. He heard people speaking around him before he was able to see them. He was still unable to open his right eye, but he was able to partially open his left eye and so he slowly tilted his head to his left. He saw Tamara watching him apprehensively. His son was at the side of his bunk gently holding his left hand. He recognized his friend, Andre…and Lieutenant Thornton was speaking with another American soldier and there was another soldier with a medical insignia, who appeared to be replacing bandages and ointments into a small medical valise.

"Mother, Mother…" Dimitri announced excitedly. "Father is finally awake!"

Tamara knelt down by the bunk and gently placed her hands on both sides of Larion's face. Her initial look of apprehension gradually turned to relief and finally she was able to offer him a timid smile. Though Larion attempted to reciprocate so as to reassure her, his facial muscles would not respond that well and he merely winced as the spasm of pain rippled through them. He attempted to mutter an apology, but the sounds which emanated past his lips were mere garbled noises.

"Andre, please tell Mrs. Sulupin that the medic has done as much as he could, but I have requested a doctor from our battalion's headquarters to come out here as soon as possible to conduct a more thorough examination," Lieutenant Thornton said. "But the good news is that he will live, but it shall take a little time for him to heal and totally recover. Fortunately, he was in pretty good physical condition to start with. That should help speed his recovery."

Thornton then proceeded to give some further instructions to Andre. Shortly after Andre translated those instructions to Tamara, she and Dimitri left. Only Andre, Thornton, and another American soldier, a Corporal, remained behind. Thornton then proceeded to relay information to Andre, who dutifully translated it for Larion. Though Andre had been attempting to introduce Larion to the English language, Larion had only been able to learn a handful of common English expressions and he was not capable of carrying on a conversation by himself.

"Andre, tell Mr. Sulupin that it was his wife who raised an alarm about his absence. By coincidence, one of my Corporals was returning to the Camp and had noticed the Soviet vehicle. The soldiers appeared to be acting suspiciously a short distance from the Camp, however, their vehicle sped off before he could investigate.

"When the Corporal heard about your absence, he advised me that he recognized the Soviet Captain and he thought he saw a glimpse of you in that vehicle. He put two and two together and we concluded that the Soviets had probably abducted you. We notified our military police to be on the lookout for that Soviet vehicle and I dispatched five of my soldiers, commanded by the Corporal, to head south to try to intercept them before they had a chance to cross over to the Soviet Zone."

Larion merely nodded his understanding.

"My soldiers came across you first. You were driving that vehicle in a northerly direction and you had parked it by the side of the road. At first, they thought you were asleep, but then it became quickly obvious that you were unconscious as a result of having been severely beaten. Then they noticed the shattered window and the blood on the right front and the right rear passenger seats. They notified our military police to check the road farther south for the three Soviet soldiers the Corporal had seen in that vehicle. Then they drove you back to the Camp for medical treatment."

Again, Larion merely nodded to confirm that he understood what Thornton was telling him.

"My men drove you back yesterday evening and our medic provided you with some preliminary treatment. Basically, just some pain medication and a muscle relaxant so that you would be able to sleep a bit easier. I have also just been advised by my staff that our military police were able to locate the three Soviet bodies by the side of the road about twelve kilometers south from where they located you."

At this point Larion started to become concerned. The three dead Soviet soldiers could force Thornton to transfer him to the Soviets and his anxiety became evident as he attempted to fidget and rise from his bunk.

"Andre, please explain to Mr. Sulupin that we have decided to handle this matter and he need not be concerned. The Soviet soldiers had committed the criminal acts of kidnapping and assault in our Zone. My superiors have decided that rather than disclosing what actually happened, it would be preferable if we just advised our Soviet allies that their three soldiers had decided to defect and their present whereabouts, including their vehicle, are unknown to us. This should put an end to this matter; however, we do not know what prior reports that Soviet captain may have passed onto his superiors."

Larion tried to muster as much strength as he could to confirm his understanding and his appreciation to the young American Lieutenant. He understood and appreciated that these Americans were trying to save his life. He tried to extend his hand to Thornton, but he was unable to do so.

"Andre, finally tell Mr. Sulupin that after he has recovered a bit more from his injuries, I would like to have an unofficial chat with him about what actually happened on his adventure. Three armed Soviet soldiers, including a Captain and two non-commissioned officers, while he was apparently restrained and yet they all end up dead while he ends up alive. It has to be an interesting tale."

Then Thornton displayed the *Walther PPK* which he was holding in his right hand.

"Seems to be an excellent weapon, Mr. Sulupin," Thornton added. "Six of the seven rounds have been used. Andre, tell him that we can also discuss the possible return of this weapon to Mr. Sulupin when he recovers, if he still wants it."

After Andre translated this final statement, Larion peered at Thornton with his partially open left eye and merely nodded his head slowly. He was not certain if he was interested in its return or not, but he did not have to make that decision at this point.

Thornton acknowledged Larion's decision with his own nod of understanding and replaced the pistol in his jacket pocket, and then he left with the other two soldiers.

*****

Over the course of next couple of days, Tamara ministered to Larion by replacing his bandages and since he was unable to chew, she spoon-fed him a broth soup. She also positioned one of the barracks' latrine buckets by his bunk so that he would be able to relieve himself, however, she had to assist him for the first couple of days. Little Dimitri merely watched his injured father apprehensively, but he was ready with a quick, reassuring smile if Larion attempted to squint at him with his one good eye. The swelling in his right eye slowly abated and he was soon able to squint through that eye as well.

The American doctor attended at the Camp after a couple of days and examined him. He told Andre to explain that he believed that Larion had suffered a serious concussion and that he would be unsteady on his feet for a while. He recommended that Larion try to commence walking short distances and Andre volunteered to improvise a sturdy cane to assist him. Both eyes seemed to be recovering well. Though Larion's jaw continued to ache with pain and he could even feel the throbbing of the nerves in the roots of his teeth, he had not lost any teeth.

All during this period of time, Larion did not attempt to have an actual conversation with Tamara. They merely smiled or frowned to convey their current feelings. When Tamara did speak to Larion, it was merely to instruct him to do something. Try to sit up or try to roll over.

However, when Tamara went to Andre's school with Dimitri, Larion attempted to exercise and coordinate his lips, jaw, and tongue so that he could try to speak again. He also commenced to practice walking with Andre's cane. His sense of balance had been affected by his injuries and in being obliged to spend the bulk of his time lying flat on his back for over a week. Gradually, he was able to limp to the barracks' latrine and the odious latrine bucket could be removed.

The first time Larion looked at his reflection in the small bathroom mirror, the bruised unshaven visage with the two blackened eyes, which peered back at him, shocked him. It seemed that he was looking at a stranger whom he did not recognize.

*****

Larion could hear Tamara and Dimitri enter the barracks. Though they were usually both solemn and quiet around him, he could hear them conversing and laughing. It gladdened him that they seemed to be normal and reasonably well-adjusted, at least when they were not around him.

"Louyna, would you like to try some solid food for lunch today?" Tamara asked politely as she bent over him. "Perhaps you can dip a slice of bread into the broth. That should soften it up for you. Would you like that, dearest?"

"I would like to try that very much, my love," Larion replied a bit awkwardly.

His voice startled her so much that she straightened up quickly and some broth spilled onto his blanket. Though his left eye was fully open, his right eye was still half shut. He had not shaved for over a week and he had a coarse dark stubble covering his face. His lips were still swollen and sore, but he was able to form a mischievous smile at the corners of his mouth. Notwithstanding his appearance, his improved health was betrayed by the twinkle in his left eye and his smile.

Tamara was flabbergasted. Dimitri was simply delighted.

"Father…Father," he squealed. "You are going to live. You are going to live."

Dimitri, in his excitement, jumped for joy and landed on his father's chest. Larion grimaced with pain, but he found the strength in his own happiness to embrace his son as tightly as he could.

"Yes, your father is going to live…" Larion replied with difficulty, since his mouth was still sore.

Recovering, Tamara attempted to disentangle the two men in her life as Larion tried to raise himself to a sitting position on his bunk without her assistance.

"And how long have you been holding this secret from me, Louyna?" Tamara asked, attempting to affect a reproaching tone. "Just how long have you been able to speak?"

"Those are the first words which I have spoken to anyone, Tamara," Larion replied. "Though I confess that I have been trying to train my sore tongue and my swollen lips to try to work together a bit better, I wanted to speak my first words only to you and Dimitri."

Tamara was simply ecstatic with joy. He remembered how surprised and happy she was when he had returned to Xhotimsk and he gave her the gift of that little gold Orthodox crucifix. But even that happiness was exceeded when he presented her with her wedding ring. She had seemed so young, beautiful, and happy then and now, she seemed to have regained that happiness again.

Tamara attempted to engage Larion in conversation as she spoon-fed him his broth. She intermittently dipped his bread and then placed it into his mouth. He squeezed and shredded it with his tongue before swallowing it.

Dimitri also attempted to question his father in between his own mouthfuls of his vegetable stew, but he did not give him an opportunity to answer because he would begin to ask another question before Larion was able to respond. Larion tried to remind himself that he should rest that afternoon so he would have the strength to respond to both of them when they came back after Dimitri's lessons.

After they both left for Andre's school, Larion decided that he would limp down to Lieutenant Thornton's office. It would provide him with some exercise and it would give him an opportunity to determine what had transpired during the period of time he had been incapacitated. He would stop by and ask Andre to come with him and assist him with the translations.

*****

"Good afternoon, Lieutenant Thornton," Larion addressed him respectfully. "Can you advise me of any developments in respect of those three Soviet soldiers?"

"Good afternoon, Mr. Sulupin," Thornton replied. "To summarize in a few words, our Soviet friends are very suspicious and they are not very happy. Basically, they advise us that they are very skeptical that three of their officers would decide to defect voluntarily. After all, they claim that it would be inconceivable that their officers would want to leave a proverbial workers' paradise for a corrupt capitalistic regime where they would simply be exploited."

"Did they raise any issues about me in particular?" Larion asked a bit apprehensively.

"Unfortunately, they did raise the issue of a possible thwarted 'forced repatriation' of a Soviet family which was supposed to be under my control, but fortunately, they could not provide me with any specific names," Thornton replied with mild satisfaction. He enjoyed countering official demands for information and cooperation, by invoking official grounds to refuse those demands.

"I have offered to provide them with access to all of our official records to assure them that we had interviewed all of our *Displaced Persons* and confirmed whether they were Soviet Citizens subject to repatriation or whether

324

they were *Stateless Persons*, who were exempted from that Protocol. Naturally, they were not prepared to accept our conclusions, but they have failed to provide us with any official written demand with a specific name to warrant an official request."

"So, as in chess, we have a 'draw'?" Larion asked, a bit relieved at the obvious impasse between the two sides.

"I play some chess, Mr. Sulupin, and I would characterize it as a 'stalemate'!" Thornton replied. "But the practical effect is the same. The Soviets are demanding that we repatriate a family which they are simply unable to identify. Since they are unable to identify who it is they think we are allegedly shielding, we are hardly in a position to comply.

"However, they have attempted to abduct you once and they may be inclined to try again. There are a number of *Displaced Persons* in this Camp who want to be repatriated because they want to rejoin their families. Those individuals are susceptible to pressure and they may be inclined to identify you, your wife, and your son."

"I understand, Lieutenant Thornton," Larion replied regretfully.

"However, I do not know if you remember that first day, we brought you back to the Camp, I told you I was curious about how you were able to escape. I told you that I would ask you about it once you recovered. Would you care to tell me what happened, off the record?"

Though Larion did not want to relive those events again, since the Lieutenant was curious and since he was trying to preserve his family's safety, he dutifully obliged.

Thornton listened carefully, but he occasionally interjected and asked some supplementary questions, nodding his understanding when that additional clarification was provided.

"It seems to me, Mr. Sulupin, that you are a very lucky man," Thornton concluded. "Had they not assaulted you, you would not have ended up in that rear footwell of their vehicle. That permitted you to rub your wrists raw and the blood from your bleeding wrists saturated that thin rope enough so that you were able to stretch it to release your hand and draw your pistol."

"You may call it 'luck', Lieutenant Thornton, I prefer to call it 'fate'," Larion replied in all seriousness. "An old friend of mine once told me, when I was much younger, that sometimes certain events occur for a reason. Sometimes that reason is an opportunity, but one must recognize the opportunity and try to take advantage of it."

"Perhaps you are right," Thornton conceded. "But speaking of that pistol…" he added, opening up the top right drawer in his desk. "Here is your *Walther PPK*. It only has one round left in its magazine, but considering it saved your life, I think you may want have it back."

Larion examined the small, sleek pistol. He remembered that he had fired it six times and those six rounds permitted him to kill three men. The fact that those three men were intent on either killing him or having him killed, no longer held much significance.

"Thank you, Lieutenant Thornton," Larion replied. "I have been forced to kill even before this war started. It was easier to justify during the war because the other people were trying to kill me. I have lost family, friends, and comrades-in-arms, and I miss them all dearly, but I am truly tired of killing. I would like to live without killing anyone else, but a former adversary provided me with this pistol so that I would be able to protect myself. An adversary who I was prepared to kill on sight. Perhaps fate has intervened to tell me that the killing is not over just yet. Perhaps I should hold on to this pistol for a bit longer."

Thornton looked at Larion and considered what this young man had just told him. Thornton had received his commission towards the conclusion of the War and he had not actually seen that much action, personally, but he had ample opportunity to view the death and devastation the war had brought. He had also heard rumors of unspeakable atrocities allegedly committed by the Nazis in their zealous pursuit of racial superiority and racial purity in various concentration camps which had been established in Germany, Poland and other occupied countries.

His superiors had circulated instructions that Nazi *SS* and *Einsatgruppen* officers could be disguising themselves as ordinary *Wehrmacht* soldiers and that all German military had to be examined thoroughly. Fortunately, the *SS* had personal tattoos with their blood group inked indelibly on the underside of their left arm, near their armpit, which simplified their identification; however, it simply was not practical to physically examine every German soldier.

There were also rumors that the upper echelons of the Nazi leadership and *SS* would be subject to an international tribunal of justices and tried for war crimes. As for Soviet Russia, even before the war, Thornton read rumors about the vile practices which Stalin had implemented to obtain absolute power and then to maintain it. It was also difficult to forget the *Non-Aggression Pact* Stalin and Hitler had entered into in August of 1939, Soviet Russia's invasion and annexation of Poland in September of 1939 and finally, its annexation of Lithuania, Latvia and Estonia in June of 1940.

Thornton wondered how individuals such as Hitler and Stalin were able to achieve such total dictatorial power. Both men seemed devoid of any empathy, scruples or human decency. Murder on an individual or a mass scale was simply a convenient tool which facilitated the achievement of their vile goals. What fascinated Thornton, though, was that both of these two reprehensible human beings seemed to attract similar personalities who surrounded them and enabled them to acquire even more power. Their amoral leadership also removed all social filters for their respective countries as well.

What a contrast these two dictators were in comparison to men like Roosevelt and Churchill, as exemplified by their respective inspiring words and deeds. Roosevelt and Churchill also attracted and surrounded themselves with individuals with similar personalities and values. But these leaders retained their moral filters. Those filters not only controlled their thoughts and guided their actions, but that of their minions, as well. Their respective countries proceeded down a more moral path.

"In that case, Mr. Sulupin," Thornton finally replied, "please accept this simple gift." He handed Larion an 'English-Russian Pocket Dictionary'.

Chapter 49

Russia's and Germany's post World War I political and monetary history paralleled each other to a large degree. In both countries, the ruling monarch was forced to abdicate. That abdication was followed by a provisional quasi-democratic experiment which was replaced by a totalitarian dictatorship. Both countries also experienced severe monetary crises which resulted in hyperinflation and several attempts to restructure their respective monetary systems.

The Mark (M) was the official currency of Germany prior to World War I, however, Germany went off the 'Gold Standard' on 4 August 1914. This simply meant that the Mark was no longer backed by nor convertible into gold. As the declared loser of the War, pursuant to its reparation obligations to the victorious Allies, coupled with the cost of the war and the post-war labor strikes, the Weimar Republic, Germany's democratic experiment, resorted to the expedient alternative of simply printing off literally 'trillions' of worthless Marks. This precipitated a hyperinflation which reached its zenith in 1923. Germany was finally forced to disavow the Mark and issue a new currency, the Reichsmark (RM) in 1924, and it remained Germany's official currency until 23 June 1948, when it was replaced by the Deutsche Mark (DM).

In Russia, after Nicholas II abdicated on 15 March 1917, the government was replaced by its short-lived democratic experiment, the 'Russian Provisional Government', whose legislative body was the 'Duma' (parliament). There was a struggle for power in the 'Duma', between the Bolsheviks (communist 'majority') and the Mensheviks (democratic 'minority').

The Mensheviks had committed the fatal error trying to continue the war against Germany and Austria-Hungary, and the Bolsheviks overthrew the last Menshevik government of Alexander Kerensky on 7 November 1917. Though Lenin succeeded in defeating his Menshevik opponents, he then had to deal with the Russian civil war and the foreign intervention prior to his death on 21 January 1924.

The Ruble (Rub) was the official currency of Russia, during both Imperial and Soviet periods. Between 1917 and 1924, the Communists had to issue a revalued Ruble on four separate occasions: 1919 – first issue, 1922 – second issue, 1923 – third issue, and 1924 – Stalin's fourth issue (the 'gold ruble' – official exchange rate – 1 Gold Ruble to 50000 Third Issue Rubles).

Considering the previous post-war history of German currency, though the Reichsmark had a deemed exchange value of approximately 2.5 RM to $1.00 (US) in 1939, the RM's commercial value in post-World War II was dubious. Essential goods were initially rationed by Nazi Germany in 1943 and subsequently by the Allies. The logic behind rationing was that the available supply of essential goods would be distributed more equitably and prices would be restricted from increasing too quickly. That logic, as with the communist dictum of 'from each according to their ability, to each according to their needs', had a fatal flaw—it ignored human nature.

Rationing in pre 'V-E Day' in Germany merely resulted in hoarding and the manifestation of a black-market economy, however, it had the same effect in the Allies' economies as well. Shortfalls in goods were made up through a barter economy and the black market, where official prices were ignored. This was aggravated by the post-war conditions in Germany where allied troops had available funds and easy access to goods such as cigarettes and chocolates.

For example, an American soldier could purchase ten 25-cigarette packs from the PX ('post exchange' – a military retail discount store) for fifty cents. A German could purchase one cigarette from an American soldier for about 6 RM to 10 RM. Those Reichsmarks could be exchanged by that American soldier for American funds or for AMC's (Allied Military Currency) at their stipulated value.

However, American soldiers preferred to purchase German cameras manufactured by Leica Camera AG, Zeiss Ikon, or Emil Busch. If a German had such a camera, he could exchange it with that soldier for about 5000 cigarettes. Those cigarettes could be sold or exchanged for goods with other Germans at an effective exchange rate of up to 20 RM per cigarette. The American soldier would mail that camera back to the United States where a friend or family member would sell it for about $600 (US), but the American's original cost of those 5000 cigarettes was only about $10.00 (US).

The Soviet soldiers, who did not have much faith in Soviet currency, preferred to purchase German wrist watches since a wrist watch was an important status symbol in Soviet Russia; however, the purchase protocol was basically the same. A modest wristwatch mailed back to Soviet Russia could be exchanged by that recipient for a cow or a horse or other limited commodities.

Cigarettes had a more stable value than the RM, since ten cigarettes could purchase: 1.5 kilos of bread, 125 grams of meat, 75 grams of butter, or 15 grams of coffee. For thirty cigarettes, you could purchase one chicken.

The 'cigarette' economy continued until the RM ceased to be the official German currency in the western Tri-Zone regions when it was replaced, on 23 June 1948, by the Deutsche Mark (DM). The replacement of the RM and the implementation of the Marshall Plan effectively neutralized the barter economy and the black-market economy was basically eliminated.

Chapter 50

After a further two weeks, Larion's abrasions and bruises had slowly faded and then finally disappeared. His overall physical condition recovered as well. He finally felt well enough to try to formulate a plan for his family's future.

He had explained to Tamara what had happened on the road when the Soviet soldiers attempted to abduct him into the Soviet Zone. She understood that they would not be able to return to Belarus, for if they did, Larion might be executed. If he was not executed, he would probably be imprisoned at hard labor for twenty-five years. At the very least, the entire family could be forced to resettle in Siberia. Their continued presence in the *Furstenwald DP* Camp was not feasible either, because some of the *Displaced Persons* who were returning to the Soviet Union would probably be interrogated about other Soviet citizens in the Camp and if he was identified, there would be a formal demand for his forced repatriation. Another threat was a possible second abduction attempt. The Soviet Captain had filed reports identifying him as a Soviet citizen, so the Soviet authorities knew about him, even though his exact identity was still unknown.

Consequently, he stopped by Lieutenant Thornton's office to advise the staff that he was going to walk to Kassel on an errand. He had been practicing his English with the assistance of the *Russian-English Dictionary* and the indispensable guidance of Andre. Though he was learning to pronounce the words in English, he was still thinking in Russian, consequently his syntax was far from eloquent.

The American soldiers, however, seemed to understand most of what he was trying to say, though some of them did smile sympathetically on occasion. He also commenced to introduce Tamara to English as well. As for Dimitri, at the tender age of four, he was learning to be multilingual since Larion tried to teach him to speak German and English, in addition to his native Russian.

As he entered the Lieutenant's office, Thornton was speaking to someone. He was uniformed, however, not a military uniform. Upon seeing Larion enter, Thornton interrupted his conversation and beckoned him to come over.

"Mr. Sulupin, I would like to introduce you to Mr. Lionel Balmelle, he is the Director of the *UNRRA* Team 505. He is officially replacing me today as the Refugee Director of this Camp. He will be processing your family's application for possible emigration to Canada."

Balmelle spoke English with a French accent, but the middle-aged, bespeckled camp director seemed pleasant and Larion willingly shook his hand in greeting.

"I no understand English good," Larion spoke apologetically. "I try learn."

"He is being modest, Lionel," Thornton replied. "He is fluent in Russian and pretty good in German. I gave him a dictionary just a couple of weeks ago and just listen to him speak."

"Hello, Mr. Sulupin. Lieutenant Thornton advises me that you and your family would like to emigrate to Canada. Please arrange to see me as soon as you can. The Lieutenant has explained your situation and the sooner we get you out of here, the better."

Larion could not understand everything the two men had just told him and he shrugged his shoulders and extended his hands, palms up, to indicate his lack of understanding.

"*Yous, votre femme et fils,*" Balmelle replied, pointing to Larion. "You come see me!" he added, pointing to himself.

Larion finally understood that the refugee director wanted him to come and see him. He nodded his head to indicate his understanding and smiled apologetically. Then he signaled to Thornton that he was going to walk to Kassel.

*****

When Larion arrived at Kassel, he immediately went to see Schalburg, for he was hoping that he would run into Helmut Seiz. Fortunately, they were both in Schalburg's poker parlor.

"*Herr* Schalburg, Helmut, *wie geht's* (How is it going)?" Larion greeted them both politely.

"Ah, *mein freund,*" Helmut replied happily. "We were just talking about you. Your poker buddies would really like to try to beat you one last time."

"Thank you, but no," Larion replied. "I got lucky twice, but I do not want to press fate too much. But Helmut, do you think that it would be possible for me to acquire a gold cross for my wife?"

"Almost anything is possible for the right price," Seiz replied confidently. "Would you like to see my black-market friends right now?"

"Go see the black marketers, but then come back here. I may have a proposition for the two of you," Schalburg said.

*****

The black marketers were puzzled by Larion's request, however, they quickly withdrew a folded satin cloth and opened it up for viewing. There were a variety of crosses, both in gold and in silver. Some were Catholic crosses, but there were a few Orthodox crosses as well. The difference was that the Orthodox cross had three cross bars instead of just one, as with the Catholic cross. There was a smaller horizontal bar above the main horizontal bar and a third lower bar which was angled downward from left to right, symbolically pointing to both Heaven and Hell.

Since Tamara's crucifix was gold, Larion decided that he would purchase a small gold crucifix to replace it, however, he was shocked at the price of 4000 *RM* since it was not that heavy, but it did come with a fine gold chain. Seiz attempted to haggle with the black marketers, however, they remained intransigent.

Larion thought about the 500 *RM* he had paid for the champagne and the small box of chocolates. The asking price for the crucifix was exorbitant, but it underscored Larion's increasing concern about the actual value of the *Reichsmarks* which he had won, so he reluctantly agreed to purchase it. He was coming to the conclusion that the paper money was essentially worthless and it was preferable for him to purchase the crucifix before the *RM* truly became totally valueless.

*****

When they returned to Schalburg's poker parlor, Schalburg had a bottle of brandy on the table with three clean glasses.

333

"Well, gentlemen, were you able to make a purchase?" Schalburg inquired politely, as he poured the brandy carefully, ensuring that each glass had an equal portion.

"My Belorussian friend must be in love. He paid 4000 *RM* for a tiny gold cross for his *frau*," Seiz replied, as he reached for one of the glasses.

"Sometimes people will accept the paper money, most times they just prefer to trade goods," Schalburg explained. "But in trading goods, at least you know exactly what you are receiving."

"That is another thing which I have just been discussing with my dear friend," Seiz replied. "These *Reichsmarks* are just paper…Nazi paper, even. And it is not a good time to be a 'Nazi anything'," Seiz added smugly as he looked at Schalburg to see if his snide comment had registered. He smiled when he noticed Schalburg's fleeting scowl. "Rumors are circulating that the Allies may even stop accepting *RM* and force us to use their *AMCs* or they may introduce a whole new currency. Then where shall we be?"

"Well, Sulupin, I believe you did the right thing. Though 4000 *RM* today may have been a high price, next week those *Reichsmarks* may be worthless," Schalburg replied.

"What do you do with your Reichsmarks, cousin?" Seiz inquired, as he took another sip of his brandy.

"I convert them into American dollars or gold as fast as I can," Schalburg replied nonchalantly. "American dollars are almost as good as gold these days."

"You said that you had a proposition which you wanted to discuss with us," Larion inquired.

"We shall need 100000 RM. How many *Reichsmarks* do you two have right now?"

"I only have 5000 *RM* left," Larion replied.

"And I have about 20000 *RM*," Seiz added quickly.

"Well, that is 25000 *RM* and I can contribute 75000 *RM*," Schalburg said. "So that gives us a required total of 100000 *RM*."

"What do you hope to accomplish with 100000 *RM*?" Seiz asked.

"What do you know about the black market?" Schalburg inquired, ignoring Seiz's question. He drew deeply on the cigarette he was smoking, exhaling the warm smoke slowly through his nostrils.

"*Meine kollegen* (my colleagues), do either of you know how much this cigarette cost me?"

When neither one responded, Schalburg advised them that it was about 10 *RM*.

"Our combined 100000 *RM* may have been a small fortune in 1939, but now it will only buy about 10000 American cigarettes. Those 10000 cigarettes would only cost an American soldier about $20.00 (US), but what would the American expect to be able to purchase for 10000 cigarettes? The going rate of exchange on the barter market would be two Leica cameras. And if you had two Leica cameras, what could you do with them? You could send them to your family or friends in America."

"But cousin," Seiz said, "I know that people are making big money on the black market. If they can do it, why can't we?"

"You have to analyze the situation we find ourselves in at this time," Schalburg replied. "*Herr* Sulupin, I have watched you play poker and you have a very analytical mind, but you are also prepared to take measured risks at the appropriate time as well. Who, in Germany at this time, has available funds to spend?"

"The British and American soldiers," Larion replied. "They are paid each month and though it is not a lot of money, it is substantially more than any other group in Germany. They also do not have much to do other than guard German prisoners of war, search for *SS* war criminals, and try to turn this country into a national brothel."

"And what do the American and British soldiers seek…that is, besides our willing *frauleins*, who are only doing what they have to do in order to survive?" Schalburg replied. "I know that they want to purchase every damn German camera that has ever been manufactured," Seiz replied. 'What they do with all those cameras is another matter."

"My dear Seiz," Schalburg replied knowingly. "Would it surprise you that they send those cameras back to America where they are resold for at least $600 (US) each. Considering that their original 5000 cigarettes only cost them about $10.00 (US), they make a profit of almost 60 times their original cost. That is how they make their 'big money'."

"But if we only have enough for two cameras, how can we make any money?" Seiz moaned with disappointment.

"I know where we can obtain about two hundred cameras; mostly Leica, some Zeiss Ikon and even some Emil Busch, and it will only cost us 100000 *RM*. Once we obtain those cameras, we can sell some of them to the American soldiers for 5000 cigarettes each or we can exchange those cameras for other goods which are even more valuable in Germany than cameras."

"Why would we need 100000 *RM?*" Seiz inquired.

Schalburg ignored the question, but added knowingly, "The American soldiers control other more valuable items than just cigarettes. Gasoline and diesel fuel, for example. Germans may still have motor vehicles, but without fuel they cannot operate them. But there is another group which has a lot of money."

"Who else has money in this forsaken country of ours at this time?" Seiz moaned.

"Some of our less optimistic industrial companies, which made billions of *Reichsmarks* duing the war, decided to convert some of their *Reichsmarks* into foreign currency and gold, which they then conveniently deposited into Swiss banks just across the border from Germany. Factories are now converting to peacetime production and they need extra fuel to operate. Fuel is a rationed commodity, but a company which can access more than its rationed share, can make substantially even more."

"So what is it that you are proposing, cousin?" Seiz asked in exasperation.

"First, we have to obtain those two hundred cameras which are presently being stored in Frankfurt. We then supply those cameras to those soldiers who guard and control that fuel. Those cameras, valued at about $120000 (US), could then be converted in $120000 worth of fuel. We offer those soldiers the cameras in exchange for the fuel. The fuel would have not cost the soldiers any money, but they would receive the two hundred cameras."

"But entry to an American fuel depot is impossible and they will not be persuaded to permit us to borrow one of their tanker trucks. Their risk would become too great. However, I can arrange for a couple of *tankwagens* (tanker trucks) to meet them away from the depot and simply transfer some of their fuel from their truck to our trucks. Their risk is small since 10000 liters of fuel would hardly be missed."

"Then we deliver that fuel to a factory in Kassel in exchange for payment in U.S. dollars and gold. Gold will always be a valuable commodity in any country and it will never lose its value. All we have to do is arrange for a couple of tanker trucks and I am working on that right now."

"And how do you propose to obtain two hundred cameras in Frankfurt, if our combined finances only total 100000 *RM?*" Larion inquired.

"I propose that we 'liberate' them," Schalburg replied tersely. "After all, they are in the current possession of some people who liberated them from someone else. I propose that we simply reciprocate their courtesy."

"And how do you gentlemen propose we split the profit?" Larion asked, since his monetary contribution was pretty minuscule in comparison to the other's proposed contributions."

"Three equal shares," Seiz quickly replied, smiling at Schalburg and quickly winking at Larion knowingly.

"Well, my dear adopted cousin, if I am putting in about three times the amount the two of you are contributing, why do you think that you two would be entitled to an equal share?"

"Because I am sure that my friend, Larion, and I shall be making up the difference in assuming a hundred per cent of the risk!" Seiz replied confidently. "I do not believe that the people who currently hold those cameras will be prepared to part with them willingly. I truly want to be fair, not only to you, but to us as well. That is why I think my proposal is fair to all concerned."

"Well, if you do not know the current location of those cameras…and if you do not know which companies would be prepared to pay for 10000 liters of diesel in dollars and gold, do you still feel that you two should both be entitled to an equal share—when I am also prepared to personally share in those risks as well?"

Before Seiz's furtive mind could respond, Larion decided to speak for both of them.

"In that case, *Herr* Schalburg, I believe a fair split would be fifty percent for you and Helmut and I would each receive twenty-five percent. My financial contribution is paltry by comparison, but I believe that you are asking us both to risk our lives, possibly more than just once. Surely our lives are worth at least a twenty-five percent share? Would that be the fair enough for you?"

Schalburg mused for a moment and then replied firmly, "If your friend…my dear distant cousin, can agree to your proposal, I would be prepared to agree to those terms."

"Oh…*meine lieben herren* (my dear friends), I agree! I agree!" Seiz stated emphatically. "After all, I am not really a very greedy man. A twenty-five percent share shall be enough for me."

"You two should also consider that the *Reichsmark* will probably be replaced by the Allies fairly soon and even this cigarette economy cannot last forever, even though it is the preferred medium of exchange right now," Schalburg explained. "Now is the time to act, but we have to move quickly."

Larion came to his final decision. "Then let's do it!" he said, as he extended his hand to Schalburg to solemnize their agreement."

"*Ja!*" Seiz quickly added. "We have all been struggling to stay alive for the past four years. It is time for the three of us to get rich."

Schalburg proceeded to refill their three glasses. Each one of them had their own questions to ask, but since Larion and Seiz had both conceded that Schalburg was going to lead this operation, they both deferred to him.

Schalburg asked Larion if he still had his Walther *PPK*. Larion confirmed that he did, but that he would require additional ammunition. When Seiz inquired what he had used the gun for, Larion felt obliged to explain what had happened with the three Soviet officers who had attempted to abduct him and transfer him into the Soviet Zone.

"*Ausgezeichnet* (Excellent)!" Schalburg exclaimed. "I knew that there was more to you than just being a very clever poker player. You were a Soviet officer, yes?"

"Just a First Lieutenant, *Herr Oberst* Schalburg," Larion replied. "However, I led a platoon in the Winter War with Finland in 1939 and I led a double platoon on the Ukrainian front when Hitler unleashed Operation Barbarossa in June of 1941. We were not permitted to retreat, even though my battalion lost almost five hundred casualties. Fourteen of us who survived penetrated the Axis lines and we fought with the partisans for the next one and a half years. Then we had the misfortune of running into you in the small town of Xhotimsk in Belarus. I, my wife, and my young son were transported to Kassel, where I helped build Tiger tanks for the last one and a half years."

"*Ausgezeichnet*, in any case," Schalburg exclaimed again. "And do you realize that I know more about you at this time, than I know about my dear alleged distant cousin here. I believe all of us should know more about each other because we shall be facing a couple of very serious risks in the days ahead."

Larion and Schalburg jointly looked at Seiz to see what he had to say in reply.

"Perhaps now is the appropriate time for all of us to share some our respective history," Seiz replied seriously. "I do not believe that any of us should proceed into this venture if he has any concern about one of the others. So allow me to explain myself a little. Though my father was a German Catholic, he had fallen in love with a beautiful young girl in our Bavarian village."

"Their only regret was that Hitler and his Nazis came to power, because she happened to be a Jew. She converted to Catholicism, more out of pragmatism than religious conviction, but there were people in the village who believed that if you were born a Jew, you remained a Jew, so her conversion was meaningless to them. As for my father, since he was so defiant as to marry a Jew, he was deemed by some to be a traitor to his race since his marriage defiled their racial purity."

"My parents never kept their secret a secret from me. It never amazed me that my two parents, who came from different backgrounds and were raised in different religions, could live and love each other. It seemed perfectly natural. I never considered myself to be either half-German or half-Jew, because in our family, it was never an issue. I was a student in Berlin when the war commenced and I loyally volunteered to join the *Wehrmacht.*"

"I fought in northern Africa with Rommel and in Italy, after Mussolini's fascist regime collapsed in 1943. Unfortunately, someone in the village decided to reveal my mother's secret to the *Gestapo* (*Geheime Staatspolizei* – secret state police), who decided to transport her to one of those concentration camps in Poland because she posed such a great threat to the *Fatherland.*"

"My father wrote and told me that he had decided to go as well. His love for my mother would not permit him to do otherwise. I can only presume that they ended up as ash, fertilizing some distant Polish cabbage field. I loved both of my parents dearly."

"When I discovered what happened to them, I abandoned my post and returned to our village. I killed that woman who had betrayed my parents to the *Gestapo* and though her death did not relieve my anguish, I must admit that it gave me some satisfaction. After that, I decided that I wanted to make enough money so that I could emigrate to Palestine. It is my intention to convert to Judaism, in homage to my parents, especially to my mother. That is all I have to say."

"You have both said enough," Schalburg replied. "Now I would like to share my brief history as well. I joined the *Waffen SS* because I was told that it was to be the most elite fighting force in the whole world. Furthermore, it was an opportunity for patriotic Germans to redress some of the wrongs which resulted from the end of the First World War. I neither hated, nor loved either the Jews or the Slavs. It was never an issue for me until I joined the Waffen *SS*."

"I joined to fight and I fought in the Benelux countries, in France, and in the Balkan peninsula. Finally, I fought on the eastern front. Somewhere along that path I realized that we had lost our way."

"However, I now know that my leaders were lost from the outset. Hatred and elimination of the Jews and the Slav's had always been the *Waffen SS's* priority, because it had always been the first priority for our leaders. Though I now wish I could have lived my life differently, I am unable to apologize for what I have done. My apology would not resurrect a single soul. I did what I did because I was a soldier and I followed orders. I also issued those same orders to other soldiers as well, because I was taught to believe that was what soldiers do."

"So, you hold no hatred for me or for Larion?" Seiz asked. "A Jew and a Slav?"

"No, I hold no hatred for either of you and I hope that you can feel the same," Schalburg replied. "But we are embarking on a venture which is not without risk and it is important for each one of us to know that we can trust and rely upon the other two."

"You never know," Seiz replied lightheartedly. "Perhaps we are all 'distant cousins' in the eyes of God."

"This is just a business venture and I want both of you to know that you can rely upon me and that I shall be relying upon you in return," Schalburg replied. "We shall need each other if this venture is going to be successful. The people who hold those cameras shall not be willing to part with them, willingly."

"Sulupin, bring that *PPK* for personal backup, but for this operation I shall provide all of us with 1941 *Police Mauser Lugers*—they have a considerably greater stopping force than a *PPK*. As you probably know, they have an eight-cartridge 9mm magazine. Each of us shall carry an auxiliary magazine as well. Our primary armament shall be *Maschinen pistole* 40s. They are short and though they are fully automatic, you can affect a low rate of fire with controlled trigger pulls. You just pull, release, then pull again, as may be required."

"The *Maschinen pistole* comes with a 32-cartridge magazine and we shall carry an auxiliary magazine as well. Please remember not to use the magazine as a grip, for it may jam the weapon's cartridge feed. Hold the machine pistol by its stock. They should provide us with sufficient fire power in close quarters."

"What about transportation?" Seiz inquired. "We shall need a small truck to transport the cameras, but how do we acquire a 10000-liter tanker truck to transport our fuel?"

"Our American friends' tanker truck has a very large capacity, but it is designed to only travel on the *autobahn*. Our German *tankwagens* come with a lower volume, but they are all-terrain vehicles. They can travel by *autobahn* or over the countryside. I shall look after this issue, but I shall leave it up to you to arrange for the small truck to transport the cameras," Schalburg replied.

"So we will transfer the fuel from the American tanker to our tankers?" Larion asked.

"I have made that suggestion to my American contact and he assures me that it can be arranged," Schalburg replied. "The first difficult part of this operation is in retrieving those cameras in Frankfurt. Once we have the cameras, we merely deliver them to the Americans' tanker and pick up the fuel. I shall provide you with the details after we get the cameras. Then all we do is deliver that diesel fuel to a factory here in Kassel and pick up our payment. That will be the second difficult part of this operation, for our *Deutsche freunde* may want to get the fuel and keep their gold."

"I can have the truck within two days," Seiz replied.

"Then we can leave for Frankfurt the following day," Schalburg replied. "I would like to leave early in the morning so that we can be back in Kassel by midnight. We can review the details respecting the cameras en route to Frankfurt and the delivery of the fuel and our payment when we return to Kassel."

"Why do we need the 100000 *RM*, if we are just liberating the cameras?" Seiz asked again.

"For payment for the information of the location of those cameras, my friend," Schalburg replied.

*****

By the time Larion got back to the Camp, it was late and dark. There was no light, not even the flicker of a solitary candle in the barracks. As Larion approached their bunk, Tamara and Dimitri were sound asleep, their arms intertwined. They seemed so serene. He huddled in his own blanket on an adjacent bunk, but he was unable to fall asleep.

The excitement of what they were going to attempt to accomplish, stimulated him to such an extent that he could not go to sleep. But even after he had eventually fallen asleep, he dreamt about the proposed enterprise and he even formulated contingency plans in the event that something went awry.

Chapter 51

Larion could feel someone gently shaking him. He felt so tired that he initially attempted to resist, but he gradually came out of his stupor and looked up to see Tamara and Dimitri looking down at him. Tamara did not look pleased, but Dimitri was smiling and beaming at this father. He was hopeful that she would say something to commence the conversation, so that he would not have to, but it was obvious that she was disappointed and upset with him, again. "I apologize, Tamara," he finally said in a tired voice as he tried to rub his eyes into focus. "My business in Kassel took longer than I had expected. I trust you did not worry too much."

Tamara declined to respond to his invitation for communication. She remained motionless and silent, waiting for Larion to explain why he had not returned as he had told her to expect.

"I am going to take Dimitri to school, but I shall come right back because I believe it is time that we had a discussion about what you are doing right now and what you are planning for us so that we may leave this despicable place. We have eaten breakfast, but you shall have to make something for yourself, if you are hungry."

Without waiting for a reply, she quickly took Dimitri's hand, turned, and walked away. Larion was grateful for her departure for it would give him an opportunity to formulate some response. He did not intend to lie to Tamara for he loved her too much to be dishonest with her, but he also knew her vunerabilities, especially her fear about their unknown future.

*****

As promised, Tamara returned within fifteen minutes. Again, she did not say anything. She merely seated herself on Larion's bunk, folded her hands in her lap, and looked anxiously at him while she waited for his explanation.

"Lieutenant Thornton introduced me to the new Camp Director yesterday. Mr. Balmelle would like to meet with us as soon as possible in respect to emigrating to Canada," Larion explained.

"I know. Andre took me to see Lieutenant Thornton's office yesterday afternoon after you failed to come back as you had promised and that was explained to me. In fact, Andre arranged for us to meet with Mr. Balmelle this afternoon, right after lunch," Tamara replied solemnly, still holding her hands clenched tightly together on her lap. Her lips were also pursed into a thin line.

"I went to Kassel to try to replace that gold crucifix I gave you the day I proposed marriage. Do you remember? You had to give it away and I wanted to replace it."

"How many times must I tell you that I am not interested in these ornaments," Tamara burst out emotionally. "They will not comfort me or keep me warm or love me. How many times must I explain that to you?"

"That I know well, my dearest," Larion replied soothingly, rising up so that he could gently caress her cheek with his hand, but Tamara turned and pulled away. Larion withdrew the crucifix from his pocket and handed it to her. "Please, Tamara. It shall please me very much if you wear it."

Tamara initially tried to slap Larion's hand away, but she stopped, assuming that to cast a crucifix away would be an act of sacrilege.

"No! I don't want it!" she replied angrily. "I don't need it! I do not want you to continue to risk your life for such trifles. They hold no significance for me."

"Please Tamara, I implore you, my dearest," Larion replied. "What I do… I do for you and for our son. Besides, if there was a risk, the risk has already been taken. Please accept this from my heart to yours."

"You know, I promised myself that I would remain angry with you and that I would remain unforgiving…but I simply cannot. But why do you continue to take unnecessary risks and jeopardize your safety and then justify those risks by saying that you did it for me and our son?"

"Any risks which I have taken, I have taken them solely for you and our family, my dearest," Larion replied soothingly. "Please accept this crucifix as token of my love for you."

Tamara finally reached over and took the crucifix from Larion's outstretched hand and looked at it.

"I suppose I should thank you," Tamara replied reluctantly, aware of the fact that Larion had persuaded her to forgive him again. "Would you undo the clasp and place it around my neck, Louyna?" Tamara asked in timid voice. She resented the fact that she was not able to maintain her disappointment with her husband a bit longer. She desperately wanted him to avoid taking unnecessary risks so that the three of them could actually fulfill their dream and live out their lives together, and possibly even watch their grandchildren grow up to become young adults.

Larion undid the clasp and placed the chain around her neck and closed the clasp tightly. Tamara reverently touched the crucifix with her right hand and though Larion could see her move her lips, her fervent prayer remained silent to his ears. He placed both of his hands on her shoulders and then reached over to kiss her cheek.

Tamara slowly turned her head so that their lips could meet. Both of them could feel the emotion surge from one to the other and then back again. Their lips parted and continued to seek out each other as they turned to embrace passionately. Larion longed to make love to her and his kisses became more demanding.

"Just wait, kind sir!" Tamara spoke abruptly, breaking off their kiss as she pulled away from him. "You have still not explained why you returned so late. It could not have been simply because you were just purchasing this crucifix."

Larion then proceeded carefully to be absolutely truthful in what he disclosed to Tamara about his meeting with Seiz and Schalburg; however, he could not bring himself to tell her the whole truth. He explained that he had been hired to go to Frankfurt in two days to pick up some goods and then return those goods to Kassel that same night. He explained that there was no point in accepting the offer of employment from Henschel, because the *Reichsmark* was essentially worthless, using the purchase price of 4000 *RM* for her crucifix as an example.

Tamara merely gasped in disbelief when Larion told her what her crucifix had cost. When Tamara asked about how he was going to get paid if the *Reichsmark* had no value, Larion explained that he would be asking for his payment in American funds. He felt that he came closest to deceiving her when he assured her that he did not intend to take any unnecessary risk; however, he reasoned in his own mind that he did not intend to take any unnecessary risk.

"Louyna, please hold my crucifix and swear that you were not gambling again."

Larion held the crucifix as Tamara had requested and swore accordingly. He was relieved that his last statement was absolutely truthful, but as he held that crucifix, he also made a silent promise to himself that this would be the final occasion when he would not be absolutely and totally truthful to his wife.

"But there is something I want you to understand, my love," Tamara spoke firmly, but in a soft voice. "I believe that sometimes you think that I am still that young, innocent teenager that you first met at the *kolkhoz* that spring day so many years ago. I think it is time that you started to see me as a young woman, a wife, and a mother. Someone who has seen more than her share of tragedy. I have witnessed the loss of my grandfather…and I have even watched my father be humiliated and executed. I have seen our friends hanging like rotting fruit from the gallows in Mogilev.

"Tamara—" Larion attempted to interject, but Tamara silenced him by raising her right palm. She was not finished and she wanted him to hear what she had to say.

"I want you to see me…not as some juvenile young, helpless doll…I want you to see me as your wife and the mother of our son. Someone who you can and should rely on, and take into your utmost confidence. Do you think that you can do that?"

"All I can do is promise that I shall try," Larion replied. "But if I see you as delicate and vulnerable, it is because you are that way in many senses and I am just trying to protect you."

After they shared a small lunch with Dimitri, they took him back to his school and they asked Andre to accompany them to see the new director of *UNRRA* Team 505 to discuss possible emigration to Canada.

"Please explain to Mr. and Mrs. Sulupin, Andre, that they have been accepted for emigration to Canada; however, they shall be obligated to sign a document…a contract, in fact, that they shall work for one year on a sugar beet farm in southern Alberta…a province…what you call an *Oblast*. Balmelle proceeded to explain that the Canadian government would cover all of their transportation costs from Kassel to the port of Hamburg, where they would be given passage on the USS General McRae, which would take them to the port of Halifax, which was located on the eastern coast of Canada. Then they would board a train and travel across the country to the *Oblast* of Alberta.

Once they reached their designated farm, they would be provided with accommodation and food, and they would also be paid $10 each per week, which would provide them with some funds to begin their new lives in Canada once their one-year service commitment had been fulfilled. Balmelle compared their prospective life as 'sugar beet farm workers' to that of the communal workers on a *kolkhoz*.

Tamara was euphoric as they walked hand in hand back to their barracks. To her, Balmelle's explanation was the fulfilment of her dreams. They did not have to worry about the cost of travelling to Canada, so there was no need for Larion to continue to gamble. This unknown country had willingly agreed to accept them, offer them food, lodging, and even pay them for their work. Most importantly, they did not have to worry about Stalin and his *NKVD*. Though Larion was happy that his wife seemed so filled with joy, his feelings were mixed.

His concern was the necessity of a contingency plan in the event Balmelle's proposal did not materialize. They were 'Stateless Persons' in a foreign country which had been devastated by war and they were totally reliant upon the kindness of other people who they did not know and who he was not prepared to trust fully. In his mind, those factors necessitated a contingency plan…and a contingency plan required financial security in some form.

Chapter 52

Seiz drove the small truck to the *Furstenwald* DP Camp to pick up Larion. He wanted to discuss matters on their drive back to Kassel to pick up Schalburg and his informant. Larion was just exiting the main office as he pulled into the Camp. As Larion descended down the three steps to the parking lot, Seiz noticed that a pretty young blonde with a young boy were waiting for him. He recognized that it was Larion's wife and son. He pulled up to them, stopped his vehicle and exited.

He could see that Tamara was apprehensive, but he was confident that Larion would not have disclosed their plans to her.

"*Grube an alle* (Greetings everyone)!" Seiz announced pleasantly. "Larion, are you ready to leave? I estimate that it is about two hundred kilometers to Frankfurt and being cautious, I estimate it may take us up to three hours to reach the city, depending on the condition of the roads, possible military traffic and road check points."

"*Guten morgen mein herr* (Good morning, sir)," Dimitri replied proudly.

"*Du sprechst Deutsch* (Do you speak German)?" Seiz asked in surprise at the child's linguistic skill.

"*Ich spreche sehr gut Deutsch* (I speak German very well)," Dimitri replied smugly, smiling up at his parents for approval, as the three adults chuckled at the boy's brazen modesty.

"We should be leaving, Larion," Seiz responded, when he was able to stop laughing.

At that point, Tamara grasped Seiz by both of his shoulders and addressed him herself with the little German she knew.

"*Kein schaden, mein mann* (No harm my man)."

Seiz looked into Tamara's earnest eyes. She was imploring him with every fiber of her being.

"Tamara!" Larion begged his wife. "Please do not embarrass me, my dearest. I promised you that I will not take any unnecessary risks."

Seiz then held Tamara by her two shoulders and looked directly into her eyes so that she would know he understood her concern and that he would protect him. "*Ja, Ich werde ihn schutzen* (Yes, I shall protect him)," Seiz replied, nodding his head to emphasis his commitment.

Though Tamara did not understand what Seiz had said, his tone of voice and his demeanor did reassure her a little, but she would say a prayer for both men before she fell asleep that night.

*****

As they drove the short distance to Kassel, Larion asked if Seiz was familiar with Schalburg's informant, who was supposed to direct them to the warehouse where the cameras were being stored, but Seiz was not familiar with the man. Larion then asked if he trusted Schalburg. "I have known him about a year and he has been fair and straightforward with me…at least to this point, but you never know. We are dealing with a lot of money…and sometimes, money makes some people act strangely," Seiz replied ambivalently.

*****

As they pulled up to the building which housed Schalburg's poker parlor, he limped out of the building and approached their small truck, which had a tarpaulin covering the back of the truck. A small, anemic-looking man came out with him. He seemed nervous and kept casting furtive bespectacled glances in all directions. He seemed extremely anxious to get into the passenger compartment in the truck as quickly as he could to avoid being seen by others.

"Gentlemen, please pick up that box in the doorway," Schalburg requested. "It contains our 'tools'. I suggest that we arm ourselves with the Luger pistols now and simply leave that box with the machine pistols in the back of the truck for now. We can arm ourselves with those machine pistols once we reach Frankfurt."

Schalburg then advised Seiz of the route he was to take. Seiz objected initially because it would add another twenty to thirty kilometers each way to the trip. Schalburg advised him that the Americans had just set up a road block on the primary road Seiz had selected and Seiz quickly withdrew his objection.

"*Herr* Schalburg!" Larion inquired. "Are you going to introduce us to your friend?"

"Actually, he is no friend of mine…merely an acquaintance who approached me recently with information he had for sale. He advises me that he knows where our friends are storing those cameras. He wanted to be paid up front, but that proposal was totally unacceptable. He will be paid as soon as we reach the destination and see the cameras for ourselves. He tells me that his name is Manfred.…I do not know his surname or even if he has a surname…and I really do not care."

"And what is our plan?" Larion inquired again.

"When we get to the warehouse, Manfred and I shall enter the building through the front entrance. Manfred has arranged to introduce me as a buyer of cameras. You and my dear cousin will be hidden in the back of the truck under the tarp, armed with the machine pistols. You will have to obtain entry into the building through one of the second story windows.

"I shall try to stall by haggling over the price, but it is imperative that the two of you obtain entry no later than three minutes after Manfred and I have entered the building. You should be able to locate us by the sound of our voices. Be sure that both of you are not in the same location.

"Once they produce the cameras, I shall curse '*Verdammt und Vernahten!*' (damned and stitched up), and then you, my dear half-Jew, and you, my dear Cossack, reveal yourselves and place our friends under control. Once matters are concluded, we shall invite our friends to load the cameras into the back of the truck and then we shall leave."

"What if they call the Military Police or the German *Polizei*?" Seiz inquired.

"They will not do that…because our friends cannot stand close scrutiny by the Military Police or the German *Polizei*. How can they report the theft of stolen cameras which they had stolen themselves, but they will try to come after us. To that extent, before we leave their warehouse, we will have to disable whatever vehicles which may be around or possibly even incapacitate one or two of them. We will have to immobilize them one way or the other to provide us with sufficient time to get away."

"And what about the second part of our operation tonight?" Seiz inquired discretely; however, Schalburg noticed that Manfred's ears immediately perked up.

"I shall be happy to discuss that with you once we leave our friend, Manfred, behind with his 100000 *RM*. After all, we do not want to give him new information which he may decide to sell to someone else, do we?" Schalburg replied.

"*Mien Herr!*" Manfred protested in vain. "I am a man of honor. I would never consider betraying a colleague like you."

*****

The drive to Frankfurt was uneventful and Schalburg took over the driving a couple of kilometers from their destination. Seiz and Larion secreted themselves in the back of the truck and covered themselves with the canvas tarp, clutching their machine pistols. Soon they stopped in front of a nondescript two-story building which was surrounded by partially demolished buildings on all sides. A pathway had been cleared to accommodate one lane of vehicle traffic. That lane led directly to a set of closed commercial doors which could accommodate vehicle traffic.

Schalburg reversed their truck and backed it up to those double doors. There was also a regular sized pedestrian door built into the right commercial double door to permit individual entry. There was only a Mercedes four door sedan parked outside in the vicinity of the building.

As instructed by Manfred, Schalburg activated the truck's nasal horn twice, followed by a further three quick blasts. Within a minute, the pedestrian door slowly opened and a bearded face wearing a Bavarian leather hat peered out and checked in all directions. The man then waved his left hand, beckoning Schalburg to come closer, however, his right hand remained concealed behind the double door. Schalburg assumed that the bearded face was armed.

As Schalburg and Manfred neared the building, three men exited through the pedestrian door. All three men were armed with pistols and Schalburg raised his arms to his shoulders in modest submission.

Larion and Seiz could hear a number of men approaching the back of their vehicle. They could hear the tarpaulin rear entry coverings being parted and then more voices. Then the men walked away. Once they heard the pedestrian door being closed, Seiz quickly lifted the rear coverings and the two men exited the back of the vehicle. They had to achieve their own entry as quickly as possible.

On one side of the building, debris from an adjacent collapsed building was heaped against the side of the building almost to the height of the second-story windows. Seiz and Larion decided that it would be their point of entry. There was only shattered glass in the window panes. Once inside, Larion gestured to Seiz that he goes to the left, while he proceeded to the right side. Their next objective was to get down to the main floor and wait for Schalburg's signal.

*****

"Alright, you fucking cripple, let's see the color of your money," the bearded face rudely commanded Schalburg to comply.

"The money is in the truck, my bearded friend, but let me show you a little sample," Schalburg replied, as he withdrew a small roll of American $100 bills. "Here, taste one if you like, but you better show me your cameras now."

"You are in my house, you *Verdammter hosen scheiber* (damned pant shitter)!" the bearded face replied. "In this place, I tell you what to do. Nobody tells me what to do."

Schalburg decided that it was an appropriate time for a dramatic pause as he assessed the bearded face wearing the silly hat and his two grinning henchmen. He was totally unimpressed.

"Manfred, you son-of-a-bitch!" Schalburg swore as he lowered his arms. "You told me that your associates were businessmen with cameras to sell, not some smelly sons-of-bitches who have not washed in a week and who probably shave in their own urine. There is no deal to be made here."

With that statement, Schalburg calmly turned around and proceeded to walk away from the odious threesome, who exchanged surprised looks. Confusion was rife in their collective criminal minds.

"*Halt! Halt!*" the bearded face sputtered. "*Halt* or I shall shoot!"

Schalburg ignored the threat and continued to walk towards the pedestrian exit. Suddenly, the bearded face changed the tone of his voice and commenced to obsequiously implore Schalburg to stop and return so that their business could be concluded.

Schalburg stopped and then he turned around slowly. He was holding his Luger pistol in his right gloved hand aimed directly at the breaded face, whose own pistol was pointed impotently at the floor of the building.

"I do not like to conduct business like this. I arrive with open hands and I am greeted with insults and threatened with pistols. I have to ask myself, are we going to act like businessmen or like bandits?"

"Dear friend, allow me to apologize," the bearded man replied ingratiatingly. "This damn war has made us forget all of the lessons our mothers had taught us about social manners. Please come back and let us all put our pistols away and just talk business."

"Well, I have shown you a sample of my money and I was told that you wanted to sell for American dollars," Schalburg stated calmly. "Now I believe that in the custom of this trade, it is your turn to show me your cameras."

The bearded face turned and addressed his two intellectually challenged minions. "You idiots, why are you still standing there. Bring out the dolly with the cameras. *Schnell*!"

The two minions dutifully shouldered their pistols and disappeared. They reappeared quickly, pushing a large dolly on which were loaded a large number of boxes containing a variety of cameras.

Schalburg quickly reviewed the boxes of cameras and observed. "I was told that you had two hundred Konica and some other high-end models. This does not look like two hundred cameras to me, *mein herr!* I presume that you are able to count to two hundred, yes?" "We had two hundred, but unfortunately, we only have one hundred and sixty-five left. But I assure you that I can count quite well!" The bearded face replied smugly.

Schalburg conducted a quick examination of the cameras which were stacked on the dolly.

"Well, all I can say is: *VERDAMMT UND VERNAHTEN*!"

At that signal, Seiz and Larion appeared from the rear and from the front with their machine pistols levelled at the three black marketeers. Schalburg also retrieved his Luger from his coat pocket and pointed it directly at the bearded face. All three of the would-be camera vendors were surprised by the turn of events, but they instinctively raised their arms high in the air in total submission.

"Manfred, *komm schnell her* (Come here quickly)!" Schalburg ordered. "Do you know how to drive a vehicle?"

'What vehicle, *mein herr?*"

"The Mercedes outside the building, you idiot. What other vehicle would I be talking about or do you think that you can outrun your friends after we leave this place?"

"But I thought I would travel back to Kassel with you," Manfred replied.

"You thought wrong, Manfred. There has been a change of plans. Can you drive or not?"

"Oh…yes I can drive, but where is my money?" Manfred replied anxiously, since he was less concerned about his safety than he was about not being paid.

"As agreed, Manfred, here is your 100000 *RM*," Schalburg replied and then he turned to the three kneeling captives who were still holding their hands above their heads. The bearded face and his two subordinates were no longer grinning. Larion removed their pistols and ensured that they were not carrying any additional weapons.

"Manfred requires the keys to that Mercedes sedan parked outside the building. I want those keys now and I do not want to ask again."

The three captives refused to speak, so Schalburg decided to let his Luger do his talking. He turned to the bearded face, who was obviously the leader of the group.

"*Mein herr*, are you going to force me to ask you again? But aren't you the one who mocked my war injury? Would you like to experience some similar pain and then learn to walk with a limp for the rest of your life?"

The bearded face foolishly elected to just glare back at Schalburg, so he pointed his Luger at the bearded face's right kneecap.

"I am told that one of the most painful leg injuries is when a person's patella is shattered and I assure you that at this range, it will shatter into a hundred pieces. They will never reconstruct it and then you will look to a future where rude people will probably insult you for being a cripple. Just because you choose to be stupidly obstinate at this moment."

The bearded face quickly lowered his right hand and retrieved the keys from his jacket pocket and proffered those keys to Schalburg with feigned contrition.

"Manfred, take those keys and then drive away from here. Remember, I never want to see your face again. If you dare cross my path or my threshold, I shall shoot you on sight between your eyes."

As Manfred gingerly took the keys from the bearded face's hand, he jumped backwards as Schalburg's Luger barked out a round behind him and the bearded face screamed with pain as his right patella shattered into a hundred pieces and his pant leg became saturated with blood.

"I do not enjoy being didactic, but I believe this is a suitable occasion," Schalburg said, directing his comments to the bearded face who was howling and writhing in pain in front of him, clutching his useless right leg. "I asked you if you wanted to behave like a businessman or like a bandit. You should understand that if you choose to act like a bandit, do not be surprised if you are treated like a bandit. I am only inclined to give someone one opportunity to decide. I do not believe in extending second chances in life."

Schalburg then turned to the bearded face's two companions.

"And you, gentlemen, are going to push that dolly out the double doors and load those cameras into the back of the truck. Make sure that you stack them neatly and then cover them with that canvas tarp. If you follow my instructions quickly and to the letter, I will permit the two of you to walk out of here, unencumbered by a shattered kneecap like your dear friend.

"*Mach es schnell!*" (Do it quickly!)

Chapter 53

Schalburg resumed control of the truck since he knew where they were to meet the American tanker truck, but he was inclined to comment on what had just happened with the bearded face and his two companions. "I think that went fairly well," Schalburg announced, with a modicum of satisfaction. "You never know what will happen when you are obliged to deal with stupid people who think they are clever."

"Well, you only had to fire one shot, so I agree, Herr Schalburg," Seiz replied.

"And what are the plans for the next phase of this operation?" Larion inquired.

"There are three Americans who will be meeting us. We decided that it would be less risk if they drove their large American *'tankwagen'* (fuel tanker truck) from the military fuel depot and just meet us outside the city limits to complete the transfer of the fuel. I have also arranged for two Henschel *Type 33 G1 tankwagens* to meet us at the same location. We shall provide the Americans with most of the cameras we have and they shall conveniently provide us with some privacy so that we can transfer the fuel from their *tankwagen* to our two *tankwagens*.

"While we are transferring the fuel, the Americans will have an opportunity to secure their cameras. After we leave to return to Kassel, the Americans shall return to their *tankwagen* and resume their journey to wherever they were going to deliver the balance of their fuel. Their explanation for the shortfall will be simple. They stopped for dinner and someone drained some of the fuel from their tank while they were eating. After all, these things are not that uncommon in Germany at this time."

"How much fuel did you bargain to take?" Larion inquired again.

"The American's *tankwagen* has a large capacity, probably in excess of 30000 liters or 8000 of their American gallons. Their vehicle has a higher capacity because it is not designed to travel cross-country, just on our auto-bahns. Our Henschel *tankwagens* have been modified to increase their capacity to 7500 liters each or 2000 American gallons. However, our *tankwagens* can travel by autobahn or cross-country, if that becomes necessary."

"How did you acquire the Henschel *tankwagens*?" Larion continued to inquire.

"You are a most inquisitive young Cossack, Sulupin," Schalburg replied. "Perhaps I should answer not only this question, but the next question you will probably ask as well. To answer your last question, Henschel is providing us with these two *tankwagens*. Henschel modified them to increase their capacity from 4500 liters each to 7500 liters. And to answer your next probable question, if you have not guessed by this point in time, our buyer is—"

"Henschel Industries!" Seiz and Larion both completed Schalburg's answer simultaneously.

"You are both very clever and perceptive," Schalburg replied with satisfaction. "I am most pleased that I had selected the two of you for this little venture."

"I do not anticipate any problems with the Americans, but what are your plans for our return journey?" Larion inquired again. "If we are going to be using Henschel *tankwagens,* I assume that Henschel is also supplying their own drivers."

"Excellent assumption, Sulupin," Schalburg replied. "Seiz shall lead our convoy back to Kassel. His truck shall be least 200 meters in front of the two *tankwagens*. If he sees any checkpoint, he will flash his brake lights three times. That will give our two *tankwagens* an opportunity shut off their lights, leave the autobahn, and proceed cross-country to circumvent that checkpoint. I shall accompany the lead Henschel *tankwagen* and you shall accompany the following one. We shall deliver the fuel at the Henschel factory at Kassel and pick up our gold. Seiz's truck shall transport us and our money back to my building."

"An excellent plan, *Herr Oberst* Schalburg," Seiz stated with satisfaction. "But after all, my dear friend, *Herr* Sulupin, was merely a First Lieutenant and I was merely a *Wehrmacht* soldier."

"No need for any false modesty, Seiz!" Schalburg replied. "Even if I am inclined to agree with you."

"And what security precautions do you want us to implement when we arrive at Henschel's factory and pick up our payment?" Larion continued his inquiries.

"It will be impossible for us to surprise anyone at Henschel, so we shall simply show up with each of us carrying our machine pistols at the ready, but not threatening in any way. I will carry on the discussion with whomever shows up on behalf of Henschel, while the two of you shall be scrutinizing the surroundings and be on guard for any problem. If any problem arises, I expect you both to respond accordingly. That means I expect you both to shoot first and think later. If Henschel presumes to try to betray us, there are other anxious buyers available, but it is important that we first survive."

"And at the risk of becoming a nuisance, *Herr* Schalburg," Larion inquired for the last time. "Exactly what is our payment going to be?"

"Yes!" Seiz echoed enthusiastically. "What is our payment going to be?"

Schalburg paused and smiled at his two business companions before answering, to heighten their respective interest.

"I have negotiated a selling price of $8 (US) per liter, which means a total of $120000 (US) for us to divide. That will be $60000 (US) for me and $30000 (US) for each of you. Not a bad payment for a 100000 *RM* investment and one night's work, don't you agree?"

"This one night's work is not over yet, Herr Schalburg," Larion replied.

*****

As they approached the rendezvous point, they could see the glare of the American tanker truck's headlights and its glistening running lights in the early evening darkness. Their truck's powerful engine was idling, gently disturbing the silence of the night with its deep-throated throbs. As Schalburg, Seiz and Larion exited their truck, the three American soldiers were leaning casually against their vehicle.

Larion made note of the fact that none of the soldiers were smoking because of their proximity to 8000 gallons of explosive fuel, but all three were carrying sidearms and each soldier had his right hand positioned in proximity to his Colt *M1911* pistol. So, though their posture was marked by unconcern, Larion concluded that the Americans were no fools and not to be trifled with.

Larion and Seiz followed Schalburg as he approached the Americans, but they had their machine pistols slung over their left shoulders in front of their chests, which made them easily accessible if any shooting started. All they would have to do is swing their weapons down and fire.

"Gentlemen!" Schalburg addressed the Americans in English. "I note that our *tankwagens* have not yet arrived, so let us conclude our business as quickly as possible. It will take some time to pump 4000 gallons of fuel from your *tankwagen* to ours, once they do arrive."

"We would like to see the cameras, then," a young corporal replied. "If you do not mind?"

"Not at all! Not at all!" replied Schalburg. "Allow me to escort you gentlemen to the back of the truck. We have Leicas, Zeiss Ikons and Emil Busch. All are brand new and in their respective boxes. As we discussed, I am proposing to give you 150 cameras of your choice."

The Americans proceeded to check some samples and then they conferred with each other. Finally, they had come to some agreement and the corporal was ready to reveal their position.

"I know that we discussed 150 cameras, but it seems that you have about 165. So we are proposing that we take them all."

Schalburg paused once again before responding. A quick refusal would not accomplish anything and a quick acceptance would cost him another 15 cameras with an estimated value of about $9000 (US). He decided to appeal to the American vaunted principle of fair play. After all, they had agreed to accept 150 cameras and now they were asking for another 15 cameras. He was also aware that the American's monthly salary was less than $175 (US) per month.

"Gentlemen, I am prepared to bargain," he replied, hoping that this concession would disarm the Americans, at least emotionally. "However, we have negotiated a bargain in good faith already. I value your respective 50 cameras at about $30000 (US) and your average annual salary is about $2100 (US). That means you can earn the equivalent of almost fourteen years salary for a couple of hours work tonight."

"But we have the fuel and you need our fuel," the corporal responded smugly. "And since you have an extra fifteen cameras, we are prepared to take them off your hands as well."

"But you are not the only contacts which can provide me with 4000 gallons of fuel," Schalburg replied knowingly.

Though Larion was able to follow some of their conversation in English, Seiz was totally lost.

He watched his American counterparts carefully, but he also watched Larion's facial expression as well. However, if Larion understood what was being discussed, his demeanor remained inscrutable.

The corporal seemed to be experienced in haggling as well and he seemed to relish this battle of wits with Schalburg.

"Well, we are the only contacts which can provide you with 4000 gallons of fuel right here and now, Schalburg."

"That is well put, corporal!" Schalburg replied. "Well put, indeed. But by the same token, we are the only contacts which can provide you with 150 high-grade cameras right here and now, as well."

Schalburg elected to take another dramatic pause. He wanted the Americans to understand that though they held a strong position, his position had a powerful leverage as well—their greed.

"But to be reasonable, I am prepared to let you have an additional two cameras each. That means you can receive 156 cameras right now, with a total estimated value of about $93600 (US). But that is my final offer. If it is not acceptable, we can part and go our own separate ways, with no bad feelings, as you Americans say."

"John!" One of the other two soldiers interrupted. "Maybe we should discuss this between the three of us. I am not interested in wasting all of the preparations which we have made, including rescheduling out timetables so that we could all be available for this run tonight."

"Alright Schalburg, we have a deal—4000 gallons for 156 cameras," the corporal replied, as the two Henschel *tankwagens* rolled up. "You guys are lucky that our tanker truck is equipped with a motorized pump, otherwise you would be hand pumping that fuel for the next four hours."

*****

As the Americans selected their fifty-two cameras each, the Henschel drivers commenced to have the fuel pumped into their two *tankwagens*. The three Americans disappeared with a fourth companion who arrived with a small covered truck. Within an hour and a half, they returned, just as the second Henschel *tankwagen* was filled up. Then the three Americans jumped up into their monstrous vehicle and slowly disappeared into the darkness of the night.

*****

"*Meine kameraden* (My comrades)," Schalburg announced proudly. "Two of our four objectives have been fulfilled successfully and there is a bonus of an additional nine cameras to divide between us with an estimated value of about $5400 (US). I suggest that I retain five cameras and you two receive two each. Is that fair? After all, it seems that I have been doing most of the work."

"I have no objection, Schalburg," Larion replied and Seiz quickly agreed.

"Now all we have to do is to deliver the fuel to Henschel and then pick up our payment," Schalburg summarized. "Seiz, make sure that you do not get too far ahead of us and that you see our vehicles' headlights at all times. If you come across any check-stop ahead, pump your brakes three quick times, twice. Once you pass that checkpoint, proceed ahead at least three kilometers and then stop by the side of the autobahn with you motor running and your lights on. Our *tankwagens* will be driving off-road without any lights, so it is imperative that we will be able to see your parked truck and know when it shall be safe to return to the autobahn."

"And what happens if I am stopped and delayed for any reason?" Seiz inquired.

"I am relying upon your ingenuity to extricate yourself out of any predicament," Schalburg replied. "You can travel must faster on the autobahn than we can travel off-road with 2000 gallons of fuel. If you are delayed, keep track of the time and try to estimate how far the *tankwagens* could possibly proceed ahead. Then just speed up and rejoin out modest convoy."

"In that case, I suggest that the nine remaining cameras be carried in your two *tankwagens*," Seiz suggested. "In case I am stopped, that shall be one less matter I shall have to explain. My truck has a convenient compartment built into the back of its bench seat and I shall conceal my machine pistol there. If they find my Luger on me, I am an ex-soldier and there are many of us moving around the country, trying to get home. If they decide to confiscate it, so be it."

"Sulupin, make sure that you check your driver for any weapons before you permit him to drive away. Check the inside of the vehicle itself to ensure that he has not hidden a pistol somewhere.

"If he refuses to follow my vehicle for any reason, either shoot him or throw him out of the vehicle and then drive it yourself. Out third objective is to get the fuel to Kassel, but we have to get there safely as well. Do not trust

361

the driver to any degree. Though we are to receive $120000 (US), the value of that fuel to Henschel is about three-fold more. Remember, trust no one."

Chapter 54

Schalburg watched his cheerless German driver carefully as he patted him down for possible weapons. He noticed that both drivers were wearing those tan 'Africa Corps' hats with extended brims. Then he checked the cab of the *tankwagen.* Satisfied that there were no weapons, he told the driver to mount the vehicle and proceed to follow Seiz, who had already left and positioned his truck about three hundred meters in front of the two *tankwagens.*

The convoy proceeded northward towards Kassel at a reasonable speed for nighttime driving and matters were uneventful. Larion estimated that they had travelled at least three quarters of the distance to Kassel when he noticed Seiz's vehicle suddenly triple flash its brake lights, twice.

*****

As soon as Seiz spied the faint glimmer of shimmering lights ahead on the autobahn, he immediately flashed his brake lights as Schalburg had instructed. He slowed the speed of his own vehicle as he approached the road block ahead of his vehicle. Fortunately, it was not the American Military Police, but the German *Polizei*. At least he would not have a language problem in communicating with the police. There were three police cars blocking the autobahn, but apparently, they were only checking northbound traffic.

*****

Larion noticed that Schalburg's vehicle immediately doused its headlights as it veered off the autobahn to its right and it quickly disappeared into the darkness of the night. Larion commanded his dour driver to follow suit, "*Schnell! Schnell!*"

When his driver hesitated, Larion pulled out his Luger and pressed the barrel hard against the driver's temple.

"*Gehorche oder Sterbe* (Obey or die)!" Larion commanded.

His driver merely snarled and tried defiantly to flash his vehicle's headlights instead. He only flashed them once before the 9 mm slug pierced his skull and he slumped dead over the steering wheel. Larion shoved his body down as he attempted to gain control over the vehicle. At the same time, he quickly doused his vehicle's headlights and veered right off the autobahn and into the dark night. He tried to unlatch the driver's door and as the door opened, Larion shoved the heavy body out of the cab as he assumed the driver's seat.

He peered into the darkness in the hope that he might be able to see the silhouette of Schalburg's vehicle ahead of him. The soft ground and the heavy weight the *tankwagen* was hauling caused his speed to reduce to thirty kilometers an hour, even though the engine was laboring noisily. Larion opened his driver's door window and tried to listen for the sound of Schalburg's engine, but his own engine was drowning out all other sounds.

Larion decided that he would have to travel farther away from the autobahn so whatever it was that caused Seiz to flash his lights, they would neither see nor hear his vehicle. He prayed that the ground remained reasonably level and free of hidden obstacles.

*****

Seiz carefully brought his vehicle to a complete stop and two German policemen approached his vehicle cautiously, their right hands on the grips of their respective Luger pistols.

"*Durfen wir ihre papiere sehen* (May we see your papers)?" The first officer asked Seiz as the other officer approached the other side of the cab so that he could watch him carefully.

"Of course…Of course!" Seiz replied as he rummaged in his jacket pockets and then his pants pockets before he was able to produce his wallet and show the police his identity papers. "What is the problem here?" he asked innocently.

The first officer did not bother to respond to Seiz's question, he merely examined the papers carefully to ensure that they were legitimate. Considering the money that Seiz had paid his forger, the papers had better stand up to their close scrutiny or he would have words with the forger when he got back to Kassel.

"What is in the back of your vehicle, *mein Herr*?"

"Nothing," Seiz replied innocently. "Please look for yourselves. I was hired to deliver a few boxes to Frankfurt and I am merely on my way home."

The second officer on the opposite side of the cab turned and walked to the back of Seiz's truck. Seiz could see the flashes of the officer's flashlight reflecting off his windshield as the back of the truck was scrutinized. Then the second officer joined the first officer on the driver's side of the truck and the two policemen shared a hushed conversation which Seiz was unable to overhear.

"What was in those boxes which you delivered to Frankfurt?" The first officer asked politely.

"The boxes were nailed shut and I do not bother to be too curious about my client's business. I was told to deliver four boxes which weighed approximately one hundred kilo each. If I opened up one of those boxes, the party to whom I was to deliver them would become aware of my curiosity and he probably would not pay me. I only get paid upon satisfactory delivery."

"Are you carrying any contraband or weapons in this vehicle?"

"I am a former soldier. I volunteered to join the *Wehrmacht* in 1939, but I must confess that I do carry my Luger. Delivering goods in Germany at this time can be dangerous. You drive a truck with a tarpaulin covering the back of the vehicle and a lot of bad people assume that you are in the black market and that you are carrying cartons of cigarettes. A man must protect himself, but please examine my weapon. It has not been fired for at least the past four months."

The second officer examined the Luger and he even sniffed the barrel. It was fully loaded and there was no smell that would have indicated a recent use. The officers exchanged glances and the Luger was returned to Seiz.

"We were both in the Wehrmacht, so we understand," the second officer explained. "These days a man...especially a former soldier has to be able to protect himself. But since you have been travelling from Frankfurt this evening, have you passed any *tankwagens* tonight?"

Without a pause, Seiz quickly confirmed that he had passed not one, but two *tankwagens* which appeared to be travelling in convoy approximately an hour earlier. They were travelling at approximately fifty kilometers an hour and their tanks had to be full since their engines were working pretty hard. He estimated that they would probably reach their checkpoint within a half-hour or less. The two officers conferred again and then signaled that Seiz was free to leave. Seiz heaved a long sigh of relief as he maneuvered his truck through the three parked police vehicles and then accelerated down the autobahn. He estimated that the police had stopped him for about twenty minutes. That would not be enough time for the two *tankwagens* to get too far ahead of him. He sped his truck up to seventy kilometers an hour and after three kilometers, he pulled his truck over to the side of the autobahn, leaving his engine running and his lights on. Then he waited.

Approximately ten minutes later, Schalburg's *tankwagen* loomed out of the gloom of the night and came to a stop behind his truck. A few minutes later, Larion's *tankwagen* joined them. As Larion's vehicle came to a stop, he jumped out to join Schalburg, who had also exited his *tankwagen*. They were quickly joined by Seiz, who was trying unsuccessfully to subdue his excitement.

"What happened at the check stop, Seiz?" Schalburg inquired.

"It was the German *Polizei*, but they were only stopping northbound traffic. They were on the lookout for *tankwagen* traffic heading north, presumably towards Kassel. I believe someone must have informed them on us."

"Perhaps it was just a coincidence, Seiz," Schalburg replied. "I am not in the mood to contemplate another betrayal on this venture."

"I believe that Helmut may be right," Larion added, explaining what had happened with his driver after Seiz had signaled a road block ahead of them.

Then they heard the driver's door of Schalburg's *tankwagen* open and as the three men looked up, they watched the driver exit the cab and start running across the autobahn to the left side of the road. His form was quickly absorbed into the darkness.

"It seems that you are both right," Schalburg replied. "And the only other party who was aware of what we would be doing tonight was the Henschel director. He was the only one who could have warned the *polizei*. Obviously, they bought off the police. The police would have arrested us and turned the fuel over to the Henschel drivers. The bribe was practically nothing because the police would not be aware of its true value. They get their fuel, keep their money, and send us to prison."

"*Diese bastarde* (Those bastards)!" Seiz spat out. "*Diese verdammten unehrlichnem bastarde* (Those fucking dishonest bastards)! They get us to risk our lives with the black marketeers, with the Americans and then when we are almost home…they want to steal our property without having to pay for it. *Diese verdammten bastarde* (Those fucking bastards)!"

"Well, since our Henschel friends want to keep their gold and steal our fuel, perhaps we can do the same," Schalburg spoke calmly, though he felt his anger was surging inside him as well.

"What do you mean?" Seiz asked. "Are you suggesting that we can keep the fuel and sell it to someone else and get their gold at the same time?"

"Why not?" Schalburg asked rhetorically. "Why not? They have tried to fuck us, so why don't we teach them a lesson and just fuck them back. As I told that bearded face in Frankfurt, people have to decide if they want to behave like businessmen or like bandits. If they choose to behave like bandits, I have no qualms in treating them as bandits."

"But how are we going to accomplish that goal?" Larion asked.

"Let us think and discuss the matter, my friends," Seiz suggested. "They would not know that we know what they have tried to do to us, so that gives us an advantage."

"Obviously, the police will be advising them that the two *tankwagens* had not passed by their road block tonight, so what will the Henschel director be inclined to assume?" Schalburg asked rhetorically. "Either we were not successful in Frankfurt or that we were somehow able to skirt past their roadblock."

"Do you think that they would still show up at the rendezvous point with the money?" Seiz asked.

"Seiz, you have to learn to think as if you were standing in their shoes," Schalburg replied. "What would they do and why?"

"I think they would be inclined to show up with the money, because if we show up with the fuel and they do not have the money in place, they would have forfeited their opportunity to purchase the fuel. There are a number of other companies in Kassel who are equally desperate for fuel."

"I am inclined to agree with Helmut," Larion interjected. "The smart decision would be to have the money in place just in case we do show up with the fuel."

"I agree with both of you, again," replied Schalburg. "But I believe that we may need an insurance policy so that Henschel shall not end up with the fuel in any case, but let me think about how we can accomplish that feat while we drive the balance of the way to Kassel."

"There is another matter which they will not know," Seiz volunteered smugly. "They will not know what has happened to their two drivers. I suggest that we pretend that we are those drivers so that we can enter their building. Once inside, we pull out our machine pistols and force them to pay us. Did either one of you notice what kind of hat both drivers were wearing? *Africa Korps Dak caps.*"

"They were both wearing that sandy-brown peaked hat with that extra-long brim…because of the desert sun. If their hats are around, we can pull them down a little bit and pull the brim down even lower to help hide our faces. They will recognize the hats, not our faces. We only have to fool them for a few seconds…just long enough to be permitted to access their building."

"Excellent observation, Seiz," Schalburg replied. "You may turn out to be officer material yet."

"I believe my driver's hat is in my *tankwagen*…though it may be bloodied," replied Larion.

"And I believe that I saw my driver's hat fall off when he scrambled to get out of the *tankwagen*. I shall check by the truck," Schalburg replied.

*****

Both *Africa Korps* hats were recovered, though one hat did have some blood spatter on its right side, it was agreed that Schalburg would drive one vehicle and that Seiz would drive the other vehicle because it would be more difficult for Larion to pass himself off as a German. He would ride with Seiz and crouch down into the footwell when they arrived at the factory.

Chapter 55

As their vehicles approached the Henschel factory's main warehouse, they could see light emanating from the interior of the building. As Schalburg's *tankwagen* approached the double main gates, he honked his horn twice…paused and then honked twice more. A man came out of the adjoining pedestrian doorway, waived and muttered some unintelligible greeting at him. Schalburg, with the extended hat rim lowered over his eyes, merely waived back and revved his engine to indicate that he was anxious to enter.

Seiz's entry was less eventful. Someone waved at him and he simply waved back and continued to follow Schalburg's vehicle. It was agreed that they would first try to determine how many men were present and if they were armed. Schalburg would then exit his *tankwagen* and then Seiz would exit his vehicle. Larion was to delay his exit briefly to give their opponents an opportunity to reveal their intentions—whether they would be merely surprised and prepared to bargain or if they were going to react violently. If their reaction was to be the latter, then Larion's delayed entrance would provide them with a further surprise they would have to cope with.

As Schalburg exited his vehicle, he looked at a bespeckled man outfitted in a white frock coat over his business suit. He recognized him to be Dr. Karl Weber, Director of Strategic Operations for the Henschel Group—the man with whom he had negotiated this transaction. Even though Weber held a doctorate in engineering, he preferred to strut around in that white frock as if he were a medical doctor at some sanatorium.

There were approximately ten other men present, half of whom wore belted holsters with Luger pistols. He then heard Seiz open up the door to his vehicle. During this period of time, Schalburg held his machine pistol in his right hand which was shielded by his vehicle's open door.

He could see that Weber was exultant. He believed that they were the Henschel drivers and that his scheme had worked. He succeeded in obtaining a critical supply of fuel which he monetized at close to half a million US dollars to their company and it did not cost them anything. He also got to keep his company's money for himself.

"Come here, Klaus, Horst...I want to congratulate you both," Weber squealed. "You shall receive a very generous bonus for what you have accomplished this day for our company."

As Weber approached him, Schalburg slowly raised the brim of his cap, revealing his face, as he slowly swung out his machine pistol from behind the vehicle door and pointed it at Weber's face. "And I am very pleased to see you again, Dr. Weber," Schalburg replied, mocking Weber's greeting. "But you do not have to give us a bonus, just our $120000 (US) in gold and currency."

Weber was so surprised that he seemed oblivious to the machine pistol pointed at his face. Schalburg believed that Weber would not have been more surprised if Hitler had risen from the dead and awarded him the *Iron Cross with Oak Leaves.*

"I...I...do not understand," Weber stuttered in confusion. "What is this? Where are Klaus and Horst?"

"Obviously, *Mein Herr* Doctor, they are not here...but we are here," Schalburg replied. "Is that a problem for you?"

"*Nein! Nein! Mein Herr* Schalburg," Weber continued to sputter. "It is just such a surprise to see you...but I assure you...a very happy surprise. *Ja! Ja!* A very happy surprise."

As Schalburg and Weber were conducting their colloquy, Seiz efficiently rounded up the remaining men, stripped the armed men of their pistols and then had them kneeling, impotently facing a wall with their hands finger locked over their heads.

"In that case, *Mein Herr* Doctor, where is our money?" Schalburg asked politely.

At that moment, three men armed with machine pistols rushed into the cavernous room and demanded that Schalburg and Seiz surrender or else. Before they could complete their threatened alternative, three separate machine pistol bursts perforated their bodies. Those three bursts had emptied Larion's thirty-two shot magazine. The bullets caused them to gyrate grotesquely as they fired their machine pistols helplessly in all directions. Their bullets ricocheted against the cement floor, the cinder brick walls, and the vaulted ceiling before they collapsed lifeless on the cold, blood-spattered cement floor.

Some of the kneeling men decided to take advantage of the diversion and rose up to run away from the mayhem. Seiz fired two quick bursts with his machine pistol and those men all fell pitifully, their bodies sprawled unnaturally on the cold cement floor.

Weber had placed his hands over his ears to block out the sound of the guns and he squeezed his eyes shut in the dire hope that he might will his surroundings out of existence.

Larion approached the bodies of the three men he had just shot. He wanted to ensure that they were dead and that they were not carrying any additional arms which some of their other captives might attempt to utilize.

"For the last time, *Mein Herr* Doctor Weber," Schalburg asked calmly, "Where is our fucking money?"

"Uh…Uh…it is not here, *Herr* Schalburg," Weber whimpered.

"Doctor, you are starting to really disappoint me," Schalburg replied. "Our agreement was that we would deliver you 15000 liters of prime American diesel and you would pay us $120000. Was that not our agreement?"

"*Ja…Ja!* That was our agreement," Weber continued to whimper.

Schalburg removed his Luger from his jacket pocket and aimed it at Weber's left kneecap. He waited until Weber looked up at him because he wanted Weber to know what was going to happen.

"Please, I beg you. Do not do this thing. I shall see that you get paid," Weber replied anxiously.

Schalburg pulled back the trigger slowly and just as Weber heard a faint 'click', his left knee cap exploded with shattered bone and blood spatter. For a split second, Weber could not feel any pain and then the excruciating, unbearable pain commenced to spasm through his leg and then through his entire body. As the pain slowly subsided, Weber broke down into tears. "I beg you, *Herr* Schalburg. You shall be paid immediately; however, it is upstairs in my office safe. Perhaps you shall permit one of my employees to assist me up the stairs?"

"Of course, *Herr* Doctor," Schalburg replied politely. "*Herr* Seiz, you guard the remaining captives. Larion shall accompany me to Doctor Weber's office."

Both Seiz and Larion noticed that it was the first time Schalburg had used Larion's first name.

*****

Weber continued to whimper in pain as he proceeded to climb the stairs up to his office. He could not put his left foot down on the steps, since that leg was totally incapable of supporting any weight. However, the slightest movement of the left leg continued to trigger spasms of pain through his entire body. Finally, they made it to his office.

It contained a large, green painted rectangular safe. The employee provided Weber with a chair so that he could remain seated as he unlocked the combination.

"Doctor, as I told you before, I am not going to ask you twice. Open up that safe and pay us our money," Schalburg ordered ominously.

Weber attempted three times before he was finally able to open the safe on his fourth attempt. As the door swung open, he pushed his chair back with his right leg to that he would not obstruct Schalburg's access to the interior of the safe.

"There it is. You will take it all, I am sure," Weber whimpered.

"*Nein*, Dr. Weber," Schalburg replied. "I am not the thief here… You, sir, are the thief. What did you plan to do? Steal our fuel from us and steal the money from your own company, is that not true?"

When Weber did not respond, Schalburg reminded him that he was not going to repeat his question and his question remained unanswered. He also reminded him that he had another knee and two elbows as well, not to mention two eyes, two ears, and a tongue. Finally, he still had his hands and his fingers.

"Yes, I must speak truthfully…no?" Weber replied. "I thought that it was a good opportunity for our company…and for myself."

"Herr Sulupin, could you come here and take a closer look at the wretch you have been working for the past eighteen months," Schalburg asked Larion politely. "And *Herr* Doctor, can you explain your moral feelings on your company's use of slave labor to build your instruments of war?"

"That is a totally different matter," Weber pleaded. "Most industrialists were not *Nazis*. We were as exploited by Hitler as they were. Hitler forced us to use slave labor, but we did pay the *SS*. We also had to feed, clothe, and house our laborers. We even had to provide them with medical treatment—all at our own expense. Hitler made us all his victims."

Larion remained silent and just looked contemptuously at the man who had caused him, Tamara, and even little Dimitri such unbearable anguish for the past year and a half.

"Perhaps *Herr* Doctor, you did not understand me fully," Schalburg spoke pedantically. "When I ask you a question, I not only want you to answer it, but I want you to answer truthfully. How much did you pay the *SS* for providing you with free labor?"

"We paid the *SS* about four *Reichsmarks* per day for each *OST* worker. After all, they also had to provide us with their guard security."

"And they also provided you with replacement workers when the *OST* workers died from being overworked, yes? Did you pay the *OST* workers anything?"

"No, they were paid nothing…but we supplied them with food, clothing, housing, and medical care."

"And if you worked those workers twelve hours a day, instead of eight or ten hours a day, it was more economical, correct? You were getting more work for each *Reichsmark* you had to pay the *SS*."

"Well, yes! But Hitler ordered us to do that."

"And tell me about the food you fed these workers."

"It was not fancy, but it was good food."

"*Herr* Sulupin, would you be so kind as to inform Herr Doctor what kind of food you and your family received? And by the way, how many hours a day and days in a week did you have to work?"

"I had to work twelve hours a day, seven days a week. If I missed a day due to illness, we were punished by having our food ration withheld until I was able to return to work. As for food, the most nutritious food we received were potato skins; otherwise, we were just provided with the rinds from carrots and other vegetables, and on a rare occasion, we might be provided with a piece of rancid meat. However, my wife learned how to prepare it so that it was edible, even though it was not very palatable."

"And how old was your son?"

"He was two years of age when we first came here and he is four years of age at this time."

"And *mein fruend*," Schalburg said. "I would like to receive your forgiveness for imposing such a hardship upon you and your family. I do not have a family now…and after going through the past five years, I am not sure if I deserve a family or…even if I deserve to live."

"You have my forgiveness, Schalburg, if you want it," Larion replied.

"And you...*Herr* Doctor Weber...do you think that you deserve forgiveness...for all your sins of omission and commission?" Schalburg asked with resignation.

"*Ja*! I deserve to live," Weber sputtered. "I have a wife, two children, and four grandchildren. You must understand, Hitler and his Nazis made us all victims...as much as your friend here."

"I have just realized something, Sulupin....I have just realized that I am tired of living," Schalburg confessed. "I truly believe that I have lived long enough. I remember someone telling me...or perhaps I had read it sometime...when I still read...that just as there is a time to live, there is a time to die."

Schalburg directed Weber to count out the $120000 payment, which was to be paid half in gold and half in American $100 bills. Then he had Weber carried downstairs. Larion sensed that Schalburg was up to something, but he could not guess what he intended to do.

Schalburg directed Larion and Seiz to tie Weber's hands, as well as the remaining six captives. Then he asked to speak to Seiz and Larion in private.

"Gentlemen, it is time to assess our current position and future prospects. I trust that the two of you realize that considering what has happened here tonight, there will be serious repercussions for all of us. Repercussions which I do not think will be bearable. So. I have a proposition to make to the two of you.

"Firstly, you may share the full $120000 (US) between the two of you. I gift you both my share. Secondly, it does not make sense that any of these remaining cretins live to testify against either of you. To that extent, I will rig my *tankwagen* with an explosive so that it will erupt like *Vesuvius*, when it destroyed Pompei in 79 AD. It should also be sufficient to ignite the other *tankwagen* and between those two explosions and the conflagration which shall follow, hopefully, it shall purify my soul and permit me to join my parents and my sister, but perhaps that may be asking too much.

"As for these *untermenshen*, I would like to take them to Hell with me, if it actually exists, as my final act of atonement. When they are gone, the two of you shall be safe. You, Seiz, can travel to Palestine and become a complete Jew. And you, Sulupin, you can take your wife and your young son and emigrate to a country which is not as besotted with hated and racism as some of these countries in Europe. But I want to thank you both for instilling some final moments of excitement into my old bones."

"Schalburg, surely you do not intend to die with these scum, do you?" Seiz asked.

"What I do not want to do is repeat my dear colleague's mistake, Seiz."

"What colleague? What mistake?"

"A dear, brave colleague of mine. Colonel von Stauffenberg. He devised a plan to assassinate Hitler on 20 July 1944. However, he made a fatal error. He planted a bomb beside Hitler at his 'Wolf's Lair', but he made the mistake of not staying to ensure his bomb exploded and killed the Nazi tyrant who has condemned Germany to a possible never-ending requiem for the sins he had this nation commit."

"I ask you to reconsider, *Herr* Schalburg," Larion implored him. "We will all have enough money to get away from here and hopefully live peaceful lives somewhere else."

"No, Larion," Schalburg replied. "As I told you upstairs, there is a time to live...and there is a time to die. This is my time to die and hopefully, my death shall ensure your respective lives. Believe me, I have absolutely no regrets with this decision. Do not make me beg you to leave or compel me to threaten the two of you with force. You are both young and you still have lives left to live."

Seiz was particularly moved by Schalburg's statement.

"Is there anything that I can do for you?" Seiz asked.

"Yes, you should go to Palestine, meet a nice darked-eyed Jewish beauty, marry her, and have many children. But if you no longer harbor any hatred for a former *SS* Colonel and you happen to have a son, perhaps you will consider naming him after me—not his first name, but possibly a second or a third choice."

"You have never told me your first name, Schalburg."

"My mother named me 'Elias', but she insisted on calling me 'Elia'."

Chapter 56

Seiz and Larion were able to locate a dilapidated Volkswagen beside the building. Though its engine would sputter and spit, it provided them with an escape from the Henschel plant. Neither man spoke for both were lost in their own thoughts. Seiz fantasized that his dream about being able to travel to Palestine was about to come to fruition. Conversely, Larion had to face Tamara's disappointment one more time.

"I have decided what I am going to do, Larion," Seiz suddenly announced, breaking the silence in the vehicle. "Travelling in Germany with all this money and gold is dangerous and I do not trust the German banks. I think I shall try to travel south to Switzerland and deposit some of my money in a Swiss bank and then take the rest so that I will be able to travel to Palestine from Italy. A large number of Jews are travelling there to set up a Jewish state for the Jewish people. What do you intend to do with your money?"

"I am not sure, Helmut," Larion replied thoughtfully. "The gold is pretty heavy and cumbersome, but my biggest problem is I have to explain matters to my wife."

"I am not sure if I can assist you with your wife, but if you would like to exchange your gold for my American dollars, I would be agreeable. This car will not be able to take me to the Swiss border, but I can drive you to the Camp and then travel back on the autobahn and retrieve my truck. My truck will be sound enough to transport me to Switzerland."

"I would like to keep three gold coins as mementos, if you don't mind," Larion replied.

"Then we are agreed, but we forgot about those nine cameras in the *tankwagens*."

"Not quite, my friend. Schalburg gave me four to hold and I secured two of them before I left the vehicle when the three guards came into the building,"

Larion replied, as he reached inside his jacket pocket and extracted a Leica. "Here is a souvenir for you and I have one left for myself."

*****

Tamara and Dimitri were sound asleep when Larion finally returned to their barracks. Though he was exhausted, he was unable to sleep. His thoughts kept drifting back to the events of the day. Being involved in the deaths of all those additional men weighed heavily on him. Though he could rationalize that their deaths were necessary, that logic did not provide him with any relief. The fact that he owed Tamara a complete and truthful explanation, only increased his anxiety. Their barracks were pretty well empty by this point in time. *UNRRA*'s repatriation and resettlement program was proceeding quickly and efficiently. Larion could not remember a more quiet night. Usually, people would be coughing or snoring or talking in their sleep. Tonight, all he could hear was the gentle breathing of his wife and his son. He was alone, with only his guilt to keep him company.

As the dawn broke over the horizon and filtered through the soiled panes on their barracks window, Dimitri was the first to stir. His movements awakened his mother, who reached over to try to soothe him, though her eyes remained shut. He could tell that she still longed to sleep a bit longer. She must have stayed up fairly late to await his return, until she finally succumbed.

"Dimitri…shush my darling boy…shush. Please go back to sleep," she quietly implored her son. "Close your little eyes and go back to sleep, my sweetheart."

Tamara's soothing comments failed to entice Dimitri to be lulled back to sleep and he continued to stir and stretch, until he finally rubbed his eyes open.

"Father! Father!" Dimitri squealed in a high-pitched voice, as he stretched out his arms so that his father would pick him up and embrace him.

Dimitri's words quickly roused Tamara from her sleep and she was equally surprised to see Larion sitting by the edge of their bunk, smiling down at the two of them.

"Good morning, my love. Have I ever told you how beautiful you look in the morning…with your disheveled tresses…your swollen lips and your blood-shot blue eyes…but you are still the most beautiful woman in the whole world to me," Larion spoke teasingly, as he leaned over to kiss her on the lips, but

Tamara turned away and Larion was only able to brush his lips against her cheek.

"Please do not be angry with me," Larion implored her sincerely. "You do not know how much that hurts me."

"You…You…Cossack!" Tamara replied, as if that was the worst epithet she could utter at the moment. "Do you have any idea about how much anguish you cause me when do go away and do these crazy Cossack things you do? I tried to stay up so that I could greet you when, perhaps I should say if you returned. But I failed and it seems that I finally fell asleep."

"Your anguish is ended this day. I swear this on my mother's soul. I want us to go see Mr. Balmelle to sign those papers and hopefully we shall be on the train to Hamburg within a day or two. Then we shall board that ship and cross the Atlantic and be in America within a week or so. Will that redeem me in your eyes?"

"I have to go to the bathroom," Dimitri whimpered. "I really, really have to go."

"Saved by your son yet another time," Tamara relented. "Go, take him to the bathroom. After all, parenting is supposed to be shared responsibility, but it seems that I have been doing the bulk of it lately."

When Larion and Dimitri returned, Tamara had commenced to prepare their breakfast. Somehow, she had been able to procure two sausages which she fried in a skillet and then she toasted three small slices of a light rye bread in the sausage drippings. She also prepared some hot water so that the two adults could drink some tea, while Dimitri had to settle for a glass of water.

Both Tamara and Larion chose not to continue their discussion while they ate their breakfast. Tamara and Dimitri shared one sausage, but the delicacy this morning was the lightly toasted bread which was flavored by the fat drippings from the two sausages. Dimitri insisted on licking his fingertips after every bite.

"Isn't Mother a wonderful cook, Father?" Dimitri asked.

"Your mother is a wonderful cook, a wonderful mother, a wonderful wife, and a wonderful human being. She is much too good for me," Larion replied reproachfully, speaking to his son, but looking at his wife. "And do you know what her most wonderful attribute is, my son?"

"What's attribute, Father?" Dimitri asked with a mouthful of toast.

"Attribute means 'quality' or 'feature', a very recognizable 'characteristic'—"

"What attribute does Mother have, Father?" Dimitri asked.

"Her very forgiving nature, my son," Larion replied sheepishly. "Her very forgiving nature."

"Dimitri, your father seems to be confused," Tamara interjected, speaking to Dimitri, but directing her reply to Larion. "Your mother used to be very forgiving, but your father has exhausted all of her forgiveness, so your poor mother has no more forgiveness to give anyone. Especially irresponsible Cossacks."

Notwithstanding Tamara's voiced criticism, Larion realized that she was prepared to forgive him one more time. He desperately wanted to hold her and kiss her and tell her again…how much he loved her. However, Larion was speechless. He did not know how to formulate a response, so he simply rose and approached her, lifted her up into his arms and kissed her. Though Tamara feigned a token resistance, she embraced him in return and kissed him fiercely…even nipping his lower lip, causing it to bleed slightly.

"Father, you are bleeding," Dimitri announced with concern in his voice.

"Do not worry, Dimitri," Tamara replied. "It is not a fatal wound…this time. I believe your father shall live to see another day. But finish your breakfast and I shall walk you to school."

Larion wiped his finger across his lower lip and examined the blood on his finger. Eyeing Tamara playfully, he placed his finger into his mouth and sucked it clean.

"And I shall be here waiting for you to return, my love," Larion replied.

When Tamara returned, Larion told her everything that had happened the previous day. Tamara simply sat quietly while her emotions swung like a pendulum from incredulity to relief and then back to incredulity again. She felt emotionally exhausted just listening to Larion's narrative of the events.

"And what a strange world! This Schalburg…he is the *Oberst* who kidnapped us from the *kolkhoz* and had us transported to Kassel."

"Yes, he is the same man!" Larion replied. "Perhaps I should say that he is the same person, but he has become a changed man. Possibly a more enlightened man who saw some of his errors and decided to atone for them."

"The same man who had three hundred Xhotimsk citizens executed as a reprisal action?"

"Yes, he is the same person, but not the same man," Larion replied. "I first met him during the second poker game and my impulse was to shoot him. I had my pistol in my left hand, under the poker table, but he knew it. He had even provided it to Seiz to give to me for my own protection in case the losers wanted to exact some retribution if I won again. Then he placed his Luger on the table and he asked me if I still inclined to fight or not.

"I would have had to lift my pistol above the table to shoot him because the table's pedestal prevented me from shooting him under the table. By placing his Luger on the table, he was prepared to assume the risk that I would not try to kill him."

"And you did not try to kill him even though he had killed three hundred of our citizens?"

"I also promised you that I would not take unnecessary risks, my love," Larion replied. "I believed that I had a chance to lift my gun and fire, even with my left hand, before he could pick up his gun and fire at me, but the odds were uncertain. Then I thought about what would happen even if I was successful. I would still end up losing because either the American Military Police would surrender me to the Soviet Zone or the German *Polizei* would charge me with murder and imprison me.

"That would mean I would still lose both you and Dimitri. So I told Schalburg that taking his life was just not worth the cost to me. But after that, I learned that he had his own principles and a man who I could trust. And fatefully, that pistol even saved my life when the Soviets kidnapped me."

"But why would he choose to die if there was a chance he could escape with his money?"

"He told me that he had decided that it was his time to die…for a variety of reasons," Larion replied sadly. "He decided that he was tired of living. I think that he felt considerable remorse for some of the things he had done during the war and he wanted to commit a final act of atonement. His most significant reason was his desire to ensure that Seiz, a Jew, and I, a Slav, would not be implicated and prosecuted. If Weber had not tried to cheat him…events may have turned out differently, for Schalburg and for us."

"Louyna, you must stop engaging in such things," Tamara pleaded. "You must stop this or I know that the next time you will not be able to come back to the two of us…perhaps I should say the three of us. The nurse at the clinic has confirmed that you shall be a father for the second time. Now you shall have two children and a wife to consider."

Larion was surprised, but euphoric at this news.

"I love you! I love you! I love you, Tamara Dimitriova Sulupina!" he yelled at the top of his voice.

"Hush, my love…hush," Tamara replied as she embraced him. "You do not want to alert the security guards or something, do you?" "Let's go to the office and sign those papers right now! Let us go and get Dimitri and then the three of us can meet with Mr. Balmelle."

"But what are we going to do about this?" Tamara asked, pointing to the bundles of bills rolled up in a dirty linen cloth.

"Take the remaining 5000 *RM* and see if you can purchase two small suit-cases, if not two, then try to purchase one. We shall carry as much of the money as we can on our person and then put the rest into the suitcase. We will have to carry whatever else we want to take in a couple of pillowcases, but is there anything that you really would want to take from this place on our journey? With one-hundred-dollar bill we will be able to buy new clothes and as much food as want, as we travel. But this money is for our security in the new world."

*****

Balmelle, Director of the *Furstenwald DP* Camp, explained the itinerary to Larion and Tamara, while Andre acted as their mutual interpreter. In two days' time they would travel by train from Kassel to Hamburg. The train jour-ney would be over three hundred kilometers and may take approximately five to six hours, depending on the number of stops the train would have to make. The City of Hamburg was Germany's biggest port, located on the Elbe River approximately one hundred kilometers from the North Sea.

They would be transported to the USS General McRae, a 'Liberty Ship', which the Americans built during the war. It had been converted to carry im-migrants to both the United States and to Canada. The journey by sea would be about one week and it would take them through the English Channel and across the Atlantic to the Canadian port of Halifax.

From Halifax, the family would travel by train to a small city in southern Alberta, named Lethbridge. That journey would be about 4700 kilometers and take at least a week. At Lethbridge, they would be met by their employer sponsor who owned a large farm south of the city. They would be guided throughout by *UNRRA* personnel.

When asked if they had any questions, both Larion and Tamara merely shook their heads to signify that they had none. All they wanted to know was when and where they were to report. Both Tamara and Larion offered profuse thanks for everything he and Lieutenant Thornton had done for them.

They were about to commence to take their first collective step towards their new life.

Chapter 57

Andre stopped by the barracks so that he could escort the Sulupins to the Camp office and bid them goodbye on their departure. His feelings were mixed. He was joyful that this young family would be able to travel to a new world and a new life, and yet he felt a sadness in his heart that they were parting and he would never see them again.

"Andre, dear friend," Larion spoke respectfully. "Please come in... We have a gift for you to repay you for all that you have done for us. Here are five one-hundred-dollar (US) notes. Keep them safe or use them as needed."

"No, I cannot accept. What I did, I did out of friendship, not out of the expectation that I would receive any payment," Andre protested gently.

"We understand that, Andre," Tamara intervened. "But this is our gift to you. Surely, you will not be so cruel as to deny us this opportunity to...help you in a small way. We accepted your help and assistance, surely you will not be so unkind as to refuse our small gesture of assistance on your journey back to Belarus?"

"Your wife is as seductive with her words, as she is with her beauty," Andre replied flirtatiously. "If I was only young again."

"Andre, behave yourself," Tamara chided him mildly in reply. "You are speaking to a happily married woman who just happens to be pregnant with her second child." Then she embraced him and kissed him on both his cheeks.

"Well, my dear, allow me to extend you both my most sincere felicitations," Andre replied. "But though I may be old, I am not deaf and I am not blind, Tamara, so I do not apologize for my comments. And I shall humbly accept your gift, albeit reluctantly."

*****

When the four of them reached the Camp's general office, Balmelle and Thornton were there to see them off as well. They were going to be transported to Kassel in a military bus with twenty-two other *Displaced Persons*, all heading to different parts of Europe.

Tamara was proudly holding Larion's and Dimitri's hands as they approached the office. While Dimitri waved enthusiastically to the small group of people who had come to see them off, Larion kept a firm grip on a small, battered suitcase.

"Please pay close attention to me, now," Andre announced proudly. "Though I have been trying to teach all of you English, I have also been trying to teach Lieutenant Thornton and Director Balmelle a little Russian, so permit me to count…*odin* (one), *dva* (two), *tri* (three)."

"*Proshchay moi druz'ya* (Farewell, my friends)!" Andre, Thornton, and Balmelle bid them farewell in unison.

After exchanging embraces and handshakes, the Sulupins boarded their train north to Hamburg. They had one open compartment to themselves, with the seats facing each other. Larion stowed the small suitcase in the luggage compartment above his head, while Tamara and Dimitri shared the opposing seat. They were all watching the people who were boarding their train and the people who had come to see them off. Their elation in finally leaving the Camp and Kassel after almost two years was diminished by the sadness they also felt in knowing that they would never see their homeland or their friends again.

Though they only had to wait another forty-five minutes before the train finally left the depot, that wait seemed interminable to Larion and Tamara. Only Dimitri remained joyous at the prospect of this new adventure.

Finally, the long train lumbered out, slowly gaining speed as the expelled steam driving the pistons gradually increased in tempo and in crescendo. As they proceeded through the countryside, the trees and the fields were a lush verdant green. It would be difficult to believe that this countryside had been engaged in a war for the past five years.

However, whenever the train passed through any municipality of any size, the ruined skeletal remnants of damaged buildings stood in stark contrast to the pristine countryside. The buildings seemed devoid of color and life. They were merely grotesque remains protruding out of the ground, stubbornly clinging to existence.

The Allied ceaseless bombing, British by night, American by day, stripped most buildings of their former structure and functionality. However, like ants and bees, the German populace swarmed to clear the streets, remove the rubble, and commence the rebuilding those destroyed towns and cities.

As the train relentlessly travelled north, they passed the cities of Gottingin, Northeim, and then they finally reached Hanover. It was a scheduled stop and it marked the completion of half of the journey to Hamburg. Dimitri and Larion needed to go to the bathroom and it was agreed that Tamara and the suitcase would remain in their compartment.

It was a pleasant relief that their train was stationary for a period of time since it permitted them to walk easily down the aisle. When the train was moving, it would occasionally rock back and forth precariously at those repaired sections where the rail line was damaged by bombs. The engineer would sound the engine's shrill whistle to caution the passengers that he was about to decelerate the train as a safety precaution. Once the repaired location was passed, the engineer would sound the engine's whistle again to announce that they were accelerating once again.

The stop also permitted vendors to board the train so that they could offer various refreshments and appetizers to the passengers. As Larion and Dimitri returned from the lavatory, a vendor was attempting to sell something to Tamara; however, she was unable to communicate with him.

Larion selected some sausage, rye bread, cheese, and a bottle of a dark beer, a small bottle of milk for Dimitri, and a small canteen of water. The cost was only 3500 *Reichsmarks*, but Larion only had his $100 (US) note to render payment. The vendor's eyes bulged out of their sockets when he saw the American currency.

He explained to Larion that he simply did not have sufficient change. Then he scurried off to discuss the matter with some of the other vendors, but Larion could see by their reaction that they would not be able to assist him either.

The vendor finally returned and asked Larion to accompany him to a money changer who might be able to break the $100 (US) note. The money changer had set up a small booth at the main entrance so that he was able to serve passengers who were both embarking and disembarking the various trains which stopped at the central station before departing to other parts of Germany, He was very suspicious and examined the bill carefully. He asked

Larion when and how he obtained the bill, and then he asked how many *Reichsmarks* Larion wanted in exchange.

Larion had no knowledge of what the exchange rate would be for a $100 (US) note, so he simply said 100000 *RM*'s. He assumed that if he was too high, he could negotiate a lower figure. As soon as Larion specified his price, he knew he had made a mistake. The money changer immediately accepted that value and proceeded to count out the exchange *Reichsmarks.* Larion dutifully counted out his vendor's 3500 *RM*s and returned to his carriage.

I think we shall have enough Reichsmarks for the balance of the journey, he mused I really should have asked Seiz or someone what the exchange rate is for a $100 (US) note. Tamara was incredulous when Larion explained that he received 100000 *RM*s. They both agreed that they should not use any more American money for it would surely attract unwanted attention.

As the train started to leave the station for Hamburg, a swarthy man approached their compartment, holding a boarding pass in his left hand.

"*Verzeihung, is hier platz* (Pardon, is there room here)?"

"*Nein, mein kleiner sohn broucht den anderen platz sum schlafen* (No, my young son needs the other seat to sleep)," Larion replied. "*Der nachst wagen is leer* (The next compartment is empty)."

"Oh, but *mein herr*, I do not like to travel alone. I prefer company and conversation," the swarthy man replied.

"*Nein, der nachst wagen is leer*!" Larion replied firmly.

The swarthy man shrugged his shoulders in disappointment and trudged to the next compartment and took his seat.

"Tamara, I think I noticed that man out on the platform when I was changing that American note," Larion explained quietly. "I am not sure if he saw that note or if the money changer told him about it, but I find his attempt to join us, when there are a few empty compartments in this car, a bit suspicious. After all, if we have one $100 (US) note, we may have more, so please be careful.

"They proceeded to eat their dinner quietly. Tamara sliced the sausage and the cheese thinly for Dimitri and placed it on a thin slice of rye bread. Dimitri found it to be the most flavorful meal he had tasted, which he continued to wash down with copious gulps of his fresh milk. The countryside continued to pass by as before. Vistas of beautiful lush green fields and forests, interspersed with depressing moments of destroyed towns. Gradually, the monotony of the wheels of the train clicking against the connected rails dulled all three of them to sleep.

*****

"*Ahem...mein herr*, would you mind if my friend and I join you?" the swarthy man asked confidently, since both he and his companion held Lugers in their right hands. Tamara woke up quickly at the sound of the voices and grabbed Dimitri with both hands and held him safely in front of herself.

"Since you ask so politely, how can I possibly refuse," Larion replied ruefully.

"*Danke, danke* (thank you)," the swarthy said as he seated himself opposite Larion. He lowered his Luger down to the seat so that his thigh would shield it from view by passersby. He examined their clothing and concluded that their threadbare clothes were of no interest to him, however, he looked up over Larion's head. He smiled broadly as he gazed at their battered suitcase. "Would you mind if I examined your suitcase, *mein herr*?"

Larion regretted that Tamara and Dimitri were with him in that compartment. He had his Walther *PPK* in his left breast pocket and if the circumstances changed, he would have been willing to shoot this cretin between the eyes. But he was not alone.

"*Nein, mein herr*," Larion replied calmy. "Please yourself."

The swarthy man started to rise up and reach for the suitcase, but he realized that he would make himself vulnerable to a counterattack.

"In that case, please rise up and get it for me."

"When you ask so politely, how can I refuse," Larion replied as he rose up and lifted the suitcase off of the overhead rack and handed it to the swarthy man.

If he was alone, he would have been prepared to shove the suitcase into his face and then shove his companion into the wall while he attempted to draw his *PPK,* but he could not take the risk at this time. His companion remained standing in the aisle with his right hand holding his Luger inside his jacket pocket, but you could tell that he was excited in having the contents of the suitcase revealed.

The swarthy man left his Luger laying on the seat beside him as he placed the suitcase on his lap and attempted to activate the closed latches to open it.

He pressed and pressed, quietly cursing, but the two latches would not release. He lifted the suitcase up in his hands to judge its weight. It was heavy and its heaviness made him even more curious and even more frustrated.

"*Derdammt! Warum offnet es sich night* (Damn! Why won't it open up)?" the swarthy man cursed.

"*Hamburg! Hamburg! Wir kommen in zehn minuten an! Zehn minuten* (Hamburg. We arrive in ten minutes)," the conductor announced as he heaved slightly from side to side as he made his way up the aisle to the next carriage.

The swarthy man grabbed his Luger, but he kept it shielded from view by his thigh and pointed it at Tamara. His standing companion with his hand in his right jacket pocket turned to face Larion. The conductor gave the group a brief passing glance, but he had to make the arrival announcements in the next three carriages and that was his immediate priority.

"I would like to commend you for not doing anything stupid, *mein herr,* but now I am going to leave your compartment…with your little suitcase. I am sure I shall find a way to open it up fairly quickly. My companion shall stay here until the train comes to a complete stop, at which point he shall leave you to join me. Allow me to wish you a happy journey, whatever your destination may be."

The swarthy man and his companion exchanged a few words and the companion nodded his head in agreement as the swarthy man waddled down the aisle of the carriage.

"Do you realize that your friend just walked out with about $40000 (US)? Do you really think that he is going to share that money with you once he finds out how much it is?" Larion asked. "If I were in your position, I would be extremely worried. Your friend has left with our money and you are standing here with your hand in your pocket. You may have your gun, but I do not think that you will ever see any money. How stupid can you be?"

"Did you say $40000 (US)?"

"Yes, I said $40000 (US)," Larion replied. "Do you know how much money that is in *Reichsmarks*, you *Dummkopf!* (dumb head). *Vier Millionen Reichsmark* (Four million Reichsmarks). And look out the window, I am sure he told you that he was going to wait for you before he got off the train, but look, he is already on the walkway with the suitcase in his hands and you are still standing here with your hand in your pocket. You are the *Kaiser* of all *Dummkopfs!*"

Before Larion could finish his sentence, the companion started running down their carriage to the adjoining carriage. Larion anticipated that the companion was convinced that his partner in crime was about to betray him and he wanted to cut him off before he reached the main exit.

"Tamara, if you would like to see what happens when two men get greedy and are prepared to betray each other; look behind you at what is about to happen on the walkway."

Larion watched as the companion got off the train and proceeded to confront the swarthy man. The companion was still holding his Luger in his right jacket pocket, while the swarthy man was disadvantaged since he was clutching the suitcase with both hands. Though he could not overhear their conversation, it was obvious that the companion was demanding that the swarthy man surrender the suitcase to him.

In exasperation, the swarthy man shoved the suitcase into his companion's face as he withdrew his own Luger. Both men seemed to fire their weapons almost simultaneously. The companion shot his Luger through his jacket pocket first, as the swarthy man, though writhing in pain, extracted his Luger from his breast pocket and fired twice as his companion was attempting to draw his Luger from his jacket pocket. The companion was able to get off a second shot as the swarthy man shot him again. Both wounded men then fell to the tarmac. The small suitcase had also hit the tarmac on one of its corners and it opened up, spilling out the bundles of $100 (US) bills onto the walkway. Almost immediately, dozens of other embarking and disembarking passengers descended upon the bundles in a frenzy. As one person succeeded in gaining control of a bundle, he was immediately swarmed by several others attempting to take it away from him Very quickly, the German *Polizei* were blowing their whistles and lashing out with their batons, attempting to restore order over of the melee on the walkway.

"Larion, those people are crazy," Tamara said breathlessly. "They are insane! Insane!"

"Greed can make many people insane," Larion agreed calmly.

"But that is your money, Louyna," Tamara observed. "Are you not upset about losing it?"

"Sweetheart, I made the mistake of not determining what was the true value of those American notes. I should have changed some of them into smaller bills or even *Reichsmarks,* so it is not a surprise that we lost them. But my darling, we still have about $10000 (US) and I also have three 1915 Austrian 4 Ducat gold coins. I do not know how much they are worth, but gold is gold, all over the world. So, we are not poor, just a bit poorer than what we were, but much wiser, and we are still alive. Look at our two would-be thieves. First they steal from us and then they try to steal from each other and now they are both dead."

Larion considered the fact that this was the first confrontational circumstance in which he had not had to kill the opponent. Ever since the Winter War with Finland in 1939, he had been obliged to repeatedly kill others in order to survive. It was such a relief that he did not have to draw his *PPK* this time. He decided that he would discard his pistol at the first opportunity. If this was the commencement of his new life, it was time to sever this last tether to his past life.

Chapter 58

Hamburg was an important member of the Hanseatic League, which was a federation of northern German 'free' cities and towns which dated back to 1358. It was primarily a commercial federation. The city, itself, was located about one hundred kilometers inland from the North Sea and situated on the Elbe River. It was deemed to be a 'free city' since it only owed allegiance to the Hapsburg Holy Roman Emperor and not to any local prince.

The Hanseatic League's decline coincided with the gradual ascendency of the German state of Prussia under rule of the Hohenzollerns. It ceased to exist in 1862 after King Wilhelm recalled Otto von Bismarck and appointed him 'Minister President' and 'Foreign Minister' on 23 September 1862. One week later, on 30 September 1862, Bismarck, made the following telling comment in a speech to the Prussian Chamber of Deputies:

"The great questions of the time will not be resolved by speeches and majority decisions…but by iron and blood."

Bismarck then proceeded instigate three quick wars: first with Denmark, then Austria, and finally, he got Napoleon III of France to declare war on Prussia in 1870. Prussia was successful in all three wars and Bismarck was able to unify the German principalities under the rule of King Wilhelm I, who he then proclaimed 'Kaiser' (Emperor) in 1871.

After Wilhelm I died in 1888, he was succeeded briefly by his son, Friedrich III, who died of cancer after ninety-nine days. His son, Wilhelm II, succeeded him and he forced Bismarck to resign on 18 March 1890.

Though Bismarck was militaristic and an exponent of achieving results through 'iron and blood', he was also cautious. Kaiser Wilhelm II was less cautious and he was also a proponent of insuring that Germany would have a 'place in the sun'…which pitted Germany's belated entry into colonialism in direct competition with the colonial empires of England and France.

Prophetically, in 1897, one year before his death on 30 July 1898, Bismarck uttered the following statement:

"One day, the great European War will come out of some damned foolish thing in the Balkans."

Archduke Franz Ferdinand, heir to the Hapsburg throne, was assassinated by an anarchist in Sarajevo on 28 June 1914, which led directly to the outbreak of the First World War. But the assassination of 'heads of state' was the norm in the later part of the nineteenth and the early part of the twentieth century. Surely the assassination of an 'Archduke' in the Balkans was not the real reason for the outbreak of the First World War, which resulted in the deaths of millions of soldiers? But perhaps it was the opportunity for England and France to neutralize the German Empire's colonial aspirations around the world and neutralize the German Empire in Europe. It was also an opportunity to dismember the Austro-Hungarian Empire and the Ottoman Empire and eliminate them as potential competitors in Europe and in the Middle East.

Chapter 59

As Larion, Tamara, and Dimitri disembarked their train, they were swept along with the crowd attempting to exit the Hamburg central train station. Balmelle cautioned Larion to watch for a man holding a sign with their family name written in Russian. As they completed their exit from the walkway which separated the adjoining parallel tracks and turned right towards the general exit, there was a profusion of individuals holding up signs in a variety of languages. Larion panicked that he would be unable to see his name, then he spotted an individual holding up a sign bearing their surname. Though they had to struggle against the flow of the other passengers in order to reach the rail and the man bearing the sign – SULUPIN, they succeeded.

After showing him their two Certificates of Identity, they were ushered away and taken to the USS General J.H. McRae and allotted three-tiered bunks as their accommodation for the rest of their journey by sea. Dimitri was given the middle bunk, Tamara the lower bunk and Larion took the third tier. In this way, either parent would be able to care for him, if that became necessary.

The 'Liberty Ships' were low-cost, mass-produced, cargo vessels manufactured to transport soldiers and cargo during the war. Between 1941 and 1945, utilizing a British design and American mass-manufacturing techniques, 2710 ships were built—averaging approximately three ships every two days.

They had a length of 135 meters and a beam of 17 meters, with a maximum speed approaching seventeen knots. The engine and the boiler were located in the middle of the ship, below the bridge. They contained five cargo holds, three forward and two astern. Between the upper deck and the cargo holds, there were five 'tween decks' to accommodate the crew, soldiers or *Displaced Persons*. The 'tween decks' were comprised of double rows of four tiered bunks with a passage between each set for the soldiers or *Displaced Persons*, while the crew was afforded the luxury of only three tiered bunks for their quarters. For wartime defense, there was a four-inch cannon at the stern of the ship for use against surfaced submarines and a couple of anti-aircraft guns situated on the bridge.

The USS General J.H. McRae was built in 1944 and initially served in the Pacific theatre, transporting troops and cargo primarily to Hawaii, but as far west as Australia and India. With the end of the War, she transited through the Panama Canal for service in the Atlantic. She was subsequently assigned to 'Displaced Person Transportation'. In 1954, she was deactivated and sold to private commercial interests and went through a variety of private owners and different names. She was eventually scrapped in Taiwan in October of 1986, after serving for forty-two years.

After enduring the train trip and even cattle cars from Xhotimsk to Mogilev to Kassel; then enduring cramped and filthy bunk beds in Furstenwald, their new quarters, though equally cramped, were clean and comfortable. They would line up in the mess hall for breakfast, lunch, and dinner, and the quality, quantity, and variety of the food was a wonderful change.

After the USS General J.H. McRae cautiously navigated the Elbe river and finally reached the North Sea, the tranquil portion of their voyage ended. Once the ship reached the open sea, it increased its speed and with that increased speed, the passengers became exposed to the undulating motion of the ship and seasickness. It affected Tamara more than Larion or Dimitri.

On fine days when the Atlantic was not being unduly traumatic, the three of them would venture out onto the top deck to enjoy the warmth of the sun and feel the salty spray on their faces. Dimitri's special joy was being taken to the bow of the ship and lifted up over the rail so that he could look down and watch as the bow of the ship sliced through the Atlantic as it continued to leave Europe and approach America. The bow seemed to cut through the ocean effortlessly. The frothy waves peeled back on either side of the bow in abject surrender against the perpetual forward thrust of the ship.

However, they also had to endure a serious Atlantic storm when the ocean's anger seemed to imitate the anger of the war they had just left behind. The huge waves tossed his little ship like the proverbial cork in troubled waters. The clouds mimicked the anger of the ocean with dark swirling clouds which spat out thunder and lightning at the little ship. But no matter how many high waves or bolts of lightning threatened to sink their ship, she bravely popped up to the surface and continued on her immutable journey to America. After a few days at sea, they had lost track of the passage of time. There was just the endless monotony of an endless ocean in all directions. One day the captain of the ship finally announced that they would be arriving in the port city of Halifax that evening. It seemed that all of the *Displaced Person* passengers went up on the top deck to await that event.

Though it was already dark, the lights in the harbor seemed to celebrate their arrival. Lights glistened and flickered from the moored ships in the narrow harbor, from the adjoining buildings and from the homes which nestled in the hills surrounding the sheltered, elongated body of water.

Different people experienced different emotions, but there was one common feeling. Relief!

Larion thought about his young son's reaction to his life to date. His life had been one of an ongoing journey from one decrepit location to another decrepit place. He wondered how his son would feel to actually stop moving and just settle down for once in his short existence, but then he thought about his own life. Since 1939, all he had experienced was war, human devastation, and wanton killing. Would he be able to adjust back to what he once knew as a 'normal life'?

The following morning, the Sulupins and the other *Displaced Persons* who were disembarking at Halifax made their collective way from the harbor to the Halifax central railway station. They would embark on the train which would carry them over 4700 kilometers to their final destination.

By the time their journey would end, they would have traversed almost half the circumference of the entire Earth. What an achievement to consider.

Though spending days and nights sequestered on two bench seats on a train was seldom comfortable or enjoyable, it was endurable. Their never-ending entertainment was to look out the train window and enjoy the ever-changing landscape of the passing terrain. The multicolored deciduous trees, then the cultivated fields bearing the varying colors of their varied crops, the lakes and rivers, the evergreen forests and then the never-ending horizontal vista of the plains.

In the course of their journey, Larion continued to study his English-Russian dictionary and he even gave lessons to Tamara and Dimitri. It was a necessary skill which all three of them had to acquire fairly quickly.

Chapter 60

Albert Nesterenko's Ukrainian parents had emigrated to Canada at the turn of the 20th century so that they could take advantage of the offer of free homestead land to any emigrant who stayed on that land, cleared it, and cultivated it. There were four Nesterenko male family members: the father and his three sons. Albert was the youngest son. Since the homestead provisions limited the allotted land to one quarter section per male, the family applied for four contiguous quarter sections under the name of the father and each of his three sons.

There allotments were situated ten miles southeast of a small city named after some Englishman, 'Lethbridge'. Over the years, the four quarter sections were gradually consolidated into one integrated mixed farm which grew wheat, potatoes, and the new cash crop—sugar beets. The Nesterenkos also developed a decent dairy and beef herd. They worked collectively and diligently, and they prospered as time went by.

Albert's two older brothers patriotically enlisted in the Canadian army to serve their new homeland in the First World War. Albert, at sixteen, was too young and looked even younger. He stayed behind to help his father manage their four quarter sections. Albert's two brothers never returned from France. They were two of the sixty-one thousand Canadian soldiers who died in that war. In all, almost seven percent of the total Canadian population of about eight million served in that conflict.

With the death of his two brothers, title to their quarter sections passed to their father and with his father's death in 1928, title to the four quarter sections became registered in Albert Nesterenko's name.

Albert became aware that the Canadian government was permitting the emigration of thousands of *Displaced Persons* to Canada under a farm worker program at the end of the Second World War. He volunteered to accept one Slavic family to assist him on his farm. He felt that it was his patriotic duty to his new homeland and by accepting a 'Slavic' family, he would be fulfilling an obligation to his former homeland by assisting one of his own in resettling in Canada.

Since the family was to be Slavic, that would facilitate communication even though he felt his Ukrainian was rusty after years of non-use since his father's death.

On 5 September 1945, Albert stood waiting anxiously in the reception area of the Canadian Pacific Railway depot with a handwritten sign with the name 'SULUPIN', printed in Cyrillic in bold black letters. He was a man of average height with premature grey hair and a face which had been weather-beaten by the summer sun and the winter wind; however, his pale blue eyes twinkled, conveying his inherent human kindness.

Albert and Larion both saw each other almost simultaneously. Larion waved his right arm in greeting and said something to a beautiful young woman who was standing beside him, and she immediately broke into a smile. The young man was carrying a young boy in his left arm. He could see a look of relief flood over their faces as they approached him. They had travelled a long way and God only knew what they must have had to endure.

"Me, Larion Sulupin," Larion introduced himself in his broken English. "This my wife, Tamara, and son, Dimitri."

"How you do, sir?" Dimitri chimed in English, as he had repeatedly re-hearsed over the course of their train journey.

"I am very well, thank you, Dimitri," Albert replied in Ukrainian. "Please forgive me for my crude Ukrainian, but I have not spoken the language for many years. My name is Albert Nesterenko."

"Oh, thank God," Tamara exclaimed. "We have travelled halfway round the world and now we are met by a fellow countryman," then she reached for Albert's hand so that she could kiss it in gratitude.

"Now, now, my dear, there is no need for such foolishness. I am not a priest or a man of importance. Now if we can pick up your suitcases, I can drive you to my farm and we can be properly introduced. My wife has prepared dinner for us."

"I am afraid that we are naked, Mr. Nesterenko," Larion replied. "We have no suitcases, only the clothes on our back."

"Well, that will not do. No, that certainly will not do," Albert said. "We are going to a clothing store to pick up some new clothes and shoes for all of you. You, Larion, shall need some work clothes and some 'going-to-town or going-to-church' clothes. And you, Tamara, you are just too beautiful to be wearing those clothes. You are young and you deserve something much better."

"We do not want to impose on your generosity, Mr. Nesterenko," Larion replied.

"Do not worry, if you have no money, I will just deduct what I spend from your weekly earnings."

"Well, we do have some money," Larion replied, pulling out one solitary $100 (US) note from his pants pocket.

"And you said you were naked," Albert responded in surprise and then added jokingly. "For this one note, you can practically buy yourselves an entire new wardrobe."

*****

Albert drove the Sulupins to a nearby clothing store. Tamara was self-conscious at the difference in her clothes compared to the other women in the store. Up to that point in time, all of the *Displaced Persons* were dressed similarly and she had lost her consciousness of the distinction in being shabbily dressed and well-dressed, but she was very aware now.

"Do not worry about anything, my dear," Albert said knowingly. "The clothes do not reveal the soul of a person. Please rummage through these racks and pick out some dresses and a coat for yourself, because our winters are cold. And then you have to pick out some comfortable shoes and warm boots for the winter…and perhaps some gloves as well."

Tamara was still very conscious of the stares they were receiving from some of the other customers in the store. Slowly, she selected three dresses and undergarments. Albert directed her to the change closet where she would be able to try the clothes on. Then he turned to Larion and directed him to the children's section so that he could pick up some clothes and shoes for Dimitri. Tamara stepped out of the change closet wearing a pretty floral-patterned dress. It was knee high with short sleeves and a prim collar which was open at her neck.

"You look beautiful, my love," Larion said.

"Go on, my dear, look at yourself in that full-length mirror," Albert added. "But you do look beautiful, as your husband just said."

"Tell that fucking bitch to go back where she came from!" an angry man yelled at Tamara. We don't need any fucking *DPs* in this country."

Tamara and Larion were confused at the stranger's anger. They had neither done nor said anything to him, yet his face was contorted with anger and hatred."

"Perhaps you should go back to where you came from, Zalarevich," Albert replied calmly.

"I am a Canadian citizen. I belong here," he replied.

"Well, my friends are lawful emigrants and soon they shall be Canadian citizens as well," Albert replied. "So why don't you mind your own business and stop making a public nuisance of yourself."

"I have my rights," Zalarevich responded angrily.

"Well, this store is my store and I have the right to refuse entry to belligerent customers," the storekeeper interjected. "And if you do not quiet down and stop harassing my customers, I shall have to exclude you and call the police."

"What!" Zalarevich exclaimed. "You are taking the side of some dirty *DP* over me?"

"We were all *DPs* of a sort when we first came to this country, so I am going to have to ask you to leave or I shall have you charged with trespassing and causing a disturbance."

After Zalarevich indignantly left the premises, Dimitri was emboldened to ask why the stranger was so angry at them.

"He is an unhappy man, little Dimitri, and he wants to go through life making other people unhappy as well. But just as with every country, there are good people, like the store owner who came to your defense, but there are also some bad people, like Zalarevich," Nesterenko replied sadly.

*****

As he drove the Sulupins to his farm, Albert regaled them with an abbreviated version of his family history. His father's decision to leave the Ukraine and emigrate to Canada. His brothers' decision to volunteer to join the Canadian army and their subsequent death during one of those inane trench battles for a few yards of enemy ground, which was inevitably retaken the following week.

Finally, he got around to explaining his farm operation. Harvesting, barring inclement weather, was going to commence in the latter part of the month. Finally, they arrived at the farm and Albert decided to show them where they were going to be living.

Their residence was a single-room building with one pot-bellied stove for cooking and for warmth. The walls were only insulated with tar paper. There was an indoor pump for water, but the toilet was a skimpy rectangular structure located about thirty yards behind their home. Tamara noticed that there was a bed with fresh linen, two pillows, and a hand-knitted comforter. She also noticed that there was a modest cupboard filled with a variety of canned goods and dry goods. She spied some spaghetti cartons.

"Pasta!" Tamara announced proudly, since Lieutenant Thornton had introduced her to this delicacy in Furstenwald. "Very good! Very tasty!" Albert merely smiled and nodded in agreement.

"Larion, I appreciate that this home is pretty modest," Albert observed. "But your first duty will be to insulate the walls and install some linoleum on the floor. If this is going to be your home, it is up to you to make it as comfortable as you can."

"Thank you, Mr. Nesterenko," Larion replied. "Actually, this looks better than the place we had lived in for the preceding two years, but if you have the materials, I am sure I can turn this modest dwelling into a veritable palace for my family."

"I have all of the required materials and the one thing we forgot to look after is a small bed for Dimitri. After dinner, I believe that we have a little bed still stored up in our attic and we can bring it over for him. I believe that my wife can also spare a small cabinet in which you can store your new clothes and belongings. But now, my dear guests…allow me to invite you for dinner with me and my wife up at the big house."

*****

Albert introduced the Sulupins to his wife. She was a short, rotund woman with a round, happy, ruddy face. She brushed her hands clean on her apron before she greeted her dinner guests.

"Please, dear friends, if you wish to wash up, the bathroom is down the hall. Then I want you all seated so that we can eat before the meal gets cold," Mrs. Nesterenko implored them politely.

After washing their faces and their hands, the Sulupins sheepishly walked down the hall to the spacious dining room, which was as big as their entire residence.

"Albert, please be seated for as long as you remain standing, our guests shall remain standing and hungry. Shame on you," Mrs. Nesterenko admonished her husband.

"I humbly apologize to you and our dear guests," Nesterenko replied. "Please dear friends, be seated and I shall say grace and then we can enjoy my dear wife's excellent cooking."

As everyone became seated, Albert asked that they all hold hands and bow their heads.

Dear Lord, we give thanks for Your bounty and Your endless love and forgiveness of our sins. We humbly thank You for safely delivering our new friends: Larion, Tamara, and Dimitri, to us today. I trust that You shall bestow upon them happiness and long life in this new country.

Everyone in the room then crossed themselves in the Orthodox fashion—forehead to heart, right shoulder to left shoulder. Then they closed their prayer in unison.

"Amen!"

Albert proceeded to pour a celebratory shot of vodka for Larion, his wife, and Tamara. So that Dimitri would not feel excluded, he had his wife pour him a small glass of apple juice.

"Larion...and please do not refer to me as 'Mr.'...my name is Albert. Please try this libation which I had personally concocted in this new world. I trust that you shall find it a warm reminiscence of the old world."

Larion took a small sip. "Excellent *soma honka*, Albert."

"And now dear friends, we shall not be able to accomplish this in one evening, but I shall endeavor to tell you about Canada and our farm, and you shall tell me about the adventure which brought you to this place. Agreed?" Albert asked.

"Agreed!" Larion and Tamara replied in unison. Then they looked at each other and smiled. For the first time in several years, they were able to sense the soothing feeling of sincere relief. Tears of joy welled up in their eyes and they leaned towards each other and shared a tender kiss.

Epilogue

Just as everything has a beginning, everything also has an end, and this is the end of the account of the brief period in the life of Larion Daneelivich Sulupin. A story of an ordinary man and the people and events in a ten-year period of his life.

It is much easier, in hindsight, to understand and assess the significance of the decisions which ended the First World War and which inevitably led to the Second World War. However, the decisions which emanated out of the conclusion of the Second World War also defined the world's post WWII history. Just as World War II was the inevitable outcome of World War I, the Cold War, the Arab-Israeli conflict, and other current issues appear to be the inevitable outcomes of the decisions which concluded World War II.

*****

The major participants in the Second World War sustained the following approximated military casualties:

Soviet Russia: 10.6 million
Nazi Germany: 4.3 million
United States: 416800
Imperial Japan: 2.12 million
United Kingdom: 384000
Italy: 301400
Yugoslavia: 446000

Stalin's Soviet Union also sustained a further estimated 16 million civilian casualties, while Nazi Germany sustained about 3 million civilian casualties. Inasmuch as Churchill was reluctant to open up a second 'western front' in France after Dunkirk and the subsequent debacle at Dieppe, it should not be surprising that Stalin would attempt to secure Russia's western frontier since Russia was invaded by: Napoleon in 1812, the Foreign Intervention of 1918-1922, and Operation Barbarossa in June of 1941 Since the second front in the west was delayed until June of 1944, it also afforded Stalin an opportunity to aggrandize most of eastern and central Europe, once the Nazi invasion was halted and then routed, albeit at a horrific human cost.

Churchill's clarion declaration on 5 March 1946, that an 'Iron Curtain' had descended upon Europe, was rhetorically accurate. Truman's subsequent declaration on 12 March 1947, of the 'Truman Doctrine' of containment of the Soviet Union, notwithstanding Soviet Russia's horrific contribution to the defeat of Hitler, was not interpreted as an act of gratitude by Soviet Russia.

Truman's decision to establish and maintain American military and economic hegemony through the threat of the use of atomic weapons was a de facto declaration of the 'Cold War', which initiated the arms race between the two countries.

After Hiroshima and Nagasaki, Stalin directed an expedited effort that the USSR obtain a nuclear weapon as well and by 29 August 1949, Stalin's Soviet Russia conducted its first nuclear test. The United States no longer possessed a nuclear monopoly. Once the Soviets and the Americans both obtained atomic and then hydrogen weapons, the focus became the development of appropriate rocket delivery systems until the saturation point of 'mutual destruction' had been achieved and neither side could rationally dare use those weapons. Therefore, the Cold War was fought through 'proxy wars', such as in Korea and Viet Nam.

In the interim, it seemed expedient to apply Bismarck's 'Realpolitik' principles whereby political decisions were to be based on 'practical', rather than 'moral' principles. Accordingly, a number of convicted Nazi war criminals, who had been sentenced to death or to lengthy prison sentences, had those death sentences commuted and those prison sentences shortened, regardless of the heinous crimes for which they had been convicted. The new enemy combatants were Stalin's Soviet Russia and America.

Pursuant to a policy of political hypocrisy, though Soviet Russia was surrounded by American nuclear missiles in Western Europe and even in Turkey, Soviet Russia's reciprocal attempt to install nuclear missiles in Cuba in 1962 almost precipitated a nuclear world war. Fortunately, John Kennedy and Nikita Khrushchev were able to resolve that dispute diplomatically. Khrushchev agreed to withdraw the Soviet missiles from Cuba in exchange for Kennedy's promise not to attempt to invade Cuba, such as the 'Bay of Pigs' fiasco, and the further promise to remove America's missiles from Turkey.

With the fall of the Berlin Wall on 9 November 1989 and the subsequent dissolution of the USSR by the Supreme Soviet on 26 December 1991, there was hope, for a while that the 'Cold War' would not only thaw, but be replaced by a more benign relationship between America and Russia.

*****

David Ben-Gurion, destined to become the first Prime Minister of Israel, was born in Plonsk, Poland, on 16 October 1886 and died in Israel on 1 December 1973. He had emigrated to Jerusalem in 1906 and had even helped form a 'Jewish Militia' in Palestine to assist the Ottoman Empire in the First World War. The 'Balfour Declaration' of 2 November 1917, had given hope to the European Jewry that they would finally obtain a home of their own after almost 1800 years.

Subsequent to the Balfour Declaration, Ben-Gurion switched his allegiance and joined the 'Jewish Legion', supporting the British forces in Palestine against the Ottoman Empire. Though England had been given the 'Mandate' over Palestine and the Trans-Jordan pursuant to the provisions of the Versailles Treaty of 28 June 1919, the Balfour Declaration was not implemented immediately.

The British 'White Paper' of 1939, provided that Jewish emigration to Palestine would be limited to 15000 Jews per year. Since that number was deemed to be totally unacceptable and non-compliant with the Balfour Declaration, it gave rise to the emergence of Jewish paramilitary groups such as the 'Haganah' and the 'Igrun' in Palestine, which took armed action against British governance.

After the revelation of the extent of the Jewish Holocaust at the end of the Second World War, groups such as the Haganah and the Igrun forced the British Government to maintain about 100000 troops in Palestine to maintain order. Eventually, the British Government referred the matter to the United Nations, which recommended a two-state solution – one Jewish, one Arab. The Jews accepted the proposal, while the Arabs rejected it.

405

After the Arab rejection of the UN Proposal, Ben-Gurion proclaimed the creation of the State of Israel on 14 May 1948, and it triggered the first Israeli-Arab War, with Israel being victorious.

The Two World Wars also resulted in diminishing England from being the pre-eminent military, commercial and colonial power in the world in 1914. Its pre-imminent position was replaced by the United States. After the end of the Second World War, England's colonial empire would gradually disintegrate as exemplified by India in 1947. India, with independence, was initially partitioned into a 'Muslim' Pakistan comprised of two separate parts on either side of the Indian subcontinent, with a 'Hindu' India in the middle.

Subsequently, between 1972 and 1974, the eastern portion of Pakistan emerged as the separate independent state of Bangladesh.

*****

Though the Vietnamese had fought the Japanese during their World War II occupation, after Imperial Japan's defeat France attempted to re-establish its colonial control over Viet Nam. It was opposed by Ho Chi Ming's communist forces. The Vietnamese forces defeated the French at Diem Bien Phu in north-western Viet Nam, on 7 May 1954. However, on 1 November 1955, pursuant to the 'Truman Doctrine', which had been expanded to contain communism all over the world, marked the commencement of the United States' involvement in Viet Nam which would last until 30 April 1975. Though the Vietnamese communists were eventually successful, the rest of Indochina did not convert to communism and the world did not end.

*****

But European colonialism and the establishment of the Jewish state of Israel did cross paths in 1956. On 26 July 1956. Egyptian President Gamal Abdul Nasser declared the nationalization of the Suez Canal. On 29 October 1956, England and France had Israel commence the Second Arab-Israeli War by invading the Sinai. England and France immediately dispatched about 80000 troops to Egypt to 'secure' the Canal.

World opinion and the United Nations compelled the British and French troops to withdraw and the Suez Canal was returned to Egypt, however,

American financial support for the construction of the Suez Canal was withdrawn, only to be replaced by Soviet financial support.

*****

At the Yalta conference in February of 1945, Stalin gave Roosevelt a commitment to declare war against Japan within three months of the end of the war in Europe. Nazi Germany unconditionally surrendered on 8 May 1945, and somewhat surprisingly, three months later on 8 August 1945, Stalin's Soviet Russia declared war on Japan and on 10 August 1945, three days after Hiroshima, the USSR invaded Manchuria.

It had been agreed between the US and the USSR that the Korean peninsula would be divided in respective American and Soviet zones of influence, as in Germany, and that the dividing line would be the 38th parallel. It was important to the Americans that Seoul, the Korean capital, would be in the American zone. Again, somewhat surprisingly, on 16 August 1945, the Soviet forces stopped their advance into Korea at the 38th parallel even though the American forces did not reach that demarcation line for another three weeks.

On 15 August 1945, the American southern zone was declared to be the democratic 'Republic of Korea' governed by Syngman Rhee. Subsequently, the Soviet northern zone was declared to be the communist 'People's Democratic Republic of Korea' governed by Kim Il-sung. This formal partition of the Korean peninsula into two separate nation states was opposed by a substantial portion of the Korean civilian population. However, active opposition was only possible in the southern democratic Korea.

The Soviets withdrew from northern Korea in 1948 and the Americans withdrew from southern Korea in 1949.

Inasmuch as opposition was more tolerated in southern Korea, wide spread resistance in the Republic of Korea's government encouraged Kim Il-sung to attack the Republic of Korea on 25 June 1950, and the communist forces succeeded in capturing Seoul two days later.

In the interim, the civil war in China between Mao's communists and the Kuomintang 'Nationalists' (1945 to 1949), resulted in the routing of the Nationalist forces on mainland China and their displacement to the island of Taiwan, where the Nationalist forces purported to establish the 'Republic of China'. In 1950, the Mao's Peoples Republic of China was actively planning for the invasion, subjugation and incorporation of Taiwan into Communist China.

As a result of the Nationalist's declaration of the 'Republic of China', the Soviet government decided to boycott the UN Security Council meetings in January of 1950. Consequently, on 27 June 1950, the Americans were successful in getting the UN to pass UN Resolution #83, which authorized a collective UN military action in Korea. Though the USSR had a 'veto power', it was unable to exercise it because of its misguided 'boycott'.

Subsequent to the UN intervention in Korea, the communist Korean forces were driven back to the 38th parallel. The overall command of the UN/American forces was under General Douglas MacArthur, who conducted the war from his headquarters in Japan. Communist China cautioned the Americans against crossing the 38th parallel into northern Korea, since it felt it had a vested interest as the People's Democratic Government of Korea was situated on its border. MacArthur was not only prepared to cross the 38th parallel, but enter China itself.

Furthermore, he was more than prepared to utilize America's nuclear arsenal. Truman had even authorized the transfer of nine Mark-4 nuclear bombs to that theatre and he had even signed the authorization for their use, though that authorization was never physically transmitted to MacArthur. Surprisingly, it was America's European allies who tried to dissuade Truman from utilizing nuclear weapons in Korea.

In the interim, MacArthur was given conflicting instructions. Both Truman and Defense Secretary George Marshall had provided him with conditional authorization to cross the 38th parallel, but only if he was certain, it would not trigger either a Chinese or Soviet intervention, notwithstanding the outstanding cautions by both of those governments not to cross the 38th parallel.

Subsequent to the UN/American forces crossing the 38th parallel, Communist China diverted the armed forces it had assembled for the imminent invasion of Taiwan and proceeded to intervene in Korea instead, driving the UN/American forces back behind the 38th parallel, with Soviet Russian pilots providing air support.

On 18 October 1950, Truman met with MacArthur on Wake Island in the Pacific in respect of the conduct of the Korean War since MacArthur refused to meet with the President on the continental US in an obvious act of insubordination. Finally, on 11 April 1951, Truman fired MacArthur. However, in the